Suzanna's Song

Book Three:
The Whitlock Trilogy

Allen Kent

For information address AllenPearce Publishers,
16635 Hickory Drive, Neosho, MO 64850

AllenPearce Publishers ©  ©

Library of Congress Cataloging-in-Publication Data
Allen Kent
Suzanna's Song
Kent, Allen
ISBN: 978-0-9964036-8-9

Allen Kent © 2018

Suzanna's Song

1

AFTON, IOWA
1867

Both men arrived on the 4:45 from Burlington, one with notice of good fortune, the other looking for trouble. As they stepped onto the platform at Afton's new rail station, its paint so fresh the air still smelled of chalk and lime, the few waiting townspeople recognized one to be a man of some means. His shoes were finely made, and he wore a fashionable, close-fitting afternoon jacket with wide, beaded lapels and a new felt bowler. At the luggage car, the porter handed down a soft leather bag the color of ripe wheat as if lowering a basket of new-gathered eggs. It matched a smaller case the man carried securely in a gloved hand. He tipped the porter generously, walked confidently through the station, and stopped on its wide front porch to inspect the neat village of white clapboard houses that stretched for five blocks to the south.

The second man was of working stock, clad in coarse wool pants and jacket, with a tweed flat cap pulled loosely over a thin fringe of hair that hinted at less beneath. His duffle, dropped carelessly onto the platform, showed that it had been tossed a hundred times before and crudely re-stitched with heavy thread along seams that had split from the abuse. Before entering the station, he approached a portly matron who was releasing a young female passenger from a smothering embrace and asked about accommodations in the village. She grasped his hand in her own fleshy paw and pulled him the dozen steps until they could see beyond the depot.

"See the two-story building there, the one that isn't the courthouse? That's the Occidental Hotel. The only one in town. Lizzy Peters sometimes lets rooms at her place on East Fillmore, but there's a grand jury in session and she's full up."

"Nothin' too serious, I hope," the working man said.

"Not for us," the woman replied. "The case was moved here from

3

Creston where they're always having some sort of town spat. This one involves horses, but that's about all I know. Better go to the Occidental."

The man dipped his head obligingly, hoisted his duffle onto his shoulder, and crossed the square of packed earth that fronted the station. He paused for a moment, then picked a street that appeared to lead in the direction of the hotel. Old-growth elms with trunks as thick as ale casks stretched late-afternoon shadows across tidy fenced yards. Mothers in gingham frocks called "Supper time!" from the railed steps of their front porches. In a vacant corner lot, boys picked up the pace of a game of shinny, hoping for a final winning goal before yielding to their mothers' calls.

This'll be a hard sell, the man thought. *None of the city squalor that makes a man restless and angry. I may just have to appeal to basic insecurity and greed.*

The two men reached the desk in the Occidental's overly decorated foyer at the same moment, one carefully placing his case on a maroon upholstered Queen Anne chair while the other dropped his duffle beside the counter.

"Please," the businessman said, doffing his bowler. "You go ahead. I'm in no hurry."

The clerk slid the registration book between them. The man in the flat cap nodded his thanks, scratched *John Griggs* across the next vacant line, and beside it *Baltimore, Maryland*.

"I may be needin' the room for a week," he said, sliding the ledger over to the man beside him.

"At the moment, we have plenty of space," the clerk said, plucking a long, notched key to room 215 from the board behind him. "A dollar-fifty a night." A wooden fob the size of a small lemon dangled from the key. The man bounced it in his hand, frowning at the inconvenience.

"We like you to leave your key at the desk when out of the room," the clerk explained apologetically. "The wooden ball is a reminder . . ."

"And a good one, I'd say," the man said. "I'll be goin' to the Whitlock mill early in the mornin'. Is it far?"

The clerk jerked his head in the direction from which the two men had come. "About twenty minutes on foot. Take the road east from the station."

The man with the bowler followed John Griggs with his eyes as the laborer mounted the stairs with the duffle slung over his shoulder, then pulled the registration log in front of him.

"Henry Rosswell," he said as he dipped the pen into the well. "I only expect to be here two or three nights. It looks like we're both going to the Whitlock place, though I may head out that way a little later. I assume there are no trams . . . ."

The clerk turned the ledger back toward him and glanced with a smile at the New York address. "Closest we have will be a Whitlock supply wagon that comes by Fife's and Cantrill's general stores each morning. If you go to Fife's, you might catch a ride out about eight." He handed Rosswell the fob-burdened key to 107.

"A supply wagon? You mean just a *regular* wagon?"

"Probably sturdier than most," the clerk said with an amused grin. "The Whitlocks haul some pretty heavy loads in them."

The guest sniffed. "Any place to get some supper? And breakfast in the morning?"

"For a dollar, Lizzy Peters will feed you with the guests at her place around the corner on Fillmore. I'd stop by and let her know she may have an extra. She serves at six-thirty, sharp."

Rosswell drew a round silver watch from a pocket in his waistcoat. "That just gives me time to freshen up. There's water and a basin in the room, I presume?"

"Just beside the window." The clerk hesitated, then asked matter-of-factly, "Something going on out at the Whitlock place?"

Rosswell retrieved his case from the Queen Anne as the clerk added, "Just seemed pretty coincidental—two people from so far away coming to see them the same afternoon."

Rosswell glanced again toward the stairs. "I think it's just that," he said. "Coincidence."

2

THE MILL

Suzanna Whitlock was not a believer in coincidence. She was not a Calvinist like Rachael Fletcher who accepted that every action was somehow foreordained by a God unwilling to trust His creations to their better judgments. Suzanna's sense of consequence had been molded out of the hard clay of the Missouri wilderness as she witnessed how every human action, no matter how seemingly inconsequential, affected all that surrounded it. Clearing trees for planting and building at her father's homestead changed the way rainwater flowed to the streams. Fields that had been prairie became marshland, chasing away burrowing animals but attracting waterfowl. Now that the family had moved to the western edge of Iowa and constructed the mill, as her workmen timbered the forests about them for lumber and rail ties, fewer bears roamed the hills and the ivory-billed woodpeckers had disappeared. Coyotes, the survivors of clear-cut woodlands, now thrived where other animals had been displaced. These fearless scavengers roamed boldly through the village at night, sorting through trash bins and thinning the cat population. There was a predictable consequence to each action that she had come to view as inevitable, a sense that the moment a stone was dislodged at the top of a hill, the shape of the stone and the bumps and obstacles in its path determined exactly where and when it would come to rest. Though that endpoint occasionally took her by surprise, she firmly believed that once the chain of events began, the end was certain.

The one bit of solace Suzanna found in her loosely-framed philosophy of inevitability was that she could sometimes serve as one of those impediments on the hillside, redirecting a stone and its eventual end place. It was not an accident that she was in the way, nor was her collision with the stone something over which she had complete control. Her being there was also shaped and solidified by a lifetime of decisions, actions, and consequences. Those experiences all coalesced in the blood rushing to her face and her spine stiffening when Reuben Hall rapped on the kitchen door and called through the screen that, "Some fella's down at the mill, handing out pamphlets and gettin' the men all riled up." It was the first of a cascade of events that she would eventually look back on as the day that changed everything.

As Reuben turned and trudged down the hill toward his work station beside the loading sled, Suzanna glanced at the wall clock on the side of the cupboard. Six-thirty. Half an hour before the steam engine rumbled to life, the belt began its whining turn, and men hoisted the first log onto the carriage that drew it into the spinning blade. David was on his way back from Plattsmouth in Nebraska where he had delivered two carloads of crossties and was negotiating a contract to supply the transcontinental rail line. She had been leaving it to her foreman, Ben Lanear, to start the men in the morning, then joined him after finishing her household duties. She folded the dough she had been kneading and shaped it into a crude loaf. With another unconscious glance at the clock, she molded it into a waiting bread pan and covered it with a damp dishtowel.

"We'd better go see what's going on," she muttered under her breath, then called after Reuben. "I'll be right behind you." But he was already halfway down the hill.

She followed the lumberman to the back of the mill but stopped before rounding the corner into the stacking yard. The morning air was still cool, and the man spoke sharply, every word carrying as clearly as if she had been standing in front of where she knew he was perched atop one of the piles of cut ties.

". . . so all the engineers has formed a brotherhood, and we expect the conductors to be followin' us next year. The whole idea is to make sure those of us in the railroad business is gettin' what we should be gettin'— a safe place to work, no more than fifty-hour weeks, some protection from just bein' let go if the boss gets some burr up his britches, and better pay for them that's been workin' longer."

"But we ain't engineers or conductors," Suzanna heard one of her men say.

"And I ain't here to talk you into joinin' the brotherhood of engineers," the voice said. "But we're all in the railroad business together. They cain't run without your ties any more'n they can run without engineers. The firemen are talkin' about organizin', and we'll be strongest when we're all in this together."

"Don't know what we'd gain from this," another of the workmen called back. "The only other jobs in Afton's at the brickyard, and we do better than them. Every man over there would sell his soul to Old Scratch to be working here."

"What if one of you gets hurt?" the organizer argued. "Then you wouldn't be here or at the brickyard, and your wife 'ud be takin' in laundry to feed your little 'uns."

She recognized the next voice as Ben Lanear. "Not at this mill," he said. She knew he had stepped forward and lifted the elbow-length stump of his left arm. "I lost this in an accident here, and the Whitlocks has made sure I can still work."

"Maybe for now," the man said. "But someone'll come in and buy this place out. It's happenin' everywhere. When all that begins to change for ya, you'll be wantin' the strength of the other brotherhoods behind ya. There's strength in numbers. You just read through this copy of the journal I've give ya here—or have one of your kids read it to ya. You'll see what we're all about. I'll be holdin' another meetin' at seven tonight at the church hall. You all come after supper and I'll tell ya more."

Suzanna drew a deep breath and strode around the corner onto the square of chip-covered ground that stretched from the open side of the lumber mill. The man standing on a pile of untreated ties in the center of the yard was perhaps a decade younger than herself—upper thirties— and, from his dress, could have passed for any of the mill workers. He looked down with amusement at the woman dressed in heavy men's work pants, boots, and shirt.

"I have to say though, brothers," he said with a light chuckle, "we haven't reached the point of hirin' women to work on the trains. 'Specially lookers like this 'un." The men looked down sheepishly, then scattered to their work stations with quick, sidelong glances back at their boss.

"You might improve things if you *did* hire a few women," Suzanna said, stopping a few yards from the stack with feet spread and arms folded tightly across her chest. "But in this case, I happen to own the train. And the men need to be starting their day. They can meet with you this evening if they choose, but I'd be obliged if you wouldn't come onto the mill property to meet with them." She turned and pointed down the quarter-mile of hard-packed lane that led to the mill and drying sheds.

"And the property begins at the crossroad up there."

The man stooped, placed a hand on the cut timbers, and hopped down from the pile.

"John Griggs," he said with a slight nod. "I'm not here stirrin' up trouble. Just lettin' your men know that the rest of us in the railroad business are lookin' after their safety and work conditions."

"And you don't think I'm concerned about those things? As far as I know, you haven't set foot here until this morning."

"Big steam engine. Whirlin' saw blade with heavy spinnin' belts. Hoists and pullies liftin' logs. Just the kind of place accidents happen."

Suzanna stiffened. "Ben showed you his arm. He caught a sleeve in the belt four years ago. You notice we have all the men wrap their forearms tight now. Their first job is to look out for each other. We haven't had a serious accident since."

Griggs shrugged. "You're welcome to come hear what I have to say tonight. We're just lookin' out for the workin' man."

"If you'd ever run a place like this," Suzanna said coldly, "you'd know that's what we have to do every day."

3

SUZANNA

Suzanna did not stay at the mill. She left Ben to manage the shouted exchanges among the men she knew would follow the stranger's appeal to join ranks with the engineers' brotherhood. She had heard about this organization—from railroad managers with whom she and David negotiated contracts for ties and trestle timber. The group had been around for over a decade, formed back in '55 if she remembered correctly, and had stirred up trouble in the east. There had been a strike against the Philadelphia and Reading Railroad that had cost half the employees their jobs. Since then, it had been a much more cooperative union, but she didn't need some troublemaker getting her men's britches in a knot.

As she climbed the hill to the house, the shrill whistle of the 7:40 from Omaha sounded from the direction of town. David should be on it. He would probably wait for Nate Carter and the mill's supply wagon and catch a ride with the teamster. He could walk the distance and beat the wagon back to the mill, but never missed a chance to sit beside one of the men and catch up on their family news. Thank the good Lord for David! He readily conceded that she was the brains of the operation. And she conceded just as quickly that he was its heart and soul.

While she absently kneaded a second loaf of bread, she sorted again through what she had heard from John Griggs. Was the mill a safe place to work? Were they fair with the men with their hours and wages? They paid a dollar a week more than the brickyard, even with the buyout plan, and the mill was cooler and cleaner. Now that the brickyard heated with fuel oil, the lot reeked of soot. The air for a half-mile around was bitter and seeped into clothing so that even on Sundays, the brick men smelled of burned oil. Her nose wrinkled at the thought, and she thrust out her tongue as if she had been given a dose of milk thistle. She could spend all day surrounded by the sharp woody tang of an oak log meeting the saw blade. On those rare days when a large persimmon or sassafras came in, she made it a point to stand beside the saw to breathe in the wood's sweet aroma. But there was nothing redeeming about the stink of the brickyard. Her men would choose the mill on its worst day over any other place in Union County.

Seven-to-five workdays, with thirty minutes for lunch and the Sabbath off? In letters from Chicago, her daughter Elizabeth wrote that ten hours were standard for mills in the city, with the half-hour taken for lunch added to the end of day. The final whistle sounding at five-thirty.

She was fully aware that with the blade, belts, hoists, and steam, the mill floor was a dangerous place. But after Ben's accident, she had not only insisted on tightly-wrapped sleeves, but that each man be responsible for a partner, keeping him away from suspended logs and whirling belts and from the blade when the drive was engaged. Nothing was serviced until the saw and engine were shut down. No degree of efficiency was worth another man's arm.

At the bottom of the hill, she heard the team of draft mules turn the supply wagon from the main road onto the lane toward the mill yard. She wiped her hands on a damp dishtowel, covered her second loaf to rise, and hurried through the house to the porch. David was on the high board seat with Nate Carter. Squeezed between them was another stranger, this man in the fashionable morning outfit of an eastern businessman.

Nate reined the team up at the bottom of the path that climbed the hill. The men clambered down, waved the teamster onward, and started the long climb to the porch. Suzanna waited for David to look up, to greet him with a wave, but the men were so engrossed in conversation that both looked only at each other and the ground at their feet.

Fifty yards from the porch, David noticed her leaning against the porch rail and his face broke into a beaming smile. It was more than the satisfied grin of a man who had been able to negotiate a good contract. He eased the other man ahead with a light hand on his back. As they mounted the steps, Suzanna stepped forward, returning the gentleman's polite nod.

David stepped between them. "Suzanna, I'd like you to meet Henry Rosswell. He met the wagon at Fife's and asked to ride out with us. He's been telling me a most extraordinary story."

Rosswell smiled politely, his eyes flitting downward over Suzanna's work clothes. She felt her face redden and she unconsciously ran her hands down her shirtfront and trousers.

"You'll have to excuse my dress," she said. "We encourage our men to wear clothing that can't get caught in the machinery. When I'm down on the mill floor, I try to do the same."

"You help with the mill work?" Rosswell asked.

"Mainly bookkeeping in the office there. But even walking through, I want to dress as we ask the men to on the floor." Rosswell's nod was not one of complete acceptance.

"Please," she said, leading them into the house's entryway. "Find a seat in the parlor and I'll get some refreshment. And I'm most anxious to hear this story."

When she returned with tea and biscuits, David and Henry Rosswell were discussing the man's travel from New York, waiting to resume his tale until she joined them. She set plates in front of each, then joined David on the sofa.

"With your indulgence," David said, "would you be so kind as to start from the beginning. Suzanna needs to hear all of this . . . ."

Rosswell sat up stiffly in his chair, set the cup on a side table with such care that she didn't even hear a *click* against the saucer, and opened an expensive leather valise. He drew out a heavy paper folder and opened it across his lap with great ceremony. Retrieving the cup and balancing it with both hands beneath the saucer, he looked up at the couple, focusing principally on Suzanna.

"I represent the law firm of Crouch, Whitman, and Rosswell of New York City. We have been looking for your husband for almost a year. You know his mother, Lydia, of course . . . ?"

Suzanna's heart leaped in her chest, fearing that something had happened to the dear woman who had become her closest female friend and confidante. But she had received a letter from Lydia only days before, mailed from Salt Lake City a week prior. No news concerning David's mother's wellbeing could be a year old without Suzanna knowing about it.

"Yes. Lydia and I are dear friends," she said cautiously.

"Then you must know that Lydia's mother was a Shipley who came to Philadelphia from England in 1793."

Suzanna did not remember the year, if she had ever been told. But she nodded her awareness that David's grandmother had been named

Margaret Shipley and had immigrated from Great Britain.

Rosswell glanced at David, then turned back to Suzanna with a mysterious smile. "Do you know why?"

Suzanna's reply was a slight shake of the head. "I know that she had recently married. I don't believe Lydia was ever told much about her parents' lives before they came to Pennsylvania."

"As it turns out, Margaret Shipley, before marrying, was an Allgar and came from a family of some breeding in Norfolk. At seventeen, she was sent to the court of King George to serve as lady-in-waiting to Queen Charlotte."

Suzanna arched a brow and turned to study her husband, who remained silent, but seemed to swell on the sofa as if the announcement gave him added importance.

Rosswell continued. "As it turns out, the queen was an avid gardener and undertook an expansion of Kew Gardens, with the assistance of a handsome young botanist named Charles Shipley. One of Margaret's duties was to accompany the queen to the Gardens when she inspected the work being done. Margaret and Charles became enamored, arranged clandestine times to meet and, shall we say, found themselves in a most delicate situation. The queen dismissed them both."

David deflated beside her on the sofa. This seemed to have been a new addition to Rosswell's story.

"So they came to Philadelphia to escape the embarrassment," she guessed.

"Not before Margaret was disowned by her father for having shamed the family," Rosswell said, glancing at the papers on his lap. "Her father, Robert Allgar, had a younger son, also named Robert, who inherited the estate and lived to a very ripe age. But the son had no offspring. Which brings me to the purpose of my visit. Robert—the son—left the estate in his will to any offspring of his sister, Margaret Allgar Shipley. Solicitors representing the estate in London contacted my firm for assistance in locating Margaret's descendants. That has led me to you."

"We were just getting to this point in the story when we reached the house," David said. "And when we saw you, I was about to ask how Mr. Rosswell had tracked us down. Perhaps he can enlighten us now."

Rosswell again laid the teacup on the side table. "It has been quite an adventure and, in all truth, has taken me into parts of the country I never expected to see. Your grandmother," he said, turning to David, "corresponded with her brother up to the time of her death. The solicitors in London found some of those letters among the estate's papers and were able to furnish an address in Philadelphia. Fortunately, your mother, Lydia Shipley, grew up in the home her parents purchased there, once they settled. She had a friend who remained close after your mother and father moved to Missouri. Lydia continued to write to the friend after you settled in the cabin along the Chariton River. That led me to the little village of Kirksville, and from there up the Chariton to the first homesteads I came across." He shifted his gaze to Suzanna, who nodded.

"My brothers."

"Exactly. And your brothers told me how to find you here."

"And why was it important to find us?" Suzanna asked, glancing again at David and anticipating the answer.

Rosswell leaned forward toward the couple. "Lydia Shipley Whitlock was the only child of Margaret Allgar Shipley. David, as I understand it, is the only child of Lydia Whitlock." He paused and smiled, quite pleased with his detective work. The Whitlocks sat expectantly while Rosswell looked from one to the other, but said nothing.

". . . and why is this important?" Suzanna prompted.

"Oh, yes!" Rosswell studied the papers on his lap with a self-important frown. "Your grandmother was left quite an estate—a country house and some acreage somewhere in Norfolk. At her death, it passed to her daughter, Lydia. That means that at her death, it passed to you."

David chuckled under his breath. "That's wonderful. But Mother is still very much alive. We heard from her just this week."

Rosswell's brow lifted in surprise and he relaxed back into the chair. "The Shattucks . . ." he turned again to Suzanna, ". . . your brothers didn't mention that when I stopped at their homestead."

"Did you ask?" she wondered.

"Well, no. I don't think so. I just asked about the Whitlock family that had lived up the river. They said David had married you, and that you were here in Afton. I assumed Lydia had come with you and had passed on."

"No. Very much alive," David said.

Rosswell glanced about the parlor. "And where would I find her?"

"Salt Lake City."

"Oh, dear!" the attorney muttered. "Among the Mormons?"

"As *one* of the Mormons."

"And are you Mormons?"

David's face soured. "No. But if we were . . . *?"*

"Oh, that would be quite alright. But I must admit I don't relish the thought of going among the Mormons. Why, one never knows what one might see. . . . And I read about Indian trouble out in Salt Lake City."

"In the Utah Territory," David corrected. "But not in Salt Lake City. In Mother's latest letter, she didn't even mention Indian trouble. And what *might* one see if among the Mormons?"

Rosswell straightened the papers in his open folder, closed it, and tucked it into his valise. "Well, one never really knows, does one?" he said dismissively. "But it appears that the adventure continues. I believe the new transcontinental railway now extends most of the way across Nebraska. I'll catch a coach from there."

David eased forward on the sofa. "Can we contact her by telegraph? Find out what she would like to do with the estate? She's old enough now that I'm sure she won't feel that she can travel to England."

Rosswell's face screwed into a tight frown. "From what I'm told by the London firm, there is an interested buyer. But your mother would need to sign any agreement to sell, and we would need to discuss who she would like to represent her in the sale."

"Then it sounds as if I should accompany you to Salt Lake City," David said, looking over at Suzanna. "I'm sure Mother will want me to handle whatever she does with the property."

Suzanna knew he was right—that they couldn't allow this New York attorney to meet alone with Lydia to arrange for disposition of what might be valuable property. But the timing couldn't be worse. She suspected David had returned with a new contract and that mill production would need to increase, just as this Mr. Griggs was trying to convince her crew that they were overworked. And if David were going to see his mother, she wanted desperately to go along.

While David was away at the war, Suzanna had run the mill, changing her daily work dress to the pants, shirt, and boots she now still wore when working near the saw and steam engine. She had become something of a pariah among the other women in town, a woman working at a man's job, dressing in men's clothing, and giving orders to their husbands. The gossipy postmistress, Charlotte Winter, had once confided, "The women know their men think you're the most attractive woman in Afton, shapely even in your work outfit and pretty as a summer morning. You shouldn't be surprised they're unhappy about you running the mill." Suzanna had bared her soul and spilled her tears through letters to her mother-in-law. Through consoling replies that came weeks later, the dear woman showed an insight and understanding that left Suzanna feeling that they somehow knew each other's every thought and felt the tender beatings of the other's heart.

Long before Suzanna knew her, Lydia had chosen to join the Mormon movement. When Mormon hunters killed David's father in a raid in upper Missouri, Suzanna and David had taken Lydia north into Iowa to meet the church migration moving west. That had been twenty years ago. Though she had often longed to hold the woman close, bless her for her understanding heart, and weep against her neck, Suzanna had not seen Lydia Whitlock since they had parted at the Mormon camp east of Afton—a place they called Mt. Pisgah. And there was a chance—a small one, she knew—but a chance that if she went to Utah, she could see Johnny.

"There are things that need our attention here at the mill," she said to her husband, choosing to wait until Rosswell was gone to express her full frustration. "Perhaps Mr. Rosswell can tell us where he's staying, and we can get back with him after we've had a chance to discuss this—just between the two of us."

Rosswell gave an understanding nod and pushed to his feet. "I realize this is a lot to get your minds around, so I'll leave you to talk it over. I'm at the Occidental Hotel, such as it is. But with this new information, I need to be on the morning train heading west. These decisions demand immediate attention and now rest with your mother."

"We will be in touch by evening," David said. "Let me hitch up a buggy. I'll give you a ride back into town."

"It's a lovely day," Rosswell said, "and the distance isn't great. I would enjoy the walk. And I see that you have a great deal to talk about."

4

JOHNNY

Beyond the pine rails of the corral, a waist-deep sea of late spring grasses rolled in easy waves to the base of the Salt River Mountains. Along the far bank of the river, black humps rose above the emerald swells like breaching sea creatures, a hundred bison seemingly unconcerned about the horses whose sleek, lighter backs dotted the landscape between the river and where Johnny Whitlock stood on the railed porch. Though snow still splotched the black peaks that framed the valley, the air was sweet with honeysuckle, clover, and prairie flax. Johnny Whitlock noticed none of this. He stood as straight, sunbaked, and sinewy as the corral's cedar corner posts and glared with dark eyes at three riders that receded north along the trail toward Three Forks.

"Damn their eyes," he muttered, hearing the hinges of the door of the log house creak behind him. Nodda moved quietly to his side, her soft moccasins silent against the bare planks. She came only to her husband's shoulder but was as lean beneath her doeskin dress as the rancher. The ebony hair that framed her round, brown face was parted in the middle and hung to mid-back in two braids, tied with strips of yellow cloth.

"The men left?" she asked.

Johnny grunted. "Just like the others. Sick with the gold fever. Some new strike up on the Salmon. We can't pay enough to keep any of them here."

"They were not good men," Nodda said in the quiet way she had learned from her Paiute mother. "One hit Cora with his glove when she got in the way. He called her a half-breed."

"You should have said something. I would've sent them packing before now."

"We needed their help—if we are taking horses to the city."

"We don't need them if they hit our daughter," Johnny said,

beginning to turn back toward the house. He stopped mid-step and peered again after the departing riders.

"Someone's coming," he said. "Looks like two wagons." Beyond the three fading horsemen, two teams pulled off the trail into the grass to let the riders pass.

Nodda followed his gaze. "The men are shouting at them. We should go see if they need help."

As they started toward the steps, the three departing trailhands spurred their mounts and galloped on. Those in the wagons watched without moving until the riders disappeared, then flicked the reins over their mules and guided them back onto the rutted track.

Johnny leaned curiously against a porch post as the teams approached, with Nodda pressed cautiously against his hip. The drivers were small, round-faced men with hats perched like acorn caps atop thatches of black hair. A young child sat beside one of the men, a ragged crop of hair brushing the shoulders of a tight, hip-length jacket. The strangers eyed them warily as the wagons drew to a halt beside the empty corral. Cora had heard the squeal of dry axles and the steady plodding of shod hooves and pushed through the door to huddle beside her parents.

The lead driver looped his reins about the wagon's brake lever as Johnny stepped from the porch, Nodda and Cora glued tightly to his hip. The child on the wagon seat scrambled into the shadows of the canvas-covered bed.

Johnny nodded a greeting. "Good morning."

The man's response was more a bow than a nod. "Good morning," he replied, his tongue stumbling awkwardly over the words.

Nodda peered at the flat bronze face with its dark, narrow eyes and leaned into her husband.

"Are they Indians?" she whispered. "From the land of the tall poles?" He nudged her into silence.

"Do you need water for your animals?" Johnny asked. "Or for yourselves? Tie up your teams and rest awhile."

The man again gave a quick, stiff bow, spoke in a high-pitched sing-song to others behind him in the wagon, and stiffly climbed from the board seat. Slowly, another small, thin man emerged from beneath the canvas and clambered down beside him, joining two others who came forward from the rear wagon. They stood in a somber line in front of their hosts.

Johnny motioned toward the watering trough. "Unhitch the mules if you like. Nodda, could you get water for our guests? Do you need food?"

The lead wagoner looked about uncertainly. "Could we build a fire? So we can cook?"

"There's a fire burning inside. You're welcome to cook in the house."

The man again bowed politely. "We can cook here. There are many of us." He spoke in the same singing tones in the direction of the wagons and the child reappeared, followed by two women, one carrying a toddler, the other a baby wrapped tightly in brown cloth. The women wore the same fitted, high-necked jackets and dark pants. They paused on the wagon seat, looking about the homestead with alert, cautious eyes, then handed the children to one of the men while they climbed to the ground. Three other children, younger than the first, eased shyly around the wagon bed from the rear, followed by another pair of women. The children huddled against their mothers' legs and lined up behind the men, staring mutely at Cora.

Johnny gestured toward the low, rectangular building beside the barn that had housed the ranch hands. "You can build your fire over by the bunkhouse." A low porch with rough benches stretched across the front of the rough log structure, giving the women with babies a place to rest. "There's wood on the side there," he said, sensing that their strange guests wished to prepare their meal without help. "Come get me if there's anything you need." He turned back to his family, ushering them in front of him toward the house. "Let's leave them be for now. We'll sit on the porch, if they need something."

While one of the men unhitched the teams, the others gathered wood and unloaded a black iron pot and three-legged stand from the rear wagon. One of the women appeared with a white cloth sack and flat, wooden box. She lowered a wide board, attached with woven rope to the rear of the lead wagon, and began to peel and slice onions on the makeshift table. Within minutes, a fire blazed beneath the kettle, filled by a bucket brigade of children with water from the Whitlock well. The woman with the box carefully measured out portions of dried egg noodles.

"We have the chicken inside," Nodda whispered, "and no ranch hands to eat it."

"Fetch it," Johnny said. Nodda rose silently and disappeared into the house. Cora slid along the bench until pressed against her father's leg, enthralled by the rehearsed way the newcomer children hurried through their assigned duties.

Nodda returned with the naked fowl clutched tightly by the feet and offered it to Johnny. He gestured with a nod toward the women. Nodda frowned with a nervous shake of her head.

"You take it," he said, nodding again toward the women. One glanced up. Her eyes widened as she spotted the bird, but quickly returned to the simmering pot. Nodda walked cautiously to the cookfire and held out the dimpled yellow hen. The cook glanced up again, looked expectantly at the man who had driven the lead wagon, then back at her work. The wagoner shuffled self-consciously toward the porch, positioned himself in front of Johnny with hands folded in front of his waist, and repeated his solicitous bow.

"You are most generous," he said solemnly. "We can accept this gift only if you will join us for this meal. Will you be so kind?"

Johnny surveyed the yard full of black-clad travelers, looked down at his daughter who had not seen children her own age since a wagon of settlers had passed nearly a year earlier, and answered with a deeper bow. "Be glad to," he said. "We've got some beans cooking inside that we can bring along . . .. But tell me. What brings you into our valley? Been a year since anyone's come this way." With a wave of his hand, he invited his guest onto the porch and to the log bench. He stood, offering the man his hand. "I'm Johnny Whitlock."

Again, the man bowed. "I am Li. We have been at the mines on the Snake River. But we were the only ones there with families. It became too dangerous."

"You are Chinese?"

20

The man bobbed formally, drawing his hands in front of his chest.

"I heard there were Chinese at the mines," Johnny said. "But none with families."

"We were in California," Li said. His English was clear, but his tongue tangled around some of the sounds. "We had stopped mining and found work feeding other miners. So we sent for our families. Then gold was found in the Idaho territory. We thought we could feed the miners there. But too many Chinese came. There is much trouble between the miners—the white miners and Chinese. We could not keep our wives and children safe."

"But why come this way? There's nothing down this valley."

Li looked south along the overgrown track that led toward a low break in the mountains. "The Mormon Trail. A wagon man on the Oregon trail told us to come this way."

Johnny frowned skeptically. "You can get there through the pass, but better on horseback than wagon. Hasn't been traveled much. You may have to cut your way through—and there'll be wash-outs. You headed to Salt Lake City?"

Li shook his head. "We will go the other way—to where the railroad is. We can cook food for the Chinese workers there. The railroad will not allow such violence."

"Does the railroad want you to come cook food? I'd be thinking they have their own cooks at the work camps."

"Some Chinese came to the gold camp from the railroad," Li said. "They say the food is very bad. Too much buffalo. No rice or noodles. We can make food in one of our wagons. The workers will come eat it."

"And you will live in your wagons and move with the crews?"

Li nodded. "We have lived in small places for a very long time."

"And if the railroad doesn't allow this?" He looked past Li toward the cleft in the distant hills, now hazy blue in the late afternoon. "We had an old trapper come through last week. Said the Chinese are refusing to work. The railroad's not happy with them."

Li gave a resigned frown. "Then we will find another place."

Cora had abandoned the spot beside her father and now raced with the other children to the stand of pines that climbed the foothills a quarter mile behind the house, returning with armloads of dry branches. The sweet tang of pine smoke hung on a light evening breeze. Johnny watched her run beside the child that had been perched on the wagon seat, shouting and pointing as she directed the scavengers to fallen trees. He gazed across the sea of grass at the dozen horses that needed to be driven across the mountains to Taylor's Cross on the Snake, or down into Utah to Logan or Salt Lake City.

"Do your men ride horses?" he asked.

Li looked at him with visible amusement.

"To ride horses, we must have horses. And some reason to ride them."

"You have mules," Johnny observed.

"We buy and sell mules as we need them to move from place to place. When we are in a place, we sell the mules to buy whatever we need."

"Do the other men speak English?"

"Not well. Only a few words the miners shouted at them. They are not words that can be used often."

"But your English is very good. Better than mine."

"I came to San Francisco by myself as a boy—when gold was discovered there. An American family took me in and insisted that I go to school rather than work in the mines. I went for three years, but the boys at the school did not want me there any more than the miners wanted us in Idaho. So I ran away to Chinatown and worked in a restaurant serving the Americans who came to eat. My English became even better, but I returned to being Chinese. I met my wife there. We now try to feed whoever will pay us to do it."

Johnny studied the pleasant round face for a moment, then said, "What if I taught you and the other men to ride and help me with the horses? You can live in the bunkhouse. We will feed you until you can help me get the horses to market. Then I'll pay you a third of what I get for them. That will be more than you can make feeding rail men, even if the rail people let you try."

Li smiled broadly and looked at his countrymen who were busy brushing down the mules and rearranging the few possessions scattered throughout the wagons. "You want to make us cowboys?"

"I need ranch hands. It takes four or five men to drive the horses across the mountains. They're selling well right now, and I have a dozen ready for market. You help me get them there, and you can each have the profits from one horse. I've been getting eighty to a hundred dollars a head at Taylor's Crossing from miners going up the Snake, and a hundred to one-twenty in Salt Lake City. I need to move them in about a month's time."

One of the women called to Li from beside the cook fire. "I believe our meal is ready," the Chinaman said. "I will talk to the others. But first, let us enjoy our meal together."

5

DAVID

They watched together from the porch as Henry Rosswell started down the hill toward the road. He walked with the careful gait and swiveling head of a man trying to comprehend, but still unnerved by, surroundings that were completely foreign. To his left, white smoke belched into a cloudless sky from a stack that pierced the roof of the lumber mill. An oak log whined as it was eased into the blade. To his right, across a quarter mile of knee-high prairie grass, James Yates turned an acre of flatland from green to black behind his team of prize Percherons and a two-bladed plow. Overhead, a red-tailed hawk soared on invisible currents, rising, rolling into a gliding dive, and rising again. David breathed deeply of the loam-scented air, sensing on the breeze that lifted the hawk the faint bite of scorched wood.

"Smells like the blade needs to be switched out and hammered," he said, his eyes still following their retreating guest.

"Ben mentioned that yesterday," Suzanna said. "We'll shut down early this evening and change it. This one should make it through the day."

David chuckled. "Mr. Rosswell was quite a start to our morning."

"Mine was interesting before you got here," Suzanna muttered, shifting her gaze toward the mill.

"So I gathered. What happened?"

"Reuben came up and said there was some organizer down there trying to stir up the men—like the ones we heard about from the railroad people. This one's named Griggs. He's trying to talk the men into forming a brotherhood of some sort like the engineers have. Gave each of them a pamphlet."

"And you went down there . . . ?"

"Long enough to hear a bit of what he had to say and tell him he needed to find another place to do his preaching. So he invited them to meet with him at the church hall tonight."

"What reasons did he give for forming this brotherhood?"

"Safety. Job protection. Better wages. Better hours. The same things we heard about from the railroad people."

"Did the men have anything to say?"

Suzanna stepped back from the porch rail and plopped heavily into one of the rockers but didn't push it into motion. "Ben spoke up. Said he'd been allowed to keep his job after losing his arm. And someone—I didn't see who—said we paid better than the brickyard."

"Do you think they'll go tonight?"

Suzanna's brow creased. "Some will. Not much else to do in Afton on a workday evening. And we know some of the men just work for the paycheck and don't have ambitions beyond that—the ones who didn't like the buyout plan when we laid it out for them."

Rosswell had reached the bottom of the lane and turned to give them a final wave. David returned the gesture and remained pressed against the porch rail. She knew he was thinking about their crew, that some felt no loyalty to them or to their workmates. They came to work on time and worked hard enough that she couldn't justify dismissing them. But they did no more than was necessary. David wouldn't say so. It had been a difference between them since he returned from the war. "Some men just want to come to work, finish when the whistle blows, and not think about it again until morning," he argued when they let their thoughts become words. "There's nothing wrong with that."

But this news—that there was an organizer at the mill—seemed more troubling. "We should ask Ben to go to the meeting and see what's said," he suggested. "We can't go. No one would say anything with us there."

"Or with Ben," Suzanna mused. "As far as they're concerned, he's us. Rueben came up to tell me, and he's rock solid. I'll ask him to go."

She pushed the rocker into motion. Aside from the rhythmic creak of wood-on-wood, there was silence for a moment. Neither seemed willing to mention the buffalo in the parlor—Rosswell and Salt Lake City.

"Oh . . ." David said finally. "I got the contract. The Union Pacific will take twice the number of ties we're turning out now each month. They're making a major push to try to beat the Central Pacific to Salt Lake City."

Suzanna stopped rocking. "We can't produce that many with the crew we have."

"We'll have to add men—and work all day Saturdays."

"That still won't do it."

"It would if we quit cutting building lumber and just cut ties. They're worth more per board foot, anyway," he said.

"And not serve our building customers? That's not like you."

"There are mills south and east of us, away from the rail lines, that are cutting building lumber. We can let them know we're getting out of the cut-board business and ask that they pick up our customers. If they meet the demand and costs stay the same, the builders won't mind."

"You've thought this all through," she said, her mouth a grim, straight line. "But I'm the one who has to find the men and change the schedule."

"I know. It's going to mean more of your time until we get production up."

"And what do you plan to be doing?"

"Well—I suppose I need to . . . ," David began.

Suzanna begrudgingly completed the thought. ". . . get out to Salt Lake City so we can decide what we're going to do about this unlikely inheritance."

"Why do you say 'unlikely?'"

Suzanna waited until he turned to look at her. "Do you ever remember your mother even *hinting* at there being money in her family? Or that her mother had been a waiting-lady to some queen? Or that your grandfather served as a royal gardener?"

"If Mr. Rosswell's right, they embarrassed the family. It wasn't something that was talked about."

"And apparently still isn't. But even as they got older? One would think that someone in Philadelphia would have known of any stain on the family."

David paused, then said what had rarely been spoken. "It wasn't the only stain. When Mother joined the Mormons and we moved with them to Missouri, her parents didn't speak to her again. I don't remember any of her letters ever being answered."

"It just seems so . . . so *unlikely*," Suzanna said. "A manor house in England in the family?"

"And mother will feel the same. That's why I need to go to Salt Lake to be certain she doesn't just turn it over to this Rosswell."

"She'll ask you to take care of it . . . ."

David nodded. "I believe she will."

"And what will you do?"

"We can decide that when we know the decision is ours to make."

"I've wanted so badly to see Lydia," Suzanna said softly.

David moved to the rocker and pulled her onto her feet, drawing her to him. "I knew that was in your thoughts the moment the man mentioned Mother. That, and a chance that you might see Johnny. But if things need to be signed over to someone, it will have to be me. And if there are problems at the mill, you'll need to be here to handle them—and will do it better than I ever could. I need to go with Rosswell tomorrow."

"The last time you left me to go that far, you didn't come back for a year. I thought you'd been killed."

"That was the war," he said. "And I did come back. This shouldn't take long, and there's no war to worry about."

"Just the Indian war Rosswell talked about."

"You're the one Mother writes to. She says that's all south of where she is. The trail to Salt Lake comes in from the northeast. We won't be anywhere close."

Suzanna unwrapped from his embrace. "Well, you'd better get some clothes together and get some of the money from the hidey hole. You can go tell your Mr. Rosswell you'll meet him at the station in the morning."

"And what are you going to do?"

"I have bread to bake and a schedule to work out," she said.

6

ELIZABETH

They called themselves "The League of Four," though on this particular summer evening, five were gathered about the oak study table in the cramped storeroom that served as legal library for Judge James Bradwell. Chicago's two-story Cook County Courthouse, a neoclassic box of gray marble with squat twin domes, filled most of a square between Washington and Randolph Streets a few blocks from the lakefront. A bold sign at every exterior door declared the building off-limits afterhours to those without special permission from the county clerk. The officer, a small, unpleasant, hawkish man who was a Know-Nothing Party carryover from before the war, had been continuously re-elected because he publicly painted such a grim and burdensome picture of his office that no prospective opponent found the position appealing. One of those onerous duties, he had personally decided, was to deny evening access to the building to all but city and county officials—and then, only begrudgingly.

Myra Bradwell was a woman not to be denied. She chose to bypass the clerk, use her husband's side door key, and depend on the good graces of Matt Jones, the night caretaker, to keep her meetings secret. Judge Bradwell had made a precedent-setting decision in a probate case concerning the meager estate of two freed slaves who happened to be Jones' parents. The ruling had acknowledged the validity of slave marriages, even when plantation records were sketchy about their legality, declaring that descendants of those unions were entitled to inherit any wealth, property, or belongings. Matt Jones owed much more to Judge Bradwell than to the self-important clerk. While Myra and her league were in session, Matt steered any night-owl workers who had passed the clerk's muster away from Bradwell's office. The makeshift library, without windows and lined floor to ceiling with law books, was the perfect hideaway for a league of women eager to study the law undisturbed and undetected.

The four regulars at the weekly gathering were as diverse in personality as they were in age. Myra was thirty-six, a sturdy woman of iron constitution, boundless energy, and indomitable will. As an apprentice in her husband's law office before his election to the bench, she had openly declared that she intended to be the first woman to be licensed as an attorney in the state of Illinois. Resistance by the state's legal establishment had thwarted her ambition but strengthened her resolve.

Elizabeth Whitlock had come to Chicago in part to escape the cloistering sameness of Afton, Iowa, and in part to find someone who could tutor her in the law. In Afton, having a "future" meant marrying her choice of the local farm boys and raising a brood of like-minded children. But a casual statement by the school mistress when Elizabeth was only eleven had so impressed the girl that whenever Judge Dawson held court in town, Elizabeth had manufactured some excuse to be near the courthouse where she could creep into the back of the courtroom to witness justice in action.

"The thing that separates us as a nation," her teacher, Miss Bennett, had observed, "is that we are governed, not by a king or emperor, but by ourselves. We have agreed upon a set of laws that we place above the commands of any ruler, and we make both ourselves and our leaders subject to this rule of law." In Judge Dawson's court she had seen those laws protect common citizens against some of the community's most influential and powerful. The rural judge had become her inspiration, and Myra Bradwell her mentor. Though a decade younger than Myra, Elizabeth now left weekly sessions of the League mentally exhausted and wondering if she was a fool to be aspiring to the woman's level of commitment and legal mastery.

The oldest of the four, Mary Livermore, was a luminary in Chicago women's circles in her own right. At forty-seven, she had achieved more than most could hope for in two lifetimes. As journalist, abolitionist, suffragette, and founder of several of the city's most admired humanitarian societies, the angular, soft-spoken wife of a Universalist minister had been the only woman granted a press pass to attend Chicago's 1860 Republican Convention. Unlike the others in the League, she had no ambition to practice law, but found a studied background in state and federal statutes to be useful in all of her activist work.

The fourth of the regulars, and the least likely, was a girl of thirteen who Myra had introduced to Elizabeth as "a young woman of impatient genius." Alta Hulett had mastered telegraphy at the age of ten and, by the time her mother entrusted her to Myra's tutelage, was working as Rockford, Illinois' most skilled telegraph operator.

"She wants desperately to master the law just as well," Myra confided. "The girl's mother can't keep her in books and asked that I take her as a ward. She's very frail. Doctors don't seem to be able to put a finger on her malady. I fear her passion may come from her belief that she may not have a long life and wishes to commit every moment to learning."

The fifth at the table on this Monday evening was Myra's nine-year-old daughter. Bessi was a precocious girl in her own right, but clearly there more at her mother's insistence than by choice. In earlier months, the four older women had completed a thorough examination of the federal constitution and papers by its framers that provided evidence of legal intent. They now plowed systematically through Illinois law and had spent the past four meetings discussing contracts: who could enter into them, their essential elements, and what circumstances might render them null and void. Bessi, who had fidgeted nervously during the entire two hours of the evening's session, had begun to doodle absently on the paper Myra had thrust in front of her for notes, but returned quickly to still indifference after a withering glare from her mother.

As Myra wrapped up the evening, Elizabeth breathed a silent sigh of her own, tucked her notes into the over-sized handbag she kept for her books and papers, and began to follow Mary Livermore into the Judge's dark office.

"Elizabeth, do you have a moment?" Myra left Alta and Bessi to re-shelve the books they had referenced and drew Elizabeth toward two chairs that faced the Judge's desk in the dim outer room.

"Please, sit with me," she said. Elizabeth dropped her bag onto the desk and took the leather-upholstered armchair farthest from the shaft of light that intruded from the library's lamp.

"You weren't your usual inquisitive self this evening," Myra said, sitting back in the other chair, propping an elbow on the arm, and pressing her chin with the extended fingers of her right hand.

"Contracts," Elizabeth answered with a weak smile. "I can't say that this is a part of the law that captures any of my interest. If ever allowed to practice, I will certainly select some area of specialization other than contracts."

Myra nodded. "A sentiment I share . . .. But it's more than that. You seem tired. Discouraged."

Elizabeth thought fleetingly about how much she wanted to share, deciding she would let Myra's questions determine what she chose to reveal. "I admit that Mondays are exhausting. I finish at Cooley and Farwell at six, barely make it to my lodgings in time for supper, clean up afterward, and rush down here to be ready to begin by eight. I must be letting it show."

She could see Myra's eyes move thoughtfully over her face in the dim light, finally settling directly on her own. "That would explain the tired," she said. "But not the discouraged."

Was that another question? Elizabeth decided it was. She lowered her eyes to the hands folded in her lap.

"I sell women's undergarments all day," she said softly enough that Myra leaned toward her. "Each Monday evening, I learn more about what I know I truly want to do with my life. And each Tuesday morning, I am reminded by a woman who insists on buying a corset she will never be able to squeeze into that I am being equally unrealistic about a profession I want desperately to fit into but may never have the chance."

Myra was silent for a moment, then relaxed back into the chair. "The last time we spoke about this, you said your Mr. Mathis wasn't anxious for you to have a profession—and didn't even favor your work at Cooley and Farwell."

Elizabeth smiled again thinly. "Robert and his mother. She's appalled that I work as a store clerk and quite disturbed when I mention a career. And Robert? He wants me to be some kind of debutant, like she was before she married."

"But you're concerned that you can't, or don't wish to, be that woman?"

"I'm concerned that I don't see anything fulfilling on the horizon, and he doesn't want me to be looking."

"A knotty dilemma."

Elizabeth nodded slightly in the shadows, feeling Myra's eyes study her thoughtfully.

"You are an exceptionally bright woman," her mentor said finally. "And I am truly amazed, and a little envious, at how quickly and completely you grasp the concepts we discuss." She paused and glanced back toward the open library door. "I brought Bessi this evening because I wanted her to see your intensity—to know that there was another Elizabeth in our lives who aspires to what she might be someday." She returned her attention to her pupil. "Could you be happy as a Chicago socialite?"

"I don't really know," Elizabeth confessed. "I have so little experience in that world. Just what I've seen when I visit Robert's family. Perhaps there is some good I could do . . . ."

"Let me ask it this way," Myra interrupted. "If you were given the opportunity to work in an area that involved you in the law—something you found truly satisfying—or could live as Robert's mother does, which would you choose?"

It was a question Elizabeth had pondered almost daily as she refolded petticoats and cotton underwear. In recent months, the answer had been clear.

"I would take the position," she said, this time with greater conviction. "Robert would have to decide if that was acceptable to him. I couldn't live as his mother does if I knew there was something like that out there for me."

"And if I were to tell you that there might be? That I know of something that appears to be just what you have been dreaming about as you cinch up those corsets?"

It was Elizabeth's turn to lean forward. "Is there such a thing? I would be *so* delighted—and so grateful."

"I can't be certain. But I didn't wish to make further inquiries until I knew you were interested if the opportunity came your way."

"*Interested?* I would be pleased beyond words. And you know I would do my absolute best to make you proud. Can you tell me . . . ?"

Myra pushed from the chair. "I have heard talk, and I'll make inquiries this week. If it develops as a real possibility, I'll tell you more. But I needed your permission."

"You have my permission," Elizabeth said, "and my undying gratitude."

Myra lifted a cautioning hand. "Let us first see if this works out," she said.

7

SUZANNA

The men shuffled nervously about the stacking yard in ones and twos rather than huddling in small groups as they usually did before the morning whistle coaxed them to their stations. When Suzanna rounded the corner of the mill, they stopped in place, glancing about to see who might be brave enough to voice aloud what most had been whispering. Edward Ransford, a loose, lanky man whose job it was, with Christian Larsen, to move fresh-cut ties to a salt brine soak to prevent rot, stepped awkwardly forward.

"Pardon, Mizz Whitlock. But we was wonderin' if we could speak to ya this mornin' about last night's meetin'—afore the day gits a goin'."

Suzanna had expected something less formal, men coming to her one at a time during morning breaks to ask about what they had heard. But a meeting with all the men was better—a chance for everyone to ask what they wanted and hear what she had to say. Otherwise, it would buzz about the mill all day like a nest of stirred-up yellowjackets. She smiled at Edward to acknowledge that this was exactly what she had hoped for.

"Why don't you all gather over by the hoist where you can sit on logs if you like. I'll drop these ledgers on the desk and be right with you."

When she returned to the yard, the men had assembled around the tripod legs of the hoist, but none sat. They stood with arms folded or hands thrust deep into their pockets, most looking embarrassed, a few, belligerent. She knew none would want to serve as spokesman, so she saved them an uneasy silence.

"Edward, I appreciate you speaking up when I came down this morning. I'd like to take what time we need to talk about your meeting. If starting time comes before we're finished, don't worry about it. Everyone needs to say what's on his mind. What were you wanting to ask about, Edward?"

Edward shuffled in place, scuffing at the thick layer of chips and sawdust that covered the yard.

"I think one of the main things was if someone gets hurt," he said. "Mr. Griggs said the mill's got no obligation to help us out or help take care of our families if one of us gets hurt."

Suzanna nodded. "That's true, Edward. Mr. Griggs is right. The mill has no legal obligation. But we do feel a moral obligation. We've been fortunate to have had only one serious accident during the time we've been in operation. And as you know, when Ben was injured, we helped the family out while he recovered, then brought him right back to work."

Ben Lanear spoke from the edge of the assembled men. "That's right. The mill's been right by me and my family."

"But what if we were hurt so as we couldn'a come back to work?" Sam Gorton asked. He was as short and thick as Ransford was lanky and worked the hoist that moved logs from the rough-cut stack to the sled. Sam still spoke with the lilting brogue of an Irishman, though he had come to Iowa near the end of the great potato famine in '51. A man who worked just for the paycheck and was known about town to spend too much of it on drink, Sam came to work sober and worked hard. "Griggs was sayin' one of the benefits o' formin' a brotherhood is that we pay a bit each month to a fund to help out if someone gets hurt like that."

Suzanna hesitated, then decided candor was the better part of wisdom. "We try our best to keep you safe here," she said. "But we have put away money over time in case we have an accident of the kind you're talking about. The fund is in the bank in Osceola."

"You've never said nothin' 'bout that before," Gorton said. "That would'a been a good bit to know about."

"If you had known about it, what would you have done?" Suzanna asked.

Reuben Hall tried to help her from the front of the group of men. "We'd a probably asked why you couldn't pay us more, if the mill was making that kind of money."

Suzanna nodded without looking at Reuben. "Exactly. We pay you a fair wage but try to keep some of what the mill brings in to plan for possible emergency needs."

A voice from the back that she took to be Willard Burgon moved to another concern. "Griggs said some company's starting to work only fifty hours. Nothing on Saturdays."

From her conversations with the railroad bosses, Suzanna had anticipated a question about hours. "We're just able to meet our production schedule as it is," she said. "In fact, with the contract David just brought back from Omaha, we will need to add men and go all day on Saturday. But I'm willing to shorten the work week to fifty hours for any man who wishes. Your pay is fifteen dollars a week now. For fifty hours, it would be twelve-fifty. That's more than the men at the brickyard are making for a sixty-hour week, so it would still be a fair wage. Just let me know during the day, and I'll adjust your schedule."

For several moments, an unsettled silence hung over the yard. Then Ben Lanear called from the back of the group. "Whistle time, men. Time to be getting to your stations. Talk to Mizz Whitlock later if you want to work the fifty hours."

"I got one more question," Gorton said brusquely. "We told Griggs about your plan where we're all buyin' the mill, a bit at a time. He said we was crazy to let you keep some of our pay each month and tell us we was buyin' the mill. 'Who knows what's to become of the mill?' he says. Believed we'd be better off getting' our full pay—and that if we ever did get the mill, we'd be getting' all the problems that we don't have to worry about now."

Suzanna felt the fine hairs on her arms bristle and her spine stiffen. She tightened her jaw to freeze the thin smile that she hoped looked unperturbed.

"Mr. Griggs was right about some of that as well," she said. "If you kept the three dollars a week that you have been contributing to the purchase plan we worked out, you would have that money to spend. And at the end of five more years, when you men own the mill, you will inherit all the problems that go with running it. We discussed all that when we presented the plan to you five years ago. At the time, enough of you voted for the plan to make it happen."

"Not me," Gorton grumbled. "I voted no."

"Yes, you did," Suzanna said calmly. "But you chose to stay and work here and contribute your three dollars a week. So you now own a portion of this mill. If you all choose, you can vote to change the plan and we will return the money to you, as we have to men who left the mill since the plan started and didn't want to keep their earned share. But you just said Mr. Griggs was encouraging you to form a brotherhood and pay something every month to help each other. Would that be better in some way than paying a little each week to own the whole mill in five years?"

"What if the mill doesn't make it for five more years?" the same voice called from the rear. "Griggs asked about that."

"Then we're all out of work," Suzanna said. "But you own half the assets right now. If we sold off the wagons, mules, engine, and other equipment, half of that comes to you. That would be better than just being out of a job." She heard grumbling from the direction from which the voice had come, but no clear rebuttal.

She moved her gaze slowly along the line of silent workers. "The mill is doing better than it has ever done. The future of the railroad looks bright, and ours is linked to it. But even if it changes, people will need lumber. If you choose to stay with our plan, in five years you will own this mill. You'll be able to work what hours you want, create whatever funds you wish to have for emergencies, and pay yourselves as much as you like. If you don't want to stay with the plan, let us know and we will return what you've contributed to the purchase. When David and I decide we have had enough mill work, we will sell to someone else, and you will have new bosses. We hope you will have a little more vision than that." She glanced over her shoulder at the idle engine and blade. "For now, let's get to work and make enough this week to cover your pay."

8

CORA

Her father hadn't learned any more of the strange language than the names of his new ranch hands. Li Bo made it too easy for him to speak to the men in English. During their first dinner with the Chinese families of chicken and noodles, the Whitlocks had been told that Li was the family name—for all four families—and that when introducing themselves, they placed it before their given names. Her friends' fathers were two sets of brothers, cousins to each other. The man who spoke English was Li Bo. His brother, Li Yan. Ji and Fan were his cousins. Her father gave instructions through Li Bo who always seemed to pass them along in much greater detail, but the men understood.

Cora's mother, who said little anyway, communicated with the women in the same way she spoke with other Indians who stopped at the ranch but were not of the language of the Paiute. The tribes all understood an elaborate dance of gestures, facial expressions, and hand signs and spoke together as clearly as if they knew every word the other was saying. The Chinese women did little with hand gesturing but were expert at acting out what they wanted her mother to do or understand. It frustrated Cora that all of them spoke little and were learning few words.

Her new friends wanted her to know the names of everything about them and were just as anxious to learn what she called them. The child that had been beside Li Bo on the wagon seat was a girl, Nuo, and she and Cora had become inseparable. During their first day together, chasing rabbits through the tall grass that surrounded the Whitlock ranch buildings, Nuo had indicated with her fingers that she was eight years old, a year older than Cora. But as they learned to better understand each other, Nuo explained that she had been considered a year old at birth, so they were very close to the same age.

Cora had lived with only her parents and a pair of black and white herding dogs for so long that having playmates filled her with an excitement she could barely keep inside. She raced through her morning chores with an energy that brought amused smiles and knowing looks from her parents. As soon as her mother nodded that she had done enough, she raced for the bunkhouse, then off through the shoulder-high grass, trailing a line of dark-suited children who followed her like a mother goose with goslings. During the first weeks, they stopped beside every new object, pointing and assigning a name. Chicken, she learned, was *ji*. Her father said it sounded just like Li Ji's name and asked, with a laugh, if Nuo's uncle was named Chicken. Nuo shook her head seriously and repeated the words, helped Cora hear the change in the lilt of her voice. It was like the subtle differences in pitch she heard in the trill of songbirds as they called back and forth across the pasture. But Father couldn't hear it.

Horse was *ma* and water *shui*. To cook was *zuo fan* with *fan* sounding a lot like Li Fan's name. Nuo again shook her head and repeated the words, her voice rising as she said one, and falling as she said the other. In frustration, she gestured dramatically left and right. "*Fan*"—hands to the left. "And *fan*"—hands to the right. To Cora's thick-eared father, both sounded like the word he used to describe the tailfeathers of the big wild gobblers that bobbed and strutted each spring in front of the hens they fancied. But Cora heard the difference and placed each in the word boxes she had created in her mind.

By the time her friends' fathers were beginning to feel comfortable chasing across the valley on horseback, she had learned to chatter in the high-pitched tones of the exciting new language. Some words she didn't remember having been told at all. She simply found herself using and understanding them, just as the Chinese children understood more and more of what she said. They chose to speak to her in English. She answered in Chinese. Sometimes they mixed the two without paying much attention to who was using which.

She helped her mother fashion buckskin shirts and leggings for the riders to wear over their thin native clothing and leather gloves to protect their hands from the coarse hemp rope that was the main tool of a herd rider. While ranching in the valley, the family had collected an assortment of broad-brimmed hats, some flat and round, others as tall again as a man's head and narrower across the front. Each of the new hands now rode with one that he had personally refashioned to his own taste.

Her father had given her one of the smaller mares when she turned five, and she now rode as skillfully as he did. She was the one who showed her friends' fathers how to cinch on a saddle, fit a bit into a horse's mouth, and guide their mounts with their knees while they threw a rope or carried a new foal. As she grew more comfortable with the new language, it was Cora who became the source of information to her parents that the reserved and eternally polite Li Bo was unwilling to share.

"Li Yan is afraid of horses," she announced as the family washed for supper one evening.

Johnny flipped water from his hands over the wash basin, suppressing a smile. "Oh? And how did you decide this?"

"I watch him. And Lily says he doesn't like to ride. He thinks his horse hates him."

"Lily?" her father asked.

"Yes. Nuo wants an English name. She likes Lily. Her brother likes Joseph."

"And *Lily* told you all this? Li Yan rides with us every day and hasn't said anything about being afraid of his horse."

"He won't say anything to *you* about it," Cora said emphatically.

"No? And why not?"

"It is his job to ride. He will not complain about doing what he's told to do."

Johnny took the towel from his daughter and looked at the girl more seriously. "You and Lily didn't decide this just from watching him ride."

"Lily hears them talking in the evening. She tells me because Li Yan is her uncle and is very unhappy."

Johnny turned to Nodda who was carrying a wooden bowl heaped with the first young potatoes of the season to the table. She frowned and gave her husband a slight shrug.

"I do not know what they talk about," she said. "Only Cora understands. She talks to the children all day."

"I don't want to make a man ride who doesn't feel safe in the saddle," Johnny muttered. "They all seem to be doing so well. And we need to start the horses south in two days." He took his seat at one end of the table as Nodda placed a platter of thin-sliced venison, cooked in onions, beside the potatoes and took the seat opposite. Cora pulled a chair up between her parents.

"The rest of the men like to ride," she told them. "Once you fixed the saddles so they could reach the stirrups, and once they didn't get sore every day, they said it is the best work they have ever done. They're excited about taking the horses to Salt Lake. Only Li Yan is afraid. I think his family wants to go with him and stay there."

Johnny dished venison and gravy onto his plate, took a piece of Nodda's flatbread from a basket, and swabbed the dark gravy. "You're certain about this?" he asked Cora.

"Chen said the same thing—that his father doesn't like the horses. His family wants to go back to California."

"Chen's only five."

Cora nodded. "So he doesn't make things up. He says what he hears."

The family ate in silence, Cora deciding she had said as much as she should but wondering what her parents were thinking. Her mother was always quiet, said little, and then very softly. Her father used supper time to talk about the day that had just passed and tell them what they would do in the day ahead. But on this evening, his thoughts were his own. He was as silent as her mother.

9

JOHNNY

They spent the morning rounding up the twelve horses that were to be sold, enclosing them in the corral beside the bunkhouse. Johnny laid back, letting his four Chinese ranch hands circle the herd and guide it down the valley into a fenced paddock. They had marked the dozen the day before with a red swab on the flank: five two-year-old mares, two young stallions, and five geldings. He opened the gate into a fenced chute that ran from the paddock to a corral behind the bunkhouse, took up a position beside the chute gate, and shouted to Li Bo to have the men cut out the sale horses and run them through into the corral.

Li Yan had ridden as aggressively as the other men in the open meadow. But in the enclosed paddock, he guided his sorrel mare to the fence, reined her in, and watched nervously as Li Fan stationed his mount across the gate to keep the brood horses in place, slipping aside as the other riders jostled their way through the packed herd with marked animals.

With the dozen successfully separated, the riders followed them through the chute. Johnny grasped the end of the top pole and threw it across the opening. He dismounted quickly and, with Li Bo's help, slid the remaining bars into place.

"Get our horses out the far gate and brush them down," he said to Li Bo. "That's all the riding we'll be doing today. I'll turn the herd back into the pasture."

The men unsaddled their mounts, threw saddles over a rail beside the bunkhouse, and waited expectantly for the rest of the day's work orders.

"We'll leave the sale horses in the corral for a couple of days," Johnny said when he rejoined the men. "They need to sort out who's going to be the boss mare. I want to get on the trail early Friday morning. Tomorrow we'll pack what provisions we'll need and decide who'll drive the wagon team. I want to take one light wagon with a pair of draft horses—pack it with what we'll need for our campsite and for meals on the trail. It's about two hundred miles. We don't want to drive the horses more than fifteen to twenty a day, depending on what kind of weather and terrain we have. They need to be in top condition when we get them to the city." He looked expectantly at the four men, careful to keep his gaze moving from face-to-face. "I'll need one of you to drive the wagon."

As if drawn by a single string, three of the faces turned toward Li Yan. He acknowledged with a quick bow of the head and stepped forward, addressing Johnny directly in Chinese with downcast eyes. Li Bo stepped up beside him.

"Li Yan asks if he may drive the wagon," Li Bo said quietly. "And he asks if he may take his own mules, and if his family may go with him. Once he has received his payment for the work he has done, he wishes to remain in the city with the wagon and his family. He is most grateful for the work you have given us, but he and his family would like to return to California and open a new eating place."

Johnny considered the information for long enough to give the impression this was new to him, then extended a hand to Li Yan. The tension in the man's shoulders slipped away and he looked up.

"You've been a very good worker, Li Yan. And I thank you for the friendship you've given my family. But I know what it means to want to go your own way. Sounds like we'd better take two wagons so we have one to bring back the supplies we need. Can your wife drive one?"

Li Bo began to interpret, but his cousin nodded his understanding. "Yes. Wife can drive," he said in English. "You been good to my family."

Johnny stepped away and surveyed the other men with a grim smile. "Will I be losing all my help with this trip?"

Li Bo spoke quickly enough that Johnny realized this had all been discussed at length. "Our families will stay, and we will come back with you." He nodded toward the other men. "We want to buy cattle with some of our money in Salt Lake City and bring them back with us. If we can work with you while we begin to raise our cattle, we can build homes in this valley. It is very large, and no one is here. We will help you with your horses. You can help us with our cattle?"

This part of the conversation was unexpected. Johnny wouldn't have been surprised to learn that all four planned to stay in the city—or that the three were willing to return for at least another season. But he hadn't anticipated the cattle and the wish to settle in. It must have been discussed out of earshot of Lily and the other children.

"There are many buffalo here," he said. "Hunters take the meat to the cities. Where will you sell your cattle?"

"If we can buy cattle in Salt Lake City, we can sell them there. There are no buffalo in California, and wagons passing through will have lost cattle along the way."

Johnny smiled thoughtfully. He'd seen the industriousness of these men and heard their stories of creating new opportunities as they were forced from one place to another. They saw in the valley a haven for a new enterprise.

"You haven't been here through a winter," he said. "The snow can get as deep as your waist."

All three men nodded. When they chose to, they understood Johnny without Li Bo's assistance.

"We have helped you cut the grass and bundle it for winter," Li Bo said. "We have grown potatoes, turnips, onions, and squash as you have done, and you taught us how to smoke and salt meat. We will build a winter barn when we return, before we build houses. If you and your horses can live through the winter, we can live here with our cattle."

Johnny paused, studying the faces of the Asian men. If they worked together, he would not need to hire more hands. And having children in the valley had been a godsend to Cora. His mind drifted north up the valley to a place where he had seen the perfect spot for a second homestead. Would they need a school? No one in the mix of families had enough education to teach the children more than the basics of reading and numbers. But his inquisitive daughter—she could learn as fast as he could supply her with books and could teach the others. And he could not hope for better neighbors.

"We'll build a barn as soon as we get back," he said, grasping Li Bo's hand and clapping him on the shoulder. "And we'll cut more hay. It's beginning to brown, but there's still good grass beside the river. We'd better ask the women what we should bring from the city if we're going to become a village."

As the men turned toward the house, Cora and Lily burst onto the porch and sprinted down the gradual slope toward the bunkhouse.

"*They're coming*," Cora shouted, waving loosely down the valley. "We saw them from my window."

To the south, dust spread like a summer storm across the sea of browning grass. Johnny squinted into the midday haze.

"Who's coming?"

"The *Newe*. It's time for the *Naraya*!"

"Ah," Johnny said, grinning broadly. "It's Washakie and his people. It's the season of the Ghost Dance. Li Bo, we will need to rope the gray stallion."

Li Bo stepped up beside him, watching the cloud sweep toward them up the valley. "Are these Indians that come?" he asked nervously.

"Shoshone. This is their valley. I give them a horse each fall as payment for being here. We will need to sit with Washakie and see what he wants to allow you to raise cattle."

"This is their . . . valley?" A deep swallow interrupted the tremor in Li Bo's voice.

"Their hunting grounds. They would say that no one owns the valley. But by agreement with the other tribes, the *Newe* hunt here. For one horse a year, Washakie allows us to stay."

"We haven't seen them here before . . ."

"They move with the seasons. In the fall, they come to the grove near the salt springs for the *Naraya*, the Ghost Dance. Most times, they come down from the north. Tomorrow night, we will hear their drums and chanting."

They stood in place as the column of a hundred men, women, and children rode toward them, many trailing pack animals burdened with bundles wrapped in skins.

"They are great horse people," Johnny said as the tribe approached. "I thought I knew horses until I was taught by the *Newe*."

The lead rider, a leather-skinned man of sixty with dark, shoulder-length hair, a prominent arched nose, wide mouth, and the high cheekbones of the plains Indians, raised his hand in greeting. Though his face was stern, his brown eyes smiled. Johnny felt Li Bo relax beside him.

"Stands Like a Tree. Are you well, my brother?"

"Very well, Washakie. I see you are strong and have many horses."

"It has been a good season. And Honeybee? She is a good wife to you?"

Johnny glanced toward the porch where Nodda now stood with two of the Chinese women. "She is a good wife and remembers the ways of her people."

The old chief leaned from his horse toward Cora, speaking to her in Shoshone. "And you, Little Many Tongues. Do you now speak the tongue of these people of the railroad who live with you?"

Cora smiled broadly, replying in his language. "I am learning it," she said. "It is more difficult than the tongue of the *Newe*."

Washakie straightened again in the saddle. "We have come for the *Naraya*. Tomorrow we will sing our dream songs."

"I have your horse," Johnny said, turning back toward the corral. "The tall gray is for Chief Washakie."

The old Indian humphed, his face furrowing. "I will not be taking a horse this season. We have made peace with the chief in Washington and are moving our people to what you call the Wind River. This is no longer the hunting ground of the *Newe*."

Johnny nodded grimly. "I have heard of this. I am sorry for the *Newe*. We will watch over the valley for you. Is this why you come from the Bear River?"

Washakie shook his head. "We have been trading skins with the Mormon chief. When we have sung our dream songs, we will go to the Wind River." He looked curiously at the Chinese hands. "These people of the railroad. They are staying here?"

"They help with the horses. They do not like the railroad or the mines. Their ancestors came from beyond the great water. These men want to stay in this valley and raise horses and cattle."

Washakie studied the three faces that looked nervously up at him. "You must all come to the *Naraya*," he said after a moment. "If you are to care for the valley, you must sing with us for good rain and tall grass. We will sing for there to be many deer and elk. When the sun sleeps tomorrow, come dance with us."

"We will come," Johnny said. "And I will bring your horse. We will still need the blessings of the *Newe* on our valley."

When they reached the grove of pines, Washakie's people had already circled the dance fire, the drums stirring them restlessly with a hypnotic beat. The *Newe* wore their finest, the women in brightly woven skirts with intricate beadwork decorating the sleeves and bodices of buckskin shirts. The younger men wore only breechcloths and moccasins, their chests painted with slashes of color, their long hair knotted into tight rolls crowned with a pair of eagle feathers, homage to the tribe's sacred totem.

As the ranch families approached, the circles spread and drew in those the tribe viewed as part of the *Newe*: Johnny to the inner ring of men, and Nodda to the outer circle of women. Cora led the Chinese families to a space between two pines where those too frail to dance sat swaying to the rhythm of the drums. Beside the fire, a tribal elder with white milky eyes and hair the color of wood ash began to shuffle about the flames, guided by the crackle and heat of the fire. With arms spread and chin tilted to the heavens, a chant lifted from his thin, motionless lips into the night sky. About him, the dancers stepped in place, mimicking his uneven shuffle and listening intently. Suddenly the men shifted left, beating the earth in unison with buckskin feet. The women and children waited until the inner ring had completed a full turn, then picking up the chant and shuffling step, matching the beat of the flat, skin-covered drums.

Li Bo leaned toward Cora. "What does the song say?" he whispered.

"It is just words," she said quietly. "Green water. Flying eagles. Tall grass. Running deer."

"What does *Naraya* mean?' Li Bo asked.

"It is the way they dance," Cora said. "The way they step." As she spoke, two women backed from the circle and took their hands, pulling the remainder of their guests into the dancing *Newe* until all but the very old shuffled and chanted, the fire casting spectral shadows against the surrounding trees like the ghosts they summoned.

10

SUZANNA

"There's a letter from Elizabeth for you," Charlotte Winter said as Suzanna approached the postal window. "It came in yesterday. Since you didn't come to town before I closed, I left it with Martha at the counter. But I fetched it back this morning." She handed Suzanna a cream parchment envelope.

Suzanna cast a quick glance toward the shop counter where Martha Fife sorted a delivery of fresh eggs by size, then turned to inspect the envelope against the light of the store's front windows. Charlotte chuckled.

"I already looked," she whispered. "I don't think Martha opened it."

"Only because Lizzy put a daub of wax on it," Suzanna muttered. "Please don't leave letters with Martha. I swear. That woman should work for the James Gang! She could open the vault at the Osceola bank and no one would know she'd been inside. When she gets hold of one of these," Suzanna waved the letter in front of her, "most of Afton knows what's in it before I do."

"I thought you might be coming later in the afternoon." Charlotte said contritely. "And I saw that it was sealed." Her face brightened and she smiled mischievously. "Martha *did* look disappointed when she saw the wax."

Suzanna folded the letter and slipped it into the pocket of her work shirt. "I need to pick up a few things and get back to the mill. Maybe I can find a few minutes during the ride back to see if Lizzy found a new position."

"I hope so," Charlotte said. "She seems so unhappy at that big Chicago store."

Suzanna read the letter, perched beside Nate Carter as he steered the supply wagon back along the east road toward the mill.

Dearest Mother:

I pray that this letter finds you and Father well and that you have taken my advice to work less and enjoy life more. I realized this week that it is the fifth anniversary of Thomas' death, and know that will be weighing heavily on your heart. But it should also serve to remind each of us that life is so fragile, and we mustn't let it pass without spending what time we can enjoying it. I suspect that with me and Johnny away, the men at the mill have become the object of your mothering. For your sake, and for theirs, find more opportunities to relax with Father.

Having unburdened myself with that little lecture, I must display some hypocrisy and tell you that I have found new employment— and I am so delighted! It appears that Illinois is not quite ready to admit members of our sex to the bar, but I continue to have that ambition and have found a position that should help with my preparation. An acquaintance from your own state, Arabella Mansfield from Burlington, petitioned to be admitted in Iowa and may find greater sympathy than we have here in Illinois, partly, I believe, because her interest is in teaching the law, rather than practicing it. I'm sure the irony in that escapes neither of us! Forgive the digression, but this fight is always near the front of my mind.

Myra Bradwell kindly arranged an interview with one of our state's senators to the United States Congress, the honorable Lyman Trumbull, who was seeking a person to manage an office here in Chicago. The senator is from Alton, down near St. Louis, but with such a strong voting population here in the city, feels a need to be represented here. I believe you would approve of him. He is of the party of Lincoln, a very congenial and moral man, and strikes me as genuinely interested in the wellbeing of our citizenry. He was aware of my interest in the law from his conversations with

Myra, and hinted that when he leaves the Senate, his intention is to open a law office here. After an hour that began as nerve-racking and ended as a delightfully relaxed conversation, I was offered the position and accepted on the spot. I returned to Cooley and Farwell the next morning and gave immediate notice.

Senator Trumbull has leased an office in the business district. My first days in the position have been revealing beyond description. I receive regular cables from the Washington Office so that I can speak knowledgably about the Senator's work. I regret to say that the press has given us little understanding of the degree of rancor and distrust that exists between the largely Republican Congress and President Johnson. At the moment, the focus seems to be on the President's efforts to replace Mr. Stanton as Secretary of War. For most Republicans, Johnson is far too accommodating to the South in his views of reconstruction, and Stanton advocates a much more severe approach. Senator Trumbull has such a commitment to what he constantly refers to as "the rule of law" and to the Constitution that he has been very hesitant to follow his colleagues in beating the impeachment drum. He has asked that I not mention the possibility to his public. If Stanton is replaced, I fear it will be difficult to keep the impeachment hounds at bay.

On quite a different matter, since his proposal in November, Robert has only again mentioned marriage once, and that was before another visit to his parents. It was a warning that his mother might broach the subject, which indeed she did. She managed to find a moment alone with me in the parlor and reminded me that I was not getting any younger. By the time she was my age, she said, she already had two children. I suggested that perhaps we had somewhat different goals in life, which seemed to confuse her more than serve as an explanation. I believe that Robert and I care deeply for each other and have much in common. I mentioned when I wrote last that he is a committed Democrat, in the mold of his employer, Cyrus McCormick, but we have managed to reconcile our differences there. Beyond that, he is still unable to accept my unwavering interest in eventually sitting for the bar, nor my desire to contribute my share to a household through satisfying work. He views the move to Senator Trumbull's office as another impediment, and I worry that we may never get past it. Too much of his life has been spent in the white-gloved company of his mother and of the women in the socialite circles in which they move. Until meeting me, he had visions of finding such a wife. He now seems torn between that vision and our affection.

I risk going on too long, dear Mother, and of tiring you with my joys, modest achievements, and continuing disappointments. But you remain my only true confidante and source of strength and reassurance. Please give my love to Father.

Affectionately,

Elizabeth

11

DAVID

The rail line from Burlington bridged the Missouri River at Plattsmouth into the newly created state of Nebraska. There, a spur branched north to Omaha. Convincing Henry Rosswell to spend another day in Afton had given David time to pack more thoughtfully and send a wire ahead to his mother. The brief message read, *"Coming to visit. Possible inheritance in England. Expected arrival in 2-3 weeks. Day uncertain. Love. David."*

The uncertainty reflected both the mode and availability of travel. The Burlington and Missouri to Omaha—one day. Berths on the Union Pacific as far as the transcontinental line now extended—two more days. Carriage, stage coach, or horseback across the Wyoming Territory into the Salt Lake Valley—eight to fifteen days. The possibility of Indian unrest once beyond Nebraska that might cause delays? Unknown. How did one plan such a journey?

They would spend the first night in Omaha at the Hendron House on Ninth Street which, in David's opinion, rivaled St. Joseph's Patee House for comfort and hospitality. Most of the business of the Union Pacific was run from a small office off the hotel's foyer. Through his business connections, David knew the railroad people who managed the Union Pacific's western expansion and thought he could get passage on one of the workmen's trains for $20 to $30. Rosswell, he guessed, would want to take the daily passenger train and pay $60 for extra comfort and a dining car. Either way, it was a fifteen-hour journey to Sidney, Nebraska, where passenger service now officially ended. David may be able to talk rail officials into letting them continue to the end of the constructed track, somewhere between Sidney and the Crow Creek Crossing in the Wyoming Territory. There, if a station was near the railhead, he and Rosswell might be lucky enough to find space on a Wells Fargo coach into the Salt Lake Valley, another $50 fare. Coach time to Salt Lake? If all went well, another eight or nine days. If they had to resort to horseback or wagon train, three or four weeks. Perhaps his telegram should have been less optimistic.

At the Hendron in Omaha, Rosswell did indeed insist on the passenger train. David used his years of service as a supplier to negotiate a half-fare. Stephen Kellogg, who managed acquisitions for Union Pacific in Omaha, granted permission for them to continue west on the supply train to the end of the line, but cautioned that it had just reached the Nebraska state line and was fifty miles short of the Crow Creek Crossing—a place they now referred to as Cheyenne City. The men might best be served by leaving the train where the line crossed the Overland Stage route at Julesburg in Colorado, picking up a coach from there.

"You'll be most likely to get a coach seat at Julesburg," Kellogg suggested. "That's also Fort Sedgwick, and there will be military personnel leaving the stage there. Wells Fargo's boasting sixty to seventy miles a day. If they're getting that kind of distance, you'll be better served not taking the train on to Sidney."

By the time their train reached the military outpost in the northeast corner of the Colorado Territory, David thanked his lucky stars that he hadn't resisted Rosswell's insistence on the passenger service. The dining car, though smothered under a blue cloud of cigar smoke, provided a hot meal every four hours and lighter fare in between. David found himself sailor-walking through the swaying cars for an hourly snack as an excuse to stretch his legs and escape the New York lawyer's incessant talk about the virtues of East Coast living and the rude backwardness of the frontier.

"How can anyone live out here among these savages?" the man muttered as the train pulled away from the station at Fort McPherson. The Nebraska outpost was little more than a loose scattering of cedar log buildings. Half-naked Plains Indians squatting along the wall of the central fort, staring in wonder at the great iron horse that belched smoke and dragged wooden houses along its trail of steel. "I see no commerce or entertainment here," Rosswell complained. "No shops or places of business. Not even a tree-lined street for an afternoon walk. I wouldn't survive a day in a place like this."

"These are rugged, independent people," David said patiently.

"They make their own entertainment—town dances and suppers. And there's a shop in one of those buildings. They unloaded three crates of supplies at the station. The people can get what they need. And as for walks on the shaded streets, they work hard enough during the day that an evening walk isn't something they're looking forward to."

Rosswell scoffed, peering through the coach's curtains with face half-hidden at the curious natives. "And look at those savages. Half animal, with their shaved heads and black, suspicious eyes." He shuddered. "I am appalled that the people allow them to lounge around their settlement."

"The settlement survives because it tolerates those men," David defended, but felt no reason to explain further.

At Fort Sedgwick, Rosswell refused to be billeted in a small room inside the fort with two low cots and straw tick mattresses. When told there was no room at the newly constructed Polley House, the only two-story structure among the cluster of whitewashed frame houses that passed for the village of Julesburg, Rosswell paced the fort's billeting office with fists planted firmly on hips, cursing under his breath. "A dozen rooms and not a single one available?" he fumed.

"You can take mine," a young lieutenant, newly arrived from West Point and assigned temporarily to the Polley House, offered. "I expected to be billeted in the fort anyway, and it won't be worse than my bunk at the Academy." He grinned knowingly at the lawyer. "If you're moving on west, I hear you've got a lot worse facing you."

"Might be safer in here, too, lieutenant," the blue-uniformed soldier in charge of billeting said with a sandpaper laugh. He was a big man, as tall as David and gnarled as the cedar logs that formed the fort's barricades. He extended a meaty hand and introduced himself as Sergeant Mills. "The town was burned to the ground two years back by about a thousand Sioux and Cheyenne." He gave Rosswell a sober frown. "We like to keep people inside the walls who are just passing through. Helps us sleep better."

Rosswell looked skeptically at David. "A thousand Indians attacked this place and burned the town? I think I would have heard about that back East." David lifted his hands, signaling that he was staying out of this discussion. His son's wife was Indian, and he had been saved from a Confederate hospital during the war with the help of both the Creek and Cherokee. If ill was to be spoken about the natives, it wasn't coming from him. And a straw mat was certainly worth a night free of the objectionable attorney. Mills led them across the fort's open parade ground toward a row of low log huts that backed against the outer wall.

"We brought the villagers into the fort and only lost eighteen people," the sergeant said. "Mainly those who tried to stay outside and defend their homes. Not much of a skirmish by frontier standards. Probably didn't get any notice in your New York papers. You remember hearings in the US Congress a few years ago about the killing of Indians at Sand Creek here in the Colorado Territory?"

Rosswell nodded vaguely. "Yes, I remember something like that."

Sergeant Mills eyes narrowed. "Well, the Cheyenne and Arapaho remembered it too. Colonel Chivington claimed his men killed five to six hundred warriors at Sand Creek." Mills glanced around and leaned toward Rosswell, lowering his voice. "Others there said there was more like two hundred, and that they was mainly women and children. They was supposed to be protected by an agreement with the troops at Fort Lyon that was only forty miles away. If I was the Cheyenne, I'd a been mad as hell myself. When they came here, they didn't seem to be looking to kill nobody—just burn the town down."

Rosswell snickered. "You sound like you've got a soft spot for these savages."

Mills' frown deepened. "You stay out here long enough, and one of two things happens. You become a Chivington who damns any man who sympathizes with Indians and tells his troops that it's right and honorable to massacre them. Or you begin to see things as they do. People are taking their land, killing their children, making them sick, and breaking every promise they make to 'em. I'm finding myself agreeing with them half the time."

"Seems like you're not in the right place," Rosswell said with a sniff.

"Or I am," Mills retorted. "And you want to talk savages? You know why this town's called Julesburg?"

Rosswell again looked to David for help, but received none.

"It's named after Jules Beni, a horse thief who made his living stealing from the Overland and Pikes Peak Express. They sent a man named Jack Slade out here to bring him in, but Beni got the jump on him. Shot Slade thirteen times not two hundred yards from here. The townspeople went after Beni, didn't catch him, but came back to find Slade walking through town all shot up. By some miracle, Slade survived. A while later, when he was at his ranch, some other agents came and told him they'd caught Beni and had him tied to a fence post. Story is, Slade went to where they had Beni hog-tied, shot his fingers off one at a time before shooting him dead, then cut off his ears. Carried those ears in his pocket the rest of his life."

Mills pushed the door of one of the low log rooms inward and beckoned his visitors in ahead of him. "You still want to stay out among the civilized?" he said to the New York lawyer.

Rosswell ducked his head into the musty, dark interior, sniffed at the air like a hound testing a rabbit hole, then turned and stalked back toward the billeting office. "For one night, I'll take my chances with the town folk," he said.

"You've got nine or ten days to Salt Lake City sitting in that rocking coach," the brawny sergeant called after him. "They don't stop for nothin'. You better get what sleep you can. This might be the best night you spend for a long time."

He turned back to David and the lieutenant. "That one thinks he's the biggest toad in the puddle," he muttered. "What a bleedin' arse hole!"

12

ELIZABETH

Senator Trumbull stopped for a day in Chicago on his way to Alton, spending the morning meeting with constituents and delivering an address from the balcony of the Tremont House on Lake Street. Both Lincoln and Douglas had launched their senatorial campaigns from that balcony, and Elizabeth had arranged the location, seeing political value in connecting her new boss to that legacy.

The speech was the first time she had really had an opportunity to study the man. His long, clean-shaven face, deep-set eyes, and naturally down-turned mouth gave the appearance of grave seriousness, even when in good humor. He lacked the oratorical passion and eloquence she had once heard in Stephen Douglas or the natural wit and homespun charm of Lincoln. But he laddered his words in such a way that his listeners could follow him, step-by-step, as he shared his deep concern with developments in the nation's capital. There was a thoughtful conviction in his voice that struck Elizabeth as more sincere than she had heard from Douglas, who she found overly dramatic and rehearsed. From her position in a curtained corner of the balcony, she studied the assembly below, knowing that she would be asked for her assessment of their response.

The Senator spoke for nearly two hours, detailing the challenges of bringing the defeated South back into the Union. Much to the displeasure of the more radical wing of the Republicans in Congress, President Johnson favored a lenient amnesty based on the Ten Percent Plan Lincoln had recommended before his death. The Republican majority in the Senate were demanding that the Southern states accept black suffrage before being fully reinstated and advocated for a period of occupation, overseen by an appointed military governor.

The Johnson plan, the Senator explained, slowing his pace as if speaking to a classroom of eager students, required that only ten percent of citizens of the rebellious states pledge loyalty to the Union. State legislatures must also ratify the Thirteenth Amendment, granting emancipation. Trumbull paused, straightened behind the balcony rail, and in the first concession to political expediency Elizabeth had heard from the man, reminded his listeners that as Chairman of the Senate Judiciary Committee, he had played a major role in shaping the popular amendment. In the crowd below, appreciative nods told Elizabeth that the point had registered.

Becoming more somber, Trumbull explained that the president had chosen to grant pardons to most of the rebel leadership and had further infuriated congressional leaders by recognizing sitting governors in four Southern states. The legislative branch, the Senator declared, was becoming increasingly dissatisfied with the president's actions, and both chambers in the Capitol rumbled with talk of impeachment.

"We must," he concluded, "proceed with caution, resisting the great temptation to allow the remaining embers of war and desires for recrimination to kindle new flame. We must not forget that we are reconstructing a constitutional republic. We have succeeded in emancipating a beleaguered race. We must not celebrate that success by unnecessarily subjugating those who resisted that emancipation. My pledge to you is that I will stand as a voice of reason in Washington—as a defender of a sorely tested constitution, a constitution that must remain the guiding beacon as we find our way out of this storm."

Elizabeth judged the applause to be sincere, but not enthusiastic. The response from the assembly seemed more troubled than angry. Those who had come to the Tremont House were among Chicago's most informed citizens, those who began their morning with a thorough reading of the *Tribune* and finished the day consuming the *Daily Journal*. Some, she guessed, included the blatantly Democrat *Chicago Times* on their reading list. They would be uncertain about the wisdom of either a conciliatory approach to reconstruction, or the harder line advocated by Stanton and many in the Republican majority.

After the senator had mixed with his supporters for what Elizabeth considered an appropriate time, she guided him to a quiet corner of the Tremont House's sumptuous dining room where she had reserved a table. As others entered, she was aware of quickly averted eyes and wondered if other diners were being considerate of the senator's privacy or were startled to see him alone with a young and attractive female companion. Perhaps she should have considered another place to critique the morning.

"I read the audience as uncertain," she shared as they awaited the soup course. "No one really seems to know what to make of the trouble in Washington."

"It's an uncertainty I share," he said quietly, nodding and smiling to passersby who were willing to acknowledge him but too polite to interrupt his lunch. "I hope you have reserved the afternoon for us to meet privately. I need your help and wisdom."

"You need *my* help?"

The senator smiled up at the waitress as she carefully placed a steaming bowl in front of his assistant. "From my brief time with you before I left for Washington and from our exchanged letters and telegrams, it's clear to me that you know the law, including our constitution, as well as I do. And I fear we are facing a constitutional crisis. I know you have been studying with Myra, and I hope you have her same keen understanding of the law."

Elizabeth looked demurely down at the spotless tablecloth as the waitress moved around the table to serve the senator.

"I am honored by your trust in me," she said quietly. "Myra has been a thorough and passionate teacher."

As soup was cleared and an entree of prime beef from the nearby stockyards laid before them, she tried to tease more information from the senator.

"I'm assuming, when you speak of a constitutional crisis, that you refer to the potential efforts to impeach," she urged.

Trumbull glanced about at the dining room's continuous flow of couples and businessmen, then turned his full attention to his steak.

"I know that I will not be able to discuss this without becoming visibly agitated," he said evenly. "I would prefer not to draw further attention. Let's finish our meal and return to the office where I can speak about this with the passion it deserves."

Elizabeth nodded her acquiescence, drew a determined breath, and attacked what would normally be enough food for three days.

She managed to slip unobserved into the storefront office across the river on North Lake Street. The senator followed thirty minutes later after shedding a constituent couple who stopped him as they left the restaurant. Elizabeth locked the door, and they pulled chairs up to the work table in a windowless back room. Elizabeth again felt the discomfort of being alone with a married man, but the senator seemed oblivious to any awkwardness. She brightened the gas lamp, drew paper from a desk drawer, positioned an ink well in front of her, and checked the nib of a quill.

"No record," the senator said, waving away the writing materials. "I just want to hear your thoughts." Elizabeth pushed pen and paper aside.

"You are aware, of course," he began, "that the president vetoed the Tenure of Office Act that prevented him from dismissing even his own appointments without the advice and consent of the Senate."

Elizabeth nodded. "But his veto was overridden by Congress the same day, as I recall." She paused, then offered without being prompted, "My personal belief is that the act will not survive an appeal to the courts."

The senator leaned back loosely in his chair and crossed his hands in his lap. "Oh? On what grounds?"

This was only Elizabeth's second face-to-face with her employer, and she had no way to gauge his tolerance for boldness. But he had indicated he desired her help.

"The separation of powers is fundamental to our constitutional government," she began, "and was central to the debate at the Constitutional Convention. There was much less discussion about what those powers should be than about how to keep them in check. The 'Advice and Consent' provision for executive appointment is very specific in its application only to the making of treaties and presidential appointments. There is an implied understanding that all powers not mentioned as restricted remain with the branch possessing administrative oversight. If my memory serves me correctly, the notes from the convention indicate that the power of the president to remove executive appointments was discussed, and intentionally left unrestricted. I believe the Court, fully aware of this history, will agree."

"Hmmm," Trumbull mused, gazing across the table with unveiled surprise and with a note of what Elizabeth read as envy. "That will be particularly likely with our Chief Justice, Salmon Chase. He is a known ally of the president. I believe Johnson may dismiss Stanton as Secretary of War sometime this month, will request consent from the Senate, and will appoint General Grant to fill the office. I am confident the Senate will *not* consent and will reinstate Stanton."

"And the president will accept the reinstatement?"

"Certainly not willingly. Grant, if he accepts at all, will hurriedly step down if the situation becomes contentious. He has presidential aspirations of his own. My fear is that the president will then make another appointment to force a test of the Act before the courts. If that happens, I am almost certain his actions will be used as provocation for drawing up articles of impeachment."

"On what grounds?"

Trumbull arched a brow. "I would think you would have thoughts on this."

"I'm curious as to your own thinking."

"On the grounds that defying the Tenure of Office Act is a violation of federal law and therefore constitutes 'high crimes and misdemeanors.' The provision for impeachment is so loosely stated that it will be construed as covering the president's action."

"And do you believe that it does?"

"Aye! There's the rub!" Trumbull said with a sardonic smile. "If you are correct—that the act will not withstand judicial review and is unconstitutional—and if I agree with that position—which I do—I cannot in good conscience vote to remove a man from office for doing something that I believe to be his constitutional right."

Elizabeth sat in silence, debating again how far it was appropriate to push the discussion. But if she were to help, she needed to know the senator's mind and soul.

"Your name is mentioned on occasion as being a future candidate for the presidency yourself. If you vote against impeachment, you will certainly alienate a sizable number of your colleagues."

"I suspect I will."

"Will other Republicans vote against the party?"

"I have no idea at this point. They have been afraid to discuss it."

"Will you risk losing an opportunity to run for the presidency?"

The cynical smile returned to Trumbull's lips. "You are a bright and ambitious young woman, Miss Whitlock. For the sake of argument, let us suppose that at some far future date, women are elected to the Senate. If you found yourself in my position, what would you do?"

The thought was not beyond the reach of Elizabeth's imagination. "I hope I would do that which I believed to be best for those I represent—and for the Union."

"And that would be?"

"I would vote for what I believe to be constitutionally defensible."

"Against impeachment?"

"Yes, Sir. I would."

"But you expect less from me?"

She felt her face flush. "No, Sir. I would not expect less."

"Then I would be most grateful if you would begin to draft a paper for me supporting that position. I hope I will not need it. But my objections to the Tenure of Office Bill when it first came before the Senate went unheeded, and I expect to fare no better in the upcoming debate."

"I will begin to work on that immediately," she said.

The Senator pushed away from the table and rose. "I plan to catch the afternoon train to Alton. You should not stay too late. I suspect that beau of yours will want part of your evening."

It was Elizabeth's turn to smile cynically. "He's off selling McCormick reapers to farmers in Nebraska."

"Then take some time for yourself. I know you have been working long hours here."

"Tonight is my evening with Myra and friends," Elizabeth said. "And with your permission, I would like to present them with a hypothetical."

Trumbull chuckled. "Your thinking and that of Myra Bradwell. What senator could wish for better?"

13

SUZANNA and ELIZABETH

Johnny's letter reached both women on the same day, carried by eastbound travelers on the Oregon Trail to South Pass and from there by rail to Chicago and Afton. Elizabeth had walked to the boarding house during her lunch break to see if the post had arrived. Suzanna rode into town at noon, hoping for a letter from David. Though unaware of the coincidence, both sat down with Johnny's letter at almost the same moment.

My Dear Family:

I know my letters are few and far between, but our life is so routine that, aside from recounting Cora's antics and what appear to us to be her remarkable abilities with riding and language learning, there is little new to tell. But I must confess that this week has been moving for me in a way that demands that it be shared.

I have written before of the Indians who move each spring and fall through the valley, led by the Shoshone Chief Washakie. They are close enough in kin to Nodda's Paiutes that they have accepted us as part of what they call the Newe—the people. Both Nodda and Cora now speak their language, and I know enough to follow along. Other Indians who pass through the valley have left us alone. I am certain that Washakie has made it known that we are not to be molested.

He told us when they arrived this week that this would be their last autumn in the valley. By an agreement that pains him to the very depths of his soul, the Shoshone will be moved to government lands somewhere north of us. He told us that he would be entrusting the valley to our keeping, to our family and to the Chinese workers I told you about who have chosen to stay and ranch with us. Last night, for the first time, we were invited to be part of their Naraya, the step dance that asks for the blessings of the spirits and of their ancestors on the things of the earth. You know that I have never been a religious man, but I truly felt the power of this ceremony.

The dance is held at night, with the tribe forming two circles about a fire: the men in an inner circle and the women and children surrounding them. Led by the tribe's holy man, they shuffle sideways about the fire, repeating a singing chant to the beat of their drummers. During a time when Nodda and our Chinese friends had joined the dancers, I stood aside with Chief Washakie and Cora, who he calls Little Many Tongues. As the tribe sang and circled the fire, the chief taught us about the power of the Naraya.

The song, he said, comes to the holy man in a vision or dream that tells him what needs to be blessed and healed by the Great Father. This night had three songs. The first was for the grasses and the water, the trees and growing plants that nourish life in our valley. The second was for the animals, the deer and elk, the foxes and the wolves, and for our horses. The third was for the eagle, asking that the great bird fly forever over us and keep us from the water ghosts and the stone ghosts who bring misfortune.

"The dream songs have power," Washakie told us. "When we sing the dream songs as we dance, the power becomes greater. The words do not tell us how things are. They tell us how things will be. They do not see the future. The dream songs have the power to make it as it will be. When we are gone, the dreams will come to you. You must come here to dance and sing and listen to what the ghosts tell you is coming."

I must tell you, dear family, that as I joined the circle, I felt the power of the songs. I knew that the holy man saw what needed to be blessed for our valley. I felt that the moving circle was more than men and women stepping together. There was the harmony of a single mind and a single voice, singing what would be.

You may be wondering as you read this if your son and brother has been too long in the mountains. Perhaps I have finally been here long enough to learn something of the wisdom and power of the people who have been here forever. I wondered, as I lay awake during the rest of the night, if the dream songs don't come to us all. The words tell us what lies ahead. All we must do is listen when they come and sing them. The quiet of the mountains has allowed me to hear my own songs and feel their power. I will write again when I have had time to consider what all this means.

My love to you all, Johnny

14

JOHNNY

The drive began six weeks later than he had intended, necessitated by the need to shape his new hands into a trail crew. Weather would not be a problem. They could reach the Great Salt Lake Valley and return before snow clogged the passes. But with August came a dry heat that sucked moisture from the prairie grass, turning it a brittle brown. The horses could live on it but would lose more weight than had they started in early July. And by the time they reached the city, most of the wagon trains passing through to California would be beyond the Mormon settlement. There wasn't a trail boss or wagon master on the trails going west who wasn't aware of the Donner tragedy twenty years earlier. The Donners had reached the Sierras in November and were trapped in the mountains where most perished and the remaining few survived by eating their dead. No party wanted to leave Salt Lake City after the first of September.

His salvation, Johnny thought, was that the residents of the city would have depleted their own herds by supplying the wagons and would be looking for replacement stock. And the railroad was surging toward the valley from both directions, if a mile or two of track a day could be considered a surge. Gold seekers passing the ranch in late June had reported that tracks from the east had made it through Nebraska, with crews now working to clear bed across the southern part of the Wyoming Territory. If they were as far as the Bear River, Johnny might be able to sell his horses there, cutting the drive almost in half. But he doubted his men could buy cattle there. And if he didn't make it to Salt Lake, he would miss seeing his grandmother.

The Chinese riders proved to be the best hands he had worked with: forever alert, always aware of the changing moods of the animals, and completely unafraid. They had learned from moving the herd around the valley that horses followed the lead mare, with the dominant stallion trailing, urging on laggards and watching for danger. If the men kept the boss mare moving in the right direction and at the right pace, the rest followed. By hobbling and tying the dominant horses at night, the herd stayed close together and calm unless they sensed danger.

As his crew shouted the marked animals into a steady trot down the valley, Johnny kept them close to the river where forage was still green and lush. At night, he found camps with a natural barrier on at least one side: a swift stretch of water, a steep embankment, or a rocky outcropping. Li Yan and his wife closed the side opposite the barrier with the wagons, the other men dividing into two camps to complete the square with the horses in the center. Each carried a Sharps rifle, surplused by the army after the war and converted to the new 50-70 caliber metal cartridges. All four Chinese riders had been trained by Johnny to shoot. Their sharp eyes and steady hands made them excellent marksmen, a skill they developed with childlike pride and enthusiasm. During the month before their departure, they had supplied enough meat to sustain the ranch families through the winter and buffalo robes for every bed in the bunkhouse.

The first six days on the trail were uneventful, comfortably covering the twenty miles Johnny had established as a daily goal. They urged the horses onto the trail by first light and stopped before the heat of midafternoon drove the mountain creatures into the shade of burrows and thickets. Johnny knew where to find good water and let the horses drink and rest before the night turned cold. Li Yan had assumed the duty of cook and, at each campsite, gathered wood as the other men hobbled the lead horses and laid out bedding.

As they neared the shallows where the Mormon Trail forded the Bear River, two men watched the approaching horsemen from the far bank. They stood a hundred paces apart, one beside a spindly tripod, the other holding a pole that extended four or five feet above his head. To the west, a dozen laborers hacked at dense brush and trees that bordered the wagon-worn trail. To the east, four canvas tents stood beside a covered wagon and a plain, pine-log building.

Johnny splashed through the river behind the trailing stallion, shouting for his trail hands to let the horses drink. He reined up beside the man with the tripod, looking curiously at what appeared to be a small telescope suspended in a metal frame.

"Afternoon to yuh," he said, leaning his elbows against the saddle horn. "You folks from the railroad?"

The man lifted his hat, using the motion to mop his brow with a damp sleeve. "Survey team," he said. "The general route's already been laid out. We're setting the exact path and marking the grade. Our Johnnies there clear ahead, and we stake out where the track's going to go."

"Johnnies?"

The man waved toward a Chinese work team. "Yeah. The coolies. That's what we call them. Johnnies."

"A strange name for Chinese workers."

"Yeah, but they have funny names that sound alike and all look pretty much the same. It's just easier to call them all Johnny. When we pay them," he said with a chuckle, "we give all the money to the gang boss and he sorts it all out.

Johnny twisted in his saddle and gazed east along the trail. "How long 'til it gets here?"

"The railroad? They're a month behind us. Maybe more. But the Central Pacific's coming east from Sacramento. The Union Pacific wants to beat them to Salt Lake and get as much of this laid out as we can before winter."

Johnny bent forward toward the miniature telescope. "What's that thing you got there?"

"We call it a theodolite. I look through it to determine changes in grade and figure direction and distance." The surveyor pointed behind him at a string of thick stakes with a red strip of cloth tied near their tops. "We notch the stakes to let the work crews know where they need to cut or fill to keep the track level."

The man's partner with the pole had walked over to join them. He looked past Johnny to where Li Yan and his family stood beside the wagon and Li Bo sat on his mount among the drinking horses. "Those coolie riders you got there?"

Johnny turned toward the river. "Chinese, you mean? Yup. Four best hands I've ever had."

"I'll be damned," the man said. "Didn't know Johnnies could ride."

"Good as anybody," Johnny said. "Better'n most." He nodded

toward the surveyor's encampment. "Mind if we set up camp beside you back there? Looks like good grass and plenty of it."

The two men exchanged a quick glance. "That's the stage station there. It's up to them if they let you bed down around them. Don't know if it would be good for our coolies to be mixing, though," the man with the pole said. "What you paying yours?"

"Nothing," Johnny said with a shrug. "Some of the horses are theirs to sell. The man with the family will be going on to California. The other three plan to buy cattle and come back up into the Salt River valley with me."

"We don't want our Johnnies getting ideas," the man with the pole said. "They been wanting more money and shorter days as it is."

Johnny looked toward the work crew whose axes and machetes were now silent. The men stood staring silently at the three Chinese riders. "We can camp down the trail a bit," he said. "But unless you lock your men up, I suspect they'll be wanting to get together. And I wouldn't worry about shorter days. My men are on the trail from sunup to sundown."

The surveyors stood silently as their workmen began to exchange whispers, then broke into animated chatter. Li Bo dismounted and walked toward the excited laborers.

"We can't be having your men interrupt our work," the man with the tripod said. "Set your camp up by ours. We'll deal with the coolies as we have to."

Johnny sat silently for a moment, then nodded. "Li Bo!," he shouted toward his foreman. "Don't keep the men from their work. We're going to camp beside them tonight. You can talk later."

Li Bo stopped, waved toward the animated collection of rail workers, and turned back to the herd, calling to his family in Chinese. Li Yan helped his wife back onto the wagon seat and the other riders turned back along the trail toward the tents and log station.

"I'll let you get back to your work," Johnny said and reined his horse around to follow the others.

"Coolie cowboys!" he heard one of the surveyors say. "Isn't that the damnedest thing!"

Johnny wheeled his mount and returned to where the surveyors leaned against their instruments. "I didn't introduce myself," he said, leaning toward the man beside the tripod. "I'm Johnny. Johnny Whitlock."

15

DAVID

Riding in a stagecoach, David decided, was at best like being a newborn lulled in a cradle with warped, squeaky rockers and, at worst, like being swept in a small skiff through boulder-strewn rapids. The coach was in constant motion, rocking gently on leather straps when the trail was smooth, and throwing its occupants, already packed shoulder-to-shoulder, hard against the sides and each other when the iron-rimmed wheels jarred into ruts or bounced over churned-up stones.

The stage was a six-passenger Concord pulled by a four-horse team that was replaced every twenty-five to thirty miles. A canvas-covered boot at the rear held luggage, and freight bound for points west was roped securely to the top. Before leaving Fort Sedgwick, David had seen a man carrying a scattergun clamber up beside the driver and tuck a mail sack beneath his seat. The coach was full, the other four passengers an Indian agent named Marler bound for Fort Laramie and three passengers David remembered from the Omaha train. Mrs. Cybil Loomis, a woman of about David's age, had been seated with them for one meal in the dining car. She was traveling to San Francisco to join her husband who had taken a position a year earlier at a preparatory school for young women. Karen and Christian Hogenson, newly married and recently arrived from Norway, were bound for Salt Lake City and spoke only enough English to introduce themselves. David sat against one window with Mrs. Loomis and Agent Marler. Rosswell sat opposite, with the Hogensons squeezed tightly in beside him. Though the seats were thickly padded and dust from the road filtered by drop-down curtains, it became apparent within the first hour that Rosswell would be the least accommodating of the six.

"Surely there must be *some* way to reach Salt Lake City other than this infernal box," the attorney groused as a rut bounced him hard between the coach's side and the reluctant shoulder of Karen Hogenson.

"I am sorry," she murmured in broken English, then continued the apology in Norwegian.

Rosswell wasn't deterred. "And this dust! My mouth tastes like mud!"

"We're all being jostled and dusted together," David said good-naturedly. "And the option would be three times as long by horseback, camping at night in the open. When the road's smooth, I find the sway soothing."

"During those brief moments," Rosswell groused. "If only we could string a few of them together."

"My option," Mrs. Loomis said, smiling patiently across at the complainer, "was three months by sea around Cape Horn. Though I've never traveled by sea, I'm sure I will find this much more tolerable."

"There may not be a new passenger at Fort Laramie," Agent Marler suggested. "That will afford more room on one side, and you can switch around."

"Three days from now," Rosswell muttered, "...if I'm still in one piece."

"If not, we'll find a suitable resting place for you beside the trail," Marler said without humor.

David redirected the conversation, leaning slightly forward to look across at the agent. "Are you replacing someone at the fort?"

"I'm an addition," Marler said. "We're having trouble with the Cheyenne, Arapaho, and Lakota up in the Powder River country. The government's trying to negotiate the set-aside of some land there as a reservation. I've been working in Nebraska and have a little experience with the Lakota. The people in Washington think I may be able to help."

"You're negotiating to give the Indians land when I read they've been killing our soldiers and raiding settlements all over the West?" Rosswell was unable to remain quiet.

Marler locked the man with a steely glare, sitting silently for several moments as the coach bounced and swayed. "You said you were a lawyer," he said at last. "If one of your clients had been living in a home for five hundred years and someone with no honest claim to the property came in uninvited during the night and chased them out, who would you favor in any subsequent dispute?"

Rosswell glared back. "We are talking here about unsettled land. Not some five-hundred-year titled estate."

"When tribes say 'These are our ancestral hunting grounds,' how does that differ from being titled?" Marler argued.

"It differs in not being established by law," Rosswell said. Mrs. Hogenson pressed closer to her husband, feeling the heat rise in her seat-partner.

Marler sniffed. "It *has* been established by law. By theirs, and more recently by ours. Then gold was discovered. Greed is a poor bedfellow with the law."

"You're as bad as that sergeant at Sedgwick," Rosswell said, pulling aside the curtain and shifting his attention away from the Indian agent to stare glumly at the passing prairie. "Is everyone out here an Indian lover?"

"Well, *I* certainly am not," Mrs. Loomis said firmly. "I took this stage with the assurance that I would not lay eyes on a red man. I was astonished to see some lounging around the train stations as we crossed Nebraska—just sitting there—staring at me with those dark eyes."

"There's a difference between reading about them in your New York papers and spending some time with them," Marler said. "I've always found them to be worthy of my trust and dependable, as long as I was the same. Whitlock, you've been silent. And you've been living near the frontier. What's your thinking?"

David had tried to dissolve into the seat as the debate raged, hoping it wouldn't come to him. But here it was. And though he had at least another week shackled to Henry Rosswell, he couldn't, in good conscience, malign the Indians.

"Very few left in my part of Iowa," he said. "We see them in Saint Joseph and Council Bluffs when they come to trade, and they're always peaceful and fair. And the truth be told, some of them saved me during the war. I have no quarrel with the red men."

Rosswell returned his gaze to the inside of the coach and to his traveling companion, seeming to see him in a new, and not particularly endearing light.

"Some Indians saved you in the war?"

David nodded. "I managed to escape a Confederate hospital in Arkansas and two bands, one Creek and one Cherokee, helped me find my way up to Fort Leavenworth."

A shout from the driver's seat pulled their attention forward. "Coming up on the Midway station," the coachman yelled. "A quick stop to change teams and give you all a chance to eat something. They usually got a mess of pork and beans cooking. Be ready to leave in thirty minutes."

The passengers pulled themselves together as if about to meet important company but knew from their last team change at Thirty Mile Ridge that they were likely to find nothing but a crude pole building and an unkempt station master. They straightened in their seat for the final five minutes, sitting in silence as the coach rolled to a stop. The driver swung down from his perch to usher his charges out onto a sun-parched prairie that stretched in every direction to a yellow line that defined the horizon.

No one joined the coach at Fort Laramie. Rosswell insisted he be allowed to sit with Mrs. Loomis during the remainder of the journey, with David wedged in beside the Hogensons.

"You people are used to riding like this," he argued, ignoring that the Norwegians had no more experience with cramped stages than he did. "Mrs. Loomis is from Boston, where carriages are certainly more comfortable. And in New York, we would never think of sending someone across town in these conditions."

Again, David remained silent, knowing that business lay ahead and not wishing his traveling companions from Europe to think that all residents of their new country were selfish boors. He did, however, insist that he and the Hogensons ride facing forward, able to look out the windows when the wheels were not churning up dust. As the coach climbed gradually into the high plains, the grass became shorter and trees disappeared, replaced by rolling, uninterrupted grasslands, then coarse brush and rocky outcroppings. The vast herds of buffalo of the prairieland gradually gave way to agile pronghorn antelope that watched them pass with fearless curiosity. For one stretch of two or three miles, a rangy coyote kept pace with the horses, loping alongside a hundred yards from the coach.

The drivers and shotgun messengers changed every twelve hours, with days and nights punctuated by brief stretch breaks to change teams and hastily inhale a meal of bean or potato soup with coarse, roughly milled wheat bread. David found that he was able to sleep for brief periods if he sat straight and away from the jarring window frame. As they climbed toward the divide where the driver told them rivers began to flow west toward the Pacific, temperatures plummeted as the sun disappeared. Heavy wool blankets, issued to ward off the chill, served as additional cushioning. They huddled in wool cocoons, their breath drifting as icy mist in the space between them. Rosswell and Mrs. Loomis sat at opposite ends of their leather-clad bench, pressed in shivering rolls against the coach side, while David gratefully drew warmth from the hip and shoulder of the Norwegian woman.

At the Bear River Crossing beyond the divide, a railroad surveying crew had nestled its wagon against the downwind side of the station, circling it with the tents of its work crew. As the driver changed horses, the surveyors joined the five travelers for mutton stew and fat-fried eggs.

"Were those Chinese men I saw by your tents?" Mrs. Loomis asked.

"We've got a mix of workers on the line," one of the surveyors said. "But those who lay track get ten dollars more a week. So the clearing crews are all Chinese."

The woman looked nervously toward the door of the log building. "Are they peaceful men?"

The second surveyor laughed. "Easier to boss than the hillbillies who signed on after the war. The Johnnies don't go getting drunk when we're near a town, and don't eat much. They send most of what they make back home—wherever that is. But the billies don't have any other ambition. These coolie men are always talking about being something different."

"Like what?" Rosswell asked.

"We had a herd of horses come through three days ago," the man said. "Most the riders were coolies and were talking about ranching cattle up north of here. Coolie cowboys! Isn't that the damnedest thing you ever heard!"

16

SUZANNA

The log crushing Willard Burgon's legs added flame to unrest that had been simmering on the mill floor since John Griggs had preached his brotherhood sermon in the stacking yard. Tempers began to boil over.

The mill used a series of winches and pulleys that lifted saw logs behind a mule team, allowing the men to swing them on or off piles that rose as high as a man's head. David had trained the log crew to work from the sides, using long peaveys and cant hooks to maneuver the logs into place. But Willard had climbed onto the stack to cant a log that hadn't fallen square onto the pile. He stepped into a gap between two thick red oak trunks just as the team bolted at a blast from the mill whistle, releasing tension on the ropes. The log pitched toward him, crushing his legs between the logs below the knees. Had the ropes not caught, the yard-thick trunk would have rolled across him down the pyramid stack. Pinned by the suspended trunk, Willard fell backward onto the pile, screaming himself into unconsciousness. While those about him stood in paralyzed shock, Ben Lanear ran toward the mule team, and Suzanna sprinted from the mill office.

"Don't lift it yet," she shouted, ripping at the sleeves of her work shirt as she ran. She clambered up the stack, glanced at Willard's chalk-white face for a sign of breath, then forced a separated sleeve under one thigh above the knee and knotted it tightly.

"Get that wagon," she shouted, pointing at one that stood harnessed beside the salt brine bath. She tore the second sleeve loose and bound the other thigh. "Now—lift it up, Ben. Slow, so I can check the bleeding. . . That's good . . . Now, two of you come up here real easy and let's get him in the wagon."

She watched in horror as the men eased the limp body from the stack, her man's crushed legs flopping like blood-soaked rags below the tourniquets. "I'm riding with him to Doc Lauder's," she said.

"Shut down the mill. No more work today."

The following morning, she called the men together before the first whistle.

"Will's going to need our support," she said, sensing as much anger as concern as she addressed the crew. "Doc Lauder had to take his legs at the knees to save his life. He's got a long, hard road ahead of him."

After an uncomfortably long silence, Sam Gorton spoke. "Is the mill gonna be payin' his family while he's gettin' better?"

Suzanna found his tone impossible to read. While she expected the men to be concerned about their injured comrade, there was an accusing note in Sam's voice.

"We are," she said firmly.

"With money you been puttin' aside?"

"Yes. The money I spoke to you all about."

"And what if he doesn'a *get* better?"

"Doc Lauder thinks he'll recover. We stopped the bleeding fast enough. Everything looked good this morning."

"And if he don't? Or if he can't come back ta work? The mill gonna support his family forever?"

"He should be able to come back to work," Suzanna said. "We can use him driving a team."

"He weren't doin' what he was supposed ta," Gorton growled. "He was up on the logs."

Suzanna felt the muscles in her face and neck tighten. She scanned the assembled men with her eyes, finding most looking at their feet.

"And I suppose none of the rest of you have been that careless," she challenged. "What's happened to you men? This is one of your workmates who's been injured!"

Gorton spoke again from the front of the assembled crew. "We've just all been thinkin' that if we weren't paying you money every month to buy the mill, and if you weren't savin' money back for somethin' like this, we could all be getting' our full pay, makin' another three dollars a week, and savin' for something like this ourselves. We'd just all be better off if we got what was supposed to be comin' to us."

It was all Suzanna could do to keep from shouting at the man. *Do you have a brain in that thick head, Sam Gorton? You, of all people, who drink most of your wages away before they even reach your wife's apron pocket?* Instead, she took the measure of the group again with a long stare, then took a step closer to Gorton.

"First of all, we will not stop putting money aside for an injury of this kind," she said coldly. "I hope none of this gets to Will or his family, or I won't be the only one who's ashamed of what I'm hearing. As for you buying our investment in the mill over time, I told you when that Mr. Griggs was here that you can vote to change your decision any time you choose. We will return to each one of you, based on your time with the mill, what you've paid into that account. You will feel like it makes you wealthy men for a week or two until it's gone. Then you'll be working for the same fifteen dollars a week with nothing to show for it. But I would take the day to think about it—and the evening to talk to your wives. They've got a stake in this too. Tomorrow morning, before we start, you can vote again. If you choose to have the money back, I'll ride to Osceola to the bank and have it for you by the end of the day. Does that satisfy you?"

From the other end of the line, Ben Lanear spoke. "We're not all favoring this, Mizz Whitlock. Some of us is fine with things as they are. And we're grateful for what you're doing for Will." A light murmuring followed, but less than Suzanna had hoped to hear.

"I understand that, Ben. But this needs to be a majority decision. Be here a bit early tomorrow and take your vote. Now, let's get to work."

17

ELIZABETH

In August of 1867, President Andrew Johnson dismissed Edwin Stanton as Secretary of War. In begrudging compliance with the Tenure in Office Act, he submitted the action to the Senate for consent, knowing that virtually all of Congress was in recess for the summer. In the interim, Johnson appointed General Ulysses S. Grant to replace Stanton, signaling to lawmakers that he expected them to acknowledge the president's right as Commander-in-Chief to choose whomever he wished to lead the nation's armed forces. Senator Lyman Trumbull was at his home in Alton, Illinois, when the news reached him. He immediately booked a seat on the afternoon train to Chicago and wired Elizabeth to meet him at the Water Street office at nine the following morning.

"All becomes progressively more contentious," the Senator said as they sat opposite each other over mugs of coffee in the curtained room. "A measure has been added to the Army Appropriations Act that requires the president to issue all military orders through the General of the Armies. While Congress has been in recess, Johnson has chosen to make several appointments to command positions in the southern states without that review. My colleagues see that as just another violation of law worthy of impeachment."

"And you view it as his constitutional right as Commander-in-Chief to make those appointments," Elizabeth guessed.

"I'm not sure what it means to be Commander-in-Chief if the president cannot make military appointments without congressional consent," the senator grumbled. "But my suspicion is that when we reconvene in January, one of the first acts will be to reinstate Stanton."

"What will the president do?"

"I believe he is hoping for it. He will dismiss him again and not request congressional approval, forcing a decision by the Court. But the House will immediately pass a resolution of impeachment and appoint a committee to draw up articles. My friends in the House tell me those articles have already been drafted. The committee will be able to bring them forward within a few days. By March, this will be back in the Senate for a trial."

"Are you getting signals from the other Republican moderates?" Elizabeth asked.

"I see most reservation coming from those of us here in the west," Trumbull said. "Doolittle from Wisconsin. Norton from Minnesota. John Henderson and James Grimes from Missouri and Iowa. They all seem to share my concern that Benjamin Wade's ambitions may discourage him from being fair and impartial in conducting the trial proceedings. As you know, Wade is President Pro Temp and, since no vice president has been appointed since Johnson took office, all that stands between Wade and the presidency is the success of this impeachment."

Elizabeth nodded. She had been following the Ohio senator's efforts to hasten admission of Colorado into the Union. Rumors from Washington suggested that Wade knew Colorado would bring two more radical Republican votes into the chamber—added security in case some of the moderates had a crisis of conscience during the anticipated trial vote.

"This is all being plotted out well in advance," she observed.

Trumbull grunted grimly. "If this goes forward, no future president will be safe if he happens to disagree with the majority of the House and two-thirds of the Senate on any measure deemed important. What, then, becomes of the checks and balances of the Constitution?"

Elizabeth scribbled hurriedly on the pad in front of her. "With your permission, Sir, I think I will incorporate those words into the position paper I am preparing. It sounds as if we may need to have it ready sooner than later."

Robert Mathis had returned from Nebraska. She met him for an early dinner at a favorite place on Halsted Street where a retired Greek sea captain named Santori had transformed his personal passion for the cuisine of his home country into a popular restaurant.

Robert arrived in a jovial and teasing mood, his handsome face seemingly on the verge of breaking into a broad smile each time they looked at each other.

"You seem especially pleased with yourself this evening," she said as the teenage daughter of the proprietor showed them to their table.

"I have good news, but I want to wait until we've eaten and can enjoy some wine while I share it."

"So, we're just supposed to have a casual chat during our meal, knowing that this big surprise is coming?" Elizabeth teased back.

"I haven't seen you in weeks. We have plenty to talk about. When you replied to my message, you said you had taken a new position. That should carry us to dessert."

"And I want to know about your travels. Your letters said you had crossed most of Iowa. I hope you had a chance to stop in Afton."

"Not on this trip. But I did see the Kohlers. They both asked after you." He hesitated, as if intending to say more about the Kohler visit, but thought better of it.

Elizabeth had first met Robert in Council Bluffs, Iowa, when she had returned to the state after receiving news her father was reported missing in the war. While several Afton men had seen him fall amid the carnage at Arkansas's battle at Pea Ridge, no body had been recovered. But the report had enticed an unscrupulous Afton lender to demand full payment on a note he held on the mill's steam engine. Elizabeth had returned home immediately to defend the family property.

Her fight had taken her to Camp Kirkwood near Council Bluffs where her father had mustered into the army, seeking records that would list him as "missing" rather than as having been "killed in action." The distinction provided important protections to her mother as long as the family still met their payment commitments on the loan.

Elizabeth had run into Robert by chance on the main street of the bustling frontier city while seeking lodgings. He had assured her that steamships on the Missouri filled all available hotel rooms with advanced bookings, but that he knew a respectable older couple in town who had a spare room. At dinner at the home of Mary and Simon Kohler, she had learned that Robert was a sales representative with Cyrus H. McCormick and Brothers of Chicago, selling reapers to the growing number of farmers across Iowa and beyond the Missouri River. Robert had accompanied her to Fort Kirkwood and provided support as she sought information about her father. She had found in the attractive young salesman a thoughtful, courteous, and intelligent admirer. When he learned that when not assisting her mother with family affairs, she lived in Chicago, he insisted that they meet again when she returned to the city. These meetings had now become weekly when Robert was in town.

After their first year of courting, Robert had begun to hint at marriage. A woman of twenty, he suggested, had reached an age at which she should be considering settling down. Elizabeth parried each advance without being discouraging. Robert was exactly the kind of man she had always imagined marrying at some point. But she fully intended to be prepared, when Illinois chose to grant permission to women to sit for the bar, to be among the state's first female attorneys. That was six years ago.

This past October, Robert had proposed. They were dining with his parents at the family's rust-brick Georgian mansion, south of the city's downtown lakefront on Prairie Avenue. Robert had come for her in the carriage and begged to have a moment alone with her in the boarding house parlor. With the doors closed and three housemates, barely able to contain their own excitement, whispering loudly in the outer hallway, he had dropped to one knee. All his life, he confessed, he had hoped to find a woman as lovely, kind, generous, and bright as Elizabeth. Would she bless an unworthy but desperately stricken man by accepting his hand in marriage? His greatest hope, he told her, was that when they arrived at his parents' home that evening, he could tell them that he and Elizabeth were to be married.

When he asked for the time alone, she was taken completely by surprise but knew exactly what was coming. Oh, she had expected it eventually, but thought she had dissuaded him from moving things along too quickly. But then, perhaps he thought five years of courtship wasn't too quickly. She took his hand and eased him to his feet, wrapping the hand in both of hers, holding it tightly against her breast.

"You know, Robert, that I love you as much as I could any man," she said softly. "And that someday I hope we can tell your parents we are going to marry. But I don't want to start a family with you away half of each month. And you know of my ambitions. When children come, I want to commit my time to family as completely as I can. But I'm not ready for that now, and don't believe you are ready to be here as much as a family would need you. That doesn't seem to me to be a good beginning to an engagement."

"I believe a promotion is coming—sometime in the next year."

"And perhaps my opportunity will come during the same time," she said. "There is talk about allowing women to sit for the bar. But let's wait until then. Surely your parents will understand that I would like a husband to be at home most of the time."

Robert appeared to understand, professing his own concern that his time away was not ideal for a family man. He was confident, he said, that McCormick planned to bring him into the home office. Until then, they could enjoy each other's company when both were in the city. But if an opportunity came to sit for the bar, might she then want to exercise her achievement by practicing the law? How might that affect family? She had been unable to answer, and dinner had been uncomfortably silent.

Nearly a year had passed since the proposal. As the frontier became civilized and extended farther west, Robert's trips lengthened from three weeks to four. The state of Illinois seemed no closer to granting women the right to practice law.

"Tell me about this new position," he said as the girl at Santori's brought bowls of spicy meat and vegetable soup. "You seem very excited about it."

Elizabeth explained Myra Bradwell's introduction to Senator Trumbull, her opportunity to manage an office for him in the city, and the trust he seemed to have in her views and judgment as the president's troubles grew in Washington. "He talks to me almost as if I'm a partner," she confided.

Robert laid his spoon aside and dabbed at his lips with a white linen napkin. "Trumbull's a Republican, as I remember," he said.

"A moderate Republican."

"You know, I'm sure, that both my family and the McCormicks are dyed-in-the-wool Democrats. I'm not sure how they will feel about you working for a Republican—even a moderate."

Elizabeth lowered her own spoon. "I wasn't aware that I need their permission," she said testily.

Robert reddened. "I didn't mean that you needed to get approval. We've talked before about the fact that you are not Presbyterian. Mother has agreed that the family can certainly overlook that, since you are Protestant. But are you Republican?"

"Just as I told you when we argued about religion, I'm not sure I'm anything. I choose in both respects to be an independent thinker."

"But surely, in this debate about the president, you have a position . . . ."

Elizabeth straightened, folding her hands in her lap. "I'm formulating one, based on what I see the constitutional issues to be."

"You and your damned law," Robert muttered, dropping his napkin into his lap. "Why can't you just . . . ." He sputtered into silence.

"Why can't I just be a good, prim, agreeable, debutante who goes to women's clubs and wants to stay at home and have babies," she finished for him.

They looked silently across the table at each other with a sadness that said more than words.

"Mr. McCormick is bringing me into the office here in Chicago in January," Robert said finally. "For good. I will be overseeing all sales activities."

Elizabeth lowered her eyes to the table. "That's wonderful, Robert. I'm assuming that was your surprise. I'm very happy for you."

He waited for more and when nothing came, said, "But you are not willing to give up this position—or your dream of sitting for the law—for us to start a family."

She raised her eyes to fix on his directly. "This is the most exciting thing I have ever done," she said with a conviction that surprised her. "And I think that if all were as it should be, it's something you would support me doing. But I'm beginning to see that even if you said you would, it would be begrudging support."

He held her gaze, refusing to let her force his eyes away. "I'll be honest. It isn't what I have imagined in a wife. This is an important position with the company. There's a lovely home available near my parents on Prairie Avenue. I can see us living there and becoming involved in Chicago society."

"Involved? What does that mean? I'm already involved in Chicago society. But like Myra is involved—as a voice for women's equality and for whatever other causes I see bringing greater justice. Is that what you've been imagining, Robert?"

The sadness on his face revealed itself in a tight smile. "No. It is not what I have imagined. Perhaps I thought that after you realized the stiff-collared lawyers of this city weren't going to allow you into their exclusive little club, you might agree to a more genteel place in mine."

She returned the melancholy smile. "It's something I can't give up, Robert. It's who I am and who I need to be."

He nodded thoughtfully, looking up pleasantly as the waitress brought plates of what the menu called *kleftiko*: marinated lamb baked with young potatoes.

"We have a lot to think about," he said after the girl had filled their wine glasses and stepped away. "But for this evening, let's think of this as having a very pleasant dinner with a dear friend."

18

DAVID

At the top of a rocky hill, the coachman reined in the team and scrambled down to free his passengers for a final stretch before the descent into the valley of the Great Salt Lake.

"This is what they call Emigration Canyon," he announced as his five charges stepped stiffly onto the hard pack of the road, shaking out what little sleep remained in their bones after a jarring overnight rumble through narrow mountain passes. "You can see the whole valley from here. About the only place I can think of where a man can get a look at an entire city."

Behind them, morning sun burst above the peaks into a clear sky, bleeding down the slopes on the far side of the valley and sweeping toward them at a pace that made them turn to marvel at the speed with which the golden orb ascended. Across the valley floor, the Mormon city lay before them in a perfectly measured patchwork, with symmetrical squares of greens and browns dotted by white houses and buildings in ocher brick. Beyond the city, the lake that gave the valley its name stretched as a pale blue sheet to the horizon, bordered by a flat expanse of glistening white. A narrow canyon cut a sharp notch into what David judged to be the north edge of the tidy desert quilt. Just beyond its point, two buildings commanded attention, even from this lofty height.

"What's the big oval place I see there?" he asked the driver, pointing toward the building.

"That's their tabernacle," he said. "Just being finished. And the white building beside it is their temple. About half done. They've been working on it as long as I've been coming through here. If you look close, you can see big wagons coming along one of them streets over there." He gestured toward the south. "They're carrying blocks of granite as tall as a man, cut out of the mountains somewhere over that way. Hard working people. I've gotta hand 'em that."

"The first sign of civilization I've seen since we left the train,"

Rosswell grumbled. "I hope the rest of their society is as organized as their city appears."

The driver laughed. "Go in and see that tabernacle on the inside. Most amazing building I've ever seen. Covers near an acre, and there's no pillars holding up the roof. Makes me jumpy, just being in there. But it's got the biggest organ you ever seen. Tall as that stand of pines over here. We'll be going right past it on our way to the station."

"How long is our stop here?" Mrs. Loomis asked nervously. "I've read there are Indian wars in the Utah territory—and some troubling things about these Mormons. I hope we aren't here long."

"We'll be changing teams and drivers here," the coachman said. "And I wouldn't be rushing myself. You'll get the best meal between Omaha and Sacramento and a good wash-up too, if you want one. And you won't be able to tell from looking at these people that they's any different from anyone else. Good frontier stock."

David turned to the Hogensons who had been silent. The young couple stood gazing down across the valley as the sun flashed against the domed metal roof of the tabernacle, arms wrapped about each other, and tears streaming down their faces.

During the descent into the valley, the horses slid and braced against the weight of the coach on the steep grade. The driver threw his weight against the wheel brake until the leather-bound wooden arm smelled of seared hide and trailed gray smoke. At the bottom of the grade, their route into the city took the stage along a broad street with two- and three-story shops in red brick lining both sides. Henry Rosswell leaned through the window, admiring the bustle of morning commerce. As they approached the central square, they passed wagons that lumbered slowly toward the construction site behind four sturdy oxen, each carrying blocks of stone half the size of the coach.

Beneath a sheltering awning of the Overland's station, men, women, and children thronged the stage on both sides, peering into the windows and pulling open the doors before the driver could clamber down to assist. Rosswell was first out, then helped Mrs. Loomis down the single step. The crowd parted for them momentarily, looking expectantly past the couple. The air around David hummed with a chorus he didn't understand, and he sat back to give the waiting crowd its prize. Strong hands reached into the coach and grasped Karen Hogenson, pulling her into the arms of a wet-eyed older couple he guessed to be her parents. A man of the young couple's age climbed into the coach and introduced himself to Christian, then embraced him as if they were reunited brothers. David's thoughts sped to the moment he had first seen his family when he returned from the war. The look in Suzanna's eyes had been more than one of love or relief. It was a look of indescribable joy and he was witnessing it again. He found that he, too, was fighting back tears.

He had composed himself by the time he found Rosswell and the two retrieved their bags. Four carriages for hire stood along the road in front of the station and David threw their cases into the back of the first. "I have an address, but I'm not sure I understand it," he said, handing a slip to the liveryman. The man glanced at the paper and chuckled.

"So you've not been to our city before," he said good-naturedly with a soft English accent. "As you saw coming down, it's laid out in squares. Each ten chains on a side, so there's ten acres in each. I'll be taking you back by the temple on what's called South Temple Street. It's the main street that runs east-west. At the corner of what we call Temple Square, we'll go south. Then the cross streets are First South, Second South, and the like. When we get to Eighth South, we turn east—across First East, Second East, 'til we get to Seventh East. That's where you're goin'. Eighth South and Seventh East. There'll be more than one house there, but that's down in the First Ward. Everyone will know everyone else."

"First Ward?" Rosswell asked.

"Aye. The city's divided into church parishes we call wards. This home is down in the First Ward."

"That street numbering system is like Manhattan," Rosswell said. "You'll just have to resist throwing in a Park or Madison Avenue when someone wants a special street."

"It's working so far," the coachman said. "And I don't see this city ever getting that big."

East Temple appeared to be the street that catered to wagon trains moving west. The broad avenue, twice the width David had expected to find in a frontier town, was lined with shops displaying all the staples of cross-country travel: new-made barrels, some empty and some packed with pickles, salt pork, or beef. Wagon wheels, spades, harnesses, and metal pails. Men on horseback rode slowly in front of the shops, looking for items they needed to complete their outfitting. Women in gingham dresses and sunbonnets poked methodically through the wares, searching for those indispensable items that would sustain them as they ventured into barren desert beyond the city.

"A fine place to have a business," Rosswell observed. "A long way to anywhere in any direction."

"As long as you can get the goods here," David said.

The lawyer peered into an open-fronted forge beside one of the shops where a smithy hammered at an orange-hot shovel head. "Looks like they're producing some of the goods themselves," he said. "Clean city. Looks like a bit of civilization."

At a corner where a street sign said "800 South," the coachman steered his team east toward the mountains, guiding the horse onto a narrower street lined with tidy brick homes. Each was surrounded by a late-summer garden and an assortment of fruit trees that had already yielded the season's bounty. Knee-deep trenches ran along both sides of the road, with side-ditches following the property lines between homes.

"Are these trenches some form of fortification?" Rosswell asked the coachman.

"Irrigation," the driver called back. "Practically no rainfall here." He chuckled to himself. "Back in Dorset, we'd get as much rain in some weeks as comes here in a year." He pointed ahead at the slope of the mountains that rose like a bulwark along the city's east side. "Canals bring water down from the mountains, and these ditches carry it through the city. People buy water shares and can turn the water onto their property for as much time as they pay for each week." He pointed at a wooden gate that had been propped into place across one of the trenches, fortified by small, sand-filled canvas bags. "That brother there is waiting for his water to come. Someone upstream has it now."

"And people honor this system?" Rosswell wondered.

"No trouble with it. This man goes and gets the water when his time starts. At the end of his turn, it's the next man's job to come fetch it from him."

As they neared the intersection where 700 East crossed 800 South, the coachman reined his carriage up beside the open trench which now brimmed with water. "It will be one of these four homes," he said, nodding at the houses that framed the corners of the crossroad. Beyond the water trench and a low picket fence, two young boys dug potatoes from mounds of brown, rocky soil. David stepped from the carriage and hopped across the ditch.

"Can you boys tell me which of these homes belongs to Mrs. Whitlock?"

The boys rose together and scrambled across the mounds of earth to the fence. "That one there," they said in unison, pointing diagonally across the intersection at a single-story frame cottage. "Granny Lydia lives over there." They grasped the top of a freshly-painted picket and vaulted over the fence. "Come on. We'll take you to her."

David followed on foot as the coachman eased the carriage back onto the street and through the crossroad. Since the coach had turned onto Eighth South, his pulse had quickened, and his heart now seemed to be straining to burst from his chest. The air seemed suddenly too thin, and he stopped in the middle of the intersection and sucked in deep breaths until the pressure in his lungs began to still his heart. He had not seen his mother since she and the Mormon wagon train left Mount Pisgah, leaving David and his young family to find a home in Iowa. A thousand miles of prairie and mountains, a war that had drawn David into service for the Union, and the responsibilities of running the mill had separated him for nearly twenty years from the woman he loved second only to Suzanna and Elizabeth. They had written with the frequency that express riders and the overland stage allowed. But letters didn't reflect the creases of an aging face or the stoop that begins to bend a frail body. His mother would now be nearing seventy. A nagging in the back of his mind wanted him to remember her as the quiet, handsome woman who had bent to kiss him as the wagons pulled away, leaving him with her blessing.

The boys were already across the dirt road and through the gate in a similar picket fence. "Granny Lydia! Granny Lydia! There's someone else here to see you!"

David followed the boys into the yard of neatly trimmed browning grass. As he stepped onto the covered porch of the bungalow, the door opened inward. Instead of a frail woman, the figure that filled the doorway was an inch or two taller than David with dark hair that waved down about his ears, deep-set brown eyes, and a smile splitting his long angular face.

"Hello, Father," Johnny said, and the two men fell into each other's arms.

19

JOHNNY

The Chinese rail workers had chopped brush until just before dusk, then hurried to the river and to their campfires to start water boiling in two black cast iron kettles. The master of the Overland station at Bear River Crossing, a grizzly, fiftyish bachelor who called himself "Two Toes Kelly," had killed a young elk early that morning and given the workers one of the shoulders. With fires spitting sparks into a rapidly darkening night, the workmen had carried the meat to the Whitlock campfire and begun slicing it into long, thin strips as they chattered with Johnny's trail hands. Johnny stood beside Kelly, leaning against a side wall of the log stage station, watching the two crews negotiate their meal preparation.

"Guess everyone asks you why you go by Two Toes," Johnny offered with a chuckle.

"Some ask. Some just stare at my boots," Kelly said. "Truth is, I froze three of 'em on my right foot the first winter I was out here. Then I shot 'em off. They started going bad on me—gettin' the rot—and I couldn't get myself to cut 'em off. So I just shot 'em off, then doused the stubs in whiskey and wrapped 'em up. Seemed to do the job, though now I tend to tip to the right—'cause of the toes, not the whiskey."

Johnny had glanced over at the man's raw leather boots, his chuckle blossoming into a hearty laugh. "Great story," he said.

Kelly traced a cross with his finger across his chest. "Gospel truth," he said.

In the middle of the trail in front of the station, the Chinese riders were demonstrating how they roped and tied a young foal before marking it with a JW brand. Johnny wished Cora had been able to come with them. More than anyone, the girl relished these animated dramas, especially if they involved riding and roping. He could see her spinning an imaginary lasso, glancing over to see if he was watching, then plunging with a delighted smile back into her pantomime.

The Chinese worker who had remained with the fires shouted that the meal was ready. Kelly, Johnny, and his men were invited to join the laborers for rice and dark tea.

"Will you come, please?" Li Bo had asked. "These men will be most honored if you would be their guest."

Johnny nodded and pushed away from the wall. It would be rude to refuse, and ruder still to ignore the request of his friends. He could finish filling his growling stomach with bread and buffalo jerky when back at his bedroll. He had looked over at Two Toes to see if he was coming.

"I always try to join 'em," the station keeper said. "Gotta be friends with everyone out here. Ya never know when ya might need help, or who will be around to help ya."

They had followed the men to their fires and watched as some continued to salt down strips of elk, hanging them over a make-shift drying rack, while the cook ladled scoops of gummy rice into wooden bowls. The surveyors remained in their wagon, the canvas flaps drawn tightly across the ends.

After finishing his bowl and finding the rice surprisingly filling, Johnny had presented the rail workers with a small bag of salt taken from a salt spring at the north end of the ranch, then excused himself to let the Chinese talk and Kelly return to his cabin. He topped off the meal with a piece of heavy wheat bread, stretched out on his bedroll, and soon fell asleep to the murmur of the nearby river and the sing-song of Chinese voices.

They had the horses moving before dawn, the team of rail workers again standing beside their campfire in undisguised admiration as the three Chinese horsemen saddled their mounts. They unhobbled the stallion and boss mare and skillfully positioned themselves on three sides of the herd, shouting the animals into motion westward along the trail with Johnny leading and Li Yan and his wife trailing with the wagons.

It had been another four days to the valley of the Great Salt Lake, urging the horses the final ten miles down Emigration Canyon in the colorless heat of early afternoon. When they reached the grid of streets that marked the beginning of the settled community, Johnny turned the herd south for three blocks before steering his riders again west, avoiding the bustle of the main avenue that ran past the temple site. Water rushed along yard-wide ditches on both sides of the road, creating a natural corridor for the trotting horses. Li Bo and Li Fan had only to ride ahead and block cross streets to keep the herd moving west.

As they approached 900 West, Johnny shouted for the men to turn the horses north. A mile ride took them out of the charted grid of streets to a natural hot spring where corrals held a picked-over assortment of cattle, horses, mules, and oxen. Beyond the stockyard, blue-gray sage stretched to the edge of the salt pan that surrounded the lake.

They drove their dozen into an empty pen, pulled the wagons up beside the corral, and tied their mounts to one of the rails. Before Johnny could search out the yard boss, a lanky man in faded denim, with a broad-brimmed hat propped back on a hairless head, approached the pen.

"These your horses?" he asked, eyeing the herd.

"Yes, Sir. Mine and my men here."

"Where you bringing them from?"

"The Salt River country up in the Idaho Territory."

The man extended his hand. "John Lingwood. I got a place down in Lehi and supply settlers going south. The Church is sending groups almost every month to homestead some new place, and I help them with teams and riding horses."

Johnny chuckled. "I know something about that. My family lived down at Fort Clara for a few years."

"That Jacob Hamblin's group? They got flooded out back in sixty-two."

"Yup. That's about when we left. Lost our home and some of our neighbors."

"You a member, then?" Lingwood asked.

Johnny shook his head. "No. We joined up with them after they left Salt Lake—when Hamblin was first taking the group down to the Santa Clara River. We liked the area around Fort Clara and found them good people to live with. My grandmother's a member. Lives here in the city."

Lingwood turned his attention back to the herd. "What have you got here? Looks like a couple of stallions, five geldings, and five mares. Are they saddle broke?"

"All but the dark stallion. And the geldings are harness broke as well."

"Look like good stock. What you asking for them?"

"One-twenty a head, except for the stallion. Since he isn't broke yet, I'll take a hundred for him."

"That's top dollar," Lingwood said.

Johnny grinned, glancing at the animals in the other corrals. "Yes, it is. But looking at what else is dragging about here, I'd say it's a fair price. And if you're selling to teams that are moving out every month, the demand must be high."

Lingwood grunted. "I need some of the mares and one of the stallions as brood stock. So I want good ones. I'd be selling the geldings and the other stallion. I'd like to be heading south out of here in the morning. Will you take a hundred a head?"

"You saw us ride up," Johnny said. "We haven't had time to talk to anyone else, and it looks to me like what's here have been pretty picked over. One-twenty and they're yours. Otherwise, I need to see what tomorrow brings."

Lingwood walked along the fence, looking over the new selection, then returned to where Johnny leaned against the railing. "You got a sale. I'll take them all and pay to keep them overnight."

"Sounds like I might of been smart to wait until tomorrow," Johnny said with a light laugh. "I didn't expect to sell out before I could even check in with the yard boss."

Lingwood shrugged. "Wait if you want. But at least give me first rights at that price tomorrow. I've been waiting here for two days for good horses to come in. There hasn't been much stock, and not many buyers. You won't do better." He looked beyond Johnny as a man with a loose paunch hanging over a tightly cinched belly and a neck and chest as thick as a pack mule's approached along the corral rail.

"You finally find something, John?" the man called.

Johnny turned and grinned broadly at the hulking yard boss. "Pete! Looks like you've had a prosperous year since I saw you last."

Pete patted contentedly at his bulging girth. "Haven't missed a meal, Whitlock. And Martha cooks like the children was still at home. These your horses?"

"All I could afford to bring this year."

"Lingwood already offered to buy them?"

"We were negotiating at one-twenty a head."

Pete waved a hand dismissively. "Take it and run. Both of you. That's fair all around."

Johnny turned back to his buyer. "If it's fair to Pete, it's fair to me. You've got yourself a sale. And this will give me a chance to get to my grandmother's tonight." He looked over at his four trail hands, then at the few rangy cattle that were scattered about the stockyard. "Pete, you have any good heifers coming in this week? We want to take some back—and a decent bull."

"None that I know of tomorrow or Wednesday, unless they just drop in like you did. But I have a bunch coming in late Thursday morning from over on the west side of the valley. Should be pretty good stock. Be here by ten, and you'll get your pick of the litter."

"What you getting for good heifers now?"

"This bunch are crossbred Spanish shorthorns, mixed with some of the European cattle the people have been bringing from the east. Pretty hardy and good feeders on light pasture. But demand is light this late in the year. My guess is they'll be asking twenty-three to twenty-five a head for something around eight-hundred pounds."

Johnny gestured for Lingwood to lead him to the clapboard cabin that served as an office. "Let's settle up on the horses. We'll be back Thursday to see what cattle you have," he said.

Johnny had visited his grandmother during each drive to the city and knew how to navigate the city blocks to her modest bungalow in the southeast part of town. She had a large garden behind the house and would be delighted to have the Chinese hands bed down among her iris and hollyhocks. And he knew they would all be treated to meals like the Asian men had never seen—and more than they ever wished to eat.

Lydia Whitlock had been a believer in the Mormon faith for nearly twenty-five years now. After fifteen years of marriage, she had stopped in a Philadelphia park one Sunday afternoon to listen to the preaching of two itinerate ministers. Their message had kindled a curiosity in the teachings of the young Mormon faith, a curiosity that had turned to interest and had led her to join the Colesville branch of the Latter-day Saints and follow them from Thompson, Ohio to Jackson County in Missouri.

Johnny's grandfather, a cooper by trade, had accepted the moves for reasons only he understood, but had not accepted the new faith. When mobsters drove the fledgling church back across Missouri into Illinois, the cooper had refused to rejoin the main body of the church in Nauvoo and had chosen instead to seek refuge in the north Missouri woods along the Chariton River. It was there their only son had met the daughter of another settler, a woman David Whitlock had once described to his oldest son as being "the most beautiful, independent, and head-strong woman I have ever met—with the exception of perhaps your sister, Elizabeth."

When Johnny's grandfather had been killed in the Mormon purge in Missouri and the family fled the state for Iowa, Lydia had chosen to become part of the great migration west. Johnny's parents had never embraced the faith and had chosen to remain in the Iowa territory, settling just south of the Mormon Trail in Afton. But once mail service was established between settlements along the trails going west and reached the city on the shores of the Great Salt Lake, Suzanna and Lydia had become regular correspondents. To the degree mail moved between the Salt River valley and either city, Johnny remained in touch with both. Whenever he could, he brought his horses to Salt Lake, spending what time he could with the quiet, well-bred, and always sensible woman who was his grandmother.

As the wagon and four riders approached the fenced bungalow on 800 South, Johnny had seen the slim, erect figure standing beside her gate visiting with a much shorter and much rounder woman. Lydia Whitlock glanced up at the men on horseback, returned to her conversation, then raised a surprised hand to her mouth as she recognized the lead rider. She spoke hurriedly to her friend and pushed through the gate, stepping across a wooden bridge that spanned the irrigation ditch to greet her grandson.

"Well, glory be!" she exclaimed. "Here, I was expecting your father, and look who comes trotting down the road. Agnes, this is my grandson Johnny. . . ." She scanned the Chinese family in the wagons and the three trail hands with an amused smile. ". . . and you will have to introduce your friends."

Johnny swung from the saddle and gave the woman a tight embrace, surprised at how good the years and hardships had been to her strong, straight back. He eased her away and gestured toward the riders. "These are my ranch hands. Li Bo, Li Fan, Li Ji, and Li Yan—and this is Li

Yan's family. We just sold our horses at the stockyard and are looking for a place to bed down for a few nights until some cattle come in. If your back garden's available, that will do just fine for us."

Agnes looked uncomfortably at the group of strangers and backed slowly along the fence. "Well, I'd better be getting on home, Lydia. I'll visit with you in a few days about the Relief Society social."

Lydia waved her friend on along the fence and took Johnny's hand. "Of course, you can all stay. You can bed down in the sitting room if you wish. Or there is plenty of room in the back. Come in and let me fix you something to eat. You can't have had much if you came in today and have been to the stockyards." She beckoned to Li Yan's children. "Come in! Come in! You must be the friends Cora tells me about in her letters."

Johnny pointed down the side of the property to a wider bridge that crossed the ditch in the middle of the block, leading to an alley between sections of property. "Li Bo, have Li Yan take the wagons across the bridge there. He'll find a wide gate in the back fence and can bring them right up to the back of the house. The rest of you, bring your horses through the front. We'll tie them along the inside." He led his mare across the short bridge and swung the gate open for his grandmother.

"The garden's gone for the summer, Johnny," she said. "And most of the flowers. Just let your horses roam inside the fence and eat what they want. The ditch runs where they can get to it across the back and has water in it now. There's a small trough by the back porch that's empty. You might ask one of the men to fill it with the pail that's beside it while we have water running."

He uncinched the girth and pulled off his saddle and blanket, dropping them onto the front porch. "Did you say when we came up that you were expecting Father?"

Lydia laughed lightly. "Yes. Today or tomorrow. It's the first time he's been here, and you've come at the same time. I think it must be providence."

"What's bringing him out here? It wasn't mentioned in mother's last letter, though that's been two or three weeks past and would have taken that long to reach us. Is everything alright?"

"I just received a brief telegram. It's something about an inheritance. That's all I know."

"I haven't seen him in . . . well, it must be six or seven years," Johnny mused.

"And I since I left you all at Mount Pisgah," Lydia said. "I've been so nervous, I can't sleep." She looked at Johnny with a melancholy smile. "I didn't ever get to see your brother Thomas. Or Elizabeth, since she's grown. She sent me a tintype from Chicago in a lovely dress with a fancy flowered hat. Isn't that just the most miraculous thing? That you can make an image like that? And, oh, my! What a beautiful young woman. She reminds me so much of your mother when I saw her last." She paused, her brow furrowing. "You're the only member of the family I've seen since I left you in Iowa."

"I have that tintype," Johnny said. "Or, I should say, Cora does. She keeps it beside her bed and calls it her 'Princess Picture.' Lizzy's become quite the city woman."

The other riders had unsaddled their mounts and Li Yan and his family had come around the house to stand shyly beside the porch. Lydia opened the front door and ushered them inside.

"My! I haven't had a houseful like this—well, ever! Let me go to the Johnson's and borrow some chairs. Agnes will be full of questions anyway. Please . . . ." She beckoned for her guests to sit as well as they could. "Johnny, stay with your friends and I will fetch some chairs over." Before he could object, she was out the door, walking resolutely toward the gate.

"Let me come with you," he called after her. "You shouldn't be carrying anything."

"Agnes has boys," Lydia called back. "Lots of them. And they will want to see your friends." She hurried out the gate and along the fence, leaving Johnny and her seven Chinese visitors standing awkwardly in the parlor.

Johnny learned that evening why his father had always spoken with such reverent affection about Lydia. She quickly learned that Li Yan's children spoke as much English as Cora spoke Chinese and used them as interpreters as she queried their mother about what the group would like to eat. There were potatoes, squash, apples, and turnips stored in bins in a root cellar behind the house. A basket of fresh eggs graced the counter in her small kitchen, the morning gathering from a dozen ducks and chickens that roamed freely through her small orchard. On shelves in a tiny pantry, tomatoes, beans, and peaches glistened through what Lydia called her "Mason jars," tall, square-shouldered bottles in clear glass with screw-on lids that sealed across their wide mouths.

"I've never seen such a thing," Johnny said, lifting a jar of halved peaches and inspecting the still-yellow fruit in the light of the bungalow's window. "How long will these stay like this?"

Lydia laughed. "I've no idea. These jars are some of the first to make it to the valley. My bishop's sister brought them from the east. He thought I would be a good one to try them. The price is that I share the fruit and vegetables, so they don't last long at all."

None to Johnny's surprise, her guests asked only for pots of water to boil their noodles.

She opened a jar of the peaches anyway and enticed the children into sampling the sweet, golden halves, letting their delight with the new discovery tempt the adults into trying them.

"They grow on trees in the back—like apples," she explained to the children, holding two halves together with forks to show them the shape of the uncut fruit. "I believe I have a book with a story in it about some children picking peaches." She led them back into the sitting room and found the book, seating a child against each hip on her small sofa as their mother prepared their meal.

The ranch hands chose to spread their bedrolls in the garden, but Li Yan was anxious to move on, if he could join a wagon train headed south on the Spanish Trail.

"I will go to California the southern route," he said through Li Bo. "Some of the men who were working for the railroad said that the Chinese are not welcome now in San Francisco. There are too many. One told me of a small town in the south of California called San Diego where land is cheap—twenty-five cents an acre. Many people come through there on their way up the coast. I think I can set up a restaurant there."

Lydia told them of a gathering place on the south side of the city, at the far end of East Temple Street, where wagon parties camped while resupplying and taking on new travelers. Li Bo and Li Yan left on horseback, returning two hours later with word that a group of twenty wagons was resupplying and would be leaving in two days for southern California. In the morning, they would take Li Yan's family back to the main market street, get what the family needed for their journey, and join the train.

Though he would have preferred to sleep outside with the men, Johnny left his Chinese hands to have a final evening together without him. He sat up late with his grandmother, exchanging the news of the past year and learning what Lydia had gathered about his parents and Elizabeth from her more frequent letters. He tried to sleep on the sofa with knees bent over one arm and head propped against the other, then yielded to the need for peaceful rest and moved to the floor.

At sunup, Li Yan harnessed his team. The children grasped Lydia's hands as their parents bowed deeply and thanked her for taking them in. With the other Chinese riders flanking the wagon, they drove back along 800 South toward the streets where they could get supplies, leaving Johnny and his grandmother waving from the corner of the fence.

"What delightful people," Lydia said quietly as she watched them go. "Such polite children—and grateful adults."

Johnny nodded. "They aren't always treated well. I hope Li Bo can arrange for the supplies without them running into trouble."

"People here are very accepting," Lydia said. "All kinds pass through, and if you want to do business, you do it with whomever comes. And I hope your father arrives today. You need to be here."

"I'll ride down to the campground and see them this evening," he said. "And you're right. I want to be here."

"While we wait, I have a cupboard door that needs to be re-hung," she said with a smile. "And I'm feeling like doing some baking." She led him back into the house, unaware that the makings of her apple pie would still be spread on the counter when her next visitors arrived.

20

SUZANNA

The change in atmosphere at the mill was palpable. There was less banter among the men. None of the hurling of friendly insults that was part of daily exchanges on the mill floor before the vote. Most of the workers now saw the morning whistle as time to start moving toward their work stations, rather than as the time the first log moved into the blade and the humming whine became a muffled scream. The two new employees Suzanna had hired to extend Saturday to a full work shift remained outsiders, with no effort by the rest of the crew to bring them into the team. As she walked through the mill to the small office each morning, Ben Lanear continued to greet her, and occasionally Reuben. But the rest consciously ignored her and begrudgingly muttered a greeting if she spoke to them.

She had known immediately when she arrived at the mill on the morning of the vote that the men had already held their own poll. They stood like twisted yellow Osage posts, their arms tightly wrapped across their chests, faces dour, and eyes downcast. Surliness masked what she knew was guilty embarrassment. No one spoke.

"Your silence and expressions tell me you have already talked this over," she said, seeing no reason to be guarded. "But before we take a vote, I feel the need to caution you again about making a decision for the short term that I believe you'll regret later."

Eyes shifted and jaws tightened as the men prepared to once again consider a decision most hoped was behind them.

"I want to remind you that you are being paid fifteen dollars a week, four more than the men at the brickyard. Three of those dollars have gone into a fund that has, up to this point, grown to be enough to purchase half-interest in the mill. In another five years, you will collectively own this company if we continue the plan as it is. So you're taking home a dollar more than the brick-workers do, and creating ownership at the same time. When the mill belongs to you, you can decide how you want to distribute the profits, and each of you will retain a portion of the ownership after you quit working. That means you'll have some income as long as the mill continues to operate." She looked directly into the face of each man, but few met her gaze.

"If I return your investment, you will cease to own that interest. As I return your money, I will have you sign an agreement indicating that you have given it up. Unfortunately, it will be all of you or none. The arrangement can't work with only a few contributors. So—let me hear what questions you have, and we'll take the vote."

Sam Gorton again spoke for the dissidents. "If we've been buyin' part interest in the mill over the years, why h'ain't we seen some of the profits comin' back to us?"

Suzanna acknowledged the question with a nod, masking the low boil it kindled in her blood.

"In a way, you have. Our understanding when we introduced this plan was that we—David and I—would take a salary as principal owners and managers during the time of the purchase. All other profits would go into a fund that buys the mill from us when we reach the purchase amount or go back into improvements. That money has purchased the steam engine, added wagons and teams to our fleet, and kept your wages high enough that you're taking home better than brickyard pay. We go over that each year when we show all of you the ledgers."

"Maybe we should have been spendin' some to have a separate bookkeeper," Gorton said, directing his comment toward the line of men beside him rather than at its target.

Suzanna felt the boil erupt crimson across her face. "If there is any question about the honesty with which we've been managing the finances of this company, our agreement certainly needs to end. We've offered you the opportunity to look over the ledgers every year. Only Ben has chosen to do so."

"They always looked good to me, and always matched up," Ben offered.

"Would, to you," Gorton muttered.

"You'll have to consider that in your decision," Suzanna said. "You're going to have to trust me to give you back what you've put in, if you aren't able to do the figuring yourself."

This time Gorton spoke directly to her. "I figure, for a man who's been workin' here since this plan started, we're owed seven hundred eighty dollars."

"The bank's been paying interest on that money," Suzanna corrected. "It's more like eight hundred fifty by now."

Gorton's brow wrinkled in momentary confusion, then he blurted, "Like I told ya, that's more'n a year's pay. Eight hundred fifty dollars! Think of what ya could do with that much money!"

"Or how quickly you might gain that much additional pay if you were dividing up profits from the mill," Suzanna said. "And you will have a source of income after you quit working."

"What if something happens to us? Like it did to Will—or worse?" Christian Larsen asked.

"Right now in our contract, that man or his family retains a percentage of the interest in the mill unless they ask that we return what he has invested. That's all written in the agreement."

Ed Ransford spoke from the rear of the group. "Suppose we was to take that eight hundred fifty dollars and put it in the bank over in Osceola like you have. And got that interest. Maybe we'd be better off than owning some part of the mill with a bunch of other people."

Suzanna shrugged her acknowledgement. "You might. But if the mill does as well as it has been doing, and if you continue to find new business for it, you will do much better than the interest the bank is paying. And how many of you honestly are going to take the money to Osceola and put it in the bank?"

"I know what I'm doing with mine," Gorton said. "A whole year's pay in one day. And money I know I have. It's time to quit talkin' and have the vote."

The vote had been ten to four in favor of discontinuing the purchase plan, with the two new workers voting for the extra salary money. The men requested return of invested funds in a lump sum. Supported by an identical vote the following afternoon, Sam Gorton created the Union County Millworkers Brotherhood. Each member agreed to commit a dollar a week to fund support for injured members and their families. The meeting was held in the yard while Suzanna sat twenty paces away at her desk in the office. She could hear every word that was spoken and Sam knew it.

"What about Will Burgon?" one of the men asked. "If we'll be taking care of Will while he gets better, our funds 'll be used up already."

"Mizz Whitlock's takin' care of Will 'cause he was hurt before we ended the deal," Gorton said. "This is for things that happens from now on."

"Whitlocks is takin' care of Will, even with us changin' the deal?" someone asked.

"That's what I worked out for us," Gorton said. He hadn't spoken to Suzanna about it at all.

"Best not anyone get hurt for a while," another voice muttered. "We gotta build up a fund."

"I got this list of safety rules I plan to give Mizz Whitlock," Sam said.

"What they say?" a voice she recognized as Ed Ransford asked.

"I got five demands," Sam said. "One: No one gets under the logs when they're on the hoist. Two: No Baggy clothes around the engine. Three: Keep all the stuff picked up from the ground around the saw. Four: Always yell out 'Clear the blade' before throwin' the belt lever. And Five: Don't be standing where a kick-out can hit you if the saw throws a board."

"Mizz Whitlock is always preaching all those things to us now," Ransford said.

"This makes them official," Sam said. "Now they're rules of the brotherhood."

Suzanna heard Ben Lanear enter the conversation. "So—what if one of us breaks the rules? What you gonna do then?"

Sam Gorton snorted. "I haven'a had time to work out all the details. But part of what the brotherhood's all about is improvin' safety."

"The brickworks has raised wages to twelve dollars," a voice Suzanna didn't recognize said. "Maybe we need to be askin' for more money. Isn't that what brotherhoods is supposed to do?"

Ben spoke again. "We're already making fifteen—and getting it all now that we aren't putting some in a mill buyout. Why would Whitlocks want to give us more?"

The same unidentified voice answered. "That John Griggs said the rail engineers walked out one time when they didn't get what they wanted."

"From what I hear, that didn't go so well," Ben said. "And they were men who knew how to drive the trains. What we do, you can learn in a day, except how to fix the engine. I'm the only one knows that. We leave here, there'll be twenty men from the brickyard here in an hour."

"So—what do we do as a brotherhood?" the voice asked.

"Protect our rights," Gorton barked. "Make sure we're treated fair."

"Good plan," Ben said. "You just take good care of us, Sam Gorton."

21

LYDIA

When the rap came to the door, she was up to her elbows in flour. "You get that, Johnny," she called. "If it's your father, he'll be just as happy to see you as me. And I don't want to be seen this way."

Johnny had answered and as she hurriedly washed away the flour and tidied her hair, she heard the excited exclamations of a father and son's reunion. In the small oval mirror that hung beside the door into the sitting room, she looked at the face that she rarely took time anymore to study and wondered how it would appear to a son who hadn't seen it since her skin was smooth and supple, and her hair still the color of ripe wheat. A smudge of white powder on her chin accentuated dark spots that seemed to have appeared since she last looked in the glass. She brushed the flour across them, hoping to soften the blemishes. Then she drew a deep, settling breath and stepped through the doorway.

The man who eased himself away from Johnny had fared no better from twenty years apart. He had refused to discuss the war in his letters. But Suzanna and Elizabeth had both confided that the wound he had taken to his side at Pea Ridge and weeks spent in the military hospital in Fort Smith had stripped weight from him that had never returned. Thick hair that she remembered as being dark and shiny as fall chestnuts had faded to the color of new potatoes, streaked with strands of pearly gray. His features had a sharpness that reflected hardship, but his gold-flecked hazel eyes shone with the same brightness she remembered when he had first told her about the beautiful girl he had seen in the north Missouri woods. As he turned to her, the eyes brimmed, and he blinked away tears, stepping forward to wrap her in his arms.

As a young man, David had never been willing to hold his mother close as he did now. He had consoled her with an arm around her shoulders and cheek against her hair when his father died. When they parted at Mount Pisgah, he had given her a quick squeeze, then released and turned away to hide tears that were an embarrassment to a young man. But now he held her like a discovered treasure, his tears flowing freely onto her neck. After a long moment, he eased her away, studying the face she had just worried over with an approving smile. His first words were what she had hoped most to hear.

"You look as beautiful as I remember, Mother." He turned to Johnny. "You said in your letters that she didn't seem to age." He fingered a strand of her hair. "A little more gray, but the same strong, beautiful woman."

"When we've both aged, we adjust our expectations," she said modestly. "But I must admit that I see the effects of the war on you. You would benefit from a little more weight."

David laughed. "It's good to be mothered again," he said, then remembered that there was another guest. "Mother, this is Mister Henry Rosswell, a lawyer from New York City. He's traveled all this distance to talk to you about an unexpected inheritance. And I believe he's quite anxious to find a hotel and book passage back to where he can get a train east. I know there's so much for us to talk about, but let's hear him out, sign what needs to be signed, and he can find a hotel. We asked the coach to return in an hour." He turned again to Johnny who had started toward the rear door into the yard. "You may want to stay for this, Johnny. It could affect you at some time."

"Would you like tea?" Lydia asked, indicating a straight-backed wooden rocker for Mr. Rosswell. He beckoned toward her small, cloth-covered table, indicating that it would be a more suitable place for what he needed to discuss.

"If you have water heated," he said. "But with your permission, I would like to explain the purpose of my visit and get this settled."

"Water is always heated," Lydia said. "It will take only a moment. David? Johnny?"

Both men nodded, and she rescued a tin of rarely-used tea from the kitchen cupboard, filled a strainer, and poured hot water through it into a blue porcelain teapot as the men settled on three sides of the table. While Rosswell drew papers from his leather case, she filled three cups, poured herself a cup of heated water, and filled a small plate with cookies from a jar of the same blue porcelain that sat at the end of the counter.

"You're not having tea?" Rosswell asked.

"I prefer just warm water," she said, feeling no reason to explain to the lawyer what David and Johnny knew from their brief experience with the Mormons—that they were counseled against both tea and coffee.

"What do you know about the reason for my visit?" Rosswell asked after they were all settled.

Lydia took David's hand across the corner of the table. "Only what David's telegram told me. Something about a possible inheritance in England. He didn't say that he was bringing a New York lawyer."

"I represent Crouch, Whitman, and Rosswell, a legal firm in New York City," Rosswell said perfunctorily. "And as you said, we have been commissioned by a London firm to represent them in the United States— or, I might more correctly say, the United States and its territories—in the matter of settling the Allgar Estate in Norfolk, England. You are aware, I assume, Mrs. Whitlock, that your mother, Margaret Shipley, was an Allgar?"

Lydia nodded slightly. "Yes. Mother said very little about her life before coming to America. But I did know her name had been Allgar."

"So you were not aware that she came from a family of some means, a family that was apparently acquainted with the wife of King George the Third, Queen Charlotte."

"No. I wasn't aware of that. And it strikes me that such a thing would have been mentioned."

"As a young woman, your mother served the queen as lady-in-waiting," Rosswell explained. "But it appears that she and the queen's gardener—or more fairly, I should say, a young botanist who assisted the queen in her efforts to cultivate unusual plants—had a bit of a tryst. She found herself in a delicate condition, and the queen dismissed them both."

Lydia smiled faintly. Her mother had been a fiercely secretive woman, to the point that Lydia and her brothers had suspected that Lydia, who was only nineteen years younger than her mother, may have been a love child.

"I can't say that I'm surprised," she said. "But I must say that I *am* surprised that if my parents left England in disgrace, Mother became heir to some inheritance."

"The estate initially went to her brother, Robert Allgar the Second. He had no children and, in his will, left his sizable holdings to any descendants of his sister, if they could be found. We were contacted about finding those descendants. That has led me to you. You are your mother's only living heir."

Lydia started. "My brothers?"

"You're not aware?"

"They were both such lively men . . . ."

Rosswell shuffled through the papers that were spread in front of him. "Both became physicians," he said after refreshing his memory. "And both chose to work with the immigrants coming into Philadelphia. Your older brother contracted cholera during the epidemic of forty-nine. It appears that your younger brother lost his life at Gettysburg. There is nothing here that indicates whether it was as a soldier or ministering to the wounded as physician."

Lydia felt David's hand tighten about her own. Her memories of her brothers had become like dreams, vivid at times but quickly fading to moments when they no longer seemed at all real. She remembered them as vital young men, the older, James, having just completed his medical training. He was talking of joining her father in practice when she and her new husband moved to Ohio to join the Mormon congregation at Colesville. Henry was only eighteen, but also talked of practicing medicine. Now they were gone. Her father, James, and Henry. There should be tears, she knew. But the thirty-five intervening years as mother to a fugitive family in Missouri, as a pioneer woman during a year-long trek to the valley, and as a widow without family in a community where family was the center of all life, had scoured her emotions to a steeled acceptance. She straightened in her chair, released David's hand, and folded her own in front of her on the table.

"Tell me about this estate," she said. "You say it is in Norfolk. My knowledge of England is such that I cannot place Norfolk."

Rosswell again referred to his papers. "It is on the east coast along the North Sea, midway up the country. Norwich is the principal city of note. This estate, as it is described, is in the western part of the county."

"And how else is it described?"

"As including a stately manor house, stables, servants' quarters, nearly a thousand acres of ground, some under cultivation by tenant farmers, some pasturing sheep. The solicitor in London indicates that a family of some means named Badgerow now leases the estate and is interested in purchasing it, though it has been several months since this communication was received."

Lydia considered the information in silence, aware of the expectant looks of the others at the table. "What does this mean . . . that I am heir to this estate?"

Rosswell arched a brow, his mouth bowing downward. "It means that it is yours. You must, of course, claim it. I am told that the estate produces a comfortable income through its farming endeavors and that all taxes are paid. Our retainer comes from the income of the estate."

"What would I do with such a place?"

Rosswell lifted his hands, palms upward. "If nothing else, sell it to this Badgerow family. It has great value."

"I don't believe this is something I want to worry about. I am very content here. And have everything I need."

"We could, if you prefer, arrange to have someone there sell the property for you and send the proceeds to you," Rosswell ventured.

David shook his head. "I don't think that's wise. We don't know who would be handling the sale. How reputable they would be. Or, for that matter, if a sale is the best option. Someone needs to go see this on behalf of the family."

Lydia again took her son's hand. "I believe this inheritance should go to you, David. Can that be done? And—would you like it?"

David didn't immediately reply and Rosswell interrupted.

"You can assign the deed to anyone you wish, Mrs. Whitlock. But you must realize that you may be giving up a substantial fortune."

Lydia settled back against the bony ribs of the chair. This man knew so little about her. She had once given up a very comfortable teaching position to marry a cooper, and a promise from her father of a comfortable home on Philadelphia's South Broad Street for a cabin in the Missouri wilderness. Her only income now was from the sewing and mending she did, from English lessons provided to new European arrivals to the valley, and from occasional care of the multitude of children in her ward who called her Granny Whitlock. Yet she wanted for nothing. Agnes stopped by daily to see if there was anything she needed. The Worthlin boys from across the street asked each week if there were chores to be done. The only empty spot in her full life was her distance from family. More money would not bring her closer to them. But it might, if the train arrived in the valley in another year, as rumored, bring her family closer to her.

"I would like this to go to David," she said firmly. "He can share whatever comes of it with Johnny and Elizabeth."

Rosswell's face vacillated between disbelief and bewilderment. "Are you quite certain about this?"

"Very certain. David . . . ?" Her son's expression signaled that he was not completely taken with the idea.

"If I accept this, I feel very strongly that I will need to go see it. And traveling to England?" He waved his hands loosely in front of him. "It's taken nearly two weeks to come here, Mother. And I've never been on a ship—or even been to New York."

Rosswell inserted himself back into the discussion. "As I said, we can have someone sell the property as your agent and send you the money. But if you were to choose to go, I can certainly assure you that you can travel there much more comfortably, and in less time, than our journey here."

David turned to his son. "Johnny, is this an adventure that would interest you? If I were to go, having someone with me would be a great comfort."

Johnny seemed to have been turning over the same possibility. "I'm afraid I couldn't," he said hesitantly. "You will need to go by spring. Winter is coming to the valley. You haven't met my ranch hands yet, but they're taking cattle back with them. They'll never survive a winter without help—and, if it's a hard one, I'm not certain Nodda and Cora could either. Foals and calves will come in the spring. I need to be there. But you should go. Mother will want you to, and no one is better suited to make a decision about the property than you are. Grandmother's right."

Lydia could see in David's eyes the options being sorted, weighed, and gradually eliminated. "Alright," he said finally, but without conviction. "I will accept transfer of the deed. I can work this out with Suzanna when I get back to Iowa. What, Mr. Rosswell, do we need to do to get this settled and you on your way?"

Rosswell lifted a page to the top of his sheaf of papers. "I first need to complete papers that indicate that your mother . . ." he nodded perfunctorily in Lydia's direction, ". . . Mrs. Lydia Shipley Whitlock, has been found and can be certified to be the sole and rightful living heir of

Margaret Allgar Shipley. I have documents from Philadelphia and from Missouri verifying that Lydia Whitlock was indeed Lydia Shipley and left the Chariton River area in Missouri in 1847 with her son David, who took up residence in Afton, Iowa. You, David, can sign a statement verifying that this woman, living in Salt Lake City, in the Territory of Utah, is your mother. That will establish right to inherit."

He slid the paper in front of David and drew a blank paper to the top of the pile. "Mrs. Whitlock, I trust you have pen and ink. Two pens, if it isn't too much bother."

Lydia rose to find writing instruments.

"David, if you will state on the bottom of that paper in your own words that you are David Whitlock, the son of Lydia Shipley Whitlock, formerly of Philadelphia, Pennsylvania and Missouri. State that you are in the presence of the living Lydia Whitlock in Salt Lake City, Utah Territory, at the time of your signing. I will prepare a reassignment of any and all properties in Norfolk, England, inherited by Lydia Shipley Whitlock, to her son David. I must prepare copies of each and will leave one with you, David, for you to take to England. Copies will be sent to the solicitor in London, who can verify signatures when you arrive. Is that clear to all?"

Lydia wasn't at all certain that it was clear, but David nodded confidently and she agreed.

"Later this evening, I will wire this information to New York. They can schedule time on the transatlantic cable to get word to London. By tomorrow, London should have this decision and will be awaiting word from you, David, about your planned visit."

Lydia leaned forward with hands on the table. "There is a wire that goes across the sea?" she asked incredulously.

"*Under* the sea," Rosswell corrected. "There have been several attempts, but last year a cable was finally laid that has been very reliable. We can now telegraph London as easily as we can send one here. Sometimes more easily, when you are having one of your frequent periods of unrest out here."

"Well, I've never heard of such a thing," she said, looking across at her grandson. "Johnny, did you know about this cable?"

Johnny's laugh was kind. "No, Grandmother. But there are so many wonders that have escaped me. I am still astonished by trains."

"And they will soon cross the continent," Rosswell said proudly. "We live in the greatest decade the world has ever known—and may ever know."

Outside, horses sounded on the hardpacked street.

"That will be the men," Johnny said. "I need to go with them to bid farewell to Li Yan and his family."

"We should have these papers finished when you return," David said. "And we will have much to talk about tonight."

22

SUZANNA

Suzanna stood alone on the railyard platform, surrounded by people she had known for most of her adult life whose discomfort at being there at the same moment irritated, amused, and befuddled her. She thought herself an observant and generally skilled student of human behavior, but for reasons that were complete mysteries to her, she seemed to have become both cause and public casualty of the changes in the work life of the mill. It had become increasingly contentious, with Sam Gorton introducing changes in what he called "work rules" almost daily. The latest had been a demand the previous Monday morning for daily production quotas that were well below the mill's normal output.

"We're thinkin' our safety's at risk when we have to be movin' as fast as you want," he had said, tossing the demand, neatly written by one of the men's wives, across her work desk.

"We've never established a work quota," she replied calmly. "You men have always worked at the pace that seemed comfortable to you, and we haven't tried to adjust it. And what safety issue have we had that was related to working too quickly? Will was injured because he was in the wrong place."

"You're always sayin' safety is the most important thing. This work rule will make it better."

She had spent much of that Sunday puzzling over what to do about Sam and his work rules and wishing she could talk to David. She knew her husband was somewhere between Afton and Salt Lake City, still on a coach, and couldn't be reached. His telegram had added vinegar to an already sour mood and as she had faced Sam Gorton across the mill office table, all of the weekend's tension rose like bile in her throat.

"I've given this a great deal of thought since you brought the demand about wanting Ben off the log sled because of his arm," she said coldly. "And I believe I have a solution to a number of our work and safety issues." She stood, reached into the pocket of her canvas trousers, and pulled out the fifteen dollars she had tucked away in preparation for this moment. "Here's pay through the end of the week, Sam. As of this moment, your services are no longer needed at the Whitlock mill. I would like you to leave now."

Sam's face had curled into a snarl. "You can't just send me packin'! I don't know any man's ever been fired from here—and the brotherhood's gonna have somethin' to say about this. I got my rights!"

"A few weeks ago, I might have agreed with you," she had said, her eyes fixed on him like two balls of ice. "You owned a stake in the mill then. But you don't now. Every request you've brought to me has disrupted our normal work, and we're falling behind schedule. And your brotherhood's a creation of your own mind. It has nothing to say about how we run the mill, and things need to return to normal. The only thing that seems to be getting in the way of our getting our work done is you. Now—do you want to take your fifteen dollars and leave, or have me go get Sheriff Billings and have him haul you away without your fifteen dollars?"

Sam had hunched into a rage, fists balled and hips pressed against the front of the table. Then his hand shot out, snatched the bills from her hand, and he stalked from the office.

"The bitch gave me the sack," she heard him shout across the mill floor. "If the brotherhood means anything to you, you'll shut this place down *now* and show her who's in charge around here."

There had been a momentary lull in the sounds of men stacking cut ties and shifting a new log onto the sled, then the trunk moved into the blade with its screaming whine and Sam was gone. No one had said a word to her through the remainder of the day. Ben Lanear had nodded with a veiled smile as she walked across the mill floor, but the others had avoided her as if she were Medusa.

She had ridden into the post office at noon on Tuesday, hoping for a mid-journey cable from David or an overdue letter from Elizabeth. Instead, she received twenty minutes of unsolicited advice from Charlotte Winter through the grillwork of the tiny cubicle that served as a post office in the rear of Fife's General Store.

"I'm a bit surprised to see you," the gossipy assistant said as Suzanna approached the window. "Thought you might stay away for a few days until the storm blows over."

"Storm?" Suzanna glanced about the shop, noticing for the first time since hurrying to the mail counter that she was the object of furtive glances from every corner of the store.

Charlotte leaned into the grillwork. "Everyone knows you sent Sam Gorton packing," she whispered. She glanced about conspiratorially. "Not that lots of folk don't think he deserved it, mind you. But he's a man with a family. And the brickyard's not going to take him."

Suzanna kept her face a mask. "Today's been the best work morning we've had in weeks," she said. "We can't have people disrupting the place, even if they're family men. If Sam had come to work to do his job and not stir up trouble, he would be out there working this minute."

Charlotte arched a knowing brow. "Still, no one's ever been sacked here before. Everyone knows that Artemus Brill goes to work at the brickyard most mornings drunk as an Irish priest. But they let him come."

"He's not encouraging the others to slow down," Suzanna retorted. "And he doesn't work for me. One of these days, Artemus will tumble into the side of one of those ovens, burn himself to where he can't work, and Will Jenkins will be giving him the sack."

"That's the other thing. A woman firing a man. Every woman in town's worried about her own husband if a woman can just sack him like that."

"So, if David had been here to sack Sam, that would have been alright?"

"I'm just saying you need to be careful. You're out there by yourself. And I hear all the threats and grumbling that go on in here over the pickle barrel."

Suzanna felt her spine stiffen and color rush to her face. She knew Sam was an impulsive man and that he had a streak of violence in him, especially when he drank. But try to harm her? Or try to do damage to the mill? She realized as she looked soberly at Charlotte through the bars of the postal window that she had let her anger and frustration obscure some of the risks.

"Do I have mail?" she asked.

Charlotte shook her head. "Nothing today. And why don't you stay out at the house for a few days. If something comes in for you, I'll have Nate bring it out with the supply wagon."

Her trip to the rail station was her first into town since Charlotte's warning.

The urgent whistle of the 11:43 stirred her from her reverie. Suzanna's pulse quickened in anticipation—of seeing a husband she missed dreadfully when he was away and of knowing she was facing another long period without him. He was slow disembarking, and she feared for a moment that she had misunderstood his wire from Omaha. But he finally stepped down from the last car, pulling his battered leather bag after him.

She held him long enough that she felt his back and shoulders relax, but he didn't pull away.

"You've had a hard few weeks," he guessed, keeping her close against his chest. "Was it my wire about England?"

She released him and held one hand while he retrieved the bag from the platform, then guided him toward the buggy at the end of the station platform.

"That didn't help," she said, but decided to wait until they were on the road to unburden herself. "Tell me about Salt Lake City—and about your mother's life there. And Johnny. I'm so pleased that he was there at the same time. And so *envious*."

David threw the bag into the back of the buckboard and helped her up onto the padded seat. "Mother's very content," he said. "In fact, as delighted as she was to see me, I almost felt as if I was intruding on her happy routine. She has friends who love her like family, and she thinks of them the same way."

Suzanna had taken the reins and urged the horse into a trot. "Did Johnny look well?" David's chuckle pulled her attention to his face. "What?" she asked, a note of concern in her voice.

"Oh, nothing. He had three Chinese ranch workers with him that he's taken under his wing."

"He's mentioned them in his letters," she reminded him.

"Yes, but Cora now speaks to them as if she'd been born one of them, and their children have learned English from her. They're turning into quite the little community."

"With these Chinese families?"

He shrugged. "They seem to get along real well."

They rode for a moment in silence until Suzanna decided he wasn't going to bring it up first.

"And what's this about you needing to go to England?"

He hesitated, then said, "Mother doesn't want the inheritance—whatever it turns out to be. She's passed it along to me. Henry Rosswell said he could find an agent in England to sell it for us and have whatever it brings sent to us here." He paused, considering his words more carefully. "I don't exactly distrust the man, but I don't believe our interests are his greatest concern."

"My sense as well," she said, giving the reins a directing tug that steered the mare left onto the road to the mill. "And I'm afraid I'm not in a very trusting mood myself at the moment."

"What's been happening?"

She kept her eyes on the back of the trotting horse. "I let Sam Gorton go. He was becoming too disruptive to the other men."

What began as an amused chuckle rolled like warm cider into David's stomach, emerging as a deep belly laugh that shook down through the seat of the shay. "Well—that explains the cold stares at the station. You've become a regular Jay Gould, and people seem to be loving you just as much."

"I'm hardly a Jay Gould," she said, dismissing the comparison to one of the country's most notorious industrialists. "But the mill's already a better place for it. I told you in my wire that the men had voted to do away with the purchase. Sam talked them into setting up some kind of brotherhood like the rail workers have and started making ridiculous demands. He's been nothing but trouble."

They rode for another moment without speaking, then she said, "Do you want to keep this estate?"

"In England? No. Unless you're feeling like you want us to get away from all this."

"Not that far away. We'd never see Elizabeth or Johnny."

"We rarely see them now."

Suzanna glanced over at him to see if there was seriousness in his objections. "You just saw Johnny. And Elizabeth was here in the spring."

He shook his head. "No. I have no desire to live in England. The railroad's most of the way to Salt Lake and should get there next year. They're talking about a stop near the Bear River crossing, and it won't be a long trip from there up to where Johnny and Nodda are. But I think I need to negotiate any sale. We can send wires across to England now, but I feel like we need to be there. See the place and talk to any buyer face-to-face."

Suzanna finally got to what she had been thinking about since the cable came from Salt Lake City. "I want to go with you."

She expected silence and was prepared to wait it out. But there was none.

"And leave the mill with the problems you're telling me about?"

"I'd be happy to have you stay and deal with them," she said. "And I could go. But I assume that since this is your inheritance, you will need to be there. And yes—leave the problems for a while. I think it might be good for everyone."

"Let Ben manage the mill?"

"We were training him for it before the vote. He knows how to manage the orders and keep the ledgers."

This time, silence. Then, "I like this idea. I was hoping Johnny could go with me, just because it will be so foreign and I hate to think of going alone. But I'd much rather you went." He turned to her and smiled broadly. "And I might need the services of a Jay Gould."

"When are you thinking you need to leave?"

"The sooner we get there the better. But Henry Rosswell thinks we should wait for spring, for a better ocean crossing."

"We can't go sooner?"

David shook his head. "The ship crossing can be long and rough. Spring is better. Plus, Ben knows the books, but he's not that good with figures. We need to find someone who can keep the ledgers."

"His wife, Anna," Suzanna said. "She's good with figures."

"You've been thinking about this," he said with a wry smile.

"Every minute since your wire came."

"Let's plan on early May, then. We can send a letter to Elizabeth, letting her know we'll be coming through Chicago. I'll wire Rosswell's firm and ask them to assist us with our passage. I think they are quite happy continuing to draw money from the estate for as long as they can."

"I'd better get more of my dresses out of the trunk," she said, looking down at the one gray-checked gingham she wore when not in her mill clothes. "I suspect English women don't dress in men's shirts and trousers."

"If we give her enough time, Bridget can sew you some new ones," he said.

She cast him a surprised glance. "You've been thinking about this too!"

"Every minute since I sent the wire," he said.

23

ELIZABETH

The meeting was Myra Bradwell's brainchild, but Elizabeth and Alta Hulett found themselves doing most of the preparation. Myra chose to call it a *gathering* rather than a convention, since a formal convention on suffrage was scheduled for the nation's capital in January, and conventions typically included men of sympathetic leanings. Myra made it clear that she wanted no men at her affair.

Elizabeth had argued against an early December date, fearing Chicago might be bundled up against one of winter's bone-chilling blizzards off the lake. But her mentor felt it important to meet before delegates went to Washington.

"The rail now comes to Chicago from every part of the country," she said. "They can get here in December, wherever they are and whatever the weather. And the time has come for a more unified and forceful set of demands. Women from the thirty-seven states need to be speaking with one voice before they get to Washington, and I am seeing some unraveling in what has never been a very tightly knit sisterhood. I will be surprised if we can get both Elizabeth Stanton and Lucretia Mott in the same room right now. Lucretia seems to find Elizabeth's friendship with George Train to be offensive to her Quaker sensibilities. And you know, of course, that while Lucretia supports the Fourteenth and Fifteenth Amendments, Stanton and Anthony oppose them unless they included women in the rights being extended to black men."

"Mr. Train doesn't seem to be a very reputable man," Elizabeth noted of the Boston shipping and rail magnate. "Perhaps Miss Mott has her reasons for disliking him."

"She does. But he has money and influence," Myra reminded her. "And right now, our movement needs both."

Elizabeth's assignment was to extend invitations to the gathering, while Alta agreed to work with Myra on an agenda. For a girl in her mid-teens, Alta had an intellect that Elizabeth found astonishing—and humbling. She had studied law with attorney and congressman William Lothrup in Rockford before coming to Chicago, and Myra was increasingly captivated by the girl's talents. Though plain in appearance and constantly troubled by illness, the spindly, awkward teen stirred in Elizabeth an embarrassing bout of jealousy. *This is silliness*, she thought to herself after bristling at what seemed overly generous praise by Myra of one of Alta's suggestions. But the realization didn't soften the sting of having to share Myra's coveted attention.

Elizabeth's first cable went to Mrs. Stanton and her associate, Susan Anthony, in New York, inviting them to an informal meeting of leaders of the women's suffrage movement, to be hosted by Myra Bradwell at her Chicago home the first week in December. Myra would arrange rooms, at her expense, at the Tremont for those she couldn't accommodate in her guest rooms. If invitees needed assistance with travel, she would also provide train fare. Mrs. Bradwell was most anxious that the two leaders of the New York movement attend, if at all possible.

Elizabeth delayed other invitations, hoping to be able to announce that both Stanton and Anthony would be attending. Susan Anthony responded by wire the following day, indicating she would be delighted to come. But Elizabeth Stanton's youngest daughter Harriot, who had come unexpectedly late in life, was now only ten. Mrs. Stanton was choosing to spend her time with Harriot until the girl was older. Miss Anthony would represent them both.

With this information in hand, Elizabeth quickly received acceptances from Lucy Stone from New Jersey, Matilda Gage from New York, and Lucretia Mott who had been informed in Elizabeth's invitation that Mrs. Stanton would not be able to attend. Angelina Grinke, an outspoken abolitionist-turned-suffragette from Massachusetts, declined citing failing health. Three young women aspiring to the legal profession who had become regular correspondents of Myra's all replied with enthusiastic acceptances: Lemma Barkaloo from Brooklyn, Arabella Babb of Mount Pleasant in Elizabeth's home state of Iowa, and Phoebe Cousins from St. Louis, Missouri.

"I also want you to include Mary Livermore, of course, and Esther Morris from here in Illinois," Myra told her when she reviewed the list. "Esther lives in the city of Peru. When I was working on the women's property rights legislation, she became one of my most outspoken supporters. When her first husband died, she was unable to inherit his property and was willing to say to our esteemed legislators what even I was too polite to say. We will need her in our fight for greater equality."

Though her response showed surprise and a trace of intimidation, Esther Morris quickly accepted. Elizabeth began to plan for twelve, including herself, Alta, and Myra. Senator Trumbull agreed to release her for four days in early December, and the three women worked on finalizing the agenda Alta had drafted.

"We plan to begin by having Susan review the Declaration of Sentiments Elizabeth Stanton presented at the Seneca Falls Convention," Myra suggested. "Susan has been doing most of the speaking for the New York activists of late and will know it well. The Declaration was developed twenty years ago but is akin to our own Declaration of Independence. It will provide a foundation for the rest of our discussion."

"We plan then to encourage the women to create a written declaration for each of their states," Alta said, her pale eyes glowing with anticipation. "Myra hopes to begin publishing what we will call the *Chicago Legal News* in January, with a first draft for the women to review. It will have a monthly column titled *Law Related to Women* and is a not-so-subtle voice for women's rights. At the gathering, we will encourage others to find similar publishing opportunities in their own states."

Elizabeth smiled encouragingly but felt another cold draught of envy pour into her stomach. Myra hadn't said anything to her about launching a publication. Of course, she was spending long days preparing Senator Trumbull's response to a potential impeachment trial, and Myra may simply have chosen not to burden her with it. "I think announcement of the publication and encouragement for others to do the same are perfect," Alta said brightly. "That discussion should fill much of a day."

"We also plan to encourage some of the younger single women to apply to law schools," Myra said. "Lemma was denied admission to Columbia because of her gender. We will make little progress with state legal boards until we can present them with credentials that make it impossible for them to challenge our training and preparation. Phoebe tells me that Washington University in Saint Louis is planning a new offering in law. Our goal is to have one or two women accepted into its first class."

The normally reserved Alta bubbled with enthusiasm. "But our *final* activity is the most exciting," she gushed, her face flushed with the first color Elizabeth had seen since the project began. "Myra has asked that I draft a bill for the Illinois legislature that we will present to the women as a model for their own states. We're calling it the 'Earnings Act.' It grants women the right to control the income that comes from their own labor. Perhaps we can get a similar draft introduced at the Washington convention."

"A wonderful idea," Elizabeth said, feeling again the chest-tightening tug, followed immediately by the hollowness of guilt. She was involved with what was happening at the highest levels in government in Washington, she reminded herself. *But, oh, how I would like to be involved in drafting that bill*, she thought. Being Myra's protégé had been the most glorious experience of her life, and she had chosen to remain in that light over a proposal from one of the most eligible men in Chicago. It wasn't regret she was feeling. Her dedication to the cause of women and to her ambitions to practice law were no less certain. It was just that seeing the laurels placed on the head of another, especially one so young, hurt in a way she couldn't explain. "Perhaps we can suggest a similar piece of legislation to Senator Trumbull. I can help him draft a federal version," Elizabeth offered, begging for some small return of attention.

"First things first," Myra said, casting Elizabeth a smile that said, "Don't feel injured, little bird. I have helped you find your wings, and there is a new chick in the nest."

The women who found their way to Myra Bradwell's gathering were as different as the stately homes that lined Michigan Boulevard: some square and sturdy, others tall and elegant, and several plain and tidily practical. Yet Elizabeth realized as soon as they came together that they were also as alike as the Iowa farm women she had grown up among— tough and resilient as post oaks, with resolute commitment to get done what needed to be done. Susan Anthony and Lucretia Mott were of the Quaker persuasion, reflecting the quiet reserve and passionate commitment to social equality fundamental to the Society of Friends. The younger women were more exuberant, displaying a brashness that had not been tempered by the years of struggle that furrowed the brows of their elders. Elizabeth took an immediate liking to Esther Morris, who appeared to be a confused wanderer in this forest of social luminaries.

"I'm not sure why I'm here," Esther confided to Elizabeth when she found her standing alone beside the doorway to the parlor, watching the other women greet and exchange war stories from suffrage campaigns.

"Myra asked for you specifically," Elizabeth assured her. "Some years ago, you spoke up publicly when denied the right to inherit your husband's property and were a staunch ally when she was championing her property rights legislation. Don't be intimidated by these other women. You have been as bold as any of them—and have made an important difference."

"And you are not intimidated?" Esther asked, giving Elizabeth a grateful smile.

"I haven't been much of a voice for anything yet," Elizabeth replied grimly. "Someday, perhaps."

Esther took her hand and squeezed gently. "Myra told me in one of her letters that you protected your father's land in court in western Iowa. That's a victory none of the rest of us can claim."

"A victory only because we have a very understanding judge in Afton—and because my father reappeared at exactly the right moment," Elizabeth said.

"Nonetheless, you belong here more than I do," Esther murmured. "I expect that I will be leaving for the Wyoming territory within another year. My husband John was seduced by the gold fever but has found since arriving there that more money is to be made running a saloon. He wants me to join him in some tiny mining camp in the mountains." She glanced up at her new confidante. "The only attraction is that John assures me that the people of Wyoming are engaged in a much livelier and more immediate debate about letting women vote."

Elizabeth turned to look at her directly. "Oh? My brother lives in the territories and has said nothing about it in his letters."

"Where is he?"

Elizabeth shrugged. "Ranching in some valley between the Idaho and Wyoming territories."

"He may not be aware of it. And I'm not at all certain the movement is nobly motivated. There are a number of freed negros and hundreds of

Chinese men in the territory. People like John are concerned that white men will lose control if they can't get more votes and control the majority. Their answer is to consider white women."

Elizabeth's smile was grim. "A devil's bargain. But if you end up going, please let me know what happens there."

"I certainly will," Esther said, releasing Elizabeth's hand and stepping tentatively into the excited mix of women.

As the day approached late afternoon and Myra felt the energy beginning to wane, she suggested that they adjourn until the morrow and reconvene after a good rest.

"I have been impressed," she said, "that we should finish our day with a song of solidarity. The girls have written words out for each of you." She led the women into the parlor to an elaborately embossed upright and perched at the stool while Alta and Elizabeth passed about the handwritten verses.

"The song was sent to me by my friend, May Wheeler," Myra announced, pounding five bold chords from the keyboard. "It is to be sung to the tune of the John Brown Song."

The women clustered more closely around the upright, holding their pages aloft as Myra repeated the chords and began to play.

Our hearts have felt the glory of the coming of the time,
When law and right and love and might shall make our land sublime,
When mount and hill and rock and rill with freedom's light will shine,
As Truth comes marching on.

Elizabeth stepped up beside Lucretia Mott, adding her voice to the chorus:

Glory, glory, hallelujah!
Glory, glory, hallelujah!
Glory, glory, hallelujah!
As Truth comes marching on.

They saw it in the shadows of that old New England Bay,
They heard it in the breezes of that cold December day,
They sent it with the echoes to Britannia far away,
That Truth was marching on.

Around her, the women's feet began to keep time with the meter of the song, shoulders swayed left-right as they marched in place. They had become a single body and single voice, the chanters of May Wheeler's dream.

The trumpet then was sounded that shall never call retreat;
Adown the cent'ries softly we hear the tramp of feet;
Today we still are marching to the same old music sweet,
Of Truth still marching on.

We're here to swell the anthem that is heard across the sea,
That equal rights in law and love is meant for you and me,
Where every law was founded on the plain of liberty.
While Truth came marching on.

Were they, Elizabeth wondered as the final chorus filled the parlor and spilled out onto the lakefront, singing of things as they were? Or was there a power in the song that declared how things would inevitably be?

The gathering, by all accounts, was a rousing success. On the fourth morning, when all but Esther Morris and Belle Babb had been taken by coach to the Great Central Depot on Water Street to catch their morning trains, Myra declared that they had achieved more than she had thought possible.

"We sent draft legislation home with each woman who represented a state yet to pass property protection laws," she announced to the four young women assembled in her parlor. "Several have committed to contact activists in states near their own to develop similar drafts. Susan promised that she and Elizabeth Stanton will publish their first issue of *The Revolution* next month and have copies ready for the Washington Convention. Lemma and Phoebe will be submitting applications to be part of the first class at the law school in St. Louis. We couldn't have hoped for a better result." She turned her attention to Elizabeth and Alta, taking each by the hand.

"You young ladies did a wonderful job. I am most grateful—and proud of both of you beyond any ability to express my thanks."

The emptiness in Elizabeth's stomach filled with warm nectar and she grasped and squeezed Alta's frail hand, completing the circle. During the week's discussions, Elizabeth had said relatively little, listening and taking mental notes that she recorded in her journal each evening. She knew that she was sitting in the presence of greatness and was, using one of her mother's expressions, watching a stone being cut out of a mountain that would roll forth, gathering momentum until it reshaped the landscape of the nation. Alta had been a vocal and aggressive participant, occasionally becoming a visible irritant to the two Quaker matriarchs who constantly reminded the women that change should never be born from hatred or violence. When Alta bristled at their gentle reprimands, Elizabeth found herself wondering if the sickly girl's passionate impatience wasn't a reflection of fear that she had little time to make her mark. As she squeezed Alta's fleshless hand, an almost imperceptible tremor added to her suspicion.

"You asked that we stay another day," Esther said, the practical immediacy that had made her a useful contributor to the week again raising its head.

Myra nodded thoughtfully. "You and Belle are in quite different positions, coming to us from smaller, western communities. Elizabeth tells me you may be going out to join your husband in the Wyoming Territory. And you, Bella, are in what is essentially an Iowa village. Your teaching at Simpson College may provide you with avenues to further the cause, and others will present themselves. I see great futures for you both. You will have to be creative and chart your own paths. We can visit about those possibilities over lunch before your afternoon trains."

In the early afternoon, as Elizabeth assisted the women with their bags to the waiting coach, she slipped Esther a card with her address at the senator's office, asking that she write if she joined her husband in Wyoming.

"It sounds like a place that needs some support and encouragement," she said.

"There is much that needs to be done in Illinois," Esther said. "We need you here."

Elizabeth laughed softly. "I am needed here like William Penn was needed in England," she said. "I am surrounded by reformers, but my particular variety may need new ground in which to sprout and flourish."

"John is being insistent, and I will undoubtedly agree to join him at some point," Esther said begrudgingly. "I have always dreamed of a life as a saloon keeper in a remote mining town."

Elizabeth smiled at the woman's self-deprecation, but her intuition told her differently. "Saloon keeper or not, I think there is much more awaiting you there," she said.

24

ELIZABETH

All of the political gunpowder stockpiled by angry Washington factions after the death of Lincoln suddenly exploded in February of 1868, touched off by President Johnson again removing Edwin Stanton from his cabinet position without consent of Congress. Three days later, on February 24th, the US House of Representatives passed a resolution impeaching the President of the United States for "high crimes and misdemeanors." The vote fell along party lines with one hundred twenty-eight Republicans voting to impeach and forty-seven Democrats opposing. Five days later, a House committee tasked with drawing up specific articles of impeachment presented a list of ten to the full body which, after floor debate, was reduced to nine. All but two were based on presidential violation of the Tenure of Office Act and the president's refusal to obtain congressional approval to remove Stanton.

Frustrated by the speed with which the government was unraveling and by what seemed interminable delays transmitting information between his Washington office and Elizabeth, Senator Trumbull summoned her to the capital. He needed, he said, to have her insightful wit and detailed knowledge of the law close at hand. His telegram promised reimbursement for first class coach fare on the Baltimore and Ohio railroad, but not for one of the luxurious Pullman cars that now provided private overnight sleeping accommodations for those who could afford to make the journey without interruption.

Elizabeth chose to divide the trip into three segments, having neither the funds nor the inclination to sleep in a fold-down berth as a train rattled through the night. Her decision was reaffirmed when she discovered that the Chicago to Baltimore Express was populated by more than its share of single young businessmen and philandering husbands, all of whom seemed bent on protecting her from every man on the train but themselves. Two hours out of Chicago, the sagging, middle-aged man pressed beside her on the red leather seat seemed to nod off. His head drooping slowly toward her shoulder, the Macassar oil sheen of his combed-over hair threatening her nostrils and the shoulder of her dress. As she reached for a kerchief to shield the satin shoulder of her frock, his right hand slipped beneath his left elbow and groped her right breast, massaging it lightly through her bodice and cotton chemise. She started upright, firing the tip of her elbow into the man's doughy neck just below the jawline. He yelped and straightened, cursing up at her while the other four passengers gazed at the pair in embarrassed confusion, but remained silent. She waited in the corridor until the next stop, then found a conductor who arranged for a seat with two elderly couples and a middle-aged widow.

Elizabeth's prior travel experience had been limited to excursions across the rolling farmland of Iowa and to the Quincy-Chicago run that rumbled along the Mississippi River through the wooded hills of western Illinois before crossing the upper part of the state to Lake Michigan. She knew that she was a child of the frontier, and that a vast continent stretched east from the Mississippi to the Atlantic. But until cradled for eighteen hours in the hypnotic, swaying arms of the train carriage, she had little understanding of the vastness and burgeoning energy of her nation. Beyond the velvet-draped windows, post-war America unfolded in a late-winter panorama that at first seemed familiar but became increasingly populated and industrial as she moved east.

It had snowed in northern Indiana the night before her departure. Neat farmsteads appeared as painted patches of white and red against a canvas of spidery black forest. Chimney smoke curled in gray plumes from stone chimneys, disappearing into the muted blue of the winter sky. Two children burst from one of the homes, sprinting across the blanket of white toward the nearby woods. The scene and the soothing rocking of the car lulled her into that twilight between consciousness and slumber. From the recesses of her drowsy memory, a young girl peeked out onto a similar snowy day in the Missouri village of Shelbyville. It was less a memory than scattered sensations and images: chasing her brother across another snow-covered field; air scented with hearth fires of hickory and cedar; a shallow ravine in the woods at the far end of the village, filled with snow that was shoulder-deep on Johnny. Did she actually remember a thick, low sycamore branch, bone white against the dark trunks of the surrounding oaks, sticking out over the ravine like the bleached rib of some giant beast? She had been little more than a toddler, but in her time-faded memory, the two of them scrambled onto the limb, then belly-flopped into the deep snow. First one side. Then the other. When packed to the point that it no longer cushioned their fall, the crushed box in the snow became a fort, capped by cedar branches Johnny cut from the upper edges of the ravine and propped against the overhanging limb. Their secret hideaway was accessible only through a tunnel burrowed between the roots of the giant sycamore. Though the images were distant and uncertain, the warmth they conveyed was as real as the snowscape that passed beyond the windows of the train. She couldn't remember there ever having been a happier time. Her father managed Jacob Randall's mercantile store. Her mother was always there when she burst into the kitchen, soaked to the skin and red as a beet root. The house smelled of baking bread and freshly washed sheets steaming over drying racks beside the fire. Then, with another flash of memory, those joyful times evaporated.

She remembered that it had been springtime—and her birthday. An old trapper had come to the house. No name. But he carried a long rifle and had given her a carved wooden horse that was still among the treasures she kept in a trunk in her bedroom in Afton. He had spoken to her father and, without taking time for any birthday celebration, the family had packed the wagon and ridden through an entire day and night.

Memories of the day that followed were among her darkest, and she shivered involuntarily against the side of the train compartment. She was hiding in the musty darkness of a workroom made of earthen blocks, huddled in the folds of her grandmother's dress. Despite hands pressed tightly over her ears, she could hear the discharge of rifle after rifle as if they had been right beside her head. From outside, one of the attackers had pulled at the plank door, prying it partway open before pitching backward, his blood spraying the snow beyond the shed. Then Johnny was running—freezing midway between the workshop and cabin as an animal cry froze him in his tracks. Elizabeth's grandmother had crawled on hands and knees into the open doorway with the young girl pressed tightly against her hip. From there, beyond the body that partially blocked the door, Elizabeth could see the raging battle. The moments that followed were burned into her soul more deeply and painfully than any in her remaining life. A tall, ragged man on a black horse had charged through the river shallows to her left, brandishing a long, curved corn knife. She had never asked about the memory, knowing intuitively that it was as painful for her mother as for herself. But she remembered the man as having only one eye, riveted on her brother who quailed in the clearing. Rifles flashed from windows of the cabin to her right. As she turned from the rider to the place where she knew her parents fired those volleys, the door of the cabin burst open. In what replayed in Elizabeth's memory as a ballet of incendiary rage, her mother swept through the doorway, grasped a flat-bladed spade that leaned against the cabin wall, and flew across the clearing to where Johnny stood. The spade whirled in her hands like the broadsword of a medieval knight, slicing into the side of the murderous rider. The horse reared and plunged, driving an iron hoof into her mother's leg and dropping her beside Johnny. Then, there was a mountain of a man . . .. In her memory he filled the entirety of the clearing and blocked everything else from view. He lifted both her mother and the boy, one under each arm as if they weighed nothing, and turned toward the cabin. The air continued to explode with gunfire and before he had taken ten steps, he straightened and arched his back with a gasping moan. Pulling his precious load in tightly against his chest, he stumbled, then slumped forward across them. It was Elizabeth's sole memory of her grandfather. He lay now in a grave beside that workshop, somewhere in the Missouri woods.

Elizabeth gasped audibly and shook herself, turning away from the winter scene beyond the train window. How had the happy image of children dashing into the snow resurrected such dark memories? Was she that unsettled by this call to Washington? By being drawn again into another brawl between selfish and hateful men? No, she decided. It was those last memories that she needed to recall. Of a woman of unfailing love and courage throwing herself into the battle, and of a man for whom no sacrifice was too great when she and her family were threatened. *I am the daughter of warriors*, she thought. *And it is my time to be courageous.*

She spent the first night in a boarding house within sight of the small dappled-brick depot in Akron, Ohio. As she climbed from her rail car and retrieved her bag, she guessed that the depot had once been buff colored, but the soot of a thousand smoke-belching engines as they idled beside the platform had dusted it sooty gray.

The proprietress of the lodging, a Mrs. Winslow, was a round, red-cheeked woman whose face had the appearance of being permanently chapped, but whose disposition was as warm as the fire that crackled in the parlor of her overly-furnished home. Elizabeth guessed the woman to be in her early sixties. Mrs. Winslow fished a ledger from one of three sideboards in her cramped dining room, spread it on the table, and had her guest sign in and present a dollar before being shown to a small corner bedroom on the second floor. The bed was surrounded by such an array of floor chests, bureaus, stuffed chairs and side-tables that Elizabeth had to hoist her luggage into a chair and squeeze around the bed to place her handbag beside a porcelain washbasin. The chamber pot sat on an end table on the opposite side of an ornate headboard where she would be certain to see it. She wondered fleetingly how she could possibly find room to use the thing, if needed, and registered a mental note to use the privy behind the house before retiring.

"You certainly have quite the collection of furniture," she said, removing her hat and placing it for the moment on one of four pillows.

Mrs. Winslow's cheery laugh shook her from top to bottom. "The combination of three households," she explained. "My late husband had been widowed once before, and I brought all those furnishings into a house that had been left to me by my parents. Then my daughter, who married a German gentleman come to Akron to work for Mr. Schumacher at his oatmeal mill, moved down to Columbus where he got a job in a brewery. 'From oats to barley,' he likes to say." She laughed more heartily, and her face glowed as red as a train conductor's lantern. "Well, she didn't want to take her furniture with her. It was a big move up for Heinrich, and she bought all new things." The woman waved an arm about the room. "Half of this was hers. And I just hate to get rid of anything."

"It's still light out," Elizabeth said, fearing that the woman might be about to relate the story behind each piece. "If the Universalist Old Stone Church is within walking distance, I'd like to visit. Can I get that in before dinner?"

Mrs. Winslow's laugh quieted. "You're one of those suffragettes," she said, her voice turning cynical. "Don't have much room for that myself. We women have enough to worry about without becoming all involved in politics and the like."

"When did your husband pass?" Elizabeth asked.

"Four years ago now."

"If it had been ten years ago, this house may not have come to you," Elizabeth said. "It did because some brave Ohio women, many who met in that church fifteen years ago, decided it was something they *should* worry about."

Mrs. Winslow's ruddy face softened and she led Elizabeth back down the stairs. "The church isn't far from here. Dinner is at six-thirty, but I can hold you a plate if you aren't back."

"I just want a quick look inside—and to sit for a few minutes," she said, slipping a hand into the pocket of her jacket and fingering a folded page. Sojourner Truth had spoken in that church at the Women's Rights Convention in 1851. A brief, spontaneous five-minute speech that had been transcribed by one of the attendees. Copies of the transcript had been a 'thank you' gift from Myra to Elizabeth and Alta after the Chicago gathering. Elizabeth had read it to the point of memory. She wished to read it again in the solitude of the sanctuary. If finding herself alone, she hoped to stand at the pulpit and declare in a loud voice, as the black woman had in response to a minister's claim that through Eve, all sin had come into the world, *"If the first woman God ever made was strong enough to turn the world upside down all alone, these women together ought to be able to turn it back, and get it right side up again! And now they is asking to do it, the men better let them!"*

The sanctuary had been scattered with parishioners and other women who Elizabeth suspected of also coming to the church to summon the spirits of past champions. In a back pew, she read silently through her transcript of Sojourner's address, envisioning the tall, sinewy negro woman standing before the convention and baring her arm as she declared, *"Look at my arm! I have plowed, and planted, and gathered into barns, and no man could head me! And ain't I a woman?* Elizabeth left the church buoyed and resolute. It was fortunate, she decided later, that the businessmen staying at Mrs. Winslow's had finished their supper when she returned. She was able to eat alone, allowing the energy to soak into her soul without feeling the need to release a spark or two on some unsuspecting male who reminded her of the masher on the train. *I will save it for Washington,* she thought.

She was at the station a full half-hour before the 9:15 overnight from

Chicago hissed and screeched to a stop beside the platform. When an accommodating young man helped her hoist her bag up to the attendant in the baggage car, she thanked him with a polite smile and reminded herself that she was not out to champion incivility and poor manners.

Pennsylvania looked much like northern Indiana and Ohio: rolling hills with stretches of naked hardwoods, their black arms stretched across blankets of untrampled snow. As the train approached Pittsburgh, pristine farmland smeared into soot-stained row houses. A sky that had been a clear, pale winter blue began to gray, and the acrid smell of coal smoke leaked into the car. The rails began to trace one of three rivers she knew joined here in what Robert had once called the Iron City. "It rivals Chicago in inventiveness," he had told her, "and has the advantage of being a center for not just iron, but tin, brass, and glass." Robert's fascination with industry had contributed as much to the cooling of their relationship as had hers with suffrage. Two obsessive people seemed destined to clash, particularly when the obsessions were so alien to each other.

Across the brown sweep of water—she wasn't sure which river— brick chimneys belched black smoke that flattened and spread as if piling beneath a sheet of glass. From a trestle bridge, Elizabeth saw two great paddlewheelers plying their way upstream, their twin stacks contributing another trail of soot to the layer that blanketed the city. In the central station, as large and lively as Chicago's, four other engines idled on parallel tracks as passengers scurried toward waiting cars to escape the cold. This was an America Elizabeth had never seen, a nation with a throbbing industrial heart that was pumping home-produced goods along its vast river and rail arteries to every part of the country.

In Baltimore, where she transferred to the afternoon train to Washington, the pulse seemed to quicken. At the Jersey Street station in the nation's capital, the beat had reached a tempo that forced her to seek shelter in an empty corner to escape the frantic crowd and catch her breath. *I am not yet the woman warrior of my imagination*, she thought, waiting for the stream of passengers to thin before hailing a porter and venturing out onto the broad boulevard that fronted the depot. The view from the station entrance again stopped her in her tracks. At the end of New Jersey Avenue on a low rise, workmen scrambled over wooden scaffolding, appearing to scrub the white stone siding of the largest building Elizabeth had ever seen. Above the marble wing that stretched in her direction, a majestic dome rose in the building's center, a towering bronze statue of a woman clad in flowing robes crowning its pinnacle. Washington had been spared the industrial fog that blanketed Pittsburgh and Baltimore, and the statue stood in silhouette against a cloudless late-afternoon sky. She lowered her case to the depot's broad step and gazed in unabashed wonder at the building and its startling bronze woman.

"Can I take you somewhere, Miss?" a voice behind her asked. Startled, she turned to face a hunched little man in a gray plaid flat cap who stood beside a closed, horse-drawn carriage unlike any Elizabeth had seen. The driver sat *behind* a small, enclosed, two-wheel passenger compartment on a high seat, looking across its top at his single horse. "Ten cents will get you anywhere in the city. Six, if it's not far."

Elizabeth returned her attention to the matter at hand. "I need to go to A Street South. A Lutman's Boarding House." She handed the man a slip with the address Senator Trumbull had given her. She would be sharing a room with a woman of about her age named Alice Patton, an aide to Illinois' other senator, Richard Yates.

"I know the place," the driver said. "Other side of the Capitol. I can have you there in ten minutes. That'll be only a six-cent ride."

She nodded and fished two three-cent pieces from her handbag. The little man hoisted her case into the carriage and helped her up beside it. "Pay me when we get there," he said, scrambling out of view on the seat behind her. "We want to be certain I get you to the right place."

The ride took her around the back of the sprawling capitol building and into its late-afternoon shadow where the temperature seemed to drop a chilling ten degrees. Without the sun on its marble sides, the stonework grayed, and the building struck her as somehow ominous. She leaned forward around the carriage side, craning to see the entirety of the massive structure as they circled. A wing mirroring the one facing the rail depot jutted out on the opposite side, giving the building a length she was certain would stretch from one end of Afton to the other.

The driver turned along the side of the new wing and back into the sunlight, then swung left along a tree-lined boulevard that led away from the Capitol. Midway down an avenue a corner signpost identified as A Street South, he reined the horse to a stop in front of a three-story brownstone with a tidy front garden behind a black wrought-iron fence.

"This is Lutman's," he said, climbing stiffly from the seat. He dragged the case down to a paved walk as she retrieved the three-penny pieces from her handbag.

"I can take it from here," she said and stood for a moment beside the fence as he turned the horse and drove back toward the depot. The sun had dipped below the Capitol dome, casting the street in cool brown shadow. Elizabeth shivered involuntarily. From her left, a young woman hurried toward her along the flagstones, slowing as she approached the boarding house.

"Elizabeth?" she called.

Elizabeth smiled. "You must be Alice."

"Yes. And I'm *so* glad to have you here. Senator Yates asked that I come meet you and bring you back to the senate chambers after supper. It's going to be a very hectic night at the Capitol." Alice pushed open the gate and stepped over to pick up Elizabeth's case. "If you're accustomed to regular work days, they just came to an end. At least for now." She waved Elizabeth into the front garden. "Let's get you settled in, have something to eat, and get back over there. The House promised the Articles of Impeachment by March fourth. That's tomorrow. But the gossip is that they may send them over this evening."

The Articles did not reach the Senate that evening. After meeting the Lutmans and eating a quick meal of fried potatoes, onions, and corned beef with six other boarders whom Elizabeth barely had time to greet, Alice escorted her back along A Street and into the newly completed House wing of the Capitol. They hurried through a narrow passage into the vast domed rotunda where the hard leather heels of their high-button shoes clicked like shod hooves on a cobbled street and echoed through the otherwise empty chamber. Elizabeth hesitated, wanting to soak in the vastness of the place.

"There will be plenty of time," Alice said, urging her forward. "And the senators wanted us back as quickly as possible."

She led her through another identical passage into the Senate chambers where most of the members still huddled in small clusters, some accompanied by aides. The new home of the United States Senate was a plush, rectangular room with rounded corners and a visitors' balcony that surrounded the entire chamber. Polished mahogany desks formed three half-circle rows, facing a marble-faced dais. Again, Elizabeth paused, letting her eyes sweep around the ornately paneled room with intricately carved double doors exiting on every side. It looked as it should, she thought. Stately, orderly, and appropriately decorous.

"There's Senator Trumbull," Alice whispered, indicating a group of three men surrounding a desk in the second row. "He's with Senator Grimes from Iowa and Henderson from Missouri." Elizabeth eased through the desks until standing quietly at the edge of his vision.

"Ah, there you are!" he exclaimed, taking her arm and drawing her forward to meet his colleagues. "This is the young lady I was telling you about. A student of Myra Bradwell's. She is as familiar with constitutional law as any person I've met and has studied rulings of the Supreme Court since it first held session." The men bowed politely, Senator Henderson running an appraising eye down the blue dress that, down to her hips, closely followed the line of Elizabeth's form.

"Such a pleasure to see a little beauty come into this otherwise gloomy place," he said, smiling in such a way that Elizabeth read his inspection as appreciative rather than suggestive. He was a tall man with a long, patrician face, high forehead, and full dark beard.

"You may recall the expulsion of Missouri's Trusten Polk from the Senate for his role in the Confederate rebellion," Trumbull said. "Senator Henderson is his replacement, and a true credit to both his state and the Union."

Elizabeth nodded to both men. "I'm most honored—and very pleased to be assisting Senator Trumbull,"

"You traveled well? And are settled in with Miss Patton?" Trumbull asked.

"Yes, on both accounts. And she said there is still work to be done tonight."

Senator Trumbull lifted a sheaf of papers from the desk in front of him. "We haven't yet received the Articles of Impeachment, but our friends in the House tell us this is what we might expect. I would be most grateful if you would read them over tonight and share your thoughts. They aren't to leave the chamber, but there are desks in the back. It appears the articles won't make it to us tonight, so I think I will retire. If you could have your summary ready for me by morning, I will be back in chambers by nine."

"May I make notes on this copy?" she asked.

"Please do. But a separate summary would be most helpful."

She worked for another hour at a desk in the rear of the chamber, realizing that to do the review justice she needed access to a law library. The senate library, she learned, was closed until eight the following morning. She returned the papers to the Senator's desk and sought out Alice who had filled the hour with reading of her own. Together they walked the half-mile back to Lutman's.

"Thank you for waiting," Elizabeth said as they clicked again through the empty rotunda.

Alice smiled at her grimly. "This city is quite safe," she said. "But there is reason to be careful in the building and try not to be alone."

Elizabeth's voice reflected her dismay. "In the Capitol?"

"The senators and representatives can be trusted. But be wary of their aides."

"I would think that anyone asked to work here would be a man of honor."

Alice sniffed. "Look at me. I'm not a pretty girl. My hair is the color of a mouse's backside and, as my mother likes to remind me, I have the shape of a sack of turnips. But several of the men—the aides, I mean— have squeezed my bottom when certain no one is looking and grabbed at what bosom I have. A woman like you, prettier than any on those cards they secretly carry about in their pockets and snigger and joke about with each other, they'll try something with you. They feel like being here somehow makes them important. No one seems willing to tell them otherwise."

Elizabeth glanced over at the woman as they made their way down the south steps and turned toward A Avenue. "Are they all like that? Surely some must be decent fellows."

Alice gave an embarrassed shrug. "You're right, of course. Most are real gentlemen. But the ones who aren't color the lot and are like bees to honey. Just don't find yourself alone with Senator Morgan's man from New York. Jackson Dandridge is his name. He thinks himself quite the dandy and loves having someone new to press into a corner."

"Point him out to me tomorrow," Elizabeth said.

Alice sniffed coldly. "I doubt it will be necessary."

Alice's words proved prophetic much sooner than Elizabeth had anticipated. She breakfasted early, arrived at the capitol at 7:45, and was admitted to the senate library the moment it opened its door.

"I'll be going for coffee," the attendant said, pushing past her back through the door. "If you need help, I'll be back in about fifteen minutes."

She found the Supreme Court records in a back corner, moved a sliding ladder into place to reach the upper shelves, and was reviewing dates on the leather spines when she heard footsteps at the far end of the stacks. She glanced down the aisle to her right to find a nattily dressed young man smiling at her from the end of the row. She knew instinctively that it was Jackson Dandridge. He had a slim, athletic frame and smooth, finely formed features. His arresting blue eyes and blond hair that waved across his forehead would normally have drawn her attention, but she felt an involuntary shiver ripple along her spine. The train fondling still pulsed in her right breast.

"Well, good morning," he said pleasantly. "My friends told me you were planning to be here early—but not that you were as beautiful as you truly are. A 'pretty girl from Illinois' doesn't do you justice. May I be of assistance?"

Elizabeth backed carefully down the ladder, carrying one of the large volumes. *Oh, please*, she thought. *Don't make me deal with this right now.*

"A very busy girl from Iowa," she said, trying to keep her voice friendly. "And I've found what I need, thank you. I don't wish to be rude, but I have a report to ready by nine, so we will have to become acquainted some other time." She had to pass him to exit the aisle and stepped confidently forward, the book held tightly across her chest.

The man's smile broadened. "A farm girl! How interesting!" he said and moved down the aisle toward her. "I'm Jackson Dandridge, aide to Senator Morgan from New York. I know the city well, and the capitol even better. I feel some responsibility to introduce you to both."

"I appreciate your interest," she said, easing sideways to pass him, "but we will need to leave the introductions and tour to another time. I really am quite busy . . . ."

He stepped across her path, his blue eyes cooling to ice. "We try to be a little more civil with each other here in the East. Surely you can take a moment to introduce yourself."

Her sense was that the shelves behind her ran all the way to the wall, bracketing a window at the far end. But perhaps there was a passage into the next aisle. "As I said," she repeated. "I don't wish to be uncivil but have a great deal to do this morning. Perhaps later . . . ." She turned, looking toward the window for a break in the shelving. Before she could move, he wrapped her from behind, his left arm about her waist and his right hand slipping beneath the volume, cupping her left breast. His chin was on her shoulder, his lips against her ear.

"You need to learn to be a little more obliging to your seniors," he whispered. "Now, we're going to take a few minutes to get acquainted. It's time for you to learn your place, farm girl."

She thought of screaming but had not heard the librarian return, and no one else enter the room. Her jaw tightened, and she released a breath to keep her breast from swelling. Dropping the book, she glanced down at her attacker's feet, lifted her right shoe a foot above the floor, and drove her heel into the top of Dandridge's instep, twisting away as she stomped downward. He shrieked and grabbed at the swirl of hair she had carefully knotted across the back of her head. She ducked away. There was no passage at the end of the stacks. She turned as his right fist swept toward her cheek, dodging instinctively and throwing up her left arm to turn away the blow. With her right hand, she hoisted her skirts and stepped into him, thrusting her knee as forcefully as she could up into his groin.

His shriek became a guttural groan and he bent into her, clutching at his privates. She picked up the dropped book and slid past him as he folded onto his knees. Elizabeth paused and bent back toward his slumping head.

"Yes, I am a farm girl," she whispered. "Do you know what a steer is? If you ever bother me or Alice again, you will find yourself roped and tied in one of these little corridors and will find your tallywags neatly clipped and hanging around your pretty New York neck."

As she approached the desk, the librarian was pushing back into the chamber, a mug of coffee clutched in both hands.

"Were you able to find everything?" she asked brightly.

"Everything," Elizabeth said, moving to a table against the wall, but within view of the desk.

It was more than ten minutes before Jackson Dandridge emerged from the stacks. He walked gingerly, bent forward at the waist and hobbling on a tender foot. His pale eyes stared straight ahead, his face flushed crimson. The librarian looked up and began to speak, then caught herself and stared in silence. As he pushed painfully through the high double doors, she looked across at Elizabeth who bent studiously over the law volume.

"Well," she murmured with a contented smile. "I see Mr. Dandridge has met our new girl."

25

JOHNNY

Spring came early to the high valleys on the eastern slope of the Idaho Territory, bringing a March thaw to heavy snow that had fallen in the headwaters of the Snake, Salt, and Grays Rivers. As the last of the ice left the Salt River and snow melted from the valley floor, Johnny watched the river widen until it poured across the lower meadows to the north of the house. As spring grass appeared, the cattle and horses moved from the corrals into pastures near the ranch buildings. He and the Li's continued to fork hay from the loft into feeding troughs, but the animals now rarely came to the barn until nightfall, and then only as they were herded in to protect them from hunting wolves and mountain lions.

It had become customary for the families to meet on Sundays for a common evening meal in the ranch house, rotating meal preparation among the women. They filled plates at the family table, then scattered throughout the house, finding seating in the great room, on stairs, and when weather permitted, on the long, covered porch. As they gathered on the fifteenth of March, Johnny called the men into the great room while the women helped Nodda prepare a meal of cornbread and baked winter squash. The evening had remained warm enough that the children still played outside in the early spring dusk.

"Tomorrow we need to load everything we can into wagons and move to higher ground," he said. "The river is rising every day, and there's still heavy snow on the upper slopes. We have tents for three of the families and can build a shelter for the fourth. The meadow up beside Jade Lake has melted off, and we can make camp there. We'll have to widen the trail for the wagons but need to get what we can out of the main floor of the house and the bunkhouse. We'll bring the stock down during the day as long as we can get them to pasture."

"You are worried about the buildings?" Li Bo asked.

Johnny nodded grimly. "We were caught once by sudden flooding when Nodda and I were first married. It came so quickly, we barely escaped. And some of our neighbors and their animals didn't. I don't want to risk that again."

"The land to the north is lower," Li Bo observed. "The water is spreading in that direction and on the other side of the river."

"But the spring melt's just starting and hasn't begun to back up where the three rivers come together," Johnny argued. "There will be more each day for at least another week. Maybe longer. What we see covering the pastures is just from the mountains around us. When the other rivers back up, it will get deeper. We're not much higher than the north meadow."

"Have you seen this happen here before?" Li Fan asked through his brother, his tone skeptical.

"No. But we haven't had this much winter snow with an early spring thaw." Johnny looked darkly from one Li to another. "If you choose to stay in the bunkhouse, I can't stop you. But things could change very quickly. I will be moving my family up to the lake tomorrow. I suggest you either pack up and come with us or be prepared to leave at a moment's notice and risk losing whatever you have."

The three men spoke briefly in Chinese with Li Bo doing most of the talking. Then he nodded firmly. "We will go. You know this valley better than we do and have lived through a flood. Tomorrow we will load the wagons. What of the squash and potatoes that are stored in your cellar?"

"We take them with us. As the water rises, the cellar will fill first."

"And the hay in the barn?"

"Most is in the loft," Johnny said. "If the water gets as high as the barn, it shouldn't stay long. The meadow up by the lake is clear, so we'll have grass."

"We will need a sentry at night for the animals," Li Ji said. "I have heard lions screaming in the night and wolves howling not far into the mountains."

Johnny chuckled. "We can rope off some corrals among the trees on the south side of the meadow, but we won't need sentries with the mules. They can smell trouble a mile away and will make such a fuss we can be up and watching before danger gets close. We'll sleep with rifles ready."

Nodda stepped into the living room. "We can eat now," she said. "Will you call the children?"

Johnny stepped out onto the porch as the men followed Nodda into the kitchen. At the north end of the valley, the pasture glistened in the twilight like a silver mirror. The water now stretched across the wagon trail.

By morning, the river was overflowing its west bank and water had moved to within a quarter mile of the ranch house. While Nodda and the Chinese women loaded wagons with what could easily be moved from the lower floor of the house and from the bunkhouse, Johnny and the men used bucksaws and axes to widen the trail to Jade Lake. Where a narrow walking bridge spanned the creek that tumbled from the lake down to the Salt River, they ramped the banks with picks and shovels to allow teams to pull their wagons through the stream.

By noon, the women had the first load started up the trail. Cora, Lily, and Joseph rode behind the stock, yelping and slapping gloved hands against their leather chaps. The horses were restless and didn't need prompting, pressed close behind the lead mare and anxious to get to higher ground. The cattle followed reluctantly, forced along the new wagon track by the young riders. As Nodda whipped the last team down the gentle slope into a swale that separated the ranch house from the foothills, the floodwaters began to creep between the buildings and the newly cut wagon track. At the lowest point, the mules splashed through water that reached their knees and lapped against the wagon bottom.

On a knoll above the small alpine lake, Nodda and the Li wives pitched tents while the men cut poles and constructed a sturdy shelter and makeshift corral. They draped the sides of the shelter with canvas tarps and topped it with pine boughs. As evening fell and the men gathered at the Whitlock tent for a meal of dark bread and boiled venison, Nodda searched among them for the older children.

"Where are Cora and Lily?" she asked nervously.

Johnny turned toward the shelter where the girls had been gathering lacy, low-hanging pine boughs for bedding. Joseph knelt in the open front of the lean-to, piling branches along one side.

"Joseph, where are the girls?" Johnny called. The boy stood and pointed past the tents toward the trail. "They rode back down to the barn," he called. "Lily left her doll in the loft."

In a single motion, Johnny and Li Bo turned and dashed toward their horses, sweeping blankets and saddles from the fence rail as they vaulted into the new corral. Within moments they had saddled up and pulled aside a top rail, jumping their horses over the lower bar.

"Put that rail back in place," Johnny shouted toward Joseph as they sprinted their mounts toward the end of the lake and the trail to the valley.

Johnny was first out of the trees at the bottom of the slope and immediately reined in his horse. A dark, slow-moving channel, a hundred yards wide, now separated him from the house and barn. In the failing light, he could see the girls standing together beside their horses at the far edge of the water, talking intently.

"Stay where you are," he shouted across the low murmur of the moving flood. "I'm coming to you."

Li Bo reined up beside him. "How deep do you think this is?" he asked tensely, leaning over his saddle to gaze at the current.

Johnny looked at the few pines that had been in the swale and now seemed to float on a sea of rippled glass. "High enough to float a wagon. I don't know that the girls can stay on their horses if they try to cross."

Li Bo grunted. "Can you?"

"If I wash off, I'll swim with the horse. We can't leave the girls there alone."

"If the water is deep, the girls cannot follow you back."

"I may have to stay with them through the night until we can see what happens to the water."

"Will it reach the barn?" Li asked, looking towards the lowest of the three structures.

Johnny shook his head. "I don't know. There has to be some level at which it all begins to pour down the Snake. But if it rises another foot, it will be in the barn. We'll stay in the house—on the second floor."

"There is nothing there to eat."

Johnny eased his horse forward into the flood, headed slightly upstream into the slow current. "There are chickens. And we may just have to be hungry for a day."

The slope dropped steeply and before the stallion was ten lengths from shore, he had started to swim. Midway across the flooded channel, Johnny felt the horse begin to struggle, his nostrils flared and breath becoming labored, his neck craning to remain above water. Johnny slid from the saddle into the icy water, gripping the horn as he kicked beside the horse. His legs numbed within seconds, and chilled fingers reached up into his diaphragm and squeezed at his chest. Had the girls fallen into this water, they would never have been able to grip their horses long enough to cross the submerged ground.

Fifty feet from the bank, the stallion's front hooves found footing and he surged forward, dragging his failing rider with him. As Johnny collapsed onto dry ground, Cora knelt beside him.

"I'm sorry, Father," she said weakly. "We didn't think the water was so deep. But it came up across our legs as we rode over. And I could tell it was deeper after we found Lily's doll."

"You did right to stay," Johnny said, pushing onto his knees and shaking what water he could from his clothing. He struggled to his feet, teetering unsteadily on the numb stumps. With a hand on Cora's shoulder, he stomped in place for a few seconds, forcing blood back into his lifeless limbs. Lily cowered at a distance, clutching the missing doll. He smiled at her and beckoned her to come to him.

"It's alright, Lily. No one is angry with you. We're just happy that both of you are safe. But I need your help to get to the house. We need to light a fire and get warmed up."

She came to the side opposite Cora and let him use her shoulder as he stepped tentatively across the remains of the winter garden to the back door.

"Get wood from the shed," he said to Cora when they reached the fireplace in the great room. He stripped to his underwear, climbed to an upstairs bedroom for a small knit blanket they had left over a chair back, and used it to dry and massage his legs. Lily stared in embarrassment as he came back down the stairs with the blanket about his waist, unsure whether to turn away or pretend that such a sight was natural.

"Lily, do you think you can catch one of the chickens?" he asked, kneeling before the hearth and piling tinder and kindling into the firebox. When the girl didn't answer, he turned to find her nodding mutely.

"See if you can catch one of the older hens," he said. "Not a rooster. It's getting dark out now. They should be roosting in the barn. Just hold it if you get one, and I'll come out and get it ready for our dinner. We'll need to stay here tonight—upstairs in the house." The girl dropped her cloth doll onto the hearth and hurried onto the porch. He found flint and steel on the mantle and sparked the tinder, blowing gently into the knotted bundle of dry meadow grass as the flame grew and spread. Cora returned with an armload of dry wood.

"I still have clothes upstairs," he said. "Build up the fire, and we'll fry up a chicken tonight. I don't want to try to cross back until the horses don't have to swim. It may be a few days."

When he returned to the great room in dry clothes, Lily stood in the center of the room with a fat hen clutched tightly in her thin brown arms. Johnny grasped the squawking fowl by the neck and, with Lily ducking away and covering her face with an arm, gave the hen a quick twist, twirling the bird like the end of a lariat. Rather than taking time to pluck the bird, he skinned and gutted it. By the time he had cut it into sections, Cora had a skillet warming on an iron grate over a bed of coals.

"Why do the floods come?" she asked as they crouched beside the sizzling bird, slicing two onions into the pan that the girls had found in the bottom of a kitchen bin. "Mother says *Si-chom-pa Ka-gon* brings the water to remind the *Numa* that she brought the people from the sea in her sack."

Johnny chuckled. "The old woman of the sea? Your mother still likes to tell you her stories."

"And you think they are like the fairytales you tell me?" Cora's eyes told him she also doubted her mother's legends.

"I do believe in the *puha*, the power in all of nature," Johnny said. "Perhaps it is part of *puha* to wash the earth when it needs to be cleaned."

"I hope the *puha* doesn't think our house needs a cleaning," Cora murmured.

"I think the water will not get much higher," Johnny said, pulling the girls close beside him as they watched the coals fade to gray and breathed in the sweet savor of roasting meat.

They slept on the second floor. When morning came, the water had not reached the house. But before it began to recede, it wrapped its cold arms around the barn, leaving it floating in a sea of icy water. The chickens remained in the loft, scratching about in the hay for seeds and insects. Rabbits had escaped the flood by retreating to high spots in the valley. Four long-legged jackrabbits darted from one hiding place to another as the girls tracked them down and chased them into the open.

Johnny sat on the porch with an old Springfield rifle that had been hidden away in an upstairs closet, waiting for one of the jacks to pause long enough in the open to become dinner.

It took four days for the water to recede enough for Johnny to feel that he could safely coax the horses back into the swale. The layer of sticks, needles, and pinecones that marked the high-water mark on the flooded trees was now suspended two feet above the waterline. By then, they were out of rabbits.

Nodda and all of the Li's crowded the bank as Johnny followed the girls into the channel, sometimes shouting encouragement, sometimes holding their breath as the horses moved into deeper water. The three rode with feet out of their stirrups, tucked up tightly against the sides of their saddles. On their smaller mounts, the girls still had water lapping against their knees. As they clambered up the far bank, their mothers lifted them from the shivering ponies and wrapped them in quilts, any scolding pushed aside for another time.

"The water didn't ever reach the house," Li Bo observed, looking past Johnny to where the barn now stood again on muddy ground. "Perhaps in two or three days, we can go back."

"If the ground will hold the wagons," Johnny said. "And something good did come from all this." He pointed out over the stretch of gray water at other mounds of green and brown earth that floated on the flooded plain. "See the other islands in this lake? We need to remember where they are. That's where you should build your homes."

"When the water is gone, we will start," Li Bo said.

"We may still have another snow."

Li Bo lifted his arms into the sun-drenched air. "I think the snow is gone for this season," he said. "And the water has answered our question. We know now what a flood will not cover."

"At least not this flood," Johnny said and turned his horse back up the trail to Jade Lake, wondering why the *puha* couldn't have waited another month to bring spring warmth to the valley.

26

SUZANNA

Suzanna and David spent late winter coaching Ben Lanear on mill operation and his mathematically-inclined wife on keeping the books. Suzanna agreed to an additional stipend of seven dollars a week for Sarah. After the woman's first week with the accounts, Suzanna wondered why she hadn't hired her years earlier. Her records were precise, simple to follow, and presented in such a way that Suzanna could see at a glance where costs might be saved and which accounts were most profitable.

"You're a natural at this," she told the woman, leaning over her new bookkeeper as they reviewed the mill's totals for the week. "And you seem to have a good understanding of what the numbers tell you."

Sarah colored to a rosy pink. "I've always been good at figures and at knowing what they mean. With the children in school, I've thought that if someone in Afton started a bank, I might find work there."

"I'll be happy to have your help here, even when we return," Suzanna said. "This has never been my favorite part of the job, but I'm better at it than David."

Will Burgon had returned to work as a wagon driver, assisted by a padded boxed seat that allowed him, with the assistance of his son, to wedge himself between two sideboards, strap himself in with a thick belt, and maintain his balance. Suzanna hitched a ride with him into town to get mail and see if the cloth she had ordered had arrived at Fife's. Bridget Whiting had promised to sew two new dresses but hadn't been satisfied with any of Fife's stock of uninspiring checks and pastel cottons.

"We need something that doesn't look like you're a farm wife from Afton, Iowa," she had said as she thumbed through a sample book from a St. Louis supplier of cloth and haberdasheries. "Or that your dress was made from a bedsheet. Dresses in the cities are moving toward a narrower silhouette, with emphasis on the bust, waist, and hips. I'll find a more exciting cotton fabric and something in a silk taffeta." She had glanced up at Suzanna and smiled slyly. "You won't need a corset, with all that work you do. But I'm afraid we will need to fit you for a bustle."

Suzanna had groaned dramatically and placed her hands on the hips of her plain gingham dress. "What women won't endure to think they look fashionable," she complained. Bridget had laughed unsympathetically. "The other women in town are going to take great satisfaction in seeing you forced out of those work trousers and into something more feminine," she said.

As Suzanna now approached Fife's Mercantile on the wagon seat beside Will, a familiar figure sat hunched forward on the porch step, clutching a bottle protectively against his chest. Sam Gorton squinted up at them through a whiskey-hazed stupor as the wagon approached.

"Well, if it isn' the gran' mis'russ of the Whitlock mill," he stammered, a stream of spittle trailing down his chin and onto the mottled front of his shirt. "To what do we owe this great honor?" He staggered loosely to his feet and swept into an unsteady bow.

"Sam, is Harriet inside?" Suzanna asked evenly.

"Oh, yes. Never lets me from her sight, now that I'm not a workin' man."

Will Burgon touched Suzanna's arm. "I'm sorry I can't help you down, Mizz. Would you like me to call someone?"

Suzanna gave his arm an understanding squeeze. "I'll be fine, Will." She turned again to Sam Gorton. "I'm sorry you haven't found something, Sam. You're a hard worker, when you put your mind to it."

"I was turned down at the brickyard 'cause of you," Sam sputtered. "Jenkins said you said I was trouble."

Suzanna lowered herself from the seat and stood a few feet from the drunken man. Two of Afton's more gossipy matrons stood lecturing each other like two country preachers a dozen steps away and quieted as if suddenly struck mute, turning toward what looked like a more tantalizing bit of gossip.

"On the contrary, Sam," Suzanna said, keeping her voice as low as her distance from the man allowed. "I told Mr. Jenkins that you were a very hard worker but seemed constantly dissatisfied with your situation—and that you freely shared your displeasures with the other workers. Was that an unfair thing to say?"

"It's the same as saying I was trouble," Sam grumbled, taking an unsteady step toward her. Harriet Gorton pushed through the door of Fife's onto the wooden porch, a woven basket looped over her arm. She looked frantically from her husband to Suzanna, then back at the inebriated man.

"Sam, I asked you to go home," she said, her voice on the edge of breaking. "Please—let's not have a fuss here."

"We're alright," Suzanna said. "And I'll say this while you're present, Harriet. We need another man at the mill. Sam's a good worker. If he can keep his drink under control and keep his displeasures with work conditions to himself, we would be happy to have him back. But no more attempts at new work rules or ways to slow things down."

Harriet Gorton looked pleadingly at her husband. "Did you hear that, Sam? The mill will take you back if you can just keep your thoughts to yourself and leave the drink at home."

Sam glared down at the bottle in his hands and, seeing it empty, flung it loosely into the street. "I'm never workin' again for some *bitch*," he spit in Suzanna's direction. "She gave me the sack. I'm not crawlin' back like a whipped dog 'cause she's tryin' to look like Saint Paddy, or somethin'."

"Sam. Please . . ." Harriet implored. "You know we need the work . . ."

"*Never*," Sam roared. "Not with her orderin' me about every day."

"We're leaving soon for what may be longer than a month," Suzanna said. "Ben will be running the mill. You can get back into the job while we're away and may feel differently when I get back. But the same conditions apply."

"You're havin' that one-arm run the place?" Sam sputtered, glaring unsteadily up at Will who had kept the wagon beside Suzanna. "It's turnin' into a bleedin' workhouse for cripples."

"Sam, *please*," Harriet pleaded. The man's wrath only increased its boil. He hunched forward, glaring at Suzanna, and waved an arm loosely in her direction. "You may be wantin' ta think twice before comin' back," he snarled. "There's no place for you in this town. You just remember that." He shifted the glare to his wife who stood, head drooping over her basket, then turned and staggered in the direction of the Gorton home.

27

ELIZABETH

Elizabeth and Alice leaned intently forward in the front row of the Senate gallery, watching tension grow as Salmon Chase, Chief Justice of the Supreme Court, entered the chamber. It was May 16th, 1868. The Senate had convened in special session for an initial vote on the Articles of Impeachment filed by the House of Representatives against President Andrew Johnson. Chase was a stern, handsome man with a prominent nose, large, well-formed mouth, and white hair that receded well above an unfurrowed brow. He had served as governor of Ohio, senator from the same state, and Secretary of the Treasury before Lincoln appointed him to the Court. He was eminently qualified, Elizabeth thought, to preside over the most important trial of the century.

Chase climbed to the dais and began to arrange papers on the senate podium, making no eye contact with the men assembled on the floor. Senators who had been whispering together in twos and threes returned to their desks and began sorting through their own stacks of documents.

Jackson Dandridge entered the balcony from a side door to the women's left, scanned the spectators until his eyes met Elizabeth's. He turned quickly away, seeking a seat as far from the pair as the gallery allowed. Alice leaned into Elizabeth's ear.

"Your friend is here. He hasn't so much as said 'good day' to either of us since you told me he met you in the library. You promised to tell me what happened."

"And I shall—before I return to Chicago."

"If the vote is settled today, you may be leaving soon. And I must know. Everyone asks why he leaves you alone when, by all accounts, you're the handsomest woman in this building. Even his friends ask."

Elizabeth glanced around at the spectators close beside them who were engrossed in the activity on the floor. She whispered back into

Alice's ear. "I haven't said anything because I don't want this to become food for more gossip in this gossipy place. So, please—wait until I am back in Chicago before you share this, if you must at all." She paused, thought fleetingly of continuing to keep the episode to herself, then said, "He grabbed my bosom from behind. I slammed my heel down onto his foot, then turned and thrust my knee into his privates. I told him that if he ever touched me or you again, I would make a steer of him."

Alice gasped audibly. *"You thrust your knee into his privates?* What did that do?"

Elizabeth leaned back, studying her roommate quizzically. Could this twenty-two-year-old woman, an aide in the United States Senate, know so little about the opposite sex? Where had Elizabeth learned such things? Helping her father or brothers clean and skin a buck deer and watching her mother fry up the pink oval meat from its sack? At the mill pond where she swam naked with the boys until Johnny began to develop fine hair on his body? When they released from the rope swing, high over the water, and the boys grabbed themselves between the legs to keep the water from slapping painfully when they hit the pond surface? Or from farmers at Fife's, kicked back around the glowing Franklin stove on frozen winter mornings, chewing the stems of corncob pipes, and planning a communal nut fry when the spring calves were castrated? Knowing such things had all been part of growing up in Afton.

"Do you have brothers?" she asked aloud.

Alice glanced about with an embarrassed frown. "No," she whispered. "What don't I know?"

Elizabeth leaned into her again. "I don't think this is the place to broaden your education."

Alice grasped her arm. "Oh, I *must* know," she said insistently.

"I should take you out into the hallway—but we will lose our places."

"Tell me here. *Please?* No one is paying us any mind. I need to know."

Elizabeth turned toward her so that their shoulders touched and she could cup her hands between them. "You know that men have that sack," she began as quietly as was still audible. Alice blushed and swallowed hard but nodded as if this was nothing new.

"Do you know what's in there?" Elizabeth asked.

"Oh, my, no," Alice whispered.

"Well, there are two . . . *balls*, the farmers at home called them. I believe they are more appropriately called testes or testicles. They are very sensitive and, if hit at all hard, cause such pain that it will double a man over and leave him virtually helpless for a few seconds."

Alice leaned back and stared across the chamber at Jackson Dandridge who judiciously avoided looking in their direction. She leaned back toward Elizabeth. "And you thrust your knee into his sack?"

Elizabeth nodded, wishing she had insisted on delaying the explanation until the two were alone.

"What did you mean? Make him a steer?" Alice whispered.

Good gracious, she thought. Don't they have cattle in Jacksonville, Illinois? She resisted rolling her eyes, realizing that as a country girl, there were a great many things about city life about which she was completely unschooled. "Do you know what a steer is?" she asked.

Alice shook her head dumbly.

"How about a bull?"

"As in, a male cow?"

Elizabeth nodded. "Well, bulls can be quite aggressive and temperamental, if left a bull. So, farmers often cut off these . . . balls . . . when the calf is young. It makes them much more docile. They then call the animal a steer."

Alice's eyes widened as though the mysteries of the world had just been opened to her. "He must have believed you," she murmured.

"I was telling him the truth," Elizabeth said.

"*Oh, my*," Alice said.

On the floor, Chief Justice Chase gaveled the assembly to order, giving Elizabeth a much-needed reprieve from delivering a basic lesson in anatomy in, of all places, the hallowed chambers of the United States Senate. And on this historic morning. She turned from Alice to hide an involuntary smile, wondering what lesson of the day would make the most lasting impression on her uninitiated roommate.

Justice Chase waited until the chamber had quieted, then announced, "The vote that will be taken this morning is on Article Eleven of the Articles of Impeachment filed by the House of Representatives of the United States Congress against President Andrew Johnson. The President of the Senate, the honorable gentleman from Ohio, Mr. Benjamin Wade, has asked that Article Eleven be considered first, since it involved what both the House managers presenting the case against the President and the President's own counsel deem to be the most serious charges." Chase lifted a paper from the top of the dais. "The article states, in part, that the President:

did, unlawfully and in disregard of the requirements of the Constitution that he should take care that the laws be faithfully executed, attempt to prevent the execution of an act entitled "An act regulating the tenure of certain civil office," passed March 2, 1867, by unlawfully devising and contriving and attempting to devise and contrive means by which he should prevent Edwin M. Stanton from forthwith resuming the functions of the office of Secretary for the Department of War, notwithstanding the refusal of the Senate to concur in the suspension therefore made by the said Andrew Johnson of said Edwin M. Stanton from said office of Secretary for the Department of War.

Chase returned the paper to his file. "Closing arguments having been concluded on Wednesday of the week just passed, this vote was initially scheduled for Thursday. But the illness of the Honorable Senator from Michigan, Mr. Howard, prevented him from being present. The serious nature of the question at hand led the President Pro Tempore to desire all present when the vote is taken. This Saturday session has been called for that purpose. The President Pro Tempore, the Honorable Benjamin Wade, has called for the question. The Secretary of the Senate shall proceed with the vote. Each senator shall reply 'guilty' to affirm and support the article of impeachment, or 'not guilty' if in disagreement with the charges of the article. Mr. Secretary, please proceed."

Elizabeth drew a pencil and folded list from her handbag, spreading it carefully on her lap. The secretary called "Senator Anthony," and the Rhode Island Republican loudly proclaimed "Guilty!" Elizabeth entered a G beside his name and began to run a tally in the right margin.

"Senator Bayard."

"Not Guilty," the Democrat from Delaware said forcefully. Elizabeth wrote NG beside Bayard and placed a stroke below the one on the right.

As she and Senator Trumbull had anticipated, Buckalew, a Democrat from Pennsylvania, voted 'not guilty,' while his state counterpart, Republican J. Donald Cameron voted to convict. The vote followed party lines until the secretary reached James Dixon of Connecticut, the first Republican Senator Trumbull believed might turn. Elizabeth trapped her breath, leaning forward against the gallery rail.

"*Not guilty,*" Dixon said loudly. Her boss had been right. A group of moderates were electing to oppose their colleagues. But would there be the ten needed to support the nine Democrats who would certainly vote to acquit? When Republican James Doolittle from Wisconsin voted 'not guilty,' the western block that Senator Trumbull had described looked as if it might hold. Two critical votes remained in question.

Though Benjamin Wade, who stood to become president if Johnson were convicted, had been encouraged, even by Republican colleagues, to recuse himself from the vote, the general wisdom around the Capitol was that the ambitious Ohio senator would not. His vote would be moot, though, if Kansas senator Edmund Ross voted to acquit, and Ross voted before Wade. Letters and cables from the far western state had flooded into Ross's office, demanding that he convict. A vote to acquit would most certainly cost Ross his seat in the next election. As the secretary moved toward the R's, Alice leaned up beside Elizabeth.

"How is your tally?" she whispered.

"Trumbull and Van Winkle will vote with the Democrats. Ross is going to be the deciding vote."

"Senator Yates is going to be so angry," Alice murmured. "He will do what he can to keep Senator Trumbull from being re-elected."

Elizabeth regarded her roommate coolly. "For what reason?"

"He isn't supporting his party," Alice said, as if the action needed no further explanation.

"What about conscience?" Elizabeth retorted, loudly enough that others in the gallery turned in their direction.

"The President has broken the law!"

"It's a law yet to be tested in the courts," Elizabeth countered.

"And there is every reason to believe it will be ruled unconstitutional."

"But it hasn't been at this time."

Elizabeth's face hardened. "That's what makes it a matter of conscience."

Ramsey from Minnesota voted guilty and the entire chamber fell silent.

"Senator Ross," the secretary called. For a heart-stopping moment, there was no response. "Senator Ross?" the secretary repeated.

"*Not guilty*," Ross said decisively. An angry murmur rippled through his Republican colleagues as the nine Democrats rose to their feet, shaking silent fists in the air.

Alice's senator, Richard Yates, was the last to vote. As he stood, he looked grimly at his colleague from Illinois. "*Guilty!*" he said and dropped heavily back into his seat.

Chase again rose behind the podium. "Will the secretary announce the vote?"

The secretary moved to the front of the dais, lifting his tally sheet to eye-level.

"The vote has been thirty-five in favor of conviction. Nineteen against."

Chase rapped his gavel decisively against the podium. "Two-thirds having failed to find guilt, the President is, therefore, acquitted of the charges presented in this article."

A muted cheer rose from the Democrat ranks, muffled by the stern eye of the Chief Justice and knowledge that ten Republican colleagues may have just forfeited their careers. Justice Chase gaveled the assembly to silence.

"Senate rules provide that any may, now that the vote has been completed, provide a brief explanation for the reasoning behind his vote, not to exceed two minutes. Does any senator wish to speak?"

Senator Trumbull was immediately on his feet.

"The Honorable Senator from Illinois," Chase acknowledged. Elizabeth drew a second sheet from her bag, written in her own neat hand, as was the paper Senator Lyman Trumbull now held up in front of the assembly. She followed as he read in a clear, resonant voice, tracing the script with her finger and aware that Alice was peering over her shoulder.

. . . and no future President will be safe who happens to differ with

a majority of the House and two-thirds of the Senate on any measure deemed by them important, particularly if of a political character. Blinded by partisan zeal, with such an example before them, they will not scruple to remove out of the way any obstacle to the accomplishment of their purposes, and what then becomes of the checks and balances of the Constitution, so carefully devised and so vital to its perpetuity? They are all gone.

"You wrote this?" Alice whispered.

"Our founding fathers wrote it," Elizabeth whispered back. "I just phrased it a little differently for the senator's speech."

28

SUZANNA

They left Afton for England on the last day of May. David had arranged for Carter Parry and his new wife Anna to stay at the house. The newlyweds had been trapped in an upper bedroom of Carter's parents' home while they built one of their own on the family farm, adjacent to the Whitlock's to the east. The young couple was delighted at the prospect of being able to step out of their bedroom into an empty house, one at which the Whitlocks had decided not to plant a spring garden. With the Lanears managing the mill, all Carter and Anna were asked to do was tend to the house, water the perennial flowers, feed the family hound Dolly and a dozen chickens, and gather their eggs before taking the short daily trek to their building site.

David and Suzanna stopped in Chicago for an overnight with Elizabeth who had returned from Washington only two days earlier. Mrs. Kruger had a vacant room and allowed them to stay for a dollar and a half, including breakfast and the evening meal with the boarders. Though David had seen St. Louis when in the war, St. Joseph was the largest town Suzanna had visited.

"I can't fathom living in one of these buildings, pressed side-by-side like this," she muttered nervously to her daughter as they walked along South Water Street beside the Chicago River. Elizabeth was giving them a walking tour of the inner city. David lagged behind, captivated by the variety of boats that plied the stale brown water. "It's like hens in laying boxes," Suzanna said. "And what if one of them caught fire? Why, they would all go up in an instant!"

Elizabeth glanced back to ensure that her father was still in sight. "I'd like to say one becomes used to it. But I get on the streets north of the river with the tall buildings on both sides, and I feel like they're going to topple over on me. Washington wasn't as bad. They haven't built up in the same way Chicago has. As one of the men I met there reminded me, I'm still pretty much a country girl."

"But you've done such wonderful things—and seen history made. We're so proud of you." Suzanna paused, then asked, "Was this man someone you found interesting?"

Elizabeth laughed cynically. "He was a masher, Mother. I didn't find him interesting at all. And *his* interest was purely in seeing how naïve I might be as a 'farm girl.'"

"Masher? What's a masher?" Suzanna asked, adding to her worry that she wasn't at all prepared for this adventure.

"It's a word I heard in the theater. It's a man who wishes to take advantage of young women."

"Ah. A knave and a scoundrel. What my father called a bounder."

"A very polished and well-educated man," Elizabeth said. "But a bounder nonetheless."

"Are you seeing anything of Robert?"

Elizabeth frowned and checked again to see if her father was staying with them. "I think he's gone his own way. And just as well. He wants a wife like his mother, a figure in society who makes a good impression at dinner parties. And I know he has a bevy of accommodating beauties chasing after him now. He will be married before the year's out."

"You sound as if you still have feelings for him."

Elizabeth walked silently for a moment, her own gaze tracing swirls on the muddy surface of the river. "It's been six years, Mother. I can't just turn off what I know was true affection. But I also can't imagine living the life of the prim, demure woman of society."

"I suspect you will find that is what most men of his breeding are looking for in a wife."

Elizabeth *humphed.* "Then I'll just have to do without a man of his breeding."

"You *do* plan to marry . . . ?"

Her daughter glanced at her with a tight smile. "If I meet the right man. But I've met some very influential women who chose not to."

"They've missed out on one of the most wonderful parts of life, then," Suzanna said. "I can't imagine life without your father—or without you and Johnny." She felt her eyes fill as scenes of another son, frail and straining desperately to breathe, forced their way across the screen of her memory. Elizabeth noticed.

"And they've avoided some of the deepest heartache," she said. Then, feeling a need to lighten the conversation, she turned to the weeks ahead.

"You must be very excited about seeing England and the home where Grandmother's family lived."

"As excited as one can be while realizing that I am also very much a country girl."

Elizabeth stopped and studied her mother who had changed for the walk into one of the new dresses Bridget Whiting had fashioned for her. "You're a beautiful woman, Mother. Well-read and well-spoken. You've learned more from life than any woman I know. And dressed as you are now, you can fit in anywhere. Don't ever feel apologetic for who you are, how you look, or how you have lived. No woman could ask for a better example."

Suzanna smiled. She was being lectured by her daughter as if she were a schoolgirl.

"I'll try to remember," she said.

29

JOHNNY

The two riders approached the knoll from the north, urging their mounts and a trailing pack mule into a brisk canter as they neared the skeleton of a cabin that crowned one of the mounds of high ground the men had spotted during the flood. Li Ji, who dragged a straight lodgepole pine from the slopes of the mountains to the west behind a pair of draft horses, stopped the team midway down the grade to watch the approaching strangers. Johnny, Li Bo, and Li Fan were barking and notching a pair of trunks that lay beside the rising log walls and took the surprise of visitors in the valley as an excuse to rest on their ax handles.

"Not trappers," Johnny said when the men were close enough to clearly see their clothing. "And not miners. They're dressed like the surveyors we saw on the Bear River—but no wagon."

"Is a train to come through this valley?" Li Bo asked nervously. "That would not be good for anyone."

"I don't think so," Johnny said. "When we were in Salt Lake, the only talk was of finishing the track across the continent. And they seemed a year away from that." He stepped forward and hailed the riders as they approached. "Good morning, gentlemen. What brings you into these parts?"

Both men swung stiffly from their saddles, looked the four builders over curiously, and approached Johnny.

"Ernst Weber," the taller of the men said. "And this is Nathanial Stone. I see you're settling here." Weber stood with the exaggerated straightness of a military man and spoke with a pronounced German accent. Nathanial Stone was a squat, round-faced man with a thick, rust-colored mustache that drooped around the corners of his mouth. He fidgeted uncomfortably, indicating he was not accustomed to spending hours in the saddle.

Johnny extended a hand and introduced himself, then the three

Chinese ranchers. "I've been here a few years. Live in the place farther down." He pointed toward the buildings a half mile south. "What brings you into the valley?"

Weber again glanced at Johnny's companions. "Who is this home for?" he asked pointedly.

Johnny indicated Li Ji. "For Mr. Li, here. And I don't wish to be rude, but why does this matter to you?"

Weber nodded toward his partner who hastily drew a paper clipped to a thin board from a saddlebag. Stone handed the sheet to Johnny. "Are you able to read, Sir?" he asked, "or could I read this for you?"

Johnny studied the brief printed message without responding. It explained that the United States Congress was expected, within a month's time, to create the Territory of Wyoming. These representatives of the US Department of the Interior were completing a census of people living in the territory to determine their interest in eventual statehood.

"What's this Department of Interior?" Johnny asked. "I can't say I've heard of such a thing."

"We manage all public lands," Weber said. "Granting of patents, Indian affairs. But in this case, our responsibility is to determine how many are living in the Wyoming Territory and poll them concerning their interest in becoming a state. Might we inquire as to the size of your family? And if you know of other families living in the valley?"

"You're saying this is public land?"

"Owned by the United States government. It will formally be part of Wyoming."

Johnny chuckled cynically. "I don't see anyone here but us. We've homesteaded this valley. And I think you've wandered a little too far west. This is part of the Idaho Territory."

Weber nodded toward the west. "It will not be when Congress passes the new act. The boundary will run right down along those mountains there. You will be in the new Wyoming Territory."

Johnny shrugged. "Doesn't make much difference to me, I'm thinking. And there are two others in my family. My wife and a daughter. As for other families in the valley, you're looking at them. Their wives and children are down at the ranch."

Stone's fidgeting extended up into his fleshy shoulders. "We aren't counting Chinese," he said, keeping his eyes only on Johnny.

Johnny leaned more heavily against his ax handle. "Not counting Chinese?"

"No. Just the people who live here."

Johnny looked at the log wall that rose shoulder-high beside him. "These men have been in the valley for two years now and, as you can see, they're building homes."

Weber straightened even more, chest out and shoulders back. "The Chinese are working as railroad workers and miners. They are not permanent and don't speak English. There are too many of them. We are not including them in this census. No Chinese and no Indians."

Li Bo stepped up beside Johnny. "And if they do speak English—and are not miners or rail workers and are building a home—do they count then?"

Nathanial Stone's cheeks glowed above his coarse mustache and he glanced nervously at the grim-faced Chinaman. Weber kept his eyes glued on Johnny. "We are not counting Chinese and Indians," he repeated in his clipped, Prussian accent. "Just proper residents."

Johnny felt the fine hairs on his arms bristle and the muscles in his jaw tighten. "And how long has your family been in this country, Mr. Weber?"

Weber's eyes narrowed, and his lips curled into a biting frown. "That is not the point, here, Mr. Whitlock. We are following our instructions. We do not include Chinese or Indians in our census."

"Then you'd better just put down one and a half people for this valley," Johnny said coldly. "My wife is Paiute, and my daughter half-Indian. And speaking as the only whole person who seems to matter in your census, I don't give a damn if we're in Wyoming or in China, or if Wyoming ever becomes a state. My advice to you, gentlemen, would be that you get the hell out of our valley."

30

DAVID

They spent only two days in New York City, long enough to visit the offices of Crouch, Whitman, and Rosswell to receive copies of the papers they needed, obtain tickets for their sea voyage, and ask Rosswell to cable the London firm handling the estate. Tickets had been obtained through London on the Cunard steamship *Russia*, sailing for Liverpool on Wednesday. The £5 fare per third-class passage was to be charged to the estate, once settled, as was £20 in English currency that Rosswell delivered to David in a sealed envelope.

"Five pounds is equivalent to about thirty dollars," Henry Rosswell informed them. "You could have traveled in the first-class cabins for three times that amount, but based on our previous travel experience together, I thought you might choose the lesser fare."

"I should think so!" Suzanna spouted. "That's two week's wages for one of our men, just for a third-class fare. How can people afford this kind of travel?"

"Working men don't take transatlantic voyages," Rosswell said dismissively.

"But there are immigrants coming every month. And I know from those who end up in Iowa that they come virtually penniless."

"That is because they sold everything they have to come," Rosswell said.

He had reserved them a room at the Metropolitan on Broadway and Prince Street, assuring them that the price of the room was also being covered by the London firm and the estate. The lavish six-hundred room hotel boasted steam-heated bedchambers, a lobby with plate-glass mirrors that a sign beneath claimed to be the largest in the world, and food delivered right to the room, if requested. The next morning, David asked that they be moved to a simple boarding house.

"I assure you," Rosswell said. "New York boarding houses are not like those we stayed in on our journey west. You have seen the rabble that fills the streets once you walk a few blocks from your hotel. That's what you would find in the boarding houses. I could have put you in the Saint Nicholas at twice the cost, so you aren't staying in New York's finest. You are only here for two days. Be happy with what you have." David acquiesced.

On their second day in the city, it was that squalor in the streets that drove them north to Central Park. A recent rain had turned a choking layer of horse manure to mush on the cobbled avenues. Urchins with shoeshine boxes chased them like rabid dogs, spotting a pair of innocents and tugging at their clothing, begging for pennies. Garbage smoldered in stinking heaps in side alleys, and people in strange clothing babbled in a hundred tongues. For David, the swirling chaos was mesmerizing, begging him to stop and sample it like some new foreign dish. But Suzanna shrank from it as if she were a child, taken for the first time to the filthy lodgings of some unsavory bachelor uncle.

Even in the refuge of the park, she clung to David as men in flat black hats covering shoulder-length ringlets passed without so much as a nod. When forced from the green sanctuary of the park by approaching evening, David hailed a horse carriage to spare her the walk back through the city. They ate in the Metropolitan's linen-draped dining room, surrounded by people who seemed not the least bit interested in anyone but themselves. In the morning, another carriage took them to the docks.

The *Russia* was already building a head of steam when they struggled their luggage up the gangway to the deck that held third-class cabins. Their tiny room was inboard, without a porthole, and smelled of lye and cigarette smoke. They slid their cases beneath the bottom berth, a two-foot-wide box with a thin mattress that lifted and latched against the wall, then hurried back to the open deck.

"I can very happily spend the rest of my life without another day in that city," Suzanna said as they walked to the stern of the ship and gazed out over the harbor. "I know this is said to be the gateway to America and our finest city. But I wish new arrivals could somehow see what lies beyond. Far fewer would allow themselves to be trapped in those godforsaken canyons they call streets."

The ship sailed with much fanfare, the dock crowded with kerchief-waving well-wishers and the families of the hundreds who lined the rail. As soon as they reached open water and the ship began its rhythmic roll and pitch, Suzanna made a hasty retreat to the bottom berth where she curled into a miserable ball. When David tried to console her, assuring her that she would get used to the constant motion and that they would fare better on deck where they could see the horizon, she mumbled that all she wanted was to be left alone. He obliged and, following his own advice, climbed back into open air.

All two hundred of the passengers seemed to have made the same decision. They crowded the open bow, filled the few common rooms, and stood shoulder-to-shoulder along the railing from bow to stern. David was surprised to see many dressed in their finery: men in afternoon jackets, vests, and top hats. Women with full bustles, elaborately decorated hats, and lace-edged parasols. He and Suzanna had chosen to dress in their everyday clothes, aware that two weeks lay ahead with little opportunity to wash. He had packed away two of his oldest home-sewn shirts and Suzanna a fading house dress, deciding they would get what wear they could from them on the voyage, then discard them. As he studied the crowd, he realized that he had allowed those in fancy dress to catch his eye, when there were more dressed as he was than like a Vanderbilt.

He found an open spot along what he was told was the starboard side beside a broad-shouldered man he guessed to be about forty: fair-haired and dressed even more plainly.

"Gives a man a bit of nerves," David said, looking over the expanse of endless sea. "Nothing but water in every direction."

"Aye. That it does," the man said. "And after a week, you'll be fearin' it will never end."

David smiled over at his fellow traveler. "I take it you've made this crossing before. And I hear a bit of the Irish in your voice. Is this a journey home?"

"Nay," the man said, turning slightly to offer his hand. "Patrick Doyle. I've been in Worcester up in Massachusetts, now goin' on seven years. Came across from County Mayo on one of the clippers.

Nine weeks at sea, and we took a right batterin'. I was almost wishin' I'd stayed and starved."

"But you've decided to go back anyway," David observed. "To see family?"

"*Get* my family. I've got a wife, Mary Catherine, and two *leanai* . . . children," he corrected quickly. "They've been livin' with me sister all this many years."

"A long time to be away from family," David said sympathetically. "What brought you to America?"

Doyle's friendly face darkened, and he glared down into the frothy wake that churned along the ship's black side. "I hate to burden ya with my own bit o' hard luck and with another man's misfortunes."

"I have nothing but time," David said. "And sharing a burden can have a way of lightening it."

As he looked up from the roiling water, Doyle's eyes relayed both gratitude and misgiving. He paused, then seemed to decide David would listen without judgment.

"I was farmin' in Ireland. Do you know the country? County Mayo's in the west." He didn't wait for a response. "Well, we were tenant farmers on the Partry Estate. Not much of a livin'. Me brother, Séamus, gave up on it during the great hunger and came to America. I stayed 'cause of me mum and da' who were gettin' on in age." He paused and glanced again at David, then asked, "You be Catholic, by chance?"

David shook his head. "Not really much of anything. There's a Methodist church in our town, but they wouldn't count us among their most faithful."

"Well, most everyone where we come from is Catholic," Doyle continued. "Have been since Saint Patrick. We had our own wee parish with Father Lavelle and were gettin' by with the help of each other. Then the estate was purchased by Lord Plunket who was also Bishop of Tuam. A bleedin' Protestant, he was. Within a year, he built a school on the estate, one that taught the children the Protestant ways. Lord Plunket wrote into the agreement with the tenants that he expected our children to attend the school. Most of us refused, and the good Christian bishop had us evicted from our farms."

David leaned more heavily onto the railing. "I'm not clear on something. He evicted you from your own farms?"

"The land belonged to the Partry Estate. We were tenant farmers."

"I don't know what that is—tenant farmers."

Doyle's expression turned quizzical. "The farmer works the land but has no title to it. The crop belongs to the owner of the estate. A share comes to the farmer for his labor. Do they not have tenant farms in America?"

"I really don't know. We have the old plantations, and I've heard of what's called sharecropping. But not in the part of the country where we live."

"Most of the land in Ireland is owned by the rich people," Doyle said. "They have the tenant farmers do their work. But if they don't like the way they're doin' it, or if they're unhappy with something else, they can evict the families from their land. That's what happened at Partry. My family went to live with me sister in Galway, and I come to America to find work. I've been workin' the mills, livin' with me brother, and savin' to bring me family. I finally saved enough to buy a wee house. I'm on my way to Galway to bring me family back."

"An inspiring tale," David said, wondering as he said it what he would find at the Allgar Estate. The thought that it was being farmed by people who did not own the land had not occurred to him. In fact, he had given the estate little thought at all. He was making an ocean crossing he had never dreamed of making, going to a land he had never planned to visit, and really had no idea what he would do when he got there. As he listened to Patrick Doyle, he realized he would be forced to make decisions about people and property he knew very little about. The thought twisted at his stomach like the pitch and roll of the ship, and he felt a sudden desire to go below and curl up on the narrow berth beside Suzanna.

That night, awakened by a swell that rocked the steamer and rolled David into the wall, he realized that he had been jarred from a dream that had recurred since before he married Suzanna. It came to him at times of uncertainty, a dream triggered by guilt or anxiety. He was again huddled in the small workmen's shack behind the owner's home at the Cochran coal mine east of Missouri's Chariton River. He had fled the family homestead after losing his father's team of prize mules to wolves while dragging a log through heavy snow to the family cooperage. The night was freezing cold, and the older miners had convinced him to warm himself with enough strong cider that he was barely aware that they had left him alone in the drafty shed. All that had come to his bleary mind was that he yearned for Suzanna and for the warmth of his home across the Chariton. That yearning, and the words of a soulful hymn. It was a verse learned at his mother's knee, a hymn he had sung on that lonesome night, swaying to the drone of his own voice until he faded into unconsciousness. He had been singing the hymn when the sea jarred him from this dream, and it continued to play in his mind as he rolled to the edge of the bunk to see if Suzanna still slept.

A poor, wayfaring Man of grief hath often crossed me on my
    way,
Who sued so humbly for relief that I could never answer nay.
I had not pow'r to ask his name, whereto he went, or whence
    he came;
Yet there was something in his eye that won my love; I knew
    not why.

David flopped back onto the bunk, rocking rhythmically as the ship swayed, the meter of each phrase of the hymn accompanying a roll of the sea.

Once, when	*my scanty*	*meal*	*was spread,*
He entered;	*not a*	*word*	*he spake,*
Just perish-	*ing for*	*want of*	*bread.*
I gave	*him all;*	*he blessed it,*	*brake.*

He could not recall having had the dream when he wasn't still midway through the song when he awoke. His feeling was that somehow the dream-song was meant to be unfinished.

The seasoned passengers aboard the *Russia* rated the crossing "comfortable." No high seas. No storms. No cold rains that kept everyone below deck. On the third day out of New York, the seas were calm enough for Suzanna to feel steady on her feet. She walked the decks for most of the day with David, holding his arm in the morning, and venturing out on her own in the afternoon. By the time the seas began to roll again the following afternoon, she had learned to sway with the rhythmic motion of the ship and spent most of her time out where she could use the horizon as a stablizing comforter. They broke the tedium with long conversations with Patrick Doyle and by finding couples with whom to visit: the Neals from Virginia who were bound for Manchester to visit Mr. Neal's cousin; the Williamsons from Pittsburgh, traveling first to Sheffield, then on to Brandenburg in Germany to study new processes for refining steel; the Jeffords from New Jersey, bound for Scotland where Mr. Jeffords had obtained a position at the University of St. Andrews in Fife.

One full day was filled with Jeffords lecturing enthusiastically on the work of St. Andrews' Rector, John Stuart Mill, whom David and Suzanna had never heard of and whose theories held no special interest for them. But the alternative was equally tedious ocean, lengthy descriptions of the revolutionary Siemans-Martin process for producing high-grade steel, or a detailed description of the Neal family tree, dating back to seventeenth century Ireland. Morning meals of porridge and noon helpings of a thick bean and salt pork soup offered little respite, and the sighting of the Irish coast was cause for great celebration.

Once in the St. George's Channel, land was visible during most of the daylight hours, giving David reason to think more seriously about what they would do, once back on solid ground.

"I hope we find Mr. Renfroe more likable than Rosswell," he confided to Suzanna as they passed Holyhead on the Welsh isle of Anglesey and turned east toward Liverpool. "This will all be so much more pleasant if we have help from someone we like and can trust."

"I feel like an onion in a flower bed," she said, glancing around the deck at passengers who had again dressed in their best clothes in anticipation of reaching port.

"Let's go below and pack up. You can put on one of your new dresses," he said. "You'll look as fine as anyone arriving in Liverpool."

"But what of the people there? What will they be like?"

David chuckled. "They're English, just as we are. These are just the ones who didn't have to escape some family scandal."

31

ESTHER MORRIS

My Dear Elizabeth:

I hope this letter reaches you and finds you well. So much has happened since we last met that I could fill a book. I will do my best to try to refrain from overwhelming you with all the dreary details of my new life and share with you at least some of its promise.

As I thought might be the case, John convinced me to join him in the Wyoming Territory. I now find myself in a mining camp called South Pass City that must be the one place on earth that God forgot to complete by the end of the sixth day. Though I arrived in July, snow still covered the north-facing slopes and, where it had melted, left nothing but bare gray rock and restless, lonely men. John learned quickly enough after a few months in the pits that the only money to be made here is from selling whiskey to those who still have not had the sense to come up into the daylight. We live on the upper floor of a cold wooden box, with a bar and tables that we call a saloon filling the floor below. John serves drinks to the rabble who crowd the place at night and to four or five laggards during the day who have abandoned the mines for the bottle. Where they find the two bits for a drink is beyond me. We refuse to run a tab, yet they always have money for drink.

I spend my life stoking two Franklins, one in the saloon and one in our rooms above, and a green enamel stove that John had his whiskey supplier cart in from Fort Bridger. I cook up a pot of antelope or venison stew each afternoon that we serve to our evening customers for the price of a drink. Some days I think it is the only thing that keeps the miners alive. The monotony of daily living is broken by regular brawls and occasional skirmishes with local Indians, mainly Shoshone and Arapahoe who still believe they have claim to this evil bit of creation. An Indian agent assured us earlier this month that the government is establishing a reservation somewhere north of us, but I can't imagine why these Indians will agree to settle there. The land north is equally barren and will have to be surrounded by army encampments to keep the natives in place.

After all of these encouraging words, the remainder of this letter may come as a surprise. You will recall that when we met in Chicago, I told you that I thought your talents were wasted in Illinois where there has been a long history of activism for women's suffrage and little result. I believe I also said that John had told me in his letters that there were rumors circulating in Wyoming that as soon as the territory gained official status, it may seek to grant the vote to women. There is an almost obsessive fear here that a constitutional amendment will be passed granting voting rights to Negros and Chinamen. Some of the good men of Wyoming are convinced that the best way to maintain control is to give the vote to the women of the territory, the vast majority of whom are white.

William Bright, who owns the saloon at the other end of what we call a town, will most likely be chosen as our representative to the Territorial Legislature. He currently is our voice in the territorial council and, though generally a man of few words, appears to have shown some leadership. I believe I have been able to convince him to introduce a measure to grant women the vote. What we need now are strong, passionate, and persuasive women in Cheyenne City who can convince other representatives to support the measure. I can think of no one, dear Elizabeth, who could fill this role more capably than you. You are a woman who has been raised on the frontier and understands the independent spirit and latent fears that drive frontier thinking. You have an appearance and manner that naturally draw men's attention, and we certainly cannot be above using our feminine wiles—those of us who still can employ them. Please consider coming west to help champion our cause. I fear that I will remain slave to this saloon and to my family of cast-iron stoves, but you are still free to move your life in whatever direction destiny demands. I pray that you will hear its call from the West and will heed the summons.

Yours faithfully in the cause,

Esther

.

32

SUZANNA

Unlike New York and Chicago, Liverpool was a city with enough history to have become comfortable with itself. There was none of the pretense that Suzanna had seen on Broadway or Water Street. Work on the docks was less frantic and clamorous. Everyone appeared to move with a steady, but deliberate, sense of purpose.

"We've been at it a good long while," Horace Renfroe said cheerfully as he led them across the dock toward a waiting carriage. "This city had been bumbling along for a good four-hundred years when your first colonists decided to leave the motherland. Oh, you'll meet some people who are still pretty chuffed with themselves before your visit's over, but most of us have a time-tempered sense for what's what and are good common folk."

Renfroe's dress wouldn't have placed him among the common: a smart, expertly tailored suit and vest in fine wool, high-heeled black boots that seemed to have avoided the mud and manure of the wharf, and a dapper top hat in silky beaver that Suzanna guessed may have been splashing in an Iowa stream only a few months earlier. But beyond his dress, Horace Renfroe was as approachable as the flower girls who lined the walk in front of the customshouse and treated his American guests as if they were the sole purpose for his being. He was a stick-thin man, lean as a pear sapling, with a long, animated face and porkchop sideburns that extended to the sides of his chin. When he spoke, his hands and an ivory-topped cane bounced with the pitch of his voice. As he described the city, they kept enthusiastic time.

"It has been said," he announced, leaning forward in the carriage to admire the monuments that lined Liverpool's Lime Street, "that had Julius Caesar returned to Britain only a hundred years ago, he would have found little changed from the time he invaded more than a millennium before. A few hovels, mud horse tracks, ignorant peasants. But we have built quite a city in this century."

"I thought you to be from London," David said, smiling at their guide's excited energy.

"Oh, aye. For the past thirty-five years. But I was raised right here, Merseyside, until I went away to university. You should have heard me then," he said, slipping into the local brogue. "I sounded just like them blokes you heard along the docks. Cambridge took some of the Scouser out of me, but not my love for our city." He swept the cane dramatically out the window at the cityscape.

"Scouser?" Suzanna asked.

Renfroe laughed heartily. "That's what we sometimes call ourselves in Liverpool. I don't know where the name came from, but you'll hear people talk about the Scousers. That would be us." He leaned forward again to better view passing buildings. "We're almost at the Queen's Arms. I've booked you for two nights to give you a chance to rest, find your land legs, and get yourselves and your clothes cleaned up. Our train leaves Thursday morning at seven. We will be stopping in Birmingham to make arrangements with Westminster Bank there to handle the money from your sale, should you choose to dispose of the estate. They keep a supply of American paper currency. You wouldn't want to be burdened with trying to carry a chest of sterling back on the ship."

David and Suzanna nodded their appreciation but were too tired and desperate for decent food to pay close attention to the solicitor's monologue.

Though Renfroe offered to commit Wednesday to showing them the rest of Liverpool, they chose to spend the extra day in their room catching up on sleep and in the hotel's restaurant stuffing themselves on steak and kidney pie and buttered scones. *I had no idea*, Suzanna thought, *how starved one could feel for decent food after two weeks of the same salty soup and dry bread.*

Their second night, Suzanna arranged for a tub to be brought to the room and filled with steaming water, carried by a brigade of kettle-bearing maids in neat, navy blue uniforms. She and David peeled away the one set of clothing they hadn't sent out for washing, and she settled gingerly into the hot bath. David knelt beside her, scrubbing away two weeks of sea salt and the staleness of their tiny cabin with a thick brown block of lye-scented soap and a coarse sponge.

"Now you," she said, letting him towel her off and massage a scented oil from the hotel dresser across her back and breasts.

"I haven't finished yet," he said, turning her into him and running the oil down across her hips and thighs. "You're still a very fine woman, Suzanna Whitlock" he murmured into her ear, then buried his face between her breasts, breathing in the fragrance of the oil.

She ran the fingers of both hands into his thick hair and drew his face tight against her belly. "We'd better get you washed off," she whispered, leaning forward to cradle him against her chest. "I don't want your smelly body chasing me around the bed, and that's where I want you as soon as I can get you there."

"I think I'm ready now," he murmured into her stomach.

"Get into the water," she said. "There's nothing a little scrubbing can't improve."

They were ready at six in the morning with freshly washed and pressed clothing and a cheerfulness that raised Renfroe's brows and gave an extra twirl to his cane.

"A good night, I see," he said with a satisfied smile. "And a full day ahead. There is still very little that is direct about British rail travel. I read in the *Times* about your great transcontinental line that will allow you to board a train in Baltimore and arrive in San Francisco a week later without ever leaving your coach. Here, we will be traveling from Liverpool to Norwich, a distance of no more than two hundred and fifty miles. But we will change trains—or I might say, regional rail lines—in Birmingham, Northampton, and Peterborough. A different fare of a few bob for every leg of the journey. But I have obtained tickets, so you just enjoy the countryside."

And enjoy it she did. Suzanna had never seen such a green and carefully tended land. Pastures walled in gray stone stretched away from the rail line, dotted with white sheep and the occasional dun-colored cow. Neat cottages in the same gray stone with roofs of lichen-spotted tile or thick straw thatch lined narrow cobbled streets. Two-wheeled horse carts carried earthen jugs of fresh milk and stacks of yellow cheeses from door-to-door. She could imagine Elizabeth

Bennet or the Dashwood sisters, women with whom she had filled the evening hours of many a winter's night in her loft above her father's cabin, crossing the wooden stiles that bridged the pasture walls or walking these quaint village streets.

The pastoral beauty was broken by the somber, smoke-belching outskirts of Birmingham. As they approached the city, the landscape faded to muted grays, the fields and cottages smothered under a film of soot that seeped into the rail car and oiled their lips and tongues. Renfroe led them through a vaporous morning fog to a cold, gray stone edifice where they spent two hours in a cavernous wood-paneled room. It was divided into smaller cubicles by waist-high partitions with swinging gates that reminded Suzanna of the spectators' bar in the Afton courtroom. They huddled about an ancient oak desk, talking in secretive whispers with a completely emotionless banker named Woolard, while around them patrons clicked across a time-worn marble floor to a row of grilled windows.

The banker screwed his face into an inscrutable frown. "Lord Badgerow is presently leasing the house and wishes to purchase it," he said quietly. "The Badgerow family has done business with us since we opened in Birmingham, and we will serve as his representative if you elect to accept his offer. The house has been valued at eight thousand pounds, and a thousand acres at two pounds an acre—or two thousand pounds. Lord Badgerow is offering the full ten thousand pounds for the purchase. There is an additional two thousand seven hundred pounds in an account that maintains the estate, half of which would come to you with the sale, since only half of estate revenue is needed to maintain the property and pay staff." He paused and waited for a response. Suzanna looked over at Horace Renfroe, then at David, who seemed deep in thought, and whose face was equally inscrutable.

"We can complete the transaction here today if you wish, and you can begin your journey back to America," Woolard said.

"We've come this far," David said. "I believe we need to see the estate. And in all honesty, I have no sense for the fairness of the offer. We will visit Allgar Hall, make a decision about our interest in disposing of the estate, and visit with Mr. Renfroe about price if we decide to sell."

The banker sat back and folded his hands in his lap. "Very well. In anticipation of a sale, we have purchased American dollars equal to the value in sterling of the property. That will allow you—if you choose to sell—to carry paper with you when you return."

David nodded. "Very sensible—and thank you. We'll stop on our return with a decision." He pushed away from the desk and Suzanna and Renfroe rose with him. Woolard shook hands with the men and gave Suzanna an expressionless nod. Their footsteps across the stone floor seemed to draw the eyes of every patron—or was it that Suzanna was still reeling from the figure tossed out so casually by Woolard? Ten thousand pounds! If a five-pound sea passage was worth thirty dollars, this Badgerow family was offering them sixty thousand dollars for David's family's estate! She could hardly imagine such a sum!

"I think the offer is low," Renfroe said as they walked back toward the station through gradually thinning mist for a late morning train to Northampton. "Those with whom we spoke in Norwich valued the estate at eight thousand pounds, so that seems fair. But Woolard's price for the land was less than we estimated. Values for similar land in the area are three pounds to the acre. And the records indicate the estate earns six to eight hundred pounds per year, after expenses. So it is a profitable enterprise. Since there is no debt and the account holds nearly three thousand pounds, I would think more than half of the escrow should come to you. I would ask eleven thousand for the estate and request all but a thousand pounds of the escrow."

"Let's go have a look at Allgar Hall," David said, taking Suzanna's hand and squeezing it lightly. "Perhaps I will decide to become a country gentleman."

33

ELIZABETH

At five cents a word, Elizabeth kept her telegram as brief as possible. "*Request one week leave. August 2 to 8. Quiet here.*" She had given the senator sixteen-hour days while in Washington and knew he was grateful. Since his vote at the impeachment trial, virtually no one had come by the office. There had been a few terse letters to the editor in the Chicago papers, and much more explicit tirades had come to the office. The general feeling among Illinois Republicans was that Senator Lyman Trumbull needn't run for re-election.

He responded by the end of the day with an even briefer cable. "*Approved. Just lock up.*" She sent a letter to Esther Morris informing her that she planned to be in Cheyenne on the Overland Flyer at approximately noon on August 4th and planned to leave again on the 7th. She hoped Esther might be able to join her during her stay. She mailed the letter on July 14th and prayed it would reach South Pass City with sufficient time for Esther to make the journey to the territorial capital. That afternoon, she booked a second-class fare on the Flyer to Cheyenne for forty-two dollars: twelve on the Chicago and Northwestern to Omaha, then another thirty across Nebraska to Wyoming. It was the equivalent of three week's wages. She chided herself hourly for being so impetuous and extravagant until she met that evening with Myra, Mary, and Alta for their weekly session.

"It is actually a very small investment if it is to determine the direction of your future," Myra said after Elizabeth confided in the women. "If I weren't so committed to trying to get General Grant to take a position on women's rights in this November election, I might offer to come with you. I have always wished to see the great frontier. But Grant seems to have decided that his best campaign strategy is to say nothing and stay out of the public eye—a wise move, I should think, for someone who enjoys drink as much as he does." The encouragement assuaged Elizabeth's concern about the fares, and she began to anticipate the journey as she had nothing in a good long while.

Fifteen hours into the trip west from Omaha, Elizabeth began to wonder if she had over-estimated her ability to endure monotony. West of Grand Rapids, the endless prairie was broken only by a brown, slow-moving sea of bison by the thousands that left a swath of bare earth, dotted by dark mounds of droppings, as they grazed and pawed their way across the grassland. By 10 p.m., it was pitch black beyond the mirrored windows of the coach and nearly as dark in the cramped car, but for the glow of a cigar that bobbed as a red dot above the seat opposite her. The other three passengers around the table that centered her compartment were all railroad men, polite and deferential, but on the heavy side in body frame and in need of bathing. She had to remind herself that growing up beside a mill pond had conditioned her to bathe more frequently than city folk, a habit she had taken to Chicago and the boarding house, much to the consternation of Mrs. Kruger.

Two of her seatmates puffed incessantly on thick, dark stogies, and a cloud of purple haze hung in the car, even when a window was cracked open. What little sleep she found was sitting upright, with the two across from her rumbling like a thunderstorm and the round bald head of the man beside her dropping heavily every few minutes onto her shoulder—this time, with no apparent desire to fondle her. He had introduced himself as George Stockton, a railroad construction engineer from St. Louis, and had the seat against the window. She did suspect that he might be choosing to tip her way rather than toward the glass to be closer to her, a suspicion confirmed when she slipped from the seat to find solitude and cleaner air in the dining car. Somehow, Mr. Stockton managed to remain upright until her shoulder again became available.

Only thirteen more hours, she reminded herself. Stops at North Platte, Julesburg, and Sidney offered a few moments on the open platforms to stretch her legs and breathe clean air, though the night platforms were drafty and lighted only by flickering oil lamps. In seven hours it would be light, the men would wake and stop their snorting. If they didn't feel in a talkative mood, she might be able to rest.

In the refuge of the dining car, she gazed out into the blackness beyond the window. To her senses, the landscape seemed inverted, with all the lights sparkling above and complete darkness below. She imagined lying on a grassy hilltop, gazing upward at the band of stardust that arched across the heavens like a pathway for the gods. She had never seen the sky so bright—and the earth so completely empty.

By dawn, they had climbed out of the grasslands into rocky, scrub-covered desert. Was this what she would find in Wyoming? Broken hills and endless tracts of sage and gnarled cedars? Then, on a low rise a hundred yards from the track, she saw what looked like a small deer, but with hooked, upright horns and white shoulders, belly, and rump.

"Antelope," the porter said, leaning across the table to point at a dozen more that grazed beside the track. "They don't seem to pay no mind to us rolling on by." There was a majesty, she decided, to the empty ruggedness of the place and in the unruffled curiosity of animals that had not yet learned to fear the tide of humanity that swept in their direction.

As they approached Cheyenne, the land again flattened into high desert, more barren and desolate than the climb into the Rockies. She felt the train begin to slow, heard the release of steam, and braced herself for the collision of cars as the string of carriages compressed. She leaned across the table toward the window to the degree she was able without crowding her bald seatmate, but saw nothing but open, brush-strewn ground. The train groaned to a stop with a final burst of steam beside a long two-story building of bare wood, fronted by a wide plank porch that reached nearly to the track. Her car came to a halt just beyond it in front of a single-story depot of the same construction. But beyond it, she still saw no evidence of civilization.

George Stockton helped her from the car and fussed about her until her bag was securely beside her on the platform.

"That's the Union Pacific Hotel right there," he said, nodding toward the larger of the buildings. "There are rooms for a dollar-fifty and the food is decent. But it can get rowdy in the evening. You may want to see if Mrs. Rollins has space at the Rollins House. She keeps a more orderly place, and it's away from the depot."

Elizabeth looked about in bewilderment. "Where would that be?"

Stockton laughed heartily and lifted her bag. "Follow me," he said and walked her through the depot. Beyond it to the north and west, hidden by the buildings along the track, a patchwork of low wooden and sandstone structures, canvas tents, and sod houses lined a modest grid of broad, dusty streets.

"Not much of a town yet," Stockton said, "but about four thousand folks now live here year-round. Not a long walk to the Rollins House but, in a dress, I'd take a wagon." He hailed a boy in his young teens who sat on a plain, weather-beaten buckboard, watching passengers leave the station.

"The lady would like to go to the Rollins House," he called, and flipped the driver fifty cents as he pulled the wagon up beside the depot's entrance.

I guess I'm going to the Rollins House, Elizabeth thought as the boy jumped from the seat and hoisted her bag into the back of the wagon. *Perhaps the railroad men don't want anyone witnessing their "rowdiness" at the company hotel.*

Near the center of town, the buildings appeared more permanent: saddle shops, two newspaper buildings, outfitters' stores, and beside the modest hotel, a jewelry manufacturer and tailor. Mrs. Rollins had only eight rooms, but two were vacant. The proprietress was a tall, severe woman with tightly knotted gray hair and stern gray eyes. She looked Elizabeth up and down disapprovingly. "Don't have many single young women coming here. I run a quiet place. No drinking on the premises. No guests in the rooms. Two dollars a day includes two meals."

"Two dollars? I only paid a dollar-fifty in our nation's capital!"

"Don't know if you noticed," Mrs. Rollins said grimly, "but you're not in our nation's capital. They'll take your dollar-fifty at the Union Pacific, but you only get breakfast."

"I hope to be meeting a friend from South Pass City," Elizabeth said more contritely, adding quickly, "a woman friend I knew in Chicago."

Mrs. Rollins softened visibly. "That would be Esther Morris, I'd be guessing. She stayed here when she came from Illinois and has when she and her husband come back over for supplies. Haven't seen anything of her for nearly a year."

"I hope my letter reached her in time for her to meet me. I sent it the middle of last month."

"If she comes, she'll be stopping here," Mrs. Rollins said. "I imagine you'll be wanting to clean up. The only bath house in town is for men only. Not a lot of women come through here needing a wash. Get settled into your room and come down to my rooms in the back. I have an old brass tub and will get some water heated for you." She winked and smiled. "Included in the two dollars."

Mrs. Rollins' rooms offered proof that the woman had a brighter and more cheerful side. Elizabeth found herself in a rear corner on the second floor, a light, airy chamber with a colorful block-pattern quilt as a bedspread and paintings of flowers decorating the walls. The porcelain washstand top, basin, and pitcher were a rose-patterned pink, the braided rug on the floor concentric circles of rose and white. It was a room decorated by a woman for other women. George Stockton would feel much more at home at the railroad hotel.

She organized her things and returned to the main floor where the proprietress ushered her into a warm kitchen where a long, hand-beaten copper tub billowed steam with the slightest hint of lavender.

"I'll leave you to get washed up," Mrs. Rollins said, draping clean towels over a drying rack beside the tub. "Supper is at six."

Elizabeth washed quickly, then leaned back to soak. The warmth of the room and water lulled her gradually to a sleep broken only by the muted clatter of pans as Mrs. Rollins began meal preparation.

"You looked so peaceful, I just hadn't the heart to disturb you," the woman said. "I'll slip out while you dress."

Besides Mrs. Rollins, four others gathered for the evening meal: a Mrs. Frazier who was on her way north to Fort Stambaugh; Mr. and Mrs. Herman who were staying at the Rollins House while finishing a dry goods store a few doors farther along the street; and a young man who stood and brightened so visibly when she entered the room that she felt an involuntary blush rise on her cheeks. He introduced himself as Thomas Spencer and invited her to take a seat beside him, opposite the Hermans. The conversation at the table was limited to brief introductions, talk about how rapidly Cheyenne was growing, and the recent granting of territorial status to Wyoming.

"That's what brought us here from Indiana," Mr. Herman said. "This is the new America. Half the country will be coming through here during the next twenty years. We plan on having them stop at Herman's Dry Goods."

Mrs. Frazier wondered what brought Elizabeth to this heart of the frontier.

"I have a friend from Illinois who, like you, moved here to join her husband in South Pass City. If our communication worked well, I'm hoping she will join us here in the next day or two."

Mrs. Rollins brought fragrant bowls of red potatoes and greens from her garden and a plate of what Elizabeth learned was buffalo meat. She confessed that the dark, lean meat would be a first for her and took a tentative bite with four sets of eyes watching with curious anticipation. The buffalo had a stronger, gamier flavor than the farm-raised beef she had grown up on in Iowa, but a rich earthiness that she quite enjoyed.

"I like it," she said, an approval that seemed to grant the others permission to attack their own plates. As Mrs. Rollins cleared the main course, Mrs. Herman filled the empty air with complaints about the challenges of acquiring needed goods for the new store. Her chatter died only after creamy lemon pudding proved too tempting for her to resist. As Elizabeth dabbed at her lips with a napkin and prepared to push back from the table, Thomas Spencer rose quickly beside her and eased back her chair.

"It's a lovely evening outside. I know you must be tired, but I was about to take a short walk. Would I be too forward to ask for your company?"

Yes, Elizabeth thought. "*You would be.*" She looked to Mrs. Frazier and Mrs. Herman for indications that it might not be a wise idea. Mrs. Frazier chose to offer her thoughts.

"I assure you, Miss Whitlock, that Mr. Spencer will be a real gentleman. It would be a very safe way to see the town."

"He's staying here rather than at the Union Pacific," Mrs. Rollins added. "That should tell you something."

"It sounds as if it would be rude to decline," Elizabeth said, smiling, and secretly pleased that the response had been encouraging. Thomas Spencer was a pleasant-looking man—seemingly well-bred and amusingly polite. A walk would be much more enjoyable than an evening in her room or sharing the parlor with the loquacious Mrs. Herman. "Just let me get a jacket. I will join you on the porch."

They walked to the right, away from the station and what sounded like a raucous after-dinner shindy at the railroad hotel. The late-summer evening remained light. There were few people on the dusty street—a lone rider on horseback and two boys chasing a hoop a hundred yards ahead.

"You've come a long way to see a friend for just a couple of days," Thomas said, looking over at her to suggest that he thought there might be more to her story.

Elizabeth returned his look without immediate answer. She noticed for the first time that his nose was slightly askew and that he had a small scar on the right side of his upper lip. Both added, she thought, to the strength of his well-defined jaw and inquisitive gray-blue eyes. *I may as well let him know why I'm here*, she decided. *After this week, we will never see each other again, and I shouldn't be a coward in speaking about the cause.*

"We were both involved in the women's suffrage movement in Illinois," she said, looking again ahead after the boys with the hoop. "Esther invited me here because she thought the territory might be considering extending women the vote."

Thomas chuckled softly. "My mother would like you. My father died when I was young, and I was raised by a *very* strong-willed and outspoken woman. If she were living, I'm certain she would be involved in your movement."

Elizabeth again glanced over at her companion. "You've lost both of your parents, then."

Thomas offered a resigned smile. "She caught consumption while I was away at the war and died before I returned. I suspect that's one of the reasons I find myself here."

"You were in the war? May I ask which side?" Elizabeth wasn't certain why it mattered, now that the terrible thing was behind them. But it did.

"I was with the Ohio Seventy-Sixth Infantry."

"My father fought with the Fourth Iowa Volunteers—mainly in the West."

"He survived the war?"

"Yes—but with some luck. He was wounded at Pea Ridge and picked up by the Rebels, thinking he was one of their own. He escaped a hospital in Arkansas and made his way back north with the help of friendly Indians."

"A fascinating story," Thomas said. "I'd like to say I'd enjoy hearing the details, but I find talk of the war distressing, even when heroic."

"I won't say more about it then, other than to ask where you served."

Thomas's lengthy silence caused her to wish she hadn't asked. Then he drew a deep breath and released it sharply through his nose. "Chancellorsville, Gettysburg, and then some of us were separated off to march with Sherman through Georgia. Do you know what a bummer is?"

She shook her head, then realized he was looking down at the street and hadn't seen her gesture. "No. I don't," she said.

"Well, the supposed brilliance of Sherman's campaign was that he moved us fast and didn't depend on supplies from the rear. He planned his marches through the most productive farming areas and fed us on what we could scavenge from the farms and merchants before we destroyed their homes. The bummers—that was my job—were the men who had to go out and find supplies. I spent the last months of the war stealing pigs, cattle, and whatever else we could get our hands on." He sniffed again cynically. "The Ohio lost over thirty-five thousand men. I was standing beside many of them at Chancellorsville and Gettysburg when they fell and, for some reason—God alone knows—the only scratch I got was as a bummer." He turned and smiled at Elizabeth, holding a finger up to the side of his nose. "A slave that I was trying to free hit me in the face with the handle of a hay fork. Broke my nose and cut my lip. He said I had no right to be taking their hogs. That they'd all starve to death if we took everything. Those were my war injuries."

"I'm sorry," she said. "It must have been horrible." They walked in silence for a few moments, then she said, "You said your mother's death may have brought you here. This is a long way from Ohio."

"I felt like I owed her everything," he said. "We lived in Newark, and my father was killed while they were digging the Ohio and Erie canal. I felt like I needed to become the man of the house, but she insisted I finish school and worked her hands to the bone taking in washing until I was out. I worked on the canal for a while, guiding teams that pulled the barges. Then the war came along, and I enlisted. By the time I got back, she was gone."

"And that led you to Wyoming?"

He laughed more lightly. "I was so tired of war and of places that reminded me of war that I went to Texas with another man from Newark to drive cattle. Over to Shreveport to the docks. Up to Sedalia in Missouri to get beef up to you in Chicago. Then to Abilene when the railhead moved west. First as a trailhand, then as a boss. I saved up some money and decided to find a place I could raise some of my own. Didn't much like Texas, so here I am."

"And have you found your place?"

He laughed again. "I've been at the Rollins House off-and-on for a month now. I started looking north—around Fort Fetterman on the North Platte, then went on up along the Powder River. There are beautiful open grasslands, but things are still pretty unsettled up there. The government's crowding the Indians into reservations, and they don't like it."

"And who could blame them," Elizabeth said.

Thomas grunted his agreement. "I'm afraid I've had enough conflict for one lifetime. I'm looking for a little more peace and seclusion. I'll be checking out the Big Horn in a few days." They had turned down a street that ran in front of a row of plain, single-story houses, a few painted white, like the Rollins House, but most still bare, weather-beaten lumber.

"We aren't far from the hall they're using for the council until a formal legislature's formed," he said. "I'll take you by there. They're not meeting now but should be this week sometime. Most of the council members are Democrats, and they're worried Grant will be elected and will appoint a Republican as territorial governor." He paused and smiled over at Elizabeth. "But now you know my story.

Tell me about your family."

Elizabeth shrugged. "We're ordinary people. I'm not from Chicago. My family has a lumber mill in Afton, Iowa, where I grew up." She smiled shyly without looking at her companion. "I had a brother Thomas. He died of some poisoning he got while working as an apprentice to a company in the East that preserved rail ties. You're like him in some ways . . . ."

"I'm so sorry," he said. "But how alike?"

"Oh, he was an independent spirit. A born adventurer. In fact, my other brother shares another of your interests. He raises horses over in the Salt River valley."

"Here in Wyoming?"

She nodded. "Wyoming or Idaho. He's an adventurer as well. Managed a station for the Pony Express in the far western part of the Utah Territory. His wife is Paiute." She glanced over to judge his reaction. He appeared more intrigued than concerned.

"You aren't seeing them while here?"

"It's not the easiest place to get to, and there wasn't time during this visit. I promised my employer that I would only be away for two weeks. Six of those days are taken by travel. Next time, perhaps."

"You haven't said anything about your employer," Thomas said. "What do you do in Chicago?"

First suffrage. Now politics, she thought. *Such a short walk, and so many chances to end a pleasant conversation with an interesting man. But it may also be a last walk, so be the courageous woman you always tell yourself you should be. And a man who has been driving cattle from Texas may very well be out of touch with issues that still divide the nation.*

"I am an aide to Illinois Senator Lyman Trumbull," she said. "I manage affairs for his office in Chicago."

Thomas Spencer stopped and turned to face her in the empty street. A curious grin accentuated the scar that creased his lip. "The Lyman Trumbull who voted against impeachment?"

She straightened defensively, without turning. "Yes. That Lyman Trumbull."

"I read his statement to the Senate after the vote. In the San Antonio Express. He was one of the few courageous men in that entire affair."

"Then you're a Democrat?"

"I'm nothing," he said, grinning. "But it was a very persuasive and sensible argument. That we can't remove a president if he's acting within the bounds of the law, just because we disagree with him."

"Then you know something about the law?" She was impressed that a man in the Territory of Wyoming had even read the opinion.

"No. But he convinced me that he did, and that others were choosing to ignore it."

"I wrote much of that statement," she said, avoiding looking at him directly.

"Well, I swan! Here I am with a lovely woman who is also smart as a timber wolf and writes papers for men in Washington. I can't say that I expected to find someone like you in Cheyenne."

"I swan? I'm not sure I've ever heard that expression."

He started walking again, pausing only long enough to be certain she was moving with him.

"*I swan?* That's something my mother said when something surprised her. I have no idea what it means and doubt she did either. But I like the sound of it. And, I have to admit, you surprise me."

"I don't think I've ever been compared to a wolf. Should I be flattered or insulted?"

"Oh, flattered! I learned while driving cattle that wolves are the smartest critters—I mean—well, you know what I mean."

"So, does it trouble you to have found me in Cheyenne?"

"No. It doesn't trouble me at all. In fact, it delights me!"

Elizabeth felt the blood run like hot tea on a cold morning into her extremities, warming her arms and hands and lightening her step. His admission seemed to fluster him and he looked ahead along the road.

"There's the building they use as the council hall," he said, pointing toward a plain, two-story building on the next corner with symmetrical rows of windows that lined both floors. "Not exactly Washington. They rent two rooms on the ground floor that are separated by a canvas partition, getting ready for when there's both a council and a senate. Plain pine benches and sawdust on the floor for all the spitting that goes on. I'm not sure it's a good place for a lady."

"I'm not asking for a seat," Elizabeth said lightly. "Just the right to vote to send someone who doesn't spit."

"And after that, maybe a seat . . . ?"

"Wyoming needs to give women the vote first."

"And perhaps you need to be here to see that it happens."

It was her turn to stop the stroll. "That's what my friend Esther said. I really came out to see if this was all more than just her wishful thinking."

"It won't happen without people like you in the territory keeping the representatives' feet to the fire."

"My hope is that she is able to get here tomorrow. She may have more news. When will you be leaving for the Big Horn?"

Thomas Spencer looked down at the few feet of street that separated them. "If you would be amenable to other walks in the evening, I think I'll stay until you have to leave."

34

DAVID

The difference, he decided, was one of energy. Though the cottages were quainter and the cobbled streets and hedge-lined pastures more picturesque, the countryside through which they passed as the train clicked and swayed from Birmingham to Northampton, then east to Peterborough and Norwich, was much like the fertile farmland they had seen in Ohio and Pennsylvania. More sheep, stone walls, and hedgerows. Fewer cattle and fewer trees. But Britain seemed to be running at about half-speed compared to what he had witnessed as they crossed the United States toward its eastern seaboard.

Perhaps England was choosing to let the homeland plod along at the pace he saw in the passing horse carts and village market squares, directing its pent-up energy into the foreign expansion he had read about in the Chicago and St. Louis newspapers that found their way to Afton. Despite her loss of the American colonies, this seemingly tranquil land was amassing the greatest empire the world had seen, controlling vast portions of continents and millions of people. How, he wondered, did a small island nation that appeared to be recently roused from an untroubled nap, exert such influence?

As they neared Norwich, the bucolic countryside gradually thickened with houses and churches, still separated by orchards and hedged paddocks. During a long sweep as the track followed the River Wensum into the city, David could see the towering spire of a cathedral and to the north, on a low rise, the blocky square of an ancient stone fortress. Horace Renfroe leaned across the seat to share the view.

"The castle was started by William the Conqueror," he said, pointing toward the fortress. "It and the cathedral date to the twelfth century. The cathedral there was completed in eleven forty-five. Norwich is a place of churches and was the second-largest city in

England after London until the woolen mills began to move to Yorkshire and cotton to Manchester. The city's been left behind a bit by industry, but as a result, has maintained much of its early charm."

Charm was the word David had been struggling for. Norwich had the same stone and cream-sided plaster cottages that gave the farmland its pastoral appeal, but nestled more closely together along its neatly cobbled streets. There was none of the filtering gray haze of Birmingham, and the city shone brightly under a late-afternoon sun.

"The age of these cities is hard to fathom," he said to Renfroe. "We think of Chicago and New York as old, but they are centuries younger—newcomers, compared to this."

"Allgar Hall is older than your cities," Renfroe said with a light chuckle. "I believe parts of the house date to sixteen forty-eight. We should be able to stay there this evening if you wish."

The solicitor had arranged for a coach to meet them at the station. The driver headed immediately west, with David and Suzanna craning through curtainless windows to watch the city unfold. The shod hooves of the carriage horse clopped rhythmically against the cobbles as they passed between the castle hill and a bustling market that smelled of fresh fish and recently slaughtered sheep, geese, and rabbits. Beyond the market square, a long, featureless three-story building of rust-colored brick scarred the medieval cityscape, plopped indecorously among the quarried stone shops and rowhouses. It clicked and hummed like a farm pond bursting with spring frogs.

"The Badgerow woolen mill," Renfroe announced. "Owned by the family that now leases Allgar Hall and the last to remain in Norwich." David peered at the dark windows until the building disappeared behind them, wondering what kind of contraptions created such incessant noise and how workers could tolerate long days inside that closed brick box.

A painted signpost announced the street along which they rode to be St. Martin's. It followed the river until the waterway turned south, then joined a broader, unpaved highroad with a similar placard— Aylsham Road. Beyond neatly trimmed hedges, sheep dotted the hillsides like puffy clouds in a green satin sky. The tidy farmhouses became less frequent and, as they approached the village of Earlham, were replaced by raw, unpainted cottages with roofs of broken thatch.

"The land seems as fertile here, and the flocks as large," David observed. "But the farms are much poorer."

"These are the tenant houses," Renfroe explained. "We're riding beside part of the estate. It adjoins both the north and east sides of the village. These are your lands."

"Then who are these people you call tenants?" Suzanna asked. "They have homes on the estate?"

Renfroe cast her a curious smile. "They farm the estate and the estate owns their homes. The Allgar family didn't actually do the farming or husband the animals. Nor do the Badgerows. The work is done by these tenants. The family leasing the hall essentially lives off their mill. An overseer manages the farm and the workers."

"A bit like a southern plantation, but with tenants rather than slaves," Suzanna muttered.

"All freemen," Renfroe declared defensively. "All can leave whenever they wish."

"To do what?" David asked. "They don't look as if they are doing well enough to start something of their own."

Renfroe looked out at a row of passing cottages where ragged children chased each other around a three-sided courtyard in a game of blind man's buff. "Some leave to go to the mills. Other men go to sea. But the landlords generally share enough of what is produced to sustain a family."

"And the portion that comes to the owner?" David asked.

"Is sold to maintain the estate. Keeping a place like Allgar Hall is an expensive proposition. Fewer of these estates survive each generation."

The carriage had entered the village and turned right at a central common where a tall stone cross with circled arms graced an engraved pedestal. Renfroe, who rode backward facing the Whitlocks, nodded toward the window. "Look ahead down the lane. You should be able to see the gates of the hall."

Ahead, a high stone wall closed the end of the street, broken by an open gate of spiked wrought iron. Beyond the entrance, neatly trimmed lawn of lush green stretched to a house front that, at a distance, filled the limits of the opening in the wall.

As they neared, the house came fully into view: another three-story brick building the color of the mill, but with much of the face hidden beneath a mask of glossy ivy that climbed to a steep tile roof. Twenty chimneys rose above the tiles in bundles of four, each stack, David guessed, drawing from a fireplace that warmed a separate room. Symmetrical wings extended forward into the lawn at each end of the massive hall, the one on the left embellished by a small round conservatory with walls entirely of glass.

"Oh, David," Suzanna murmured. "This place is bigger than our entire mill floor. How many people can possibly live here?"

"There are five in the Badgerow family," Renfroe answered. "And, of course, the house staff.

The lane turned left immediately beyond the gate and looped around the acre of lawn to three brick steps that rose to a high oak door. To their right, two men walked side-by-side down the sloping lawn, each pushing a wheeled cylinder braced between two arms at the end of a long handle. The face of the cylinder was crossed by metal blades that snipped the grass at an even height and threw the clippings forward into an attached wooden tray.

Suzanna reached across David to point at the mowers. "What a marvelous thing! It clips and catches the grass as it's pushed along."

As they alighted from the carriage, the central door opened and five women and a man dressed in uniforms of black and white hurried out, forming two lines on either side of the steps. Behind them, a well-fed gentleman of middle age in a light afternoon jacket and an attractive woman in a fashionable, high-collared purple dress, stepped formally to the center of the porch. Renfroe hurriedly alighted and helped Suzanna down onto the gravel drive, then stepped aside as David bent through the low door. The solicitor led them up the steps and bowed slightly to the waiting couple.

"Lord and Lady Badgerow, allow me to introduce Mr. David Whitlock and his wife, Suzanna."

Badgerow stepped forward, extending a fleshy hand to David as his wife bent into a quick, bobbing curtsy.

"So delighted to have you here," Badgerow said, his voice as round as his belly and full of good humor. "May I present my wife, Rebecca. We were pleased to learn that you decided to come see the place, but hope you do not find it so much to your liking that you choose to turn us out and become Englishmen."

"I believe we are quite happy where we are," David said, grasping Badgerow's hand firmly and acknowledging Rebecca with a pleasant nod. "I think we could put half of our small town in this house and still have room for visitors." He turned and looked down the steps at the wait staff who stood nervously with hands folded in front of them. "I didn't have a chance to meet these people on the way up." While the Badgerows stood in surprised confusion, he stepped back to the drive and walked along the line of servants, introducing himself to each. "We're probably as English as you are," he said to the butler. "Just a few generations removed."

"I hear the effect of those generations in your accent," Badgerow said as David returned to the doorway. "I believe you are the first Americans we have had in Earlham. Everyone will find you quite the novelty. But please come in. You have had a long journey and will want to rest." He guided them into a wide, oak-paneled hallway with a broad staircase rising in front of them in its center. "Supper will be served at seven. If you are not too tired, we can then have a cigar and discuss business over a glass of sherry. Godwin can show you to your room. The dining room is just to the left here. We will see you in just over an hour."

The butler took their cases and climbed stiffly in front of them to the second floor where he led them into one of the wings and a bedchamber as large as the Whitlock living room. A high bed with an ornately scrolled headboard in rich mahogany stood centered against one wall with a matching dresser and wardrobe filling the wall opposite the windows. A white, rolled-arm settee and matching chairs framed three sides of a mahogany coffee table near the door.

Godwin placed their cases beside the wardrobe, nodded formally, and indicated a curved metal handle beside the bed. "Just ring if I can be of service," he said and hesitated just long enough for David to ask, "What's on the floor above?"

Godwin's brow furrowed until he realized he was being asked about the rooms on the third level. "Ah. The service staff have rooms above," he said and waited for further questions. When none came, he hastily left the room.

"I wonder if these furnishings come with the house?" Suzanna wondered aloud. "There must be hundreds of dollars of value just in this room."

"We'll have to ask Renfroe," David said, pulling aside heavy fringed curtains. The window overlooked the lawn they had circled as they arrived. The men with the clipping machines had finished their work and the grass stretched to the open gate, smooth and even as carpet.

"So, the way this works, as I understand it, is that these tenant farmers raise whatever is grown here, the overseer sells the sheep and produce, and the farmers are paid enough to keep them healthy, but not enough to move elsewhere. The rest comes to the house to pay staff and taxes, cover expenses for running the place, and, if there is excess, accumulate or be invested."

Suzanna nodded, moving to stand beside him at the window. "There were the six serving staff when we arrived—and the men working on the lawn. They must be gardeners. Even assuming that includes all the help, this would be a costly place to run."

"If they pay their people anything," David muttered. "The staff live and eat here, so they may not get much in wages."

"More questions for Renfroe," she said. "Let's get cleaned up and dressed for dinner."

35

ELIZABETH

The Esther Morris who climbed from the buckboard in front of the Rollins House was not the cream-complexioned woman with delicate hands that Elizabeth remembered from the Chicago gathering. Her face had been leathered and creased by mountain sun, her hands hardened feeding the cast-iron stoves, and her straight mouth given a slight downturn on the left side, even when she smiled. A high-collared dress of dark blue added to her look of severity. She greeted Elizabeth with the embrace of a woman who had been too long without feminine company. Easing her away to arms-length, Esther inspected her younger friend from head to toe.

"Just as beautiful as ever," she said, glancing at Thomas Spencer who stood beside her. The two had been talking quietly on the low porch of the Rollins House when the carriage arrived, catching a few private moments before entering for dinner.

Elizabeth felt a flush creep across her cheeks, welcoming the timing of the compliment.

"I'm so please and relieved you were able to come," she said to Esther. "This is Mister Thomas Spencer. He is also staying with Mrs. Rollins and has been kind enough to show me around Cheyenne City."

"What there is of it," Esther said with a grim laugh. "A pleasure, Mr. Spencer. I'm Esther Morris—from South Pass City." She turned to a tall, sober-jowled man who had arrived with her and had helped her from the wagon. His thick mustache drooped unevenly over the corners of his mouth and his deep-set eyes studied the young couple uneasily beneath bushy brows.

"May I introduce Mr. William Bright. He's been selected to represent South Pass City in the Territorial Legislature. We arrived just in time for tomorrow's meetings."

Bright bowed stiffly and pushed past them into the house.

"He isn't much for talking," Esther muttered, following him with her eyes. "We rode by wagon to the rail stop at Bridger's Pass, and I've never enjoyed so much quiet. Fortunately, there were others on the train who were open to conversation." She looked again approvingly at Thomas Spencer and released Elizabeth's hand. "You two continue with whatever you were talking about. I'll let Dorothy know I've arrived. I need to freshen up before dinner."

Elizabeth walked her to the door and saw her into the parlor, then returned to Thomas.

"I can see why you like her," he said with a playful smile. "She's just like you."

"And what am I to understand from that?" she asked.

"Nothing hidden. No restraints."

"And is that good or bad?"

"You won't hear any complaints from me," he said. "Now, I think we should also get ready for dinner."

Mrs. Rollins had prepared a pair of prairie hens she had purchased from a hunter who came to her kitchen each afternoon with his kill of the day. Esther appeared in the same dress she had worn on the train but had tied up her hair and dabbed herself with a heavy rose perfume. William Bright appeared just as he had climbed from the wagon and sat stiffly opposite Esther at the ends of the table in a seat usually taken by Mrs. Rollins. With her table full, she now took her supper in the kitchen.

"Mr. Bright will be recommending to the council tomorrow that they prepare a bill to extend voting rights to women when the territorial legislature is officially formed," Esther announced when the guests had finished a soup of creamed potatoes and were passing the plates of roasted hen.

"Whatever for?" Mrs. Frazier said, looking at the man from South Pass City with open curiosity. "We have managed just fine without it for this many years. And I'm quite sure I don't want to be troubling myself with it now."

"Some of us feel quite differently," Elizabeth said quickly. "The possibility of suffrage for women is one of the reasons I came to Cheyenne. To do what I could to support it." She looked across at Mr. Bright with an approving nod which seemed to encourage him to speak.

"Damned Congress went too far when they made citizens of them Niggras," he said. "Now they's going to be givin' them the vote in our state, if we become one. We need all the white votes we kin git. Even women."

"I quite like the idea," Mrs. Herman said, lifting a thin strip of hen breast onto her plate and glancing around quickly to see if others had been served before taking more. She returned the fork without seconds and passed the plate to William Bright, adding, "We need more young women like Elizabeth to come to the territory. She's the only single woman I've seen while here—other than the six over at Flo's who entertain the railroad men. Letting women know they can vote in Wyoming may be just what our new shop will need."

Bright took two pieces of meat without checking other plates and grunted his agreement. "We do need more women," he said. "Need 'em for marryin', and for school teachin'."

"I might offer another thought," Elizabeth said, anxious to take advantage of the moment. She looked pleasantly at Mrs. Frazier. "I suspect that, whether we favor it or not, we all would agree that suffrage for women is eventually going to come. The first state or territory to approve it will make history—will forever be remembered as the enlightened place that truly believed in equality. Everything I hear or read about Wyoming presents the territory as a place of freedom and adventure. What greater way to convince people that Wyoming is truly free," she said, turning to Bright, "than to say that every person can vote."

"Every *white* person," Bright corrected. Elizabeth began to protest, but a stern glare from Esther warned her to accept what progress she could.

"Another thought," she said, deciding to flatter instead, "would be to do as you suggested, Mr. Bright, and include in your bill that any woman who comes to Wyoming to teach school will be paid whatever a male teacher is paid. That would make the message much more appealing."

"Don't know that we have any men teachers," Bright said. "So that wouldn't be much of a promise."

"It also wouldn't be difficult to do then," Elizabeth said.

"Can't do nothing until we're approved by the gov'ment," Bright said. "But I want people to be thinkin' about it. We need more white votes than we'll git from the Niggras and Chinee."

Elizabeth glanced again at Esther Morris. "Do they allow guests to sit in the room when you have your discussions?"

Bright shrugged. "We sit around a big table for now. Been a few people sit along the sides of the room. All men. But I ain't heard no rule against women coming in. You thinkin' of comin' tomorrow?"

"I've been so impressed by what I've heard you say, Mr. Bright. I'd very much like to hear your proposal to the council."

Bright straightened in his chair and looked about the table with satisfaction. "Well, I 'spect they'd let you sit in," he said. Thomas's warm hand cupped Elizabeth's beneath the table and gave it a gentle squeeze.

The council chamber was no more than a bare room with a long plank table surrounded by straight-backed wooden chairs. The men who surrounded it represented every image of frontier Wyoming: railroad men; newly established businessmen from Cheyenne and Laramie City, dressed respectably in eastern suits; miners in heavy blue denim pants and cotton shirts who had made their way into the territory from the gold fields of California; buckskin-clad trappers who had given up their nomadic lives to settle with an Indian woman or rescued prostitute on a ranch in one of the state's fertile river valleys. All turned to look at Elizabeth and Esther as the women entered the room, and all continued to look appreciatively at the attractive young blonde in the sky-blue dress.

William Bright, through force of a personality that he had kept hidden from the dinner guests, appeared to have captured the support of the council and sat at the head of the table. He stood as the women entered.

"These ladies asked permission to watch what was goin' on today," he said officially. "I don't think there's no rule again' it. Anyone has objection?"

Several of the men frowned disapprovingly, but none spoke. One of the ranchers pushed two of the unfilled chairs away from the table, against a side wall.

Bright rapped a gavel against the pine surface of the table, called the meeting to order, and had a suited businessman who sat to his left take a quick rollcall. Fifteen council members were present. A second man, also in a suit with wide, gray stripes, read the minutes of the previous meeting which dealt primarily with needed preparation for a more formal organization, once the territorial governor was appointed. Bright asked if anyone had changes.

"We talked about what we might do to keep all the Negros and Indians from being able to vote," one of the miners said. "And the Chinese. I didn't hear anything said about that."

The man who read the minutes nodded. "I left it out. Didn't think we'd want that written down." There was a general mumbled assent from the rest of the council.

"We'll just leave them as they are," Bright said. "And I 'spect these women are here for the first thing I have on my list for today. It's related." He looked sternly about the table, then down at some notes he had scribbled on a scrap of paper.

"If this new amendment passes in Washington—and I 'spect it will—we may not have any control over what men vote in the state. Black men. Red men. Yellow men. Any men." He paused to allow the thought to simmer, then placed both hands on the table and frowned thoughtfully. "What I've been thinkin' is that all the women who'll be coming to the territory—and to the state, when we get statehood—are goin' to be white women. School teachers. Women to work in shops. Some comin' out to git married or who's already married. So, I propose that we begin to write up a bill to be ready when we have ourselves a real legislature—after a gov'ner's appointed—that will allow women to vote in Wyoming. And to git some of them women school teachers to come out here, we make it the law that women school teachers in the Wyoming territory will get paid as much as any man teaching school."

"We don't have no men school teachers," one of the leather-clad ranchers objected. "In fact, we got any school teachers at all?"

"Two school marms here in Cheyenne," one of the businessmen said. "And I believe one in Laramie. No men that I know of."

"Won't be hard to make that happen then, will it?" Bright said, keeping his eyes away from the women.

"But here's what we want to write on our record of the meeting," he added. "We're tellin' folk back east that this is the land of freedom and adventure. Where things kin happen and are possible that you just kin't do out east. What better way to let folks know that than to say, 'We're ahead of ya'll with our thinkin'! This is the land where women kin vote, just like a man, and kin make the same money."

"White women," the man who had objected to Negros, Indians, and Chinese interjected.

"White women," Bright agreed.

"Some of you have Indian wives," one of the businessmen said. "How do you feel about them not being able to vote?"

"Don't think mine'll care," a trapper said.

There was silence in the room for a long moment, then one of the ranchers said, "Don't make no difference to me if women vote. Only one of them up where I am, and she thinks like I do." There was a general murmur of assent.

"I'll git some help to write somethin' up, then," Bright said. "We'll have it ready for our new gov'ner when he gets appointed." He looked over at Elizabeth and Esther. "You women really interested in what's goin' to go on today, or you heard what you came to hear?"

Our cue, Elizabeth thought, and looked over at Esther who was already rising. "Thank you, gentlemen," Esther said. "You will all be an important part of history."

The men at the table initially looked puzzled, then began to nod and backslap as Esther's words sunk in.

"Damn right!" a miner exclaimed. "History bein' made here today!"

Thomas was waiting when they left the building. "How did it go?" he asked, looking first at Esther, then locking his eyes on Elizabeth.

"Perfectly," she said. "Mr. Bright presented our dinner conversation of last evening as a personal conviction."

"And seemed to get general agreement," Esther said, wrapping Elizabeth in a sisterly hug. "I'm certain we will see a proposal to the legislature as soon as it's formed. In fact, I may be asked to write it. I'm so grateful that you are here!"

"It would be a shame," Thomas said, taking Elizabeth by the hand, "if this were to come up in the legislature and one of its greatest champions weren't here to support it." He turned again to Esther Morris. "Would you mind, Esther, if Elizabeth and I walked alone for a while? I'm thinking I should go west—and have a look at the Salt River Valley."

Esther took Elizabeth's other hand and gave it an encouraging squeeze. "I hear it's a beautiful place," she said. "Perfect for raising cattle. You two go on. I'll see you at supper. There's a lot of planning that needs to be done before next year."

36

SUZANNA

Supper at Allgar Hall was an extravagant contrast to the simple meal served to the six guests squeezed about the modest supper table in Mrs. Rollins' dining room. Mr. Badgerow, Suzanna learned, was the youngest son of one of Britain's many earls and, as such, was entitled to call himself "Lord," which he insisted be used by service staff. "M'Lord" sat at one end of a polished mahogany slab that Suzanna decided was at least as long as their Afton parlor. Lady Badgerow commanded the other end, dressed in elegant eveningwear, with two strands of pearls about her delicate neck and earrings to match. Suzanna and David had a side to themselves, easily within shouting distance, but not within reach. The Badgerows' three children, two boys and a girl, sat opposite, close enough that they could touch fingertips if they stretched their arms to full length. As servants moved officiously across the polished hardwood floor to reach the muffling carpet beneath the table, the richly paneled chamber echoed like Pruitt's Cave in the bluff south of the mill. Then, once soup was served, they stood like mannequins along the wall and there was such deathly quiet that Suzanna hesitated to lift her spoon from the steaming broth for fear a careless slurp might draw every eye. The staff, two rigid men in black and a maid with a frilly white apron, were ready, she was sure, to drag her from the hall if she unwittingly violated some undisclosed social norm. The five Badgerows had mastered the art of soundless sipping, adding to the distress of being the first to break the silence. The youngest of the boys, a ruddy-complexioned lad who had announced, when introduced, that he was thirteen, finally lifted the pall with a question.

"You live in the American West? The Wild West?" he asked, directing his question to David.

"We live near the western edge of the established states," David said, relaxing with his own display of relief from the stifling quiet.

"But we are near the center of the continent. The real *wild* West is beyond us—toward the mountains. Our son lives there."

"Are there red Indians there?" the daughter, who was sixteen and had introduced herself as Rachael, asked. "The savages we read about?"

"Not where we live" David said. "The Indians in our area were moved south and west. But where our son Johnny lives, they still have some freedom to move about. The ones in his valley are not savages at all, but very friendly and helpful people."

"I've read about bloody massacres—both of whites and of the red men," nineteen-year-old Collin offered. "Some quite recent."

"It still happens," David admitted. "They are steadily being forced by the government from their tribal lands onto reserves. Often, not willingly."

"Do you visit your son often?" Lady Badgerow asked Suzanna from the distant end of the table. Conversation, Suzanna realized, was much easier than she had imagined in this vast, still room.

"The train now goes to within about a hundred and twenty miles of his home," she said. "Four days by train, then another three by wagon. We haven't been able to leave our mill long enough to make the journey. Perhaps when we return home . . . ."

"Four days by train . . ?" Lady Badgerow wondered. "My gracious. How far is it?"

Suzanna looked uncertainly at David. "Eight-hundred fifty miles? Nine hundred?"

The children gasped audibly. "How far is it to London, Papa?" Rachael asked.

Lord Badgerow frowned solemnly. "One hundred miles, I should say. Perhaps, One-twenty."

"And to Edinburgh—in Scotland, Papa?"

"Three times that far, I should think. Perhaps, four-hundred."

The girl stared in disbelief across at Suzanna. "And it is more than twice that far from where you live to where your son lives? To where the red men are?"

Suzanna smiled at the girl. "It's a vast country. Nearly three thousand miles across. And most of it remains unsettled. We don't even have a train that crosses the continent yet."

"You must remember," Lady Badgerow offered, "that the colonies have only been without British rule for less than a hundred years. Civilizing the continent will take time."

One of the men in black stepped up beside Suzanna and removed her soup. The serving woman replaced it with a plate of roast lamb and potatoes.

"Your mill," Lord Badgerow asked. "Would it be a woolen mill or cotton?"

"Lumber," David said. "We mainly produce the wooden cross ties that support rail tracks for the western expansion. And cut some lumber for building."

"Fascinating," Badgerow said. "And where do your trees come from?"

"We're surrounded by forest. We can cut and haul all we need from within ten to fifteen miles of the mill."

"Fascinating," Badgerow said again, and they ate in silence until the meat plates were removed and replaced with cooked cabbage and carrots, fresh dinner rolls with butter, three choices of fruit jelly and marmalade, and sweet pickles.

"So much to eat!" Suzanna said, surveying the new dishes and feeling her bodice tighten against her sides. "...and it's all so delicious," she added quickly.

"What would you have for supper?" Lady Badgerow asked, waving the maid over to re-fill her wine glass.

"Whatever we can prepare easily when we finish at the mill," Suzanna said, knowing that she was inviting more questions.

Lady Badgerow sent a look of surprise the length of the table to her husband. "What do *you* do at the mill?" Her voice was curious and incredulous.

"David works with the men. I manage the ledgers," she said.

The quiet click of forks and knives fell silent. Suzanna looked quickly about the table to find five pairs of puzzled eyes studying her face.

"Oh, my!" Lady Badgerow said finally, and an uncomfortable silence settled over the table until a serving of cream-covered cakes with fresh fruit topping and cups of dark coffee finished the meal.

Lord Badgerow pushed contentedly back from the table. "You

must be exhausted," he said. "We will gather for breakfast at nine, then I will show David about the estate while Rebecca shows you the gardens, Suzanna."

"With your permission, I would like to see the estate with you," Suzanna said, then turned quickly to Rebecca. "I am, of course, very anxious to see the gardens. Perhaps after touring the farm . . . ."

Badgerow's shrug suggested he was past trying to understand this American couple. "If you wish," he said. "Nine o'clock for breakfast, then."

A hedge, as high as a man's reach, separated the back gardens of the manor house from fields of grain that were just being harvested. As the carriage horses moved at a slow trot along a boundary lane, men and women swept long-handled scythes through what Suzanna recognized as wheat on one side of the lane and a finer-grained crop on the other. Children scurried across the fields behind their parents, gathering up sheaves of cut stalks and tying them into bundles with hemp cord.

"What is this corn with the feathery top?" she asked Lord Badgerow, who rode facing her in the open carriage.

"Barley," he said, lifting a silver-topped walking stick in a wave to one of the farmers who leaned curiously against the curved arc of his scythe. Badgerow turned to the man who rode beside him, a rugged-featured fellow with an unruly shock of dark hair splaying from beneath a broad-brimmed felt hat. "Jarvis, what do we do with this barley, once harvested?"

The overseer frowned nervously across at Suzanna. "Now the rail joins most o' country, we send a good lot to breweries in Staffordshire," he said in a broad accent that Suzanna strained to understand. "What's left goes to sheep and cattle."

"I see that everyone in the family helps," she said. "These children . . ." she began. ". . . are there schools?"

Jarvis chuckled through a ragged row of stained teeth. "Nay, Ma'am. They's farmers," he said.

Beyond the fields of grain, they stopped in a courtyard surrounded by five simple cottages. Their plastered walls were newly splashed with whitewash, but their thatched roofs, thickened over centuries by fresh layers of reed, now appeared to Suzanna to be a dark, living mass atop the peasant homes. Two ancient women, mirror images in black dresses and fringed bonnets, sat knitting in rough wooden rockers. They looked up through filmy eyes but without a hitch in the rhythmic click of their needles. In the courtyard, children too young to bundle sheaves chased a litter of kittens while the mother cat stretched languidly at the feet of one of the matrons.

"They's five families here, and five o'er other side o' pastures," Jarvis said. "Them's takin' care o' sheep."

David had been silent since they left the house, watching the field workers with a brow-furrowing intensity that Suzanna recognized as troubled thought.

"Are there smaller, independent farms here?" he asked as the carriage jolted again into motion.

Jarvis frowned thoughtfully. "Aye. A few. Some o' old estates been sold off. But a bloke needs a good fifty acres to make a livin', mind ya."

David nodded silently and continued to gaze out over the farmland as it turned from fields of golden grain to rockier pasture, surrounded by hedges of thorny brambles. When the carriage again pulled to a stop in front of the steps of Allgar Hall, he helped Suzanna onto the gravel drive, thanked Lord Badgerow and Jarvis for the 'most enlightening' morning, and asked if he and Suzanna could be excused for a walk through the grounds. He led her across the neatly clipped lawn toward the front gate.

"I could almost hear your mind working," she said. "What are you thinking?"

"I'm thinking there's no reason for one man to have all this," he said. "Especially a man who has no idea what happens to the crops he grows. The Badgerows make enough from their mills to maintain this estate—or could at least support it with half of what these farmers produce. But the people doing the work are given a pittance."

Suzanna chuckled softly. "I knew that was what was troubling you. But if we lived in the American South, it would be much the same. Or in the North, but with factories rather than farms. It seems to be the way of the modern world. You've become too much of a frontiersman."

"A casualty of war," he said.

"What does the war have to do with this?"

He stopped their stroll and turned to her with a grim smile. "I don't think I've ever said anything to you about this, but one of the great tragedies of war is that the men who fight and die to protect the wealth of nations aren't those who benefit from their sacrifices. Most of the soldiers who fought beside me were common men. Dirt farmers like these peasants. If they lived, they went home to scratch out a meager living doing what they were doing before being conscripted. The only victory they'd won was freedom to remain poor."

"So . . ?" she said, glimpsing where this was going, but only vaguely.

"So, this estate is being handed to us. We haven't done a thing to earn it but are going to leave here wealthier than we ever dreamed of being. . .. "

"Or have really had any desire to be," she added.

"Exactly. So why not share some of that good fortune with the people who have made this place profitable and not just with those who have benefited from their hard work?"

Suzanna turned and looked back across the expanse of lawn toward the sprawling manor. Lord Badgerow stood in the parlor window, hands clasped behind his back and eyes following the couple.

"What are you thinking?" she asked.

David turned her back toward the gate and eased her into motion. "There are ten of these peasant families. And a thousand acres. Suppose we arrange with Renfroe to deed fifty acres to each family. They could choose—pasture and an equal portion of sheep and cattle, or cultivated land to grow crops. Half the animals stay with the estate and half the land. We reduce the price by the value of the land and, from the figures Renfroe showed us, the estate can support itself on half of what it produces each year. We could even agree to leave enough in the estate account to support it for several years beyond what normal maintenance would require—to make this more palatable to the Badgerows."

Suzanna had seen enough of the idea developing to have anticipated problems. It was a skill that both impressed and infuriated her husband, and she tested him now.

"What if the tenants don't wish to farm on their own?"

"Why wouldn't they? Some of the land's fallow and they could put more sheep on these pastures. On their own, they could produce more than they are now, and keep the increase."

"You forget the men at the mill," she said. "We offered them the chance to own the whole thing. Most of them voted to continue to work for a weekly wage. It seems to be the nature and disposition of many men to choose security over opportunity."

David gazed out over the expanse of lawn that had darkened to forest green as billowing clouds with swollen underbellies rolled in from the west.

"It's going to rain," he said absently. "If you aren't opposed, we'll present the idea to Renfroe. If some of the farmers don't want to keep the land, they can sell it back to Lord Badgerow for what he's offering us."

"And if he doesn't want the place—with only half the land?"

David shrugged. "We can stay longer and see if there are other buyers. It appears to have been a popular property. My guess is that he will. His money comes from his mill, and he wasn't the least familiar with the farm's return. If I understand the figures properly, half the land will more than cover the cost of maintaining the estate. And he and his family want the status of owning this place."

Suzanna turned with him and they started up the broad lawn toward the house. "I would very much like to get this settled," she said.

David grunted in agreement. "We'll present the idea to Renfroe this evening. He can talk to the tenants and to Lord Badgerow. Perhaps we can start home before the week is out."

"While we're here," she said hesitantly, "I had hoped we could see more of this country. I remember my grandfather saying that our family name wasn't originally Shattuck, but Chaddock, and that his parents came from a town called Tyldesley in western England. I doubt we will ever be here again, and I would very much like to go there before we return home."

David chuckled. "I think we should do it. To be honest, I wanted to come here partly to see where I came from. That should be no less important for you."

She grasped David's hand and hastened their steps toward the house as thunder rolled beneath the overhanging clouds. As she looked toward the manor, the full figure of the English lord still filled the parlor window.

37

CARTER PARRY

Carter Parry slumped back on the Whitlock's parlor sofa and scratched at his temple with three fingers of his left hand.

"I don't rightly know what woke me up," he said to Sheriff Billings who faced him across a cherrywood coffee table from a satin wing-armed chair. The sheriff was perched on the front of the cushion, elbows propped on the ends of the curved arms and hands holding a dusty hat between his knees. His brow drooped with a worried intensity that told Carter and Anna Parry that he didn't like the thoughts that were simmering beneath his thinning salt and pepper hair.

"I could hear the crackling as soon as I opened my eyes," Carter said. "It was like being at the bonfire on the Fourth. All the popping and snapping. We sleep in the Whitlock's bedroom upstairs and had the window open and the curtains closed. I could see the light dancing against the curtains as soon as I looked that way. And I could smell fuel oil."

Billings leaned even more intently forward. "Fuel oil?"

"Yeah. The wind was coming up the hill from the south, and I could smell fuel oil. Not that scraped-bone smell of whale oil. This was fuel oil—like they're bringing in from Pennsylvania. That thick, leaves-a-taste-in-your-mouth smell. I was helping unload some barrels from a train in the spring, and one broke open. I know the smell."

"It was the horses woke us," Anna said. "The work teams. They were making a real ruckus down in the corral behind the log stacks. That's what I heard first."

"And when you went to the window?" Billings asked.

"Just the wagons was on fire when I first looked out," Carter said. "The whole string of them, one behind the other. I saw the man moving about. And just as I got to the window, the mill went up. With a big *whoosh*." He threw his hands in the air in a dramatic finger-burst. "All at once. Not like a fire would spread normal-like."

"And then the log pile," Anna added. "Right after it."

"And then the man disappeared?"

"Yeah. Behind the burning mill."

"You recognize him from up here?"

Carter hesitated. "No—not really."

"And you headed down the hill to free the horses . . ." Billings said.

The young man nodded. "More to keep them from running off. They'd already broke out of the corral and was splashing about in the mill stream. Anna threw a bridle on Maisie and came after me."

"You see anybody lurking around when you got down there?"

Carter shook his head. "I got a rope around Whitlock's big chestnut and led him over to Pa's place. The others just followed along. I didn't figure I could do nothing about the fire, but I could save the horses."

"You did right," Billings said grimly.

"By the time I got back with Anna, there was nothing left but burning timbers on top of that steam engine," Carter said. "The log stack was burning, but slow. Them oaks was still green and would have been hard to light without something on them. I thought I could still smell some of the oil in the air."

"Real strong when it started," Anna said.

"When are the Whitlocks due back?" the sheriff asked.

"At least a week. Maybe more. They sent a cable two weeks ago saying they was visiting some other places. They wasn't sure how long that would take."

"Any way to cable them back?"

Carter looked at his wife and both shook their heads. "They wasn't too sure exactly where they was going. We have the name of a law place in London. They might be able to reach them."

Sheriff Billings brooded into the carpet for a long moment, then rose stiffly. "I don't think we should try for now. They need to finish their business and will be back as soon as they can anyway. Worrying about this won't get them here any sooner and will just add trouble to their journey." He looked past the seated couple at the cloud of black smoke that still rose from the log stack. "Maybe I can have this figured out by the time they need answers," he said.

Carter stood with him. "Only one place in town you can get that much fuel oil."

"Two places," Billings corrected. "Fife's and the brickyard. My guess is Henry's store. I wonder if he knows it's missing?"

38

ELIZABETH

Before her train crossed into Nebraska, Elizabeth was composing a resignation letter to Senator Trumbull. She had decided to become a resident of the Territory of Wyoming. Her first hour after leaving the station in Cheyenne had been spent compiling two lists: one enumerating reasons that leaving Chicago would be a mistake, and one supporting the move. List One included eleven items: Wyoming is a barren, inhospitable place; Cheyenne is a town full of saloons, ruffians, and railroad men—few women; I love my position with the senator; I enjoy being involved in politics; I would miss Myra Bradwell and the group of strong women that surrounds her; Chicago is a lively city; I am only a day by train from Afton; Chicago has become a center of industry, where America is growing and experimenting; famous people come to Chicago and I have been able to meet some of them; there are lectures and lyceums where I first heard Stanton, Emerson, and William Lloyd Garrison; I know the city and feel comfortable there.

Her list of reasons for moving to Cheyenne had only four entries: It may be the first place to approve the vote for women; I can make a difference here; I would be closer to Johnny and family; Thomas Spencer. As she compared the lists, she realized that she had compiled them only to make an appearance of being objective and that this wasn't about being rational. It was about items two and four on her short list: making a difference, and Thomas Spencer. And if there weren't the prospect of suffrage passing in Wyoming, Thomas would at least be reason for another, longer trip back.

As her coach clicked and swayed through dry, brush-mottled country, Elizabeth relaxed against the maroon leather seatback and gazed at a tribe of antelope that stared back, statue-still, a hundred yards from the track. Thomas was so unlike Robert Mathis. Oh, they were about the same in height: several inches taller than herself. But where Robert was slender, Thomas was, well, solid. Not heavy, but broader in the chest and hips, with sturdier legs. Robert had always struck her as polished: walking, sitting, even standing with a relaxed effortlessness that she attributed to practiced cultivation. When she walked through the streets of Cheyenne beside Thomas, his long strides had been more efficient than refined. He constantly found himself several steps ahead and slowed self-consciously to allow her to catch up. But he always had.

And Thomas had a genuine politeness about him that was the kind ingrained in a young man by a mother who wanted her son to be mannerly, not by the stern command of a governess or by lessons in etiquette that were part of the ritual preparation for the first cotillion. It was this courtly veneer, she realized, that she had never found comfortable about Robert—her sense that if scratched too hard, the elegance might peel away. She had never been certain what might lie beneath. With Thomas, each time they met on the porch, she could see that he had spent a good part of the previous hour scrubbing away every speck of dirt and smoothing what creases he could from a new shirt he had talked the Hermans into selling him from their unopened stock. There was nothing to scratch away from Thomas. Though always anxious to present himself at his simple best, the man who met her on the porch was genuine through and through. And she liked what she saw—very much.

When he had seen her off at the station, he hadn't proposed, but had made his interests clear. "I'll be here at the Rollins House off and on while I'm searching for that ranch. And when I find it, I'll be letting you know where I am. Nothing would make me happier than to learn you've been asking after where to find me." She hadn't promised that she would come looking. Only that he had given her much to think about. And part of that "much," was looking back at her in the expanse of sage-covered desert she passed through and in the curious eyes of a family of pronghorn. Beyond a man who she knew cared for her deeply and for whom she had developed an affection more genuine than any she had felt before, could she find among this thin scatter of people and crude sense of frontier civility outlets for the other passions she knew animated every fiber of her being?

Her mother had found them in the village of Afton. Or more honestly, her mother had forged them from raw material she had had to quarry herself—and at some personal cost. Afton had not been far enough west that all of the sheen of traditional sensibilities had been buffed from those who settled the town. The rough grittiness of what she had seen of Wyoming seemed to have worn away all pretense. What was left was sometimes raw and unpolished. But she saw in Esther Morris a woman who was reshaping that unfinished clay in her own image. The territory may be the only place in the whole of the nation that Elizabeth could do the same. And if Johnny's descriptions were more than fanciful exaggeration, there were places of majestic beauty to be found in the territory. Thomas, she was certain, would find one of those places.

She turned again to her letter. She would post it from Omaha, letting Senator Trumbull know that she was taking two days to check on the family home in Afton, but should be back in the city by the end of the second week as promised. She wanted him to have as much notice as possible that, after an appropriate time for him to find a replacement, she would be leaving her position and returning to Wyoming. She remembered with a wry smile the words of Jackson Dandridge in the stacks of Washington's senate library. "It's time for you to learn your place, farm girl." Perhaps she finally had.

39

DAVID

Lord Badgerow made no pretense of disguising his displeasure with the Whitlock proposal.

"You wish to give portions of the estate to the laborers?" he sputtered, his jowls quivering and heavy brows curling inward over his nose. "I may be able to see my way to offering three dollars per acre, but reduce the amount of land by a quarter?"

"A relatively small portion," David said evenly. "We met with the farmers last evening and only three elected to accept the gift of land for growing grain. Three brothers, if I remember correctly. And two of the shepherds—who I believe were father and son. The others chose to remain in your service."

"You met with the tenants without my consent? Without Jarvis present?"

Suzanna took an involuntary step forward and managed to get out an "*Excuse me, . . .*" before David grasped her elbow and eased her back.

"Mr. Renfroe and I thought it best that the men feel free to make their decisions without you or Jarvis present. And I might remind you, Sir, that they work for the estate, not for you, Lord Badgerow."

The Englishman's nose wrinkled only once with suppressed rage, but his lower lip continued to tremble. "Jarvis, did you know of this meeting?"

"No, m'Lord. I knew nothin' of it." The overseer leaned moodily against the wood-paneled wall of the dining room where Horace Renfroe had papers lined neatly along one side of the table. "Three brothers. That would be McAvoys," he said. "Doesn't surprise me none. The three of 'em thinks they can work the land together. The father and son? That would be the Clines."

David glanced over at Renfroe who stared soberly at the tabletop, his hands squeezed tightly into balls against its polished edge. He had

225

also opposed dividing the property but had agreed, when pressed, that the land was David's to do with as he wished.

"We did not give them choice of land," David said, turning back to Badgerow. "The two hundred fifty acres will be taken from the east side of the estate, farthest from the hall. In fact, it serves to square the property more evenly. The farmers agreed that if they are not able to work the land profitably, they will offer it back to the owner of Allgar Hall for the price you have offered to buy it from me. If they do not succeed, you may be able to reacquire it all again within a few years at reasonable cost."

"This diminishes the value of the estate," Badgerow complained. "I will have to reconsider my offer."

David nodded. "As you wish. It does not reduce it substantially and rather than take seventeen hundred dollars from the escrow, I will agree to fourteen hundred. That reduces the value of the lost land to the two hundred you initially offered. You seemed to have little concern about what the land was producing as long as it covered expenses. It should continue to do so quite easily. And I gather that most of your wealth comes from your mills. This should make very little difference to you."

The English lord sniffed. "This is so *American* of you. These are not some black men for you to come liberate. Are you trying to compensate for your failure to patch your beleaguered country back together?"

David's first thought was a retort, a comment about how the slave trade had been a thriving business in colonial America while all had still considered themselves English. But further angering his prospective buyer served no useful purpose.

"It was something I believed needed to be done," he said simply. "If you would like to purchase the estate with the adjustments in land and price Mr. Renfroe has described, we would be delighted. If not, we will make it known that it is to be sold with the adjusted description. I'm certain others will have interest." At Renfroe's suggestion, he then excused himself and left the solicitor to soothe the irate peer and see if he could finalize a sale.

Suzanna led him to the edge of the broad sea of lawn that separated the house from the gate to the village. She still smoldered over the exchange in the dining room and watched without comment as the same men with the clipping machines followed each other like plow mules across the green expanse. He stood behind her in silence, letting the heat dissipate into the cool morning air.

"See how they stripe the grass as they pass, as if pushing along some wide paint brush of a deeper shade," she said finally. "And what is left is like fine carpet. We never see anything like this in Iowa."

David couldn't suppress a smile. The woman's boundless curiosity had temporarily defused her anger. "This grass has been tended and clipped for centuries," he suggested. "And watered by an afternoon rain almost every day of those hundreds of years. This lawn is as ancient as the house."

"And such an extravagant use of land," she said, letting her thoughts drift back to the morning's meeting. "One of these farmers you're so set on liberating could make a living just from what we have in front of us."

"I suspect extravagance is the purpose," David mused. "To be able to leave so much land idle. A sign of a place of means."

Suzanna turned from her inspection. "And of a man who doesn't wish to forfeit some of those means."

David shrugged. "Renfroe will go over the particulars with the changes we've made. Lord Badgerow won't be pleased, but he will agree. He wants the place badly and is losing little."

"A quarter of his holding."

"A quarter of an amount he had trouble remembering when asked. If that Jarvis weren't standing beside him, I think he'd have no idea what the estate included or produced. Badgerow doesn't need it at all."

"And if he agrees? We really haven't talked seriously about what we will do with so much money . . ."

Finally, he thought. She is allowing herself to consider having a fortune. "And what would you do, Mrs. Whitlock? Build a larger, finer house?"

"Whatever for?" she said with a genuinely puzzled frown. "We have more than we can care for well right now."

"We could hire help. A cook. Someone to clean."

She sniffed, turning again to the mowers. "And we could carpet the pasture between the house and the mill with finely clipped lawn and have two men with clipping machines walk up and down until it's thick and rich as carpet."

"We could," he said.

"And what would that add to the world?" she muttered. "Two fat and lazy mill owners and two acres of useless grass."

Behind them, Horace Renfroe stepped through the high door onto the porch. As they turned, he wiped his brow dramatically, gave them a curt nod, and smiled broadly.

"It appears we will need to decide what to do with our fortune," David said softly and led Suzanna back toward the waiting contracts.

40

ELIZABETH

Sheriff Littlefield pulled a plain wooden chair over beside the iron grate that served as door to the single cell in the dank cellar of the Union County courthouse.

"Don't be gettin' too close to the bars, Miss Lizzy," he said. "Ole' Sam's coming out of a mighty deep drunk and he thinks critters are crawling all over him. I don't want him going mad on you here."

Rust spotted the metal bars where a thick crust of black paint had chipped away or been rubbed thin by sweaty hands. The stench of urine and feces rolled like swamp gas from a bucket in a rear corner. Elizabeth leaned forward on the chair, peering between the bars at the slumped figure on a soiled cot that filled the rest of the back wall.

"I'll be alright with Sam," she said to the sheriff. "Can you give us a few minutes alone?"

Littlefield shrugged. "I'll leave the door to the stairs open. You call out if he starts gettin' nasty." The big man ducked through the doorway and trudged heavily up the stairs.

Elizabeth sat in silence, waiting for the figure on the cot to look up. When he didn't, she called across the shadowy cage.

"Sam, do you know who I am?"

The sagging head didn't move.

"Sam. This is Elizabeth Whitlock. I would like to know what happened."

Still, the head didn't move. "I know who you are," he said, his voice tired and beaten.

"Tell me about the fire," she said. "I saw your wife at Fife's. She told me you claim you didn't do it."

"She not believin' me though," he said, head still hanging.

"She said she isn't certain you would remember."

Sam Gorton's head slowly began to wag from side to side. "Oh, I remember. I was dying sick. She'd throwed me out and I was lyin' with a gut ache beside Fife's back fence. It's right there back 'o our house." He looked up for the first time, his eyes reddened by drink and scraped raw by the coarse rub of his knuckles.

"I lay there all night—even after I heard them all ridin' out toward the mill. I was there 'til old Joe Tanner come across me and called the sheriff."

"Were you aware enough to know that you didn't go to the mill?" she asked.

"I was too cramped up to sleep. I just staggered out back to the fence and lay down again' it. Then I don't remember nothin' 'til they found me. I know I didn't go nowhere."

"Everyone in town says you threatened to get back at Mother. They all seem certain this was your way."

Sam belched sourly and wiped a stream of spittle from his lip with the back of his hand. "If I'd a wanted to git to your mother, I'd a burned the house. That's what I told the sheriff. Burnin' the mill just hurts all me mates."

"Who else would have done this, Sam?"

Sam Gorton scoffed and slid the back of his wrist beneath his nose. "No one here would believe me if I told 'em. I'm not the only one hates your mother."

"One of the other men?"

The scoff curled into a sneer. "You need to be talkin' to Black Nate. He can tell you who else."

"Old Black Nate? He's never had anything against Mother."

"Ain't Nate. But you know where Nate's been workin' these twenty year. He cleans up in the brickyard after the others leave. Hears ol' Will Jenkins cursin' and a carryin' on about how your family was closin' him down. Can't find good workers 'cause they're all at the mill. He gets them that don't want ta work and don't stay."

"Will Jenkins? No one would ever believe that . . . ."

"That jus' what Nate says. 'Specially when it come from the only Niggra lives round here."

"Did Nate tell this to Sheriff Littlefield?"

Sam scoffed again until it bent him into a cramping cough. "By Jesus, no! You think Nate's gonna say something about Will Jenkins? He said he can't be losin' his job over this, and don't want two hangin's."

Elizabeth sat silently, staring through the bars at the bent figure. There was more than defensiveness in Sam's anger and resignation. He was like a man who was accepting a beating for a fight he hadn't picked. But Will Jenkins . . .?

Sam interrupted her thoughts. "And who'd think of usin' fuel oil to start the fire? If I was startin' it, I'd a found some dry cedar limbs and stacked them up under the wagons and beside the mill wall. Wouldn' leave no stink. Only two places got that much fuel oil. Fife's and the brickyard."

Sam had been thinking about this, hoping that at trial he would have the chance to point another finger.

"Who's representing you, Sam," she asked. "Who is your lawyer?"

There was nothing here to scoff about. The man again bent forward into his beaten slump. "No one here goin' to stand up for me 'gainst the Whitlocks," he said. "I'm gonna have to speak for myself."

"Judge Dawson has to appoint someone for you," she said.

"It ain't happened. Just me gonna have to say me own piece."

Elizabeth scraped the chair back across the concrete floor and stood. "I'll see if I can find you someone," she said. "I'll talk to Judge Dawson."

Sam again straightened on the cot. "Why're you wantin' to help me?"

Elizabeth stepped forward, grasping two of the flaking bars. "Did you light the fire, Sam?"

"No, Ma'am. I didn't light no fire."

"Then you need some help," she said.

Though the window in Judge Dawson's cramped chambers was open, no breeze fluttered the cream lace curtains. Flies that had sought shelter from the Iowa summer blaze by buzzing beneath the raised sash quickly retreated, assaulted by the room's smothering stillness. Elizabeth's bodice clung to her breast with embarrassing definition and she held her handbag up in front of her chest as Dawson's eyes involuntarily wandered in that direction. The only redeeming grace in the cellar below was that it was twenty degrees cooler.

The magistrate with the full, white lambchop sideburns had been more than accommodating when, six years earlier, he had allowed her to argue a case against a money lender who was after the family mill. He now seemed completely unsympathetic. The judge sat across a cluttered desk, his robes hanging limply from a hook beside the door that exited into the courtroom. His own high-collared shirt clung just as revealingly, but with considerably less appeal, against his soft chest and belly.

"The circuit has me in Afton this week, then on the road for the next three," he said, wiping his glistening brow with a soaked kerchief. "I hold court in three counties now—Adams, Union, and Clarke—and will be in Creston next week and Osceola the following. Sheriff Littlefield wanted this case tried quickly and the matter resolved. As you've seen from your visits about town, there is a great deal of upset."

"I understand no one will represent Sam," Elizabeth said.

Judge Dawson dabbed irritably at the tip of his dripping nose. "I ordered George Greer to take the case and he refused. Defied my order, even after I threatened him with contempt. When P.J. Goss heard it was your mill that was burned, he refused as well. Said he had done enough damage when he represented Rufus Hays when he was trying to foreclose on your place. And he said that since he's from Clarke County, I couldn't order his service. Jefferson Talbert from Creston will be serving as prosecutor. If I weren't so damned angry about this myself, I'd have tried harder. But Gorton can defend himself."

"He has a defense," Elizabeth said abruptly.

Dawson lowered the kerchief and studied her with tired, rheumy eyes. "Have you been to talk to him?"

"I have. Just now. I met his wife in Fife's and she convinced me Sam honestly doesn't believe he burned the mill."

"I've heard she isn't certain herself."

"But Sam is. He claims someone else had a motive."

Dawson arched a white, bristly brow. "I don't believe this is something I should hear now, but are you suggesting that you should defend him?"

"I would like to."

Dawson leaned forward, his elbows clearing two spaces on his desk. "You may not. No question this time."

"You allowed it in the Hays case."

"That was a family matter—and a civil dispute."

"And this isn't a family matter? It was our mill that burned."

"Still, I will not allow someone who has not been admitted to the bar to represent the accused in a criminal matter."

"Then assign him counsel."

Dawson huffed his exasperation. "I have made every reasonable effort. No one will defend the man."

"Will you object if I sit at his table and give him advice?"

Dawson spread his hands, palms toward the ceiling. "Elizabeth, I think sometimes that you just want to find any excuse to show how bright you are. This is foolishness—and working against your family's own best interests. But no. I can't keep you from sitting with Mr. Gorton. But you can't say a word to the court."

"I'm not sure how it is in our best interests to send Mr. Gorton to prison," she said. "Especially if the mill was burned by someone who might be better positioned to provide restitution."

"Ah!" Dawson said, returning the kerchief to his forehead. "So, this may not be an act of complete selflessness."

"I see it as an act of finding justice," she said. "And I would like to ask something of you in preparation for the trial. Are you familiar with the case of the Commonwealth versus Webster? The Massachusetts Supreme Court. I think the year was 1850."

"Don't try to school me in the law, Miss Whitlock."

"I have no desire to school you, Judge Dawson. I know you to be a religious student of the law and spend a great deal of time staying current, even after all your years on the bench."

"And don't try to flatter me," he said, a slight smile curling between his mutton chops. "But yes. I am familiar with the case and know what you're implying. Judge Shaw, who rendered the opinion for the court, went to great length to differentiate between direct evidence and circumstantial evidence and cautioned that jurors must consider whether a chain of circumstantial evidence might apply to others as well as to the accused. He argued that jurors must be allowed to exercise judgment based on what he referred to as 'reasonable doubt'."

Elizabeth nodded. "And this case is purely circumstantial. There will be much room for reasonable doubt."

Dawson shook his shaggy white mane. "I think it a miscarriage of justice to advise a jury to somehow weigh the degree of their uncertainty and lean in favor of the accused. They hear the evidence. They exercise their best judgment. I should not play a role in shaping that judgment."

"Even when the accused is supposedly presumed innocent?"

"Until proven guilty," Dawson said. "The process of the trial provides that proof—or fails to. Not my instructions."

"I would ask that you at least consider informing the jury that reasonable doubt may be cause to acquit."

"It is not my role to interfere with jury deliberations," Dawson said with a note of finality.

"Very well," Elizabeth said testily. "I'll see you in court."

The next twenty-three hours, much of it with businesses closed and the town tossing in uneasy sleep, gave Elizabeth little time to determine if Sam Gorton was worthy of her help. Before leaving the courthouse, she asked Judge Dawson's clerk for a sheet of paper, envelope, pen and ink, and scribbled a quick note to Thomas Spencer.

My Dear Thomas:

Please excuse the brevity of this message, but I find myself involved in a family crisis of sorts and have a list of pressing details that must be addressed before I can return to Chicago. The family mill burned and, as I mentioned, my parents are abroad. I must do what is needed to get family affairs in order, plus I have an uneasy feeling that the man charged with the arson may not be to blame. I did not want the days to pass, however, without writing to let you know that I am missing you terribly and I have determined that, as soon as I can address waiting commitments in Chicago, I will return to Cheyenne. I see my future as being there among the strong women who are fighting for a voice in our affairs of state. My hope is that I will find you there when I return.

Most affectionately,

Elizabeth

She knew that she was being far too forward and was presuming too much. But she had little time, and Thomas claimed to appreciate a plainspoken woman. Perhaps her message would see just how acceptant he was.

She took the letter by the postal window in Fife's, received assurance from Charlotte Winter that it would be on the afternoon train west, and stood for the few minutes it took the assistant post mistress to inspect the letter carefully and query her about who this Thomas Spencer might be.

"Just back from Wyoming and sending letters to a gentleman there," Charlotte said with a knowing wink.

"Business," Elizabeth said, smiling politely.

". . .that couldn't wait until you are back in Chicago," Charlotte observed, turning the letter in her hand as if it might reveal its secrets.

"I will be delayed here a few days, and Mr. Spencer is expecting information as soon as I return. I needed to let him know of the delay." Elizabeth wondered fleetingly why she felt any need to explain to the woman, but getting out of Fife's store often meant reaching a degree of impasse with Charlotte.

The explanation seemed to suffice, and she made her way south along streets that grew shabbier as she neared the brickyard. She found Will Jenkins back among the domed ovens, shouting instructions to a shirtless youth who fed coal with a short scoop shovel into the fiery mouth of a furnace.

"Now, we want it low and steady 'til the water smoke stops coming out," Jenkins shouted at the novice brickmaker over the roar of the fire. "You shout at Hansford when you think the smoke's starting to clear. He'll tell you if it's time to stoke up the fire. Might be another three or four hours." He turned and saw Elizabeth standing with a hand shielding her face from the searing heat. She thought she saw a glimmer of panic, but if there at all, it passed as quickly as it had come. He flashed a friendly smile and strode to where she stood.

"Miss Elizabeth. How nice to see you. Have your parents returned?"

"Not yet, Mr. Jenkins. I would think they are on their way back, but we've all been traveling, and our cables have missed each other."

"I'm terribly sorry about the mill. Such an unfortunate bit of madness. Are you here for the trial?" He turned and shouted at his laborer. "Not too fast! Steady, low heat until the vapor clears."

"I am, and I hoped you might help me," she said. "I'm trying to understand what happened at the mill. Sheriff Littlefield said fuel oil was used to start the blaze." She glanced beyond him at the flaming kiln. "For some reason, I thought you had converted your kilns to oil."

Jenkins followed her gaze. "Just two. We can't get a supply that's dependable enough to fire all the ovens." He pointed across a wide, flat yard where hundreds of the clay blocks stood on their sides in a herringbone pattern on a bed of rolled sand. "Those ovens over there are oil-fired. These four on this side, we still fire with coal."

"It would have taken pails of oil to start the fire the sheriff described," She said. "Has any of yours gone missing?"

"Littlefield asked the same," Jenkins said, the narrowing of his eyes asking why he was being asked again, and by a young woman. "None missing here. He didn't tell you?"

"I didn't ask," she said. "I've just been curious where Sam would have found all that oil without it being missed."

"May have been saving it up," Jenkins offered, though Elizabeth had already learned from Sam's wife that she managed what little money the family had, and there had been none for stockpiling fuel oil.

"Might have," she said. "It must have been purchased from Fife's. I'll stop in and see if Henry sold him more than he needed this past winter. I wouldn't think he'd be buying any lately, the weather being warm as it is."

Will Jenkins' gaze remained suspicious. "Why are you wondering where Sam might have got his oil? Can't see that it makes a whole lot of difference."

Elizabeth looked directly into Jenkins' eyes. "It's just struck me as strange that a drunk with no money and no real way to haul buckets of oil a mile to the mill managed to douse the wagons and building. I've been wondering if someone else was helping him?"

"I had some of the same thoughts," Jenkins said, his eyes not wavering. "But Sam denied everything and didn't point at anyone else."

"That's what I've been told," she said. "Very curious."

She caught Henry Fife just as he was latching the door to the mercantile at 6:00 p.m. His greeting seemed more genuine than Will Jenkins'—and more sincerely troubled. *He must be in his mid-seventies*, Elizabeth thought, cringing inside as she watched his trembling hand fumble with the key from his permanent stoop.

"Terrible reason to have to come home, Lizzy," he said, finally able to find the slot and give the key a painful turn. She fell in beside him for the short walk along West Fillmore to the Fife home, slowing her steps to match his deliberate shuffle. "Terrible thing for Afton," he added. "We've always been such a peaceful little town."

"I'm trying to learn what I can about what happened," she said, taking Henry's arm at the elbow and steadying his halting step. "The sheriff said Sam doused the mill with fuel oil before he burned the place. Had he been buying more than normal from you?"

She wasn't certain whether Henry stopped, or just paused to catch his breath. "Less," he said, without turning to her. He forced himself back into motion. "In fact, I was worried about them this winter. They back up against the shop, you know. On Polk. Sam drinks away all their money, and Harriet's been saving every penny she can from the sewing and washing she does. I think they went back to burning wood. I'd have given her some. But she's a proud woman, that Harriet."

"So you haven't sold them any for some time . . . ."

"Can't remember when she bought some last."

"Has any been taken from your yard?"

Henry shook his head so slightly it was no more than an exaggerated tremor. "The sheriff asked me that. I keep the barrels against the back fence, and they all leak some. But when we checked, I had about what I expected."

Henry paused again for breath and Elizabeth tightened her grip on the fleshless arm to steady the man.

"I just can't fathom how a man in Sam's shape got that much oil out to the mill without someone noticing," She said, mainly to herself. "And where he got it."

Henry Fife coughed into a frail, bony fist. "That's figuring it was him," the old man said.

Elizabeth was staying with an old school friend, Nancy Stormer, who lived two blocks south and farther west on Scott in a home that had been her husband's parents'. It was typical Afton, a two-story white clapboard with a railed porch across the full front and a door that entered directly into the parlor. Nancy had moved her twins into her bedroom and given Elizabeth the second upstairs room. Lawrence Stormer was a furniture maker, as his father had been, and kept a shop of the same white weatherboard behind the house. The family was waiting supper when Elizabeth returned, and Lawrence dominated meal conversation with questions about Wyoming and what she had seen as she traveled west.

"You could load a train car of your oak furniture and sell it in a day in Cheyenne City for three times its price here," Elizabeth said as they finished a dessert of tart apple dumplings and sweet cream.

Lawrence laughed a deep baritone laugh. "It's good to have a Whitlock back in town," he said. "Always thinking about something new to sell and someplace new to sell it." He smiled down the table at his wife. "But there's always a good idea in what they say. If I can bring on another lad, we may be able to get a carload ahead." He pushed back from the table. "I'll read to the girls tonight. You two settle in the parlor and catch up on things."

Alone with Nancy in the sitting room, surrounded by the simple, straight-lined oak and maple furnishings that had come to Iowa from Pennsylvania with Lawrence's father, Elizabeth again expected the conversation to turn to her life in Chicago, a subject that seemed of endless interest to her old classmate. But instead, Nancy's thoughts were on Afton.

"You're poking about in tomorrow's trial, aren't you, Lizzy?" she asked as soon as they were settled.

"There's something about it that isn't right," Elizabeth said. "I don't see how Sam could have done this the way they said he did."

"He needs to have done it," Nancy said seriously.

Elizabeth had been admiring the pleating that Nancy had sewn into the dress of one of the twin's dolls. She placed the porcelain figure on the cushion beside her.

"I don't understand. He *needs* to have done it?"

Nancy glanced uncomfortably toward the door and spoke in a raised whisper. "If it wasn't Sam, that means it was someone else from Afton. Sam is okay—and everyone loves Harriet. But he's gotten really mean with his drinking. Everyone thinks she'd be a lot better off without him."

"*Nancy?*" Elizabeth's retort was both surprised and accusing. "I talked to Harriet today and she seemed completely committed to Sam and getting him out of this mess. And if he didn't do it, he shouldn't be convicted."

"*Lizzy*, he burned your mill! Why do you have to be Miss Salmon Chase and have to be the great lawyer? Let things be as they are. The jury will decide if Sam's guilty."

"The jury will know only what they're told."

"*Lizzy?* You aren't going to get in the middle of this like you did with old Rufus? This is different."

"Yes, it's different," she said. "Judge Dawson won't let me represent him."

"You *asked?* To speak for Sam Gorton?"

"No one else will. He's having to defend himself."

"That's 'cause everyone knows," Nancy said.

"Then why have a trial?" Elizabeth retorted. "Why not just ship him over to Fort Madison?"

"Yes. Why not? It would save this town a whole pot full of grief. And you think they're going to find anyone who doesn't think Sam did it? They've picked the jury. I know all twelve of them. Not a man there who would let Sam go."

Elizabeth sat in silence for a moment, her hand returning to finger the doll's ruffles.

"I'm going to sit with him tomorrow," she said finally. "He deserves at least that."

41

DAVID

The London solicitors determined that the safest way to get Ben Lanear's cable to the Whitlocks was to forward it to the bank in Birmingham. David and Suzanna had stopped in the city on their way to Manchester, confirmed the sale with Mr. Woolard, and asked that the banker hold the proceeds until they returned from their visit to Tyldesley. The cable reached Mr. Woolard two days before they returned.

In the small Lancashire town near Manchester, Suzanna had learned from the local vicar that the Chaddocks came from the nearby village of Leigh.

"I serve that parish as well," the churchman said, "and remember seeing the name in the records there. I believe most of the Chaddocks left in the middle of the last century, but you'll find them there in the churchyard."

Leigh was little more than a collection of brown thatched cottages surrounding a picturesque gray stone Norman church. A wizened caretaker led the couple through a neatly kept graveyard to a row of moss-covered headstones pressed tightly against a low stone wall that separated the churchyard from the pastures beyond.

"This would be the Mary and Jonathan you're asking about," he said. The inscriptions on the rounded granite markers were barely legible, worn to vague impressions and partially covered by lichen.

"I believe these are my grandfather's parents," Suzanna murmured, kneeling in front of the weathered markers and scraping at the moss with a fingernail. She carefully traced the faded dates with her fingers. "The names and dates would be right."

David crouched beside her. "It does say Chaddock," he observed.

"That's what Father told me," she said. "My grandfather couldn't read or write. My mother taught my father. When someone finally was able to write the name, it must have come out 'Shattuck.'" She remained for a moment with head bowed. When she stood, David noticed that her eyes had filled, but she stepped ahead of him as they returned to the church and had blinked the tears away by the time they thanked the old caretaker.

They spent a week fifty miles north and east in the West Riding of Yorkshire, visiting the village of Haworth where the Brontë sisters had lived and written their brooding novels of strong women. In the mornings, when mist still blanketed the low hills and dew glistened on the heather, they walked the narrow paths that crisscrossed the moors as Suzanna recounted the sisters' tales that had animated her own imagination and sustained her heart and soul while David had been away at the war.

"These were the friends of that terrible and lonely year," she said. "When I was younger, it was Jane Austen who kept me company. I've never been able to explain to you how lonely it was as I was growing up—to be the only girl living in that cabin along the Chariton with three brothers and no mother." She turned and took his hand, pressing it against her cheek. "Reading—and Jane Austen—sustained me until my own Mr. Darcy moved upriver."

On a bare stone outcropping overlooking the mist-shrouded English village, they sat surrounded by the graying sage of late summer. Without warning, Suzanna leaned into David's shoulder and began to sob as she hadn't wept since the day her youngest son was buried. He pulled her more tightly against his chest and they sat without speaking as the mist thinned and lifted above the moor and morning sun brightened the stone cottages and the Brontë parsonage below.

"It has been so good to come here," she whispered finally. "To England, to Allgar Hall, and to Leigh and Haworth. I don't believe we really know who we are until we understand where we came from."

They returned to Birmingham to find the previously emotionless Mr. Woolard waiting anxiously in his cold cubicle. He rose as they entered the bank, snatching the telegram from the desk and clutching it to his chest as if protecting a national secret. His round face glistened with perspiration, and he glanced furtively through his round, rimless glasses from David to Suzanna.

"I fear I have bad news," he said before they could be seated.

Horace Renfroe had met them at the Birmingham station and taken them to the bank. He answered before the couple could speak.

"Lord Badgerow has withdrawn his offer," he guessed, pausing behind the leather-upholstered chair that he had pulled out for Suzanna.

"Oh, no, Mr. Renfroe," Woolard stuttered. "He accepted the sale on your terms, and I have your money." He stepped toward David and extended the telegram like a courier passing along a cable from the War Department that a son had fallen in battle.

Suzanna's heart dropped into her stomach. It must be one of the children. Elizabeth or Johnny. After Thomas's death, the one great fear that haunted her dreams was that she would lose another child before her own death. David's face reflected the same unspoken dread. He unfolded the yellow form and scanned it quickly. Anger clouded his face where she feared she would see despair.

"What is it?" she asked.

David handed her the telegram. "It's from Ben," he said simply.

She quickly read the seven-line message.

Mill burned last night. Fire set. All lost but engine. Can be repaired. Got six weeks of ties. Will fill orders til gone. Await instructions.

Suzanna's mouth tightened into a hard line and her eyes sparked. "Sam Gorton," she said.

"Ben would have said if they knew Sam did it," David said.

"Sam vowed he'd get back at me. This was his work."

"We don't know that. But we need to get something back to Ben. We don't need a roof over the whole floor to get the mill in operation. The heat will have warped the blade, but he can have a new blade and belts within a week. That will give him time to put a shed over the engine to keep it dry until we get a proper mill rebuilt. He should be able to start cutting again before the place is completely closed in."

Bitterness ran like vinegar over Suzanna's words. "I think we should let it go. If the men had stayed invested in the mill, Sam wouldn't have dared burn it. They brought this on themselves. We don't need this trouble."

David knew better than to put a hand on her shoulder—or touch her at all at a time like this. She would jerk away and the temperature would flare another ten degrees. He had learned to read her face like the gauge on the side of the engine boiler. She was well up into the red zone. Renfroe and Mr. Woolard had quietly eased out of the cubicle, leaving the couple standing beside the desk.

"The town needs the mill," David said quietly. "And there's no sin in the men wanting a secure job rather than the risks that go with trying to run the place. This will have convinced them of that. And we're the ones who have committed to the orders. Not filling them won't hurt the men at all, aside from the pay. But it's the Whitlock mill that won't be getting the work done, and that's what the railroad people will remember. We need to get it up and running before we get back or run out of stock."

His reasoning threw just enough water on the flame to create a head of steam. She stood in silence for a moment, her eyes fixed on some point on the dark brick wall of the bank and her mouth curling firmly downward.

"I'm through with it," she said finally. "You tell Ben what you want, but if we rebuild, it's yours to run."

There was no sense arguing. And nothing to be gained from more talk until the needle again worked its way into the green.

"Let's settle up on the estate. I'll find a place to send a cable." He waved across the chest-high partition at Renfroe.

"You can take care of that too," she said. "I'll be waiting outside." She lifted the hem of her skirts with a decisive jerk, pushed through the cubicle's swinging gate, and drummed her leather heels across the marble floor while the Englishmen shuffled uneasily.

42

ELIZABETH

Beside her on a straight chair, Sam Gorton shivered uncontrollably. Fear and withdrawal wracked a body that, once small but solid, was now bent and frail. She had convinced the judge to let her use the morning to clean him up, get his hair trimmed, and find him some decent clothing. But there was no disguising the tremors. Elizabeth placed a quieting hand on his arm beneath the table.

"Take some deep breaths," she said quietly. "You need to be calm. When the judge asks for your opening statement, just walk over to the jury, look at all of them as steadily as you can, and say 'All I have to say is that I didn't burn the mill. I was passed out drunk behind my house where they found me. I don't know who it was, and nobody else seems to either. They are just pointing the finger at me because I got fired from the mill and said some things I shouldn't have. But I am not guilty, and you will see that they don't really know who did this." Then come sit down.

Sam nodded absently. She wasn't certain where his mind was, but it wasn't on remembering a simple opening statement. Judge Dawson had just finished giving brief instructions to spectators, advising them that he wouldn't tolerate outbursts or catcalls.

Jefferson Talbert stood in front of the jury, reminding them what a law-abiding town they enjoyed and that a breach of the peace, particularly one against one of Afton's most respected families by a man who had shown personal malice, couldn't be tolerated. Several noted citizens, he explained, would testify that they had heard Sam Gorton threaten Suzanna Whitlock in front of Fife's store. An eye witness would place Gorton at the scene of the fire, and the sheriff would testify that when the suspect was found, he smelled of fuel oil and claimed to have no memory of the past hour.

"The evidence is somewhat circumstantial," he conceded in conclusion. "But when following a threat of revenge, this circumstantial evidence will be sufficient to demand a verdict of guilty!" He gave the jury one final nod of unwavering confidence and strode back to his seat without looking at the pair behind the defense table.

Elizabeth leaned into Sam, whispering reassuringly. "Your turn, Sam. Don't try to remember exactly what I told you to say. Just tell them as honestly as you can that you didn't do it, and there is no real evidence that you did. You will show them that before the trial is over."

Sam stood unsteadily, feeling his way along the side of the table until he had to release it to reach the center of the space in front of the bench. He stood there with quivering chin, blinking furiously until able to control his voice. A quick glance at Elizabeth brought a reassuring nod.

"You folks all know me," he said haltingly. "And I know for the last while I been a no-good sonofabitch. That's the truth of it. And I said some things to Mizz Suzanna that shouldn't 'o been said. I can'a be sayin' that I didn't, and there's no need to be bringin' people up here to say I did. But sayin's a sure bit shy of doin', and I swear to you on my mother's grave that I didn'a burn the mill." Elizabeth had cautioned him not to say, ". . . and you folks know I couldn't do something like that." Some of them might be quite certain that he could, and she didn't want to plant the thought.

"Don't know who did it," Sam said, shaking his head with a look of confusion. "But it wasn'a me. Other folks has as much reason to want it gone as me. Maybe more. We'll show you there's no real evidence to show it was me, and that's all it takes—you not knowin' for sure who done it."

He turned back toward the defense table. "You see who's sittin' with me? That's 'cause she isn'a so sure I did it herself and thinks somebody aught'a be helping me show you that. She calls it 'reasonable doubt.' That's what we'll show you." He turned and marched back to his chair without touching the table. He had done better than she had thought possible.

Jefferson Talbert called Emma Harper and Violet Hallman to the stand and tried to keep them focused on his question, while both much preferred to recount in painful detail the argument they had been having when Suzanna met Sam Gorton in front of Fife's mercantile.

"We saw Suzanna coming down the street in the wagon," Emma Harper said, ignoring the jury and looking beyond the prosecutor at the room full of inviting spectators. "I remembered when Johnny came back from being off with the Pony Express. He brought that Indian wife with him, and I was reminding Violet how everyone was so full of opinions about her. Well, you might all remember that she dressed like an Indian. Never talked. Why, it was just like having a real Indian woman living right here in our little town—until they left."

"Miss Emma, please just address the question about what Mr. Gorton said to Mrs. Whitlock," Talbert said patiently.

"I'm getting to that," Emma said, waving off his direction. "I promised to tell the whole truth, and this is all part of the whole truth." She lifted her head a little higher to draw the attention of the courtroom.

"Well, Violet was certain Johnny's wife was Mexican. Someone he met in California. And I said to her, 'Don't you remember what she wore? That leather dress made from deerskin?' But she insisted Mexicans wore that same kind of dress in California. I was about to march her back into Henry's store—he's been to California, you know—and have him tell her what Mexican women dress like."

"And then you heard the exchange between Sam and Suzanna Whitlock," Talbert prompted.

"Well, not right then. We stopped talking about it when Will and the wagon got close. We didn't want to embarrass Suzanna—and we were impressed by how they had Will strapped up in that box on the wagon seat."

"And when you *did* hear the exchange? What did Sam say?"

"Well, I'm not there yet," Emma said indignantly. "Harriet came out of Fife's while Suzanna was talking to Sam. Suzanna said they were going to be gone for several weeks, but if Sam could manage his temper and his drinking, the mill would take him back. Suzanna thought he had been a good worker when the man wasn't overcome by drink."

"And then Sam said . . ." Talbert prompted.

"He said, 'You should stay away because you aren't wanted in this town.'"

A murmur passed through the spectators and rippled through the jury box.

"And what did you understand that to mean?"

Judge Dawson glanced quickly at Sam and Elizabeth, then seemed to remember that he had instructed the defendant's counsel not to speak. "You shouldn't answer that question, Emma," he instructed. "There was no real way for you to know what Sam meant by that comment."

"Oh, I know what he meant," Emma said, eyeing her followers beyond the spectator rail. "He meant that he intended to do her harm!"

Elizabeth leaned quickly over to Sam. "Stand up and say that you object," she said. "Now!"

Sam pushed himself to his feet, hands again braced against the table. "I object," he said and looked back uncertainly at Elizabeth.

"She can't know what you were thinking," Elizabeth said. "Ask the judge to instruct the jury to ignore her comment."

Sam dutifully passed along the objection.

"Sustained," Dawson said, but Elizabeth saw in the twelve faces that the threat had been heard, believed, and filed away. She thought fleetingly of advising Sam to ask the woman in cross-examination how she could possibly know what he meant or had been thinking when he said Suzanna Whitlock was not wanted in Afton. She was certain there were a number of people in the crowd who shared the opinion but would never view saying so as a threat. But it was anyone's guess what Emma would say. *Follow Myra's advice and don't ask a question for which you aren't certain of the answer*, she thought. She let Emma be dismissed without challenge.

Talbert had only slightly less trouble keeping Violet Hollman on track.

"I *did not* say that Johnny Whitlock's wife was a Mexican," she insisted before he could ask his first question. "I said I thought she was Spanish. There are a lot of Spanish in California, and I thought she looked very Spanish."

"And what do you remember Sam Gorton saying to Mrs. Whitlock?" Jefferson Talbert asked.

"One of the things Emma forgot was that Sam told Suzanna he hadn't been hired at the brickyard because of her. He was very upset."

"I did not forget that," Emma called defiantly from her seat behind the rail. "Mr. Talbert made me hurry. I would have said that."

Judge Dawson rapped sharply with his gavel. "You had your say, Emma. Please—no more comments."

"I did *not* forget," Emma muttered, loudly enough to be heard but avoiding another reprimand from the bench.

"And there was one other thing she forgot," Violet said with added satisfaction. "After he told her she wasn't wanted in Afton, he said, 'And you just remember that.' I think that was the most threatening thing."

Judge Dawson asked if there would be cross-examination and Sam again declined. These women knew too much and talked even more.

Carter Parry was called to the stand and recounted seeing the man silhouetted against the wagons as they burned beside the mill. "I couldn't make out his face, but I could see his shape real good. Not a big man. About the size of Sam there."

"And what did he do?"

"He disappeared behind the mill. Then the whole place went up— the saw logs with it. I could see he was setting fires all over the place."

"And did you see him come back out?"

"No. He must have left from the other side of the mill, where I couldn't see."

Elizabeth had prepared Sam for a brief cross-examination. "This man you saw," he asked, looking down at the notes she had written. "He looked about my size?"

"Yup. Pretty much your size, Sam."

Sam studied his notes. "You know most the men in town, Carter. Are there any others that's about the same size?"

Carter hesitated, looking for help from Jefferson Talbert who showed no sign of what he wanted his witness to say. "Yeah. I can think of some," Carter said finally.

"Who are some of them?" Sam asked.

"I don't know. I can think of three or four."

"Will Jenkins for one?" Sam asked, looking at his notes.

Carter glanced about nervously and said nothing.

"Objection," Talbert shouted, surging to his feet. "Will Jenkins isn't on trial here." Elizabeth suppressed a smile.

"Overruled," Judge Dawson said wearily. "The man's identity was uncertain but his stature was raised by the prosecution as a way he might be identified. The defendant is just pointing out that there are others his size in town. Carter, answer the question."

Carter's eyes dropped to his boots. "Yeah. Will Jenkins is about the same size."

"This man must 'o been carryin' round buckets of fuel oil," Sam said. "Was he movin' around pretty fast?"

"What I saw, he was moving about pretty fast," Carter said.

Sam looked down at his sheet. "Not much like an old drunk who could barely stand up," Sam muttered and walked back to his seat beside Elizabeth.

Jefferson Talbert called Sheriff Billings who recounted finding Sam lying beside the fence between his yard and Fife's storage area, smelling of fuel oil.

"Henry's never too sure how much oil he has back there," Billings said. "Some of it leaks. He could have had a couple of buckets taken and wouldn't have known it."

"And who lives across the fence?" Talbert asked.

Billings pointed at the defendant. "Sam and Harriet."

When Talbert turned over the witness, Sam again carried his notes to the witness stand.

"How hard would it have been to lift buckets of that oil over the fence," he asked the sheriff. "That fence is higher than me or you."

"I'm not saying it went over the fence," Billings said.

"If it went out the front, what difference does it make who live over the fence?" Sam asked.

Billings shrugged nervously. "It makes a difference if someone's found lying on the other side of the fence, smelling like fuel oil."

"When you found me, what kinda shape was I in?"

"Barely conscious—like you'd been trying to drink yourself to death."

"In the kind of shape to be runnin' around the mill yard carryin' buckets?"

"You could of got a bad drunk on after you did it," Billings said coldly.

"You saw me about every day that week, Sheriff. Threatened to throw me in jail a couple o' times. Did you ever see me when I could o' been runnin' round carryin' buckets of oil?"

"A man can do surprising things when he's got a mind to. I knew a man who walked five miles with a bullet clean through him. And I seen a man lift a wagon off his son when it slipped its axle and crushed the boy's leg. You could'a done it, if you was in a rage, Sam. And you smelled of oil."

"What was the ground like under me when you found me?" Sam asked.

Billings' brow furrowed. "Don't know what you're asking."

"Like everyone said, it's right through the fence from those leakin' barrels," Sam said. "Wasn't there lots of oil on the ground there?"

"Some, I suppose."

"And if Harriet kicked me outta the house 'cause I was too drunk to stand up, and I staggered out the back and passed out along the fence, where would I have been?"

It was Billings turn to sit in silence.

"I'd a been lying in the oil just where you found me—that's where. And I'd a smelled like someone who'd been laying around in it," Sam said, and marched again back to Elizabeth who squeezed his arm under the table.

Jefferson Talbert's summation was brief and to the point. "The defendant had motive, had threatened the Whitlocks, had opportunity to get the needed oil, and had time to commit the crime. A man fitting his general description was seen at the scene, and they found Sam smelling of fuel oil behind the fence where the oil is stored. The evidence is, as I said when we began, circumstantial. But the circumstances are overwhelming. Sam Gorton burned the Whitlock Mill to carry out his threat." The prosecutor stood for a silent moment and scanned the two rows of jurors with a resolved frown, then turned his withering gaze on Sam Gorton as he returned to his chair.

Sam stood without looking at Elizabeth and marched to a position immediately in front of the jurors' box.

"I got only one thing to say," he began, his voice without tremor or uncertainty. "I did not burn the Whitlock mill. Simple as that. Nothin' you heard from anybody said I did. Could 'o been anyone little as me. And you all know others wanted that mill gone worse than I did. That's where me mates worked. T'weren't me." He returned to the defense table and dropped into his chair, elbows propped on the scarred oak top.

Elizabeth drew a long silent breath and looked steadily at Judge Dawson. *Do what's right here*, she thought. *Give the jury instructions that allow for reasonable doubt.* He cast her a quick glance, and she knew he would not.

"You have heard the case against Sam Gorton," Judge Dawson said, leaning slightly toward the twelve citizens of Afton. "And you have heard Sam's denial. I will now dismiss the jury to deliberate. We will be in recess until they have reached a verdict." He rapped his gavel and stood, leaving the bench without ceremony while the bailiff ushered the jurors into a side room and Sheriff Billings moved to the table to escort Sam back to his cell.

"What happens now?" Sam asked as Billings grasped his arm and lifted him from his chair.

"We wait," Elizabeth said.

The wait was much shorter than she had anticipated. Twenty minutes after leaving the courtroom, the jurors announced that they had reached a verdict. Elizabeth had planned to slip out for a quick lunch with Nancy Stormer, but Ben Lanear caught her before she could push through the gate into the spectator seating.

"You were pretty quiet in here this morning," he said, smiling broadly. "They not letting you talk?"

"Dawson's rule," she said. "Since I'm not legally a lawyer, I can't defend a client."

"Too bad for Sam. But I was surprised to see you up there. Everyone was."

"He deserves a defense. And I'm not convinced he did it."

"You're the only one," Ben said. "But I came up to tell you I got a cable from your pa. They're on their way back. He asked me to start rebuilding the mill."

"Does that surprise you?"

"It did some. When the men voted to get out of buying the mill, I think your ma was pretty upset."

"I'm sure they want what's best for the town," Elizabeth said.

Well, yeah. I'm sure they do." He paused, then said hesitantly, "Your ma is letting me pay the men from the bank. But she didn't say nothing about using bank money for other things. Can you go to the bank with me and tell them it's okay for me to get some money to buy supplies?"

"Certainly, Ben. We can head over there after . . . ." It was then that the bailiff entered the courtroom to announce that the jury had reached a verdict.

"That was mighty quick," Ben said, watching the first of the jurors file back into the courtroom. "Is that good or bad?"

Elizabeth walked back to the table and returned her leather case to its afternoon place. "I'm not certain," she said. "It could either be very good for Sam, or very bad."

Judge Dawson reentered from his rear chambers as Sam Gorton was ushered back into the courtroom by the sheriff. Without waiting for spectators to reassemble, the judge gaveled court back into session and asked if the jury had reached a verdict.

Steven Rissler, a farmer whose land adjoined the Whitlock's on the west and who, in stature, could easily have been one of the four or five Carter Parry had thought of while giving testimony, was serving as jury foreman. "We have, Your Honor," he said soberly.

"Please read the verdict," Judge Dawson instructed.

Steven Rissler unfolded a sheet of paper with great ceremony. "We, the jury, find the defendant, Sam Gorton, guilty as charged."

Sam's head drooped to his chest and new tremors shivered across his back and shoulders. Sheriff Billings was immediately beside him. "Don't lose heart," Elizabeth whispered. "I'll see what can be done." She glanced back at Ben Lanear who was one of the few spectators who had made it back into the building. He shrugged. "You're the only one," the shrug said.

43

SUZANNA

From the porch on the hilltop, Suzanna watched men hoist long slabs of corrugated tin onto the oak skeleton of the mill's sloping roof. While two workers held a sheet in place, a third punctured it above the wooden ribs with a steel punch and a fourth drove nails through the holes to secure the roofing. A second crew worked the row above, lapping their sheets over the row below and snugging the tops against the ridgepole. With half the roof in place, one of the younger men now scrambled over the completed end with a pail of thick tar, daubing black pitch over each nail head to waterproof the surface.

The fire may have been a blessing, she thought as she watched the northern slope of the roof take shape. The old shakes had begun to warp and crack from twenty years of Iowa winters. She had worried each summer that an errant cinder from the engine's boiler would set the tinder-dry shingles aflame. Ben's new plan lengthened the floor to keep the saw logs, once loaded onto the sled, under roof as well as the engine and blade. It would be a much better mill than had burned to the ground.

David stepped out onto the porch beside her, gnawing a cold, partially eaten drumstick.

"Looks like they'll have it finished today," he said, stripping away the last piece of meat with his fingers and tossing the bone to the drooling hound that had climbed lazily onto the porch and now sat with sad, pleading eyes.

"Don't give chicken bones to Dolly," Suzanna scolded.

David put an arm about her waist and pulled her closer. "You're becoming a demanding woman in your old age," he said.

She jabbed an elbow into his ribs. "A year younger than you, and always will be. And one of us has to be demanding. When this work is finished, we'll have the best mill in Iowa. And you want to just turn it over to the men—the same bunch who didn't want to run it four months ago."

"Men who didn't think they could give up a fifth of their wages each week for something that wouldn't happen for another five years."

"It took us ten to make it profitable," she said defensively. "And it cost us a son along the way. Even without the three dollars, they were making more than Will Jenkins paid his men. They need to learn that you can't have everything without sacrificing something."

"The solution we worked out asks that of them," David said. "If we decide we're through, Ben and Sarah will take over the management. The mill will pay us a hundred a month until we're paid with interest. If it nets more than that after the men are paid, they share the profits."

"It will net more if they run it right." She paused, then said, "Are you certain you've had enough?"

She felt his shrug. "I've got to keep doing something. Sitting up here in one of these rockers all day would drive me to drink. But if you're sure *you've* had enough, I don't want to be running the place without you."

Suzanna was silent for a moment. It was hard to get a clear picture in her mind's eye of why she couldn't spend her days again on the mill floor, and harder still to put that picture into words. Someone in her town—probably Sam Gorton, possibly someone else—hated her enough to burn the mill. If it was Sam, she had helped create the drunken, bitter man. When he had stood up to her, defended the organizers and argued against the buyout, she knew she had wanted him gone. Looked for reasons to get him off the crew. Oh, he had willingly given her all the reasons she needed. But if she had done things differently, taken the time to talk to him alone, been more patient? Would he now be locked away over in that square block of stone on the Mississippi they called a state prison?

And if Elizabeth was right? That it wasn't Sam? That meant someone else wanted the mill gone—or the Whitlocks gone—badly enough to burn the place. That was even harder to fathom. She couldn't think of any way she could have injured anyone that deeply.

"Do you think Lizzy was right about Sam?" she said finally.

"You're still brooding over that?"

"I'll always brood over it."

"I don't know. Everyone in town thinks he did it."

"Except Liz—and maybe Harriet. And Liz said Henry Fife wasn't so sure."

"Judge Dawson was willing to give a light sentence. He'll be out in a year. Maybe less. Long enough, Dawson thought, to dry him out good and well."

"And then what?"

"Ben said they'd take him back at the mill if he's sober and does his work."

Suzanna sniffed. "And you think he and Harriet will want to stay here? Will be *able* to stay here?"

"If they choose. People love Harriet. If Sam comes back dried out, they'll do what they can to help him."

"People around here aren't all as softhearted as you," she said cynically.

David didn't answer and she knew he was thinking, *Or as hardhearted as you.*

"Do you think Lizzy could be right? That Will Jenkins might have burned it?" she said, her mind still sorting through reasons someone might want her gone.

"Will's never been outright hostile," David mused. "Always a little resentful, but not a mean sort."

"Liz thought he might have seen Sam's little display on the street as good cover for burning it himself. Everyone in town knew about Sam's threat, with Emma and Violet standing right there."

David shook his head. "I'm not sure it matters now. The mill's being rebuilt. We kept up with orders. And we can live comfortably without it if we decide."

"But Sam's in jail," she reminded him.

David chuckled. "I think Dawson was right. As long as Sam doesn't get himself killed over in Fort Madison, a year locked away may be the best thing that could happen to him."

At the far end of the drive that led up from the mill road, a light, one-horse buggy turned toward them up the hill. The driver, a tall, lean man, wore a dark, flat, wide-brimmed hat that hid his features. The horse was a distinctive brown and white paint.

"That's the carriage horse from the livery," David said. "Someone must have come in on the train. Are we expecting one of the railroad people?"

Suzanna eased away from him and walked to the rail. There was something about the man's straight-backed carriage on the seat that she recognized: long legs, spread but relaxed; loose arms managing the reins. She hadn't seen it in years . . . ." She released the rail and dashed toward the steps that descended to the drive.

"*Johnny*!" she shouted, hoisting her skirts and continuing down the hill toward the buggy. The driver reined up as he approached and jumped from the buckboard.

"I didn't expect to find you waiting," he said with a hearty laugh and lifted his mother into a whirling embrace.

They stayed on the porch, rocking in the chairs David had said would drive him to drink and inspecting the work of the men on the roof. Johnny had learned the mill had burned from a Thomas Spencer who had shown up unannounced on horseback. Suzanna sat beside her son, clinging to his hand, but glanced over at her husband at mention of the name. Neither chose to say anything.

"I rode out the next morning," he told them. "Went to the railhead on the Green River and they let me onto a supply train to Cheyenne. Mentioning the Whitlock name carries some weight with those railroad people. They knew about the mill being burned and were impressed you'd kept up with orders. In Cheyenne, they got me onto a passenger train to Omaha, then one to Afton. I've been sitting for four days."

"Before we go in, let's walk down to visit our Thomas," Suzanna suggested, pulling Johnny with her as she pushed out of the rocker. "That will stretch some of the cramps out. Tell us about Cora."

As they walked toward the massive red oak that shaded the grave, he told them about the girl's horsemanship and her skill with language. "She talks to the Chinese as well as they talk to themselves," he said. "And she's the closest thing we've got to a schoolmarm. The other children and their mothers come to our place every morning after chores. She's got them all speaking good English and learning their numbers."

When they reached the gravesite, they stayed outside of the fenced plot, but stood for a moment without speaking. Suzanna pulled Johnny protectively to her side.

"Tell us about this other Thomas," she said finally. "This Mr. Spencer. Lizzy mentioned him when we stopped in Chicago but didn't want to say much."

"He came into the valley from the north," Johnny said, looking up into the canopied branches of the oak that cast dappled light over his brother's grave. "He'd followed the Lander Cutoff from South Pass, so the first place he came to was Li Bo's. Bo and his daughter Lily brought him down to the ranch. He'd no more than given me his name than he mentioned Lizzy. Said he was her friend."

Suzanna released him and turned with her back to the white pickets, hands folded in front of her. "Elizabeth was making plans to go back to Wyoming. Though she didn't seem to want to tell us much about him, I'm sure this Mr. Spencer was part of the reason."

"I approve," Johnny said, grinning to show that he knew how little that mattered. "He's a right sensible man. Helped us finish up a corral at Li Ji's place the day he arrived, even after riding all day. When I said I needed to come back to help with the mill, he offered to bunk down in the barn and help out 'til I got back."

"Sounds like a man who wants to impress Liz's family," David said with a chuckle.

Johnny nodded. "You're right about that. And he wanted to spend some time up in the north part of the valley. Said he'd liked what he saw as he rode through and didn't seem put off by what we told him about the winters. He's looking for a place to ranch."

"So Elizabeth said."

"I rode out the next morning, so we didn't talk much."

"I think Liz's experience with Mr. Mathis in Chicago has made her cautious," David said. "We didn't push. She'll tell us what she wants when the time's right."

Suzanna glanced back at the weathered stone that marked the resting place of her younger son. When Elizabeth had mentioned a new interest and said his name was Thomas, she had felt the hand of melancholy squeeze her heart, but with a twinge of hope—of resurrection.

"This other Thomas," she said, her voice trailing down the hill on the afternoon breeze. "Tell me what he looks like."

Johnny's mouth bowed downward. "A regular sort of fellow. A little shorter than I am—but strong as a work plug. And handles a horse well. While we were working on the corral, he knew what needed to be done without being told and got right on it. The kind of man you like to work with."

"But what kind of work does he do?" Suzanna asked. When prodded on the matter, Elizabeth had managed to say nothing.

"He was in the war, Father. And he drove cattle in Texas. Managed to put some money aside. He's looking to start a place of his own in Wyoming. That's about all I know." He hesitated. "You said Lizzy will be coming through on her way back out there. Ask her about him." Johnny looked past his mother at the men finishing the north side of the mill roof. "Well, Pa," he said, "I could use some work that will wear me out. If you were headed down that way, I'll go with you. I don't hear the saw . . . ."

"It's shut down while the men are on the roof," David said. "Your mother and I are thinking we may not work the mill any longer. You remember Ben Lanear? He's been running things while we were away and did a right nice job. We may turn it over to the men and let them buy it from us."

Johnny had started toward the path but stopped and looked back at his mother.

"I thought you'd given that a try."

"New day. New circumstances," David said.

"And what will you do?"

Finally, someone had spoken the question that had been churning in Suzanna's head like the old millwheel. She looked to David for help, but he was lost in his own uncertainty.

Johnny stepped back toward them. "Join Lizzy when she comes west. Pack up what you want from the house, sell the place, and come stay with us." He glanced back over his shoulder at the men who were clambering down from the roof, leaving it to the tar dauber. "Come build a saw mill in the valley. There's no oak or maple, but we've got pines longer than the mill floor—some hard and some soft. And good cedar. More people will be coming and will need lumber."

David looked up at her, raised a brow, but said nothing. Was he suggesting this was hers to decide? He walked to his son, threw an arm across the broad shoulders of the Wyoming rancher, and turned him again toward the path. "Let's get this mill finished first," he said. "You can tell me more about this valley of yours while we work."

44

CORA

She had never seen a train. Just pictures in the books her father brought back when he took horses to the city. And he told her stories of sitting in a small wooden building on wheels—a building as long as the ranch house, but narrow as her bedroom, with benches lining both sides for people to sit on. This room, pulled by a black machine the size of two hay wagons, moved across the prairie faster than her horse could gallop, but sometimes slowed when climbing through the mountains until you could walk beside it. The pictures in her books of locomotives showed a great iron tube with a high smokestack at one end and a small open shed at the back for the driver. Three iron wheels on each side ran on tracks of steel—three, her father told her, because a single iron wheel on metal tracks slipped too much for the train to move forward. He had tried to explain how a cylinder of solid iron that he called a piston moved back and forth inside the locomotive in a smaller tube to drive the wheels. But she had decided he didn't understand it that well himself, and she knew when to quit asking.

But the giant, smoke-belching machine that shrieked like a hundred mating eagles as it scraped to a stop beside the Bear River was larger and more entrancing than anything her imagination had created. Had she not been there to meet her grandparents and her auntie, people she also knew only through her father's stories, she could have spent the day climbing over the enormous black beast, discovering for herself how throwing wood into a firebox at the rear of the tube could make the locomotive move on its own.

Her mother and father walked her beside the track to one of the rolling rooms just behind an open-topped box that held wood. Her father called the rooms "carriages," and this one was lined from end-to-end with windows, with a door at the end that opened onto a small porch and iron stairs. She took her father's hand and pressed tightly against his leg. She was not certain what a white grandmother would look like. As old as the oldest of the Shoshone *pia*, the ancient mothers with dim eyes and hair the color of aspen bark? Their faces had the skin of dried frogs, and the oldest sat silently at the ghost dances and stared into the fire without blinking. Her mother told her they lived in the place of dreams. Would this grandmother be like that?

The first woman through the door was not old at all. No older than her parents, but with a paler face than Cora had ever seen and hair the color of corn silk. Her eyes were as light and blue as the sky and matched a dress that showed her to have a shape that drew Cora's eyes immediately to the woman's hips. Her top, beneath the tight-fitting dress, was like any woman's. But where other women swelled with a smooth roundness at the back, this woman had the bottom of a well-fed hog. It stuck out behind her to double what Cora had ever seen and was covered by piles of the bright blue cloth. The woman stood for a moment on the small porch, looking over the waiting party with a wide smile. She fixed her eyes on Cora for a brief, delighted moment, then hunted through the crowd until she found Thomas Spencer. He stepped to the side of the iron stairs and helped her carefully down, her lifted skirt showing feet that were no larger than any other woman's but wrapped in hard shiny black.

Thomas had been staying with them since he came into the valley and, at supper each evening, always spoke of her Aunt Elizabeth. This, Cora decided, must be Elizabeth. Mr. Spencer had assured her that her aunt was one of the most beautiful women he had ever laid eyes on. As he drew the woman to him and kissed her cheek, Cora studied the face to see what a beautiful woman looked like. Her aunt's skin was smooth as polished river stone and had never seen much of the sun. Her nose was less pronounced than Cora's father's, and much narrower than her mother's. She had to agree that the woman's eyes were the most beautiful eyes she had ever seen, and she understood how the Blue-Eyed Mary blossoms that colored the lower meadows in the spring had earned their name. These eyes had none of the gray of Mr. Spencer's and were hard to look away from, once she looked your way.

Her study was interrupted as a second woman stepped from the carriage. Cora glanced back quickly at her Aunt Elizabeth, recognizing that this new woman was her grandmother and that someday Elizabeth would look exactly like her. The new woman's hair and eyes had lost some of the shine but remained light and soft. Her skin hadn't escaped the sun and was the color of pinion nuts. This woman's simple dress hung straight on her hips, without the billowy bump that disfigured her daughter. There was nothing cautious about this woman. She stepped onto the porch carrying her own worn leather case. Her eyes immediately found Cora's and the girl saw them fill with tears that were quickly blinked away. Father stepped forward to take the case and help her down the iron steps. The woman held Father in a tight hug, squeezed Cora's mother not so tightly, then turned and squatted on her heels in front of her granddaughter.

"Hello, Cora," she said with a smile that quivered just enough to confirm that her eyes had truly shown tears. "I am Suzanna. Your grandmother. May I have a hug?"

Cora stepped shyly into the woman's arms. They were strong, but gentle. As she wrapped her own about the woman's back, she felt a sinewy firmness that was like her own willowy body. Grandmother was a woman who liked to be out of the house.

"Can you introduce me to your friends?" her grandmother asked.

Cora began to turn but stopped to study the man who had followed the women from the train carriage. He was as tall as her father, but with straight, graying chestnut hair while Father's was a mass of dark curls. Her grandfather's face displayed a light ring where a hat had shielded it from the sun. The skin beneath was almost as fair as Elizabeth's. Cora glanced unconsciously at her father, surprised that two fair-colored sires had produced such a bay colt. She looked quickly back at her grandmother who watched her curiously. She took the woman's hand and led her to her friend Lily who bowed shyly.

"This is my friend, Lily—and her father and mother. They have a ranch by ours and raise cattle." She raised Suzanna's hand slightly. "This is my grandmother, my pa's mother. She's coming to live with us 'til we can build them their own house." The Li family bowed deeply, and Lily's mother stepped forward and presented a small doeskin bag with a row of Chinese symbols centered along each side in purple dye.

"It says 'Good fortune for your life'," Cora explained. "Lily's mother made it for you and has one for Auntie Elizabeth."

"It's *beautiful*," Grandmother said. "Please thank her for me."

"She knows what you're saying," Cora said softly. "You can tell her." Lily's mother smiled shyly and bowed again.

"And you can read this writing?" Grandmother asked Cora.

Cora nodded. "It's not like our writing." She pointed at the row of symbols. "These aren't letters, like a, b, c, d. This one that looks like a person standing next to a cabinet with a box on it? That means 'good fortune.'"

Her grandmother looked at her without speaking, but Cora saw surprise and wonder in her face. *Good* surprise and wonder, and it made her happy.

Grandfather came up beside them with her father, who told him again who everyone was. "Li Bo's brother and cousin stayed with the animals," her father said. "We have four wagons, so we should have room for everything."

The men who were building the railroad were mostly Chinese and had talked to Li Bo and his family when they arrived early in the morning. They had all crowded around Cora when they learned she could speak to them and wanted to know if people talked in Chinese where Li Bo lived. But they had been told by the track boss to get back to work.

The railroad had built a triangle of track before it crossed the river and the black locomotive backed the rest of the train onto one side of the triangle. While they watched, the engine moved forward again with great puffs of smoke belching from the chimney and hot steam shooting between the iron wheels. It moved again out onto the main track and stopped, now pointed in the other direction.

"Everything's in the boxcar behind the Pullman," Grandfather said. "The three flat cars of ties are our final shipment. In fact, most of the last car was produced by the new Union County Lumber Mill."

"Let's get the wagons up to both sides of the boxcar," Father said. "We can unload out both doors."

With her father's permission, Cora and Lily scrambled into the open car. While the men moved heavy oak dressers, tables, and bedframes, the girls carried wooden crates packed with pots and pans, hidden treasures wrapped in bedsheets, shoes, and leather-bound books to their mothers and to Auntie Elizabeth who packed them into the wagons. Her aunt had disappeared behind one of the wagons for a few moments and had somehow removed the lump that had been her behind. When she saw Cora's surprised stare, she laughed as if she had heard a funny story and pointed at a basket-looking thing with a belt that Cora guessed cinched around the woman's waist.

"I hope I'm through with that thing," her aunt said, taking a box of equally uncomfortable-looking shoes from her niece. "And most of these, too. What we won't do to be fashionable!"

"Can you girls step to the side for a moment?' her grandfather asked. He and Father slid a flat wooden crate from the back wall of the car toward the door, keeping it on edge. Through the slatted sides, she could see two silver-blue disks that were as tall as she was, with hexagonal holes in the center and what looked like hooked teeth clawing from the outer edge. Thomas Spencer followed, carrying a roll of wide leather strapping. Behind them, still in place against the wall, a stack of cupped and slotted wooden wheels were piled beside long, upright posts with square pegs circling both ends like the petals of a stubby wooden flower.

"What are those things?" Lily whispered in Chinese.

Cora shook her head. She could see at a glance that the wooden petals at the end of one pole were meant to fit into the slots around the edge of the wheel that sat on top of the pile. "It's a gear, I think," she said, remembering her father's demonstration with two slices of a spruce limb he had notched with a chisel.

"A gear?" Lily asked.

"I haven't taught you that yet," Cora said dismissively.

"I thought you might bring the old millwheel on one of the flatcars," her father said to Grandfather.

"It had been sitting dry for too long," Grandfather said. "Pretty badly cracked, with bugs in most of it. We'll build a new one when we see what the stream's like."

"There's a low fall near the bottom of what we call Cub Creek Canyon," Father said. "A good flat place on one side that could hold the mill. Easy place to haul logs."

Li Bo came to help them, and they carefully carried the crate to one of the wagons and braced it firmly upright along the side of the bed.

"Best if it rides on edge," her grandfather said. "The things seem to want any excuse to warp."

The boxcar filled three wagons and half of the fourth. Her parents drove one of her family's wagons and Thomas Spencer the other, with Elizabeth beside him. Li Bo and Lily's mother drove their own, and her grandparents drove Li Ji's team, the wagon with the half-load. Cora, Lily, and Joseph sat on bedding that filled the front of the bed behind the older couple.

"Not a good trail," her father warned as he flicked the reins over the backs of their pair of jennies and started the team away from the locomotive. "With these loads, we'll have to take it slow. Probably four full days. Maybe five."

Her grandfather laughed and called after them. "We've nowhere else to go, and time doesn't matter." Grandmother turned and leaned back toward the children from the high seat.

"Are you three ready for four days on the trail?" Her forced smile showed that she wasn't very pleased at the thought herself.

"We've already done it," Cora said. "Sometimes we get down and walk with the mules. You can do that if you get too tired."

Lily leaned toward her, keeping a shy eye on the woman who sat above her. "We were going to sing the song of my grandmother to your grandmother," she whispered in Chinese.

Cora looked at Joseph, who nodded. Together, the three began a slow, melodic tune taught to them by Lily's mother to sing the newcomers into the valley. The music seemed to roll with the gentle sway of the wagon and the children rocked with it. Suzanna Whitlock turned on the seat and lifted her feet over between the girls, humming with them as the children began a second verse.

"What a beautiful song!" she said as they finished. "Is this one Lily taught you?"

"My mother," Lily said. "It was taught to her by her grandmother. It is a very old song."

"Will you teach it to me?"

Lily and Joseph nodded enthusiastically.

"Do you know what it means?" Grandmother asked Cora.

"Most of it," she said.

"Tell me. It will help me remember it."

Cora eased again into the gentle swaying motion, fitting English words she had practiced for just such a question into the melody as Lily and Joseph hummed along.

Beside the old pathway, by the goodbye house,
The green of beautiful grasses goes far into the sky.
Evening wind moves the tree branches.
There is a song from a flute.
The sun sets behind the shadow of mountains.
At the end of the sky, at the corner of the world,
My friends are scattered there.
After we leave tonight, I wait for a new dream.

"The words are beautiful, too," her grandmother said, her eyes again misting. "And just right for our journey. As we leave tonight, I wait for a new dream."

AUTHOR'S NOTES

In the notes to *Wild Whistling Blackbirds*, I claimed that arguably no decade shaped the destiny of the United States more profoundly than did the 1860s. The Civil War and the accompanying influences of President Lincoln's assassination, emancipation, reconstruction, and the Johnson impeachment trial would probably qualify the decade for that honor without embellishment. But add in the brief experiment of the Pony Express, the opening of the West through completion of the transcontinental railroad and telegraph, the trans-Atlantic cable, and rapid advances in industrial technology, and you have the makings of a truly transformative era.

After reading *Blackbirds*, a local attorney friend, Dwight Douglas, suggested several other ways in which the decade served to reshape the nation. The railroads gave rise to efforts to organize labor, efforts that quickly spread into other dangerous and unpleasant work environments such as the fledgling steel industry. Rapid industrialization created labor shortages that drew millions of new immigrants to both shores and into the cities. It was Dwight's suggestion that in Book III, a labor organizer for railroad workers should come to the Whitlock mill and stir up trouble, and that the Whitlocks might be pioneers in providing an employee buyout opportunity.

I learned shortly after beginning work on the book that Dwight was critically ill with pancreatic cancer. I hurried through an initial draft to give him a chance to see his suggestions in print while he could still offer a critique. His wife, Bonnie, had to read the final chapters to him because of his failing condition, but we were able to discuss the novel two weeks before he passed away. Dwight was a great student of history and had a particular interest in how our nation had survived one crisis after another because of its reliance on the rule of law. That theme also appears throughout *Suzanna's Song*. When we spoke, I was using a working title Dwight didn't care for. *Suzanna's Song* came to me some weeks later and immediately seemed right. I hope he approves and am most grateful for his suggestions, critique, and support. His approval of the draft was sufficient reward for the work that went into the book.

I have tried again to be as faithful to history as the plot allowed but have taken a few liberties. To my knowledge, Myra Bradwell did not hold a "gathering" in Chicago of the luminaries in the women's movement prior to the Washington Convention in 1868. But I needed to bring Elizabeth and Esther Morris together before Esther moved to Wyoming, and the gathering provided a setting for one of the book's "dream songs." Alta Hulett had not moved to Chicago by the time this meeting was held, but I found her such a compelling young woman that I hastened her education and contribution by a few years.

The Ghost Dance that underlies the theme of the book is of uncertain origin and undoubtedly sprang from the circle dances of the Northern Paiute and other ceremonial round dances of Rocky Mountain and Northern Plains tribes. After the time in which this novel is set, a Paiute leader named Wovoka developed a cult-following around the dance, claiming that if performed properly and at the right times, it would lead to great prosperity, peace, and freedom from white expansion. Wovoka popularized the dance to the degree that it is now largely associated with his movement. But it precedes his time as a means of invoking blessings and guidance from the world of spirits.

I attempted to portray the Johnson impeachment as accurately as space allowed. Lyman Trumbull and a handful of Republican senators, largely from the Midwest, voted against impeachment for constitutional rather than partisan reasons. None was re-elected. Trumbull's explanation for his vote was read into the Congressional Record, though Elizabeth Whitlock obviously wasn't its author.

The Jules Beni and Jack Slade story about how Julesburg was named is as accurate as a bringing together of various legends permits. There are differing accounts of how many times Slade was shot and of how he executed Jules once the man was captured. But I found it the perfect story to unnerve a fussy New York lawyer like Rosswell and a great anecdote about early frontier justice.

Cheyenne in 1868 truly was a collection of tents, crude adobe huts, and rough clapboard buildings spread along a half-dozen dirt streets beside the new rail line. The Union Pacific Hotel and rail station were its architectural gems, but several of the streets did offer boarding such as the Rollins House and the beginnings of commerce such as a Herman's dry goods, a tailor, and a jeweler. The city grew exponentially over the next decade as Wyoming approached statehood and as land speculators, ranchers, and businessmen took advantage of its location on the transcontinental railroad. The state's somewhat tarnished motives for pursuing the vote for women is basically accurate, though motives varied and champions like Esther Morris played a significant role in shaping policy. Esther is credited with having planted some of the seeds of women's suffrage in the mind of William Bright, the territorial legislature's representative from South Pass City. Esther eventually became Wyoming's first female justice of the peace when South Pass City's justice, R. S. Barr, resigned in protest over the vote which extended suffrage.

Johnny's valley between the Idaho and Wyoming territories would be approximately where Star Valley in Wyoming is now, though I again took liberties with some of the geography and with the history of its settlement. When I was young, my grandfather took us fishing in Yellowstone in the summers and we usually drove from our home in central Utah up through Star Valley. From my first visit, I was struck by the peace, natural abundance, and beauty of the place. It seemed the ideal setting for a Whitlock family reunion.

Jane Austen wrote and published her novels early enough that they may have reached a teenaged girl on the Missouri frontier in the 1840s, and the Brontë sisters wrote early enough for their work to be available to a lonely Civil War wife. I am not certain that these books penetrated the American frontier within a decade of their publication. For the purposes of *Suzanna's Song*, accept that they did. Suzanna would have loved and been moved by them.

Did Sam Gorton torch the mill? Your guess is as good as mine. But a year in Fort Madison was probably the best thing for him, his wife, and the village of Afton.

Many of the surnames in this novel and in the trilogy of Whitlock books come from my own genealogy: Whitlock, Shipley, Shattuck, Burton, Allgar, and even Rosswell and Griggs. They were strong, courageous pioneer people who played small, but important roles in shaping what our country has become. I owe them a deep debt of gratitude. I am honored to dedicate this final Whitlock book to their memory and to its contributor, Dwight Douglas.

Visit Allen Kent's website at http://AllenKentBooks.com
OTHER NOVELS BY ALLEN KENT

Unit 1 novels
The Shield of Darius
The Weavers of Meanchey
The Wager
The Marburg Mutation
Straits of the Between
Ring of Thorns

The Whitlock Series (Historical novels)
River of Light and Shadow
Wild Whistling Blackbirds
Suzanna's Song

Colby Tate Mysteries
Murder One
Eye for an Eye

Mystery/Thrillers
Backwater
Guardians of the Second Son

Young Adult Adventure
Switch